Sword of Forgiveness

Winds of Change

This book is dedicated to everyone who believes that God won't forgive them.

Sword of Forgiveness
Winds of Change
by Debbie Lynne Costello

© 2015 by Debbie Lynne Costello

Published by Wakefield Press

ISBN: 978-0-9861820-1-3
E-Version ISBN: 978-0-9861820-0-6

All Scripture is taken from the King James Version of the Bible.

Edited by Susan Lohrer
Cover Design by The Killion Group, Inc.
www.TheKillionGroupInc.com

Acknowledgements

Books are the efforts of so many people and this book probably more than most. I always want to give God the glory first and foremost as He gave me the desire in my heart to write and the story to put on paper. I want to thank my wonderful husband who was the first person to encourage me to write a book. Thank you, Joe. I love you! I'd like to thank MaryLu Tyndall who read what my story was about and believed in me, mentored me, and connected me with the ACFW and so many wonderful people. To Kathleen L. Maher who saw this story in its raw and unpolished form and fell in love with it. She has walked every step of this road with me, reading SOF more times than me I think. Her insight has been invaluable and her friendship irreplaceable. Thank you, dear friend. You'll never know the impact you've made. A big thank you to Deb Kinnard for all her medieval expertise, Laurie Alice Eakes for putting up with the gazillion questions I always threw at her, Melanie Dickerson and Linore Rose Burkard for being prayer partners and for being willing to look over this story. Thank you, Susan Lohrer, for your undying support and edits on this book, not once but twice. You saved me from the head-hoppers. All of you played an important role in Sword of Forgiveness and have become precious friends to me. I'm blessed by you.

Lastly, I want to thank my family who has stood by me, cheered me on, and believed in me. You'll never know how much that means to me.

Glossary

Bailey – an open area inside the castle complex, the bailey contained the domestic and other necessary buildings of castle life. An inner bailey laid in an area inside the main castle and its safety, while the outer bailey was outside the main castle defenses, making it more vulnerable should there be an attack.

Blood-lust – strong desire to kill.

Bolt-hole – a hidden door in a castle used for escape.

Caitiff – wicked man.

Chattel – owned, personal property.

Chausses – chain mail garment that covered the legs and feet.

Chemise – long loose undergarment for women.

Chivalry – a moral system which combined a warrior's character, his knightly piety, and his courtly manners which together gave a notion of honour and nobility.

Circlet – decorative head piece.

Cooper – person who makes and repairs barrels and tubs.

Coif – in terms of armour, a coif is a piece of chainmail that is draped over the head and neck, covering and protecting them. In essence, a coif combines the helm (head protection) and the gorget (throat protection), although it could also be worn underneath a helm and/or gorget for added protection. It was often used in combination with a hauberk.

Cote-hardie – a dress under a surcoat.

Courtly Love – a time when many marriages were not for love, courtly love followed rules and allowed a man and a woman to outwardly show their affections for each other.

Dais – raised platform.

Dearling – endearing term such as darling.

Demesne – part of the estate of the lord of the manor for his own use and support and often sub-leased.

Destrier – warhorse.

Forge – furnace/oven.

Fortnight – 14 days.

Garth – small enclosed or fenced area.

Great Hall – multi-purpose room where meals were taken, guests received, business conducted, and even used as sleeping quarters when needed.

Hauberk – long tunic made of chain mail used for protection.

Headrail – a square, oblong, or round piece of fabric placed over a head and wrapped around a woman's neck and shoulder and held in place by a circlet or crown.

Hoodwinked – deceived or duped.

Keep – fortified tower in the castle.

Man at Arms – a well trained professional soldier.

Mantle – a lush cloak that would be fastened in front by a large brooch, buckle, or pin.

Master-at-Arms – the man responsible for the training of soldiers at a specific castle.

Mews – housing for falcons and hawks.

Pater – father.

Plait – a braid or plait of hair.

Sennight – 7 days.

Serf – a member of lowest feudal class and an agricultural laborer who is bound under the feudal system to work on his lord's estate.

Solar – private sitting room often found above and used by family and close friends. Solars could be connected to bedrooms.

Squire – shield-bearer or armour-bearer to the knight. Squires are promoted from the rank of page at about the age of thirteen or fourteen, they were then trained further in knightly pursuits. The squire was a candidate for the honor of knighthood, and learned from the knight he was squire to by performing any tasks that the knight might require.

Stuff – a quilted material that is used under chainmail
Surcoat – cloth dress that covers an underdress. Surcoats were also made of leather, and worn over armor during heraldry period they might display the coat of arms.
Trencher – trenchers were used to serve and eat food, much like modern day plates. Stale loaves of bread (or stale crusts of bread) were used to soak up food and eat it. Leftover pieces of trenchers were often given to the dogs or distributed to the poor as alms.
Troubadour – musician and poet that entertained
Tunic – the medieval equivalent of a shirt. A tunic was usually longer and looser than a modern shirt.

Villein – a tenant who paid dues and/or services to his lord in return for land.
Wimple – headdress
Yestereve – refers to last evening.
Yesternight – refers to last night.

Prologue

Cumberland, England, 1398

Brithwin gazed at her father's grey, lifeless face as she crossed the room. Other than a pinprick to her conscience, there was no sorrow. She faltered. Was his chest rising and falling? A dull roar filled her ears, drowning out her pounding heart. She gasped. Nay. Nay! Hadn't the priest said his soul was at rest? Hadn't she watched as the icy fingers of death slowly robbed him of his last breath?

A shudder slithered through her body. Was it a sin to find relief in his death? He couldn't hurt her anymore. Surely God would not find fault with her. Perhaps her father's sudden passing was God's punishment for all the wrongs he had done her. The shuffling of feet brought her contemplations to a halt.

"It's all right to grieve, dear one—the tears will help you heal." Pater, a follower of John Wycliffe and branded a Lollard, laid his hand on her shoulder.

Brithwin pushed aside her conflicting feelings. "You know there is no sorrow in me for his death. Only relief that he is gone and anger for what he has done."

"Don't let bitterness consume you. It will do your father no harm, but it will slowly drain the joy from your life, my child."

Brithwin turned her head away from her father's still form and looked into the empathetic eyes of a man who had suffered far greater than she at her father's hand. She spoke the words anyway. "If anyone has a reason to be bitter, it is I. Isn't a woman's lot always bitterness?"

"Nay, Brithwin, you must forgive, just as our Lord

forgave. Remember what you have learned. Reach down in your soul and let this hate go. No good can come of it."

Dropping her gaze, she let his words pervade her thoughts. Could she forgive her father for the suffering dealt her at his hand, as Pater had done? It was the right thing to do. Uneasiness fluttered inside her, and memories poured down on her like a driving rain—her father's cruel words, her head snapping back as his knuckles connected with her cheek, but worst of all, the darkness that surrounded her when he chose the dungeon as her punishment. She would not, could not, forgive him. It was too much to ask. Brithwin turned and walked to the doorway. She paused, knowing her words would not please her Lord. "We will bury him today. With no one to mourn his death, I see no reason to wait."

Hours later, dark, menacing clouds filled the sky, threatening to open up and pound rain into the open grave. A crash of thunder shook the ground and Brithwin flipped her hood over her head. The few people in attendance moved restlessly, glancing at the sky. She'd not required the servants' presence at the burial, but some had come anyway out of loyalty to her. And she was here only out of obligation. A biting northern wind whistled through the trees. It seemed a fitting day to bury her father.

The priest's sermon droned on like a persistent bee. She shifted her feet to get the blood flowing through her legs, and a chill slid down her back. She drew her cloak closer as numbness swept over her mind and body. Today she was free of her father's tyranny. She should feel joy. But closing her eyes, she only wished the day behind her.

Pater's cough broke through her thoughts. She lifted her gaze. The priest had said his final words and stood in attendance. The wind picked up, slicing through her garments. Brithwin turned to shield herself and made her way back to the castle.

Before she reached the cover of her home, the rain began to fall along with an unexpected sadness as heavy as a millstone tied around her soul. Were these God's tears for a man no one loved?

Chapter 1

Two weeks later

Brithwin jerked out the weeds, noticing too late that half the stems she'd pulled were herbs. Too busy fussing to herself as she tucked the damaged plants back into the ground, she didn't see Thomas until he cleared his throat.

"Lady Brithwin, you wish to speak to me?"

Brithwin pushed herself off her knees to stand. When had she scooted from her stool and knelt in the dirt? She glanced up to see him frowning at her soiled gown. Raising her eyebrows, she wiped her muddy hands down her sides. "I have heard you sent a messenger to the king. Is this true?"

Thomas Godfrey, the captain of her guard, stood with his feet braced apart, arms folded, and face rigid. "It is as you say, for you need a strong husband." His firm voice gave her no hope of persuading him otherwise.

She narrowed her eyes. "You have wasted no time in searching for one."

His eyes softened under bushy dark brows. "I know you feel you can run this castle, Lady Brithwin, and you have done well, indeed, while your father lay abed ill. However, you know very well that King Richard will not allow you to hold these lands in your own right. What I did, I did for you."

Staring at her soiled hands, she shifted her feet. "You did for me? The last thing I want is another man to treat me like chattel."

With his arms still folded over his chest, he looked like a father firmly instructing a child. "And that is why I have intervened, and hopefully not allowed fate to decide."

She fisted her dirty hands and shoved them on her hips.

"I would rather give up my position here and live with the villeins."

"You are too naive, milady." Thomas drew in a deep breath and let it slowly escape. "You are a lady, and though I have no doubt you could survive anything after what you have been through, you would never be happy—not when you'd never be able to make a difference in your people's lives."

He spoke the truth. She would not want to see another cruel lord come in and abuse the people she loved so much. But to be under a man's iron fist again was too much to ask of her after enduring her father. Tears burned behind her eyes. She bit her bottom lip, refusing to let them fall lest Thomas should see them and think her weak. "You are a man. You could not understand how I feel." She swallowed a lump forming in her throat.

Tenderness softened the hard lines of his face, and the hard warrior who remained a constant in her life seemed almost vulnerable. "From the day your mother died and your father turned his back on you, I have looked after you. That is what I am doing now. You are like my own child."

Brithwin sighed. "I need no more men to look after me. You are enough. But I suppose it is out of my hands. We will wait to see what the king says." She knelt back down to tend her plants, dismissing him.

"Very well, milady." Thomas walked away grumbling.

She shook her head. Not even Thomas understood.

Brithwin sat on her stool and closed her eyes. What was she to do? When her father died, she had promised herself no man would own her again, yet who could defy an edict of the king?

†††

Royce Warwick and his men trudged down the muddy, rough-cut road. The rain had quit, but the men, along with their horses, were sodden and exhausted. Each step the animals took, their hooves sank into the sucking wet muck, draining more strength from them. They pulled their legs out only to sink down again, slogging along step by slow step.

The gates of Rosen Craig came into view, and they never had been so welcome. The past month away at his father's behest had not resulted in good news. Royce's dreams of settling the dispute peacefully and coming home to relieve his father's anxious mind of the rumored uprising—dashed. Yet he looked forward to discussing with his father the course of events that had taken place. Lord Rosen Craig's wise counsel would put his mind at ease or give him advice for future incidents.

Royce had still to dismount and shed his riding gear when his faithful servant met him, coming through the gate of Rosen Craig.

The servant doffed his hat, wringing it in his hands. "Master, I have distressing news."

"Surely, Fendrel, it can wait until I greet my father and mother." He swung off his destrier and handed the reins to the servant. "Take Shadowmere to the stables and see he gets a thorough rub down."

"B-but, s-sir." The man stood before him with reins and cap in trembling hands but not doing Royce's bidding.

Royce frowned. "What say you?"

Fendrel flinched. The man must have something weighing on him to be so anxious to speak. He waggled his head back and forth. "'Tis not m-my place, sir."

"Out with it, man." What was wrong with the man? First he wishes to give him news then he changes his mind?

Fendrel stepped back. "Y-your f-father and m-mother are d-dead."

Royce's innards twisted. Surely he hadn't heard him right. They were both doing well when he left. "Dead?"

The color drained from the servant's already pale face. He nodded.

Royce staggered back from the blow that hit him. He couldn't breathe. It was as if painful bands tightened around his chest, sucking out all the air.

"Where is Bryce?" Royce forced the words out as he scanned the grounds. He needed to talk with his brother. Find out what happened while he was away.

Fendrel's eyes welled with tears. "I'm sorry, Lord Rosen Craig."

Royce swallowed back the bile that rose in his throat and swung on his heel, heading for the castle. He didn't want to be lord of Rosen Craig. That was his father's job and then Bryce's. Yet only one thing would cause the servant to call him Lord Rosen Craig.

Silence in the near-empty great room testified to the truth. Royce dropped into a chair on the dais. All eyes rested on him. His companions sat, anxiously awaiting his directive. Royce closed his eyes and rubbed his temple, willing away the tears that bit at the back of his eyes. *Why them? 'Tis I that have sinned.*

He drew in a deep breath. When he rode away a month ago to investigate the rumored border uprising between his people and the Scots who'd been coming down causing problems, he had planned to be gone only a fortnight. But the unrest had taken much longer to control.

He opened his eyes. Simon, an aged comrade, sat to his left and gazed on him with understanding. The man's friendship and wise guidance had meant much to him through the years, right below his father's.

Sitting on the dais to Royce's right was Jarren, his long-time friend and fellow knight, and beyond him, Royce's uncle, Lyndle, lounged back in the chair with arms crossed over his chest.

"All of them?" Royce choked out the words.

"Aye." Simon laid his hand on Royce's shoulder and squeezed. He seemed to search for what to say. "My words are inadequate, I know, for you have suffered a great loss today. A terrible evil has fallen upon us." He shook his head. "We all grieve the loss."

"How could this happen?" Royce tightened his fists, his nails digging into his palms. Had a sickness swept through the castle?

The word echoed in his mind as though rolling through a cave—*how*. Moments ticked by before he realized he had spoken his thoughts.

Simon's eyes filled with unshed tears and his voice grew thick with sorrow. "We know very li—"

Lyndle leaned forward and elbowed the old man aside. "I woke to the scream of your mother and hurried to your parents' room, but when I arrived, they were both dead. While your father slept, someone ran a sword through him. Your mother's neck was broken." His voice cracked. "She must have woken and seen her attacker. When I looked for your brother, Bryce, he, too, was found in his bed, soaked in his own blood."

Bile climbed in Royce's throat and he fought to keep it down. "Did you see any of the attackers?"

Lyndle looked down at his hands as he spoke. "I saw the men as they rode out of the gates. One of them wore the Hawkwood colors."

The words hit Royce like a joust stick at full tilt.

Jarren raised a single eyebrow and stared down the table at Royce's uncle. "'Tis a bold move when the king is calling for peace between his lords. And how did they breach a well-guarded castle?"

Lyndle pulled his shoulders back. "The gatekeeper was found dead, and the guard's food was laced heavily with wild poppy."

Simon snapped his head up and gaped.

Was this the first he had heard this? Royce's gaze darted to Lyndle. "Did you alert the guards in the hall?"

"I ran to make aware the guards outside." Lyndle shifted in his seat. "But when none answered my call, I came in to wake the men in the hall."

Royce slammed his fist down on the table. "Are you saying we have a traitor within our gates?"

Lyndle's gaze shifted to Jarren then back to Royce. "I-it would seem so."

Breath wouldn't come. Swirls of color descended over his vision, blurring all reason. *My family—saints above! How could this happen?*

Clenching his jaw, Royce sucked air into his searing lungs. He needed to keep a straight mind. He couldn't allow his grief to cloud his judgment. "How long since the search was mounted?"

"Search?" Lyndle looked around cautiously.

"We have a traitor among us and no one has sought him out?" Royce's voice rose with each word.

Jarren cocked his head. "Why would men of Hawkwood kill your family?"

Lyndle shrugged. "Perhaps they sought to increase their holdings."

Royce pushed away from the table. Putting his weight on his hands, he leaned forward and looked down the line of men. "Jarren asks a good question. As we rode out these gates to put down the skirmish with the Scots, the king's messenger met me with a missive. The king has given me Brithwin, the heiress of Hawkwood, to be my bride." As the words left his lips, a leaden weight sank to the pit of his stomach. If his betrothed had devised this, the scheming wench would pay for the blood spilt at Rosen Craig.

Chapter 2

A month had passed since her father's death, and Brithwin had heard nothing from the king. Until now. Just as she'd begun to think God heard this one prayer—that the king was too busy to bother with her. But deep down she'd known better. A castle as large as her father's held too much importance, and as surely as his tax collector's annual appearance, the king's decree had now come.

Standing in the great hall, every muscle frozen, Brithwin took the missive bearing the royal seal from her servant. She ran her fingers over the uneven wax and studied its signet. Within this letter lay her destiny. Making her way to her favorite chair, she sat in front of the large stone fireplace at the far end of the hall. Something told her she would want to be sitting when she read this.

Thomas, who'd been giving her an update on the state of things, followed quietly beside her and spoke as she sat. "Do you mind if I remain?" He tipped his head toward the missive.

Brithwin nodded for him to sit in the adjacent chair and opened the letter. Letters from the king were not common, so when the servants found the missive while cleaning her father's room, they brought it straightway. The seal had been broken, indicating her father had read the contents. "Father had not shared this with you?" She studied Thomas's face.

"No, I knew nothing of its delivery."

She skimmed the paper, her fears becoming reality.

The king was pleased with a marriage between her and Sir Royce Warwick of Rosen Craig. A tear rolled down Brithwin's cheek as she read the missive. She quickly brushed it away. Her father's punishments had taught her to hide emotions that showed her weak. With Thomas's gaze on her and not trusting her voice, she handed him the letter.

He scanned it quickly and let out his breath. His words faltered, as if he were unsure how she might receive them. "Lady Brithwin, when I wrote the king and informed him of your father's impending death, I suggested an alliance with Sir Royce would be welcomed. But when I thought we'd gotten no response, I feared the king had not considered my request."

Heat crept into her face. "You told the king I *wanted* to marry this—this stranger? Why, when you know I do not wish to marry him or anyone else?"

"Have you forgotten all I told you when your father died? Has the short time of running Hawkwood caused you to ignore your place as a woman? A woman cannot own a holding as strategic as this. 'Tis not done. You will marry, either by conquest or by decree."

Her hands gripped the arms of the chair, turning her knuckles white. "I see no difference between the two."

Thomas leaned forward in his chair, elbows propped on his knees. "Sir Royce is a good man. I knew him when he had just earned his spurs. We served as knights together at Landower Castle. Sir Royce will treat you well, for he is honest and loyal. A better man I do not know."

"You sing his praises well, though it matters not. It seems I have no choice in the matter. No amount of valor can make me admire a man who forces my hand in marriage." If she were ever to marry, she'd want a man who would love her and care about her thoughts and desires.

Thomas spread his hands open before her. "Milady, you know I would never intentionally cause you distress. I have only your best interests at heart."

She would not concede to the compassion in his voice while her life dangled on a precipice. *Distress?* To be again at a man's mercy may as well be a death sentence.

His voice softened. "I pray you will not be angry with me, Lady Brithwin. I did what I must and suggested a man I respect."

"I need to think." Exhaustion seeped into her bones. "I will eat my meal in my room. And I wish not to be disturbed."

Brithwin pushed herself up from the chair and moved toward the staircase.

Thomas called to her before she reached the steps. "Think about what I have said, milady."

"Aye, I shall." She turned and ascended the stairs.

†††

Royce called together several of his men and sent them throughout the area in hopes of discovering who might have betrayed their lord and lady. Surely someone besides Lyndle had heard something—the drumming of hooves, perhaps, or a glimpse of men carrying Hawkwood's standard. When he had finished talking with his men, he strode out of the hall, mounted his horse, and rode to the graves of his parents and brother.

He was still there on his knees, sword resting across his thighs, when Jarren approached. Royce cupped his hand over the metal hilt, staring at the new grass rising from the freshly turned earth. "Do you believe in reaping what you have sown?"

Jarren squatted next to him. "Your family's deaths are no fault of your own."

Royce fingered the blade. "I had looked forward to getting the border skirmish behind me—to coming home, taking a wife, having my own castle to run. I had great hopes Lady Brithwin and I would fall in love, have strong boys"—a smile touched his lips— "and perhaps a pretty little girl or two, and oversee our land with fairness as husband and wife."

"Don't be hard on yourself. You're a good man. And who is to say you still will not have all those things you so desire?"

Royce shook his head. "Nay, they are not to be mine."

"Even *if* the tale Lyndle tells is true, you need not hold it against Randolf's daughter."

"You doubt Lyndle's veracity?"

"Let us just say it merits further investigating. But Lady Brithwin—I expect she knows nothing of this."

"That very well may be the truth of things. She is most probably an innocent. More the reason this marriage never should have been suggested. Not now. You know as well as I the sins I carry—how much blood is on my hands."

"How could we have known the Scots were innocent and came out armed only to protect their village?" Jarren shook his head. "You can't hold yourself accountable for something you knew nothing of. Edmond is the one to blame if you must lay blame at someone's feet. Had he not attacked them, they would have stayed in their homes."

Edmond. Royce's body stiffened at the name. The last time he had encountered Edmond was to defend innocent lives, but he had come upon the bloody scene too late. He and his men had chased Edmond off but not before the viper had left a trail of carnage through the town.

"You can't keep blaming yourself for another man's evil deeds. Edmond may not have been present this time when we fought the Scots, but his hand remained in it. The fight with our border neighbors was no chance meeting. We both know Edmond set us up."

"And because of that, commoners lost their lives. Will that man forever be a thorn in my side?"

Jarren cleared his throat. "I fear so. 'Tis why I sought you out. He and his knights came by Rosen Craig two days before your parents' deaths and told your family you had fallen to the sword while in the north."

"Are you certain? What could he gain by such a lie…unless…he came to appraise the security of the castle? If that be the case, then 'tis possible he works for my betrothed's father. Are you certain 'twas him?"

"Aye, 'twas he and his men who brought the news." Jarren shoved himself up to stand. "There is no question. He bore the scar you gave him at our last rendezvous."

✝✝✝

Royce spent two weeks mourning his family before leaving Rosen Craig. He'd left strict instructions to keep his family's death quiet until he had a chance to evaluate Hawkwood's people. As they rode onto Hawkwood land, he spoke to his men. "Remember, until I know what we ride into, I am still Sir Royce to you men. No one is to call me Lord Rosen Craig. We will see if anyone knows I am lord without us informing them." The weight of guilt lay heavy on his shoulders. His father and brother were the ones worthy of the title, not he.

Nearing the portcullis of Hawkwood, he scanned the walls and took in his surroundings. To see everything in fine array as he and his men rode into the inner bailey was a pleasant surprise. The gate had stood closed and well-guarded upon their arrival, knights walked the curtain wall, and men practiced mock battles in the field. Hawkwood did not appear weakened by a sickly lord—it was protected and well organized. He dismounted and his men followed suit. The stable boys emerged to take the horses' reins before his feet had hit the ground. With good fortune, the rest of the place ran with the same efficiency.

Initially, King Richard's announcement of Royce's upcoming nuptials had pleased him. At least until he'd learned of his family's murder. But even at that, seeing the castle up close sent warm currents through his blood. He was to be the new lord of this impressive structure.

The sound of his name interrupted his thoughts.

"Royce Warwick, it has been ages." Thomas slapped him on the back and smiled.

Royce grinned at his old friend. "Thomas, 'tis good to see you. I was not aware you were located here."

Thomas raised his eyebrows. "Did the king not tell you 'twas I who sent a request and suggested you for Lady Brithwin's husband?"

"Nay, the missive held no details. But then, Richard is the king." He grinned.

Jarren joined them, and Royce introduced the two men. "Jarren, this is Thomas, a friend from many years ago. We served together at Landower Castle."

They exchanged a few words, and Jarren turned to Royce. "Would you like the men to have a look around and acquaint ourselves with the surroundings?"

Royce nodded to him. "'Tis your new home. Go over the defenses—I will want a report."

Jarren strode toward the stables.

Thomas puffed up. "You will find the defense and security of Hawkwood well in order."

Royce nodded. "I am impressed by what I see."

"Come, I will show you around."

The two men headed toward the large, wooden doors giving them access to the castle. Inside, Royce was once again impressed. It was obvious the old lord had wealth, with all the luxuries the dwelling had. A well-maintained fireplace large enough for a man to walk in sat deep in the wall opposite the dais. White cloths covered the tables, and intricately carved chairs, stained a deep brown, sat on the raised platform. Beautiful tapestries portraying courting couples, village scenes, and hunts hung on the whitewashed walls. Royce took in the splendor of the room.

"I wish to speak with Lord Randolf." Royce dragged his gaze away from the brightly colored tapestry hung behind the lord's chair. "'Tis important I get this matter behind me."

Thomas gaped at him then shook his head as if to expel the words. "I—I assumed you knew he died."

"Died? I knew he was sickly, but I didn't think my tarrying would keep me from meeting him."

"His health had declined over the past few months. However, he took a turn for the worse and passed in a few days. He's been dead nigh on to five weeks now."

An ice-cold chill wrapped around Royce. And why did they not find his death important enough news to send to him? That would have put Sir Randolf's death just days before his own family's. "Who has been in charge since the lord's death?" If Hawkwood's colors were seen fleeing Rosen Craig, then who gave the order?

"That would be your betrothed." Pride filled Thomas's voice. "Milady is an intelligent and ambitious woman, quite capable of overseeing things here."

He searched his old acquaintance's eyes for guile. There was none. Could his betrothed have given the orders and kept them from Thomas, knowing him to be an honorable man? Had Thomas not just said she was ambitious? Royce balled his hands.

He longed to slam his fist into something. Anything. He needed to feel pain to help take his mind off the ache within. Less than two months ago, he had left Rosen Craig a happy man, anxious to put down the uprising and get back to marry. But all that had changed.

Movement to his left caught Royce's eye. A pretty maid stepped out of the hall.

Royce glanced around for his betrothed, but didn't see anyone dressed like the lady of the castle. The maid strode toward them. The top of her head barely reached his chin. As she drew closer, Royce's body warmed. She wasn't just a simple beauty. Her long chestnut hair flowed carelessly around her face. Intelligence flashed in her sea-blue eyes. But it was the challenge in the way she looked at him that he found so startling. What maiden regarded a lord as though she were his equal?

†††

Each step drained Brithwin of hope that the man in front of her was not her betrothed. He held himself as a lord would and dressed in fine clothes *and* appeared to know Thomas. He stood eye to eye with Thomas, making him a hand taller than most men. The muscles in his arms and chest gave proof of a warrior who wielded a sword. Hair black—no, deepest brown—touched his collar with the slightest hint of waves. His straight nose, square jaw, and strong chin gave him a look of authority.

Brithwin refused to glance down at her soiled dress or push back her unplaited hair—evidence that she'd spent the morning outside pulling weeds in her garden. She tipped her chin—she was still Lady Brithwin, regardless of what she wore. With any luck, her neglected appearance would turn the man away. If the situation were not so dire, she'd laugh. The only reason he agreed to marry was to take that which was hers.

"Lady Brithwin, meet your betrothed, Sir Royce Warwick."

Interest flickered in his enthralling golden-brown eyes, but it quickly vanished at her introduction and what replaced it made her shiver.

Brithwin broke the painful silence that followed their introduction with a slight nod of her head. "We welcome you to Hawkwood, Sir Royce."

†††

Ice ran through Royce's veins. His betrothed? He gaped, wide-eyed, wishing she lacked in beauty. She was not a maid nor an angel, but the devil in disguise. But oh, what a lovely disguise. He would have to strengthen his resolve until he could find proof of her innocence or her guilt. If she tantalized his senses dressed in these ragged clothes, he could not imagine what she would do to him adorned in a beautiful gown.

Royce looked at this exquisite creature and knew his trials had just begun. If she had ordered his family's murders, then surely she would try to use her womanly wiles on him to get what she wanted. Every time he gazed upon her beauty, he would need to remind himself of the possible blood on her hands.

Defiance blazed in her eyes. Perhaps a sign of her guilt? The woman needed to learn her place, and now would be a good time to teach her that he and he alone was her lord. His slow gaze raked her from head to toe. When he had finished, he chose his words carefully. "I hope this is not the way my betrothed always dresses. Go, clean yourself up before my men get the idea you're a servant and expect you to serve as such."

Chapter 3

Brithwin gasped. Had she heard him right? Glancing at Thomas, she knew she had, for the scowl on his face told of his displeasure. This was the man Thomas held in high esteem? The one he believed had more honor than most? What sort of man spoke in such a way upon meeting his future wife? Aversion spread over Royce's handsome face. His contempt for her was obvious—the same as her father, who had despised her.

Why did he not walk away if he deemed this marriage so distasteful? She glanced at her filthy clothes and sniffed. No matter how unattractive he found her, if he refused the union he would forfeit the prize—Hawkwood.

Brithwin gave him a cold stare just as he had weighed and examined her a moment earlier. She would have turned on her heel except she feared it would appear she made haste to do his bidding. Heaven forbid! She deigned to waste her words on him. "If you will excuse me, *my* castle demands my attention." She turned and marched away, sure to hold her head high.

††††

"Aye, your betrothed is quite a lady. She has not only the skills of a woman but the command to keep this place running smoothly."

"Humph." Royce stalked out of the mews and headed toward the stables when he spotted the garth. "What is this fenced area?" He pointed to a small sectioned yard with narrow rows.

"It is our garden. We grow many herbs, some for cooking and others for healing. The garden is off the kitchen, and Marjory, our cook, grows a goodly assortment of spices."

He added quietly, "And milady loves her flowers—she comes here whenever she is troubled."

Could a woman capable of ordering the murders of three people hide behind the guise of innocence? Such a person could love nothing or no one but herself. "She sits out here often, then?"

"Lady Brithwin?" Thomas let out a chuckle. "She does not come out here to sit. She is the one who cares for the garden."

That explained her soiled hands and clothes when they met. The question was, what had troubled her so today that she sought out a quiet place where she could think? His impending arrival? Perhaps she considered him a problem that needed solving. Perhaps *he* had better watch his back.

After inspecting the grounds and parting with Thomas, Royce strolled toward the great hall for the evening meal. Jarren caught up with him. They briefly compared notes on different aspects of the castle.

As they entered the hall, Royce lowered his voice as he spoke to Jarren. "Find out what you can about Thomas. He is an old friend. I trust him not to be a part of this, but I would like to know my trust is not misplaced." When Royce had finished speaking, he turned to see Brithwin sitting on the dais in the lord's seat, casting him a cool, appraising stare.

The woman challenged him. He didn't know whether he should laugh or send her to her room without dinner. This lady had backbone, and she would not submit to him like the simpering little fool he'd expected to find here.

Very well. He would have to cross the line she had drawn.

✝✝✝

A hush fell around her. It was obvious everyone waited to see the outcome of what was sure to be a confrontation. Whispers, "She sits in his seat!" wafted through the air.

Thomas had tried to convince Brithwin not to sit in her father's chair. The lord's chair. He had warned her she should not put Royce to a test of wills. Her betrothed's long legs took him quickly toward the dais, his fists clenched and jaw muscles bunching. Her pulse betrayed her, rapid at the collar of her dress. She swallowed.

She should have listened to Thomas.

Royce stopped directly in front of Brithwin and looked her up and down. "I see you took my advice. You clean up rather well." He spoke loud enough for half the hall to hear him.

The heat in Brithwin's cheeks spread through her face. This was not going as she hoped. She had wanted to show Royce she would not be easy to rule. The smirk on his face told her he noticed her blush.

"It has been a busy day, so if you will excuse me, Lady Brithwin, I will take my meal in my room. For future record, I have carried men with full armor off the battlefield, so a little rebellious wench is but a trifle for me." He started out of the hall, stopped, and slowly turned back to her, a predatory glint in his hawkish eyes. "And Lady Brithwin," he said softly, "tomorrow be sure not to sit in my seat unless you wish to be bodily removed."

The sound of indrawn breaths and the shifting of bodies in their seats reached her ears. Her face burned. She hated him.

Who did he think he was? He was not her husband—yet. Maybe she wouldn't marry the arrogant knave. Thomas was wrong. This man was not honorable. So why should her principle hold her to such a farce of a marriage?

If she did not care so for her people, she would flee to her kin in Scotland and forget her integrity. However, after meeting Royce Warwick, she knew she could not leave her people to his mercy because she was sure he had none.

What a fool she was to think a man ever would treat her with respect. They were all the same. Save for Thomas and Pater, men were out for no one but themselves, and a woman was no more than chattel in their eyes.

Well, she would not let anyone treat her like a piece of property. Men like him treated their horses better than their women and valued them more, too. She had been down this road with her father, and she didn't wish to travel it again.

Bands of tightness wrapped around her chest. The futility of her wishes to escape this marriage crushed her heart, but she would not allow Royce to crush her spirit. She drew in a deep breath and pushed her shoulders back. She would stay strong.

Still fuming when she left the great hall, she stomped to her chambers. Her body ached from the tension she'd held in all day, and she looked forward to the bath she had ordered in her room. It would relax her tight muscles, ease her nerves, and give her some much-needed peace and quiet to think. She reached the top of the stairs and turned the corner. Approaching the door of her room, she heard the sloshing of water. Elspeth, her lady's maid, now prepared her bath, and the water would be lovely and hot. Brithwin stepped into her room. "I won't need any assistance tonight, Els . . ." Her words stopped dead on her tongue. All she could do was blink and clutch the door.

"Ah, Lady Brithwin," Royce's smooth voice carried across the room. "My thanks for sending up the bath."

She bid her feet move but they wouldn't obey.

He tilted back his head and smirked down his nose at her. "Would you close the door? I feel a chill."

The nerve of the man. He'd already taken over her room. And in her bath! Brithwin's eyes dropped to the hair on his tanned chest, which glistened above the water. Her stomach fluttered and she pressed her palm against it. She couldn't just stand here, and she certainly wasn't about to walk away without saying something and let him get the best of her twice. She took a steadying breath and prayed he wouldn't see her tremble.

Forcing a smile she hoped didn't look false, she spoke as sweetly as she could. "I wanted to see how well *you* cleaned up."

With his jaw dropped and disbelief in his eyes, she sailed out of the room, grasping the drying cloth as she departed and leaving the door open—a genuine smile creeping across her face.

Chapter 4

Royce fumed in the tub, staring at the open door while goose flesh rose on his arms.

"Brithwin." He waited to see if she'd answer or appear back in the doorway, knowing full well the little vixen wouldn't. "Brithwin!" Silence.

You'll know who your master is when I am finished with you.

There had been so much to do and see to since he had gotten to Hawkwood, he'd not taken the time to learn the servants' names. Now he wished he had. The only maid he could recall was Brithwin's lady's maid.

"Elspeth!" Royce bellowed the woman's name. This time, giggles tinkled from down the hall.

"Wench, come here. I'm in need of your assistance." The giggles ceased and he could just imagine the two women scurrying away. Royce let out a growl. The servants disrespected him just as their lady did.

He'd catch his death, as cold as the room was becoming. He glanced at the bed where his clothes lay in a pile— unreachable. Nothing lay within an arm's reach for him to cover with. The bed had covers. He let out a low growl as he stood and water dripped from him. Snatching the cover off the bed, he sent his clothes plummeting to the floor. He wrapped the cotton fabric around his waist as he hurried to the portal. As his hand pushed the door closed, his wet feet slid out from beneath him. He landed on his back, smacking his head on the floor. Dazed, he lay there until the blackness dissolved and his sight returned.

Gingerly, he sat up and fingered the knot rising on the back of his head. He'd best not see that woman again tonight.

No telling what he would do to her. Taking hold of the wall to steady himself, he stood and walked to the bed. He fell on the soft mattress as the room spun. On the morrow, he would deal with Lady Brithwin.

The next morning when Royce came down to break his fast, Thomas sat eating. Royce rubbed his head and winced when his fingers brushed the painful goose egg. Royce had been around the chit for one day, and already he felt like he'd lost command. Well, it was time to take it back. The lord's chair stood empty and he headed for it. Brithwin would understand when she saw him taking his proper place. It would be pure joy to see the look on her face.

He settled into his chair, said a few words to knights walking past, and his food was served. Before taking a bite, he turned to Thomas. "This castle runs with efficiency. I am impressed."

Thomas set his goblet down and cocked his head. "'Twas not always so, not until Lady Brithwin took on the running of things. I'm thankful she pleases you."

Royce forced down the bite of food he'd taken. That statement greatly exaggerated his feelings. "Speaking of Lady Brithwin, when will she grace us with her presence?"

Thomas nodded to a servant to fill his tankard. "She has eaten and is already about her duties."

The smile faded from Royce's face. The day was early, the hall remained full, and still people filed in for the morning meal. She avoided him. Well, he would change that. "I wish to see this marriage performed as soon as possible."

"When were you thinking, my lord?"

"I see no reason to delay. She should have had time to prepare." His gut roiled as he said the words, but his king had ordered this marriage and his country needed a strong lord on this borderland. A thought niggled somewhere in his mind. Could an alliance have been formed between her and the border Scots? He would seek out the truth of who had murdered his family, and when he found it, justice would be swift.

Thomas leaned back and pushed his plate away. "Some things have been readied. Without knowing the details of your arrival, 'twas difficult to plan all."

"I see you have a chapel. I have yet to see a priest."

"Father Bronson resides near us. However, another lord had need of him. A death, I believe. He went to console the family and perform the funeral. He should return on the morrow."

He took a bite of meat and swallowed. "Very good. We can have the wedding ceremony in three days' time."

"What of the banns?" Thomas's voice was firm. "They must be read."

Royce set down his knife and shrugged. "'Tis the king himself who said we must not tarry. Let the priest read them each day and again on our wedding day."

"And what of your family? I know they live but a day's ride from here, but even if we sent a messenger in the morning, I doubt your family could arrive in time."

Royce's heart flinched at the unexpected mention of his family. "I am the only one left in my family. Bryce and my parents were murdered"—he searched Thomas's face for guilt, found none, and let out his breath —"recently."

Thomas stared in disbelief. "I am sorry. Who was responsible?"

Again, Royce studied Thomas. The man seemed to harbor no guile, but he'd wait and see what Jarren unearthed in his investigation about Thomas. "My thanks for your concern, but I would rather not speak of it."

"Of course, my lord."

Royce sighed. Back to the title he didn't deserve, but he would do all in his power to earn it.

†††

Brithwin stayed in the mews long after Thomas came to speak with her about the shocking news of Rosen Craig's murders. She had sent out an archer to bring back a hare for her favorite falcons, Talon and Lioness. Lioness improved daily from a malady, and Brithwin offered her a chunk of the meat, hoping to coax the falcon to eat a bite of her favorite food. With encouragement, Lioness accepted the treat. Talon eyed Lioness and the meat then hopped toward Brithwin and took a chunk from Brithwin's gloved hand.

The birds picked at the meal as she considered the news Thomas had brought her from his conversation with Sir Royce—Lord Rosen Craig. She would need to keep his title in the front of her mind when she spoke, but in her heart he would never be her lord.

Even with the bad taste in her mouth for Royce, she did have sympathy for him. To lose one's whole family would be horrific, particularly since Thomas had said Royce was especially close with his brother. Perhaps that explained his short temper and impatience—much different than the laudable man Thomas described. Grief could cause a person to act out of character, and Thomas had vouched for his honor and chivalry. She'd seen sorrow addle her servants and the villagers before, although she never had experienced its effects herself.

Maybe she'd been too hasty in judging him. A wee bit of guilt gnawed at her for walking out and leaving the door open last night. Brithwin ran her hand over Talon, and he leaned against it, enjoying the contact. Well, maybe *guilt* wasn't the right word. The look of shock on his face! No, she had felt naught but pure satisfaction to best him in a game of wits.

There was much to consider. If Royce's imperious behavior was due to grief, then how could she not forgive him? Christ did say to forgive seventy times seven. Part of her wanted to forgive Royce and do what she knew to be right—to offer her fealty. The other wanted to hold fast to the wrong he'd done her and gain the upper hand.

If she wanted anything other than animosity in her marriage, she would need to disregard her pride and forgive him regardless of whether he asked or wanted it. Her stomach knotted as she left the falcons and went to speak to Royce.

She found him out in her garden. Maybe they did have something in common if he sought out the comfort of a garden when his heart was heavy. That gave her hope, and she smiled as she approached him. He was handsome. Her words fled. She gazed at her feet, waiting for those elusive thoughts to return. Finally they did.

Raising her head, she looked past him. "Can we speak?" She nodded to the garden bench.

†††

Royce strolled over and waited for her to sit. It was obvious Thomas had spoken to her about his family. The way she avoided looking him in the eye fueled his belief she may be guilty. He longed to grab her and shake her until she confessed to her vile crimes. "What do you want?"

"You wish to marry in less than a week's time?" She continued looking across the garden. Anywhere but at the man she'd so grievously wronged.

"The *king* wishes it." Certainly not him.

Brithwin clasped her hands. "Thomas tells me you have recently lost your family. I am sure the king would allow a grieving period."

Royce flew from the bench and began to pace. Why would she offer this? The woman must have an ulterior motive. Did she not loathe him yesterday? He stomped across the well-manicured aisle and back as he considered the possibilities. The kindness she showed could only be a ruse to throw him off and make him believe her blameless. He would not fall prey to her charms. He swung to face her. "Yes, I am sure you would like that. It would give you more time to plot against me."

She looked away, probably because her guilt weighed so heavily.

He could not control the thunder rolling through him. He knew she could possibly be innocent, though that was unlikely. If only he could cause her to break and spill forth with the truth. "What would you believe if you received the information given to me? Your men were seen fleeing Rosen Craig. *You*, my lady, are the one who gives the orders here, are you not? So do not play innocent with me!"

A low growl drew his attention to a large, grizzled wolfhound standing beside his mistress. Its hackles were raised.

She jerked her head up to meet his gaze for the first time. Those sea-blue eyes had turned frigid, and her small hands resting in her lap curled tightly into white fists. Her anger condemned her. "I do not *play* at anything, Sir Royce."

She sucked in a breath, and he chose not to correct her on his title.

"No. What you play is far more dangerous. Do you deny responsibility for my family's death?"

"I believed your bad behavior was due to your grief, but now I see you have gone mad." She stood. "I deny nothing, for I have nothing to deny. You insult me, sir!"

She wouldn't defend herself, more evidence she was guilty. She stomped away with her back stiff and arms swinging. His pent-up fury burst forth before she reached the kitchen. "Henceforth, you may address me as 'My Lord.' And, my lady, we wed in three days' time."

She slowed but didn't turn around. "Aye"—she paused

—*"my lord."* And she stomped into the kitchen.

†††

Brithwin had to tell her feet not to run as she scrambled for the stairs and her old room. She dreaded another confrontation, and going to the lord's chamber was definitely asking for one.

Her whole body trembled as she struggled to slip the heavy oak plank into its latch. After several attempts, she managed to secure the door. Grasping the recently doused torch off the wall, she plunged the end into the fire. Back in its holder, the candle sent a soft yellow glow over the room. She hated the dark. Her father could be thanked for that. Brithwin staggered to her bed and collapsed on it, telling herself she would not cry as she swallowed the lump in her throat and drew in deep breaths. Willing her hands to stop shaking, she pulled the wimple from her head. Feelings were a difficult thing to master, but she'd gotten good at it. However, at the moment, she was finding it a challenge to tamp down the tears.

No sooner had she settled onto the bed when scratching started at the door. She turned her head away and ignored the noise until pitiful whines joined in. With a sigh, she pulled herself up, padded across the room, lifted the latch, and opened the door. Thor, forever faithful, gazed at her with sorrowful eyes. He seemed to know when she needed him. "Come in, my friend." She coaxed him onto her bed and curled next to him. The bristly grey fur belied the hound's soft, comforting nature. Wrapping her arm around Thor, Brithwin knew this would be one of her last evenings nestled next to her companion.

She had no choice but marry—to defy the king would mean prison or death. The wedding would be in three days with or without her approval.

She would have to harden her heart as she had under her

father's cruelty. Though short, her freedom from male dominance had given her peace. Now, Royce had shattered that peace, for she'd be under an iron fist again—married to a man who believed her guilty of his family's murder. Lord have mercy on her. What would he do to her when she became his wife? Perhaps he believed an eye for an eye. That would be far better than the cold, dark dungeon. Brithwin wrapped her arms around her middle, trying to rid herself of the tremor that still shook her body.

She couldn't sink into despair. She must trust God to give her time to adjust and strength to endure a new marriage.

†††

The wedding day arrived too quickly. Elspeth stood before her with a gown draped on outstretched arms. Its fabric, the color of a beautiful summer sky, was adorned with a delicate gold braid around the neckline, sleeves, and hem. Tiny pearls, sewn in an intricate swirled design down the front of the gown, twinkled in the morning light. She touched the fine fabric, letting it run through her fingers.

She should be angry with Thomas for disobeying her and getting her a gown. She knew she had displeased her guard at arms when she informed him she would wear one of her old gowns, for her wedding was no celebration. Oh, the brooding look he'd given her. Brithwin smiled. But when she'd suggested she wear her black gown, he'd rolled his eyes. How could she be angry with him? This blue gown was exquisite. It was as if Thomas knew her heart, for he must have put much consideration into the colors and style, not to mention the cost of the gown.

Elspeth broke her thoughts by pulling the gown from her touch and laying it across the bed. "Milady, your bath awaits."

After disrobing, she touched the water with her toe and

stepped into the tub. The warmth soothed more than just her skin. "The gown is lovely." A sigh escaped her lips as she sank farther into the water. "Thomas must have ordered this made weeks ago. It was kind of him. I just wish it were a happier occasion."

Elspeth's gaze shot to the door and she lowered her voice. "Don't let your betrothed hear that! 'Tis rumored milord has a beastly temper."

"I really don't want to do this, Elspeth." Her trembling hands caused ripples in the water. "I do not want to live the rest of my life with a man who hates me."

"We'll have none of that talk." Her maid knelt beside the tub. "He will realize he is wrong. Give it time. You are too kind for him to believe such a beastly thing once he is better acquainted with you. Now, let's get your hair washed and you out of there before the water cools and you catch a chill."

Brithwin had managed to avoid Royce since she rushed out of the garden, but she couldn't avoid him much longer. Once out of the bath, she donned her best linen chemise, embroidered with tiny flowers around the neck and hem. After pulling on her knitted wool hose and securing them with knee garters, she picked up Thomas's gift and slipped it on.

The gown, as soft as a kitten's fur, was the finest garment she had ever worn. Fitted to the hips where the voluminous skirt was adorned by tiny pleats, the surcoat, darker blue than the cotehardie it covered, had an exquisite gold belt that hung low on her hips. Still, for all its beauty, she felt melancholy.

Poised on the chair, she donned her shoes while Elspeth fussed with her hair.

"Milady, please stop your fidgeting."

"I'm sorry, Elspeth. I can't help it."

"Now, for the final touch." Her maid placed a gold circlet on Brithwin's head. She moved back and clasped her hands in front of her. "Ye are beautiful, milady."

Brithwin rose up and clasped her maid's hands. A knock on the door drew their attention. "It appears we finished none too early." She squeezed Elspeth's hands. "Thank you, you are too good to me."

Thomas's voice came through the wood. "It's time, milady."

Brithwin let go of Elspeth's hands, stepped out of the room, and took Thomas's arm.

Taking a slow pace, she tilted her head and looked at him. "Thank you for the lovely gown, Thomas. 'Twas kind of you."

"The gown?" He blinked. "Oh, aye, the gown."

Thomas sounded surprised she would thank him. He must have thought she was still upset. It was wrong of her to have been so unkind to him for encouraging the king to decree this marriage. He was right. If not Royce, it would have been someone else.

"Lady Brithwin, you look beautiful." Thomas's eyes shone with pride.

"Thomas, I wish there were a better choice."

His brow crinkled and his face softened with understanding. He slowed his steady strides and pulled her to a stop. "It will all turn out well. Wedding fears are not uncommon, even in people betrothed since childhood. You must garner your strength from God above. The Lord will never forsake you. Remember that always, for it is a treasure you should hold close to your heart."

If only she could have Thomas's faith. It seemed to come so easy to him, while she struggled with the simplest truths. For as hard as she tried, she failed to imagine God's love could help her bear this union.

"I shall try, Thomas." Her voice came out in a strangled whisper.

Chapter 5

Royce gazed down from the church steps as he waited for his bride to appear. His mind shifted to three days prior when Brithwin had huffed out of the garden with her head held high. His betrothed had too much pride. Yet, she bewitched him like no other—beauty, intelligence, confidence—qualities that also made her dangerous. Especially if he let down his guard.

The woman vexed him. What man desired to spend his days watching his back? He let out a growl. The priest, standing beside him, frowned. Vexed or not, King Richard's eyes were on the benefits the marriage would bring him, not on Royce's reluctance.

At Brithwin's approach to the church, wearing the blue gown he'd bought for her, thoughts flew from his mind. A queer pain hit his chest, robbing him of his breath. None could rival her beauty. Chin tilted high, shoulders back, and hips swaying, Brithwin looked like royalty. And somehow she looked innocent in all her splendor.

Innocent! He shook himself mentally to get his thoughts in order. It would do him well to remember she could very easily be like Eve in the Garden of Eden, plotting to deceive him, to trick him into letting his defenses down. He couldn't let her beauty cloud his senses, for surely she would use her womanly wiles against him in any way she could.

†††

Brithwin wished the day was over as Royce said his vows.

"I take thee, Brithwin, to be my wedded wife, to have and to hold, from this day forward, for better, for worse, for richer, for poorer, in sickness and in health, 'til death do us part, if holy church it will ordain, and thereto I plight thee my troth."

The words couldn't mean anything to him. He'd made it clear how he felt. It would be by God's mercy only that he might honor one of the promises.

When her turn came, she replied where expected, all the while longing to be a spectator. That is, until he lowered his head and his lips tenderly brushed across hers to seal the spoken vows.

Suddenly, she was there. The awareness of his hands on her upper arms sent her senses on alert. He broke the contact, and she could still feel the impression of where he had held her. Lips tingling, she ran her tongue over them. He was the first man whose mouth had touched hers. He'd been so gentle, she almost could deceive herself into believing he could be kind.

Brithwin's body stiffened. Respect was something she'd never get from him as long as he believed her a murderer. To live in a marriage where her husband held so much hatred and animosity toward her would be unbearable. She needed to forget her pride and convince him of her innocence—but he'd made it clear he would never believe her. All her protests would be wasted words.

Royce took her arm and guided her into the church for mass. She drew her shoulders back and marched to the front, taking her seat. Settled beside Royce, Brithwin couldn't concentrate on the priest's droning words, and they became mere noise filling the small building. Married—her vows spoken before both God and man—her fate was sealed and she must move forward. She glanced at Royce, who stared straight ahead. A muscle flexed in his jaw. Could God make anything good come out of a marriage neither participant wanted?

†††

When the service finally concluded, the town folk filed from the church. Brithwin stopped beside Royce on the steps. He spoke to her people. "Let me present to you Lady Rosen Craig." They all cheered. "You are all invited to come to Hawkwood to celebrate with us." A roar of excitement went up among the crowd.

Had he just invited every servant, freeman, and villein to remain and partake of the meal with them? Most of these people never had eaten in the castle hall. And judging by the pleasure of his invitation, it appeared Royce had made a calculated move, for if she knew her people like she thought she did, he had just won them over.

Struck by a moment of outrage, she drew her brows together—how warmly her people welcomed him. Where was their loyalty to her? How could they betray her after all she had done for them?

Brithwin let her gaze roam over the crowd with a frown. *Where* did he think he would seat everyone?

They made their way through the bailey, his hand still possessively on her arm, accepting the kind words and congratulations from the swarms of people.

The great room was a buzz of activity, with men scurrying around, moving tables closer together and opening floor space. Her people filed in, many finding seats on the floor, while others crushed together on benches, and to Brithwin's astonishment, although it was very tight, they all fit.

With everyone seated, the food came out. Pork, beef, mutton, and poultry filled the tables. Sauces garnished the meats, while an abundance of fruits and nuts were heaped upon platters. Sweet custards and delicacies topped off the tables. It was a feast like none she ever remembered.

The troubadour that Thomas had hired for the evening made his way to the center of the room, entertaining with his ballads of chivalry and courtly love. Even with the distraction of music, she couldn't keep her mind from what the evening would hold. Her stomach twisted—she needed air.

Brithwin glanced at Royce. He had not spoken a word to her since they'd sat to eat. Now, with the meal finished, he was not seeking her company—she had no reason to remain in her seat.

Brithwin stood to leave. Royce's hand shot out and he seized her wrist as though he owned her. "Leaving so soon?"

The deep growl of her faithful wolfhound came from behind her. It renewed her courage. With a tip of her chin, she met his eyes. "I need fresh air. I find it stifling in here."

"You will go nowhere without asking my permission first, my lady." He tightened his hold as she tried to pull away. "Do not challenge me in this. I assure you, I am much stronger. If you defy me, you will only humiliate yourself."

Brithwin flopped down. She wouldn't ask him for permission. This was her castle. The only home she'd ever known.

As luck would have it, she didn't have to feign submission long before an altercation erupted and duty called Royce away. Brithwin quickly slid from her seat and hurried to the back stairs. They were better concealed, and he was less likely to see her. All she had to do was make it to her room where she could lock the door and be safe.

†††

Royce approached a group of men overindulging in ale and throwing punches. He glanced around for one of his men to help break up the scuffle and glimpsed Brithwin scurrying along the wall toward the back stairs. Turning back to the boisterous group, Royce summoned Thomas, already making his way to him.

"Take care of this for me, Thomas," Royce yelled as he hastened toward the front stairs.

†††

Brithwin rushed into her room and slammed the door. The heavy plank securing the latch leaned on the wall next to the door. As her hands grasped the oak board, Royce's voice rumbled like a violent storm behind her.

"I'm glad to see you hurrying up to be with me."

Brithwin yelped. Swinging around, she held the board as a shield. "How did you—"

His lips curled. "Get up here so quickly? Ahh. I saw you sneak to the rear steps. I wasn't aware you were so anxious for this evening."

Brithwin's throat constricted. Her hands tightened on the board, and she took a step back. "Stay away from me."

Royce glanced at the thick board in her hands. "Give it to me."

"Nay." As the words left her lips, he reached for the plank. She flung it at him and pulled the door handle.

Royce grabbed for the flying board but not fast enough. The board glanced off his forearm and slammed into his temple.

Brithwin cringed but continued to tug on the latch. A bolt of hot fear shot through her, twisting her insides and obstructing her thinking. She had to get out. She jerked on the handle until her arms were weak. Why wouldn't it open? Her gaze flew from the top to the bottom of the door.

Royce's foot, planted at the base of the door, barred her escape. Following his boot up to his muscular body, where his thick arms folded over his broad chest, Brithwin released the door handle and backed away. As he secured the door with the board, her mind filled with the image of rabbits caught in small game traps.

Royce turned. Blood trickled down one side of his face. Those golden-brown eyes now narrowed at her, full of dark foreboding. She glanced around, frantically seeking an escape. And then she saw the window.

†††

Royce's head ached from the impact of the board. He couldn't believe that the little imp had gotten the better of him.

The board in place, he turned to deal with Brithwin, but she'd backed against the wall, gaze wild and darting around the room. He knew the moment his wife saw freedom by the way her roaming eyes fixed on the window. She broke free and dashed away.

With long strides, Royce closed the distance, grasping her gown before she reached her escape. He pulled her toward him as she tried to jerk the fabric from his clutch. Spinning around, she came face-to-face with him and let out a small gasp. He felt pity for her when she drew up her arms, protectively covering her face as if he would strike her. Her body stiffened at his touch, but he did not relent. He had to establish lordship over her proud, defiant ways.

Sweeping her into his arms, he headed to the bed. To his surprise, she drew still and compliant in his embrace. A visible pulse throbbed at her neck, and her eyes went wide. He shook himself out of their mesmerizing hold.

"You would jump from a window to your death rather than remain in here with me?" Royce raised one eyebrow. "No, do not answer that."

She was beautiful. Blood pounded in his ears. He did not want these feelings she caused. Disgust, directed at himself, consumed him. Brithwin was a deceiver, and he would not fall prey to her bewitchment. He must remain unfeeling toward her. He couldn't become a love-struck pup—not with the woman suspected of arranging the murder of his family. He was like Adam tempted with the forbidden fruit. No matter that *he* had forbidden the fruit.

†††

Brithwin's heart thudded erratically as Royce's arms cradled her—and imprisoned her in their grip. A morsel of kitchen conversation snapped into her mind—the giggles behind servants' hands as they gossiped about wedding nights. She cringed and lifted her eyes to see him, wanting to know his intent. Pain splayed across his face. Those captivating brown eyes no longer blazed but now looked straight into her, seeking . . . The scent of sandalwood and leather beset her nose, causing her stomach to riffle. She bit her bottom lip. His embrace wasn't so frightening.

Warmth rose in her face, and the heat consumed her. Her lips parted. This man caused so many different emotions to run through her and put her mind into a jumble. In a matter of minutes, she'd gone from angry, to scared, to something she couldn't name.

Her thoughts ended abruptly as her body hit the bed, and his arms came down on each side of her, caging her in. The irritation had left his face, replaced by satisfaction.

She would wipe the smug look off his face. He may be stronger, but she had learned many lessons on defending herself against a man. She'd had to.

Her father had never been her defender. No one had to wonder for long about how he felt about her. When knights and nobility traveled through, often spending the night, they took his aversion for her as an open invitation.

Indeed, when Brithwin was but fourteen, Thomas had walked in the kitchen as a knight caught her unawares and pressed her against the cook's table until the hard wooden edge bit into her back as he tried to steal a kiss. Thomas flung the man off her and beat him until she worried he would kill the man in his rage. The next day, he took her aside and taught her several effective ways to defend herself. Lessons she took seriously.

She tensed her leg to drive her knee upward.

Chapter 6

Royce gazed down at his beautiful wife, trapped between his arms and the bed. Brown hair swirled in a chestnut-colored halo around her head. He longed to run his hand through the silky curls. His gaze wandered to her lips. Lips as soft as flower petals. They were like a siren, beckoning him to taste their perfection.

As if to weaken his resolve, she tenderly touched the wound on his head. Red, slick blood stained her fingers. Her gaze darted to her bloodied hand and back to him. If only she were innocent... He lowered his head, giving in to the desire to feel her lips touch his.

The yearning he experienced quickly fled at the threat of her next action. Royce brought his lower leg down on hers, preventing her from jabbing her knee into his groin. One glimpse of her eyes and his heart softened. Wild, rounded in fear, they reminded him of a cornered animal's.

He eased the pressure of his leg over hers slightly, still keeping her confined so she couldn't unman him. He had to stay in control and resist her beguiling ways. A knight could never let his guard down or turn his back on his adversary, and right now he had to remember that his wife very well may be his enemy.

Yet he could not help but admire her spirit and so much more.

"Remove yourself from me and from this bed." Brithwin ground out her words and tried to roll out of his grip.

Royce leaned down and increased the pressure across her shins. "You mean, remove yourself from me and this bed, *my lord.* Moreover, why would I want to do that? You near knocked me out cold with the board."

"'Twas an accident, and well you know it." She hesitated until his eyebrows rose. A shiver sliced through her body. She'd not give into fear. "*My lord.*"

Brithwin lifted her hands to push him off her, but he grabbed her arms again. "Accident or no, I think I will stay here."

She scowled. "What do you want?" She waited defiantly. "My lord."

He gazed down at the amazing woman he held. Any man would be proud to call her his wife—she had so many fine qualities. What *did* he want? He wanted her to be innocent of his family's blood. He wanted a bond with her like his parents had. He wanted to feel worthy of a fine woman and the blood washed from his hands. But none of that was to be his.

And none of that was for her ears to hear. He shook his head. "You were told not to leave without my permission."

Brithwin pulled, trying to free her hands. "You had gotten up, so how was I to ask?"

Royce kept his grip firm. "You took advantage of my leaving. You should have waited until I returned."

"How was I to know how long you would be?"

He knew what she was about but wanted to hear it from her lips. "Why did you not come look for me?"

She slanted her head. "Now, that is the crux of the matter, isn't it?"

His head ached as he imagined the torture of spending the rest of his life married to this devious beauty. "It is that. Now, tell me why you were in a hurry to get here."

Brithwin lifted her chin, sinking her head farther into the bed. "If you will let me go."

"*If* I do, will I have to dodge flying objects, guard the door and window, or protect myself from being unmanned?"

Brithwin's lips twitched. "On my honor, I will behave."

"What say you if I tell you I do not believe you have any honor? You have given me no reason to believe you have any. Only reasons to believe you don't." Even as he said the words, he knew they weren't true. She'd showed nothing but honor since he'd been at Hawkwood. His only grievance was an unsubstantiated accusation.

Her face clouded. "If I had no honor, I never would have married *you!*"

Aye, a man like him, who'd shed so much blood. He steeled himself against the rolling waves of guilt. "Explain yourself."

"I married you because of my people." Her words came out short and terse. "I could not leave them to your wrath should you have come here and discovered you were short a bride."

"I am supposed to believe you would have left—you didn't want this marriage?" He scoffed. "I think you were too greedy and did not expect me to find out about your little plan." Royce bent over and spoke in her ear. "So, now that things are not going as you had planned, I imagine you would like to escape."

As he pushed himself away, fury flashed across Brithwin's face. "Are you going to let me up or not?"

Royce cut a hard look at her and a long pause ensued.

Brithwin's eyes narrowed until they were near shut. "*My lord.*"

Royce lightened his hold on her arms. "I will release you, but you are only to sit on the bed and not to move. I am faster and stronger, and next time you defy me, I will punish you. Remember that."

As he stood and stepped back, Brithwin swung her legs over the side of the bed. He readied himself to capture her again should she bolt.

She glowered at him. "You are wrong when you say I

wanted this marriage. I wanted no man in my life. Relief was what I felt when my father died. All men are the same. You care for none but yourselves and your pleasures. A woman is naught more than chattel in a man's eyes, easily discarded. I know, for I have lived it. I was quite content here these past months, running Hawkwood without a husband to interfere."

"You ran this castle on your own?" Royce let out a snort. "Are you not forgetting your steward?"

Brithwin sat straight and folded her arms in front of her. "I dismissed him, for he was not honest with his dealings."

Royce leaned his shoulder against the large wooden post on the bed. "Is honesty that important to you?"

Brithwin tipped her chin up. "Aye, it is, along with trust."

Royce read the truth of it in her eyes. "Who keeps your accounts?"

Brithwin started to push herself up and appeared to think better of it. "*I* do. Pater taught me how to read and work with numbers."

Royce choked. She could read and write? What other surprises did she hold? Royce ran his fingers over the cool metal on the hilt of his sword. "If you did not want this marriage, why did you have my family murdered? You did not deny it when I asked you."

Brithwin sprang from the bed and faced him. "I said I had nothing to deny, and if you think I am capable of such a thing, you are a fool!"

Royce pushed away from the post before answering. "Do not ever call me a fool again, my lady," he whispered. "Or you will find your fears justified."

††††

Brithwin squared her shoulders and lifted her chin. So he had noticed her fear. Well, he never would see it again. Showing fear made her weak—lessons from her father left an impression she did not forget. He'd fed off the terror he enjoyed inflicting on her. She had overcome it—all of it. Even the one horror he found extreme pleasure in. It had taken her a long time to hide the panic that went through her when he sent her to her own personal prison. But once he no longer saw her fear, he lost interest in her.

"Your threats mean nothing to me. I am sure I have lived through worse." She squelched a shudder threatening her body. She could not let him see her tremble or give him any hint of the way her stomach convulsed.

Royce's hand dropped from his sword and he stepped forward. "What do you mean?"

Brithwin fought the urge to step back. "Only that you do not know me nor do you understand what my life has been."

He studied her face. Apparently, her answers were not to his liking. Perhaps she was a bit too vague. She stifled a smirk.

His gaze remained riveted on her. "What was your father like?"

She tapped her foot. "It matters not what he was like, for he is dead."

"Then what of your mother? I have never heard mention of her."

Brithwin sighed and looked away. "I never knew my mother, for she died giving birth to me."

With the lightest of touches, his hand cupped her chin, drawing her gaze back to him. Royce's brown eyes glittered with curiosity. "So your father raised you alone?"

As if he'd realized he'd given too much away with that touch of tenderness, Royce swept away invisible lint from his shirt. But she saw through his pretense. The questioning had gone on too long for her liking, anyway. She needed to gain control of the conversation before she became vulnerable.

"You said you came up here because I left without

saying anything. I will return with you, if that is what you wish."

An uncomfortable silence followed as he scrutinized her. "You may remain in here." He dropped into a chair and leaned his head back.

She folded her arms in front of her. "What are you doing?"

He didn't bother to move. "Waiting."

She tapped her fingers on her arm. "For what?"

This time he raised his head and glared at her. "For time to pass. Now go to bed."

Brithwin raised her chin. "I will not! Not until you leave."

"'Tis fine with me. Sit there, but do not speak."

She stomped to the bed and perched on the side while he glowered at her from the chair. Brithwin refused to squirm under his fierce perusal.

After what seemed like forever, he unfolded himself from the chair and walked out of the room, his boots tapping on the floor. She darted over and locked the door behind him. She'd had enough surprises for one night.

No sooner had Royce left and she'd taken a few steps away, than a knock sounded on the door.

"Milady?"

Brithwin hurried over and let her maid in.

"Help me out of this gown, Elspeth." Her maid loosened the ties binding the dress together and held the garment while she stepped out. With the gown neatly folded, Elspeth laid it on a chair with her belt and circlet.

"Was he mean to you, milady?" Elspeth dropped her gaze to the floor. "I do not wish to be too forward."

"You are more than my maid. I know you ask because you worry." Brithwin sighed. "No, he has not been cruel. Although he tests my patience." A clipped bitter laugh escaped. "But no more than I test his, I assure you."

Elspeth's hand went to her chest. "The servants all say he is a fair and just lord, unlike your father. They are all pleased he has come."

The words hurt. Even though she wanted fair treatment for her people, a part of her felt loyalty had swayed.

Remaining in her chemise, Brithwin excused Elspeth and stretched out on the bed. She never should have let Royce know he could frighten her, but he'd caught her unawares, and once the fear had gotten a foothold, it was difficult to overcome. Yet he'd done nothing but talk. Her father would have devoured her had he seen that kind of weakness in her. Could she be so lucky that Royce was different, or did he play a game to leave her wondering…worrying? The unknown could be far more terrifying.

But even though he'd done nothing more than talk, how could he be as honorable as Thomas said when he got angry with her for such a minor infraction?

Brithwin opened her eyes to the night's darkness. Bolting out of the bed, she caught sight of the smoldering fire with its hot coals. The orange embers pulsed from bright to dull, and she hurried to stir them. When a flame burst forth, she placed a piece of wood on the small flicker and blew lightly.

A shiver ran through her body. It wasn't the cold that bothered her, it was worse—a black, moonless night. She hated being alone in a dark room. How many times in the warmer months when a fire was not feasible had Elspeth lit a torch and placed it on the wall in her room? Heaven knows what her father would have done if he had found out. This time, she couldn't stop the shudder rippling through her body.

She stared at the log as it took on the flames. Elspeth

must have believed she would sleep in the master chamber this evening—otherwise there would have been a fire.

Royce would expect her, it being their wedding night. She should go. But it was not as though he liked her. He barely tolerated her. The heat from the rising flames warmed her face. Had he not told her to remain on the bed? If he became angry and came to retrieve her, she would remind him of his words.

She put a second log on the fire, sending up tiny sparks. Light now in the room, she climbed into bed and lifted up a silent prayer.

God, it seems I come to You most when I am in need, and here I am again. Please be with me. Give me the strength and wisdom to see things as I should and to know what to do.

†††

Royce raised himself from his chair. He hadn't returned to the wedding festivities but instead had gone to his new solar to think. His gut still roiled from the evening. He should be thankful for his wife's innocence in some areas—her confusion as to why he remained with her in their bedroom was not an act. He'd met more than his share of ladies *playing* innocent. But her bewilderment, as he allowed an appropriate span of time to pass to give an impression to the servants of their consummation, had been genuine. Knew the lass nothing of the ways of a husband and wife?

It may be his wedding, but he didn't feel like celebrating. As he stepped inside his room, the weight of a suit of armor settled on his shoulders—the burden that always assailed him once alone with his thoughts.

To go along with the burden, it was as if a blacksmith hammered in his head. He picked up a clean white cloth from the table and dipped it in the water bowl beside it. The cloth nettled the bloody cut on his temple. He winced, removing the dried blood. He rinsed the cloth and folded it, pressing the cool fabric against his pounding forehead.

He dropped down on the chair next to the fireplace, stretching his legs. The unnecessary fire crackled, and flames licked high into the air. The heat encompassed him like the warm arms of a loving father. Royce closed his eyes, forgetting—until those arms became bloody and he peered into the empty sockets of a man he loved. Grief tormented his soul. If he had not been delayed from returning to Rosen Craig, he could have saved them all! He wanted their murders vindicated. Could his new wife be an accomplice to this heinous crime? He needed the truth but he didn't want *that* to be the truth.

He shook away the vision of his father, and Bryce pushed his way in. He missed his brother. Bryce would never have the chance to marry his betrothed—but at least she'd not be a widow.

'Twas strange that Lyndle hadn't mentioned Clarice when he was there. He would have to make a point of asking about his brother's betrothed next time he and Lyndle met.

And here he sat, wondering if he'd married his brother's murderer. Royce tossed the warmed cloth to the hearth. He raked his hand through his hair, no longer convinced Lady Brithwin had done it. The evidence said guilty, however his gut said innocent. He'd always trusted his inner voice, but with the tragedy at the uprising, he could no longer trust himself.

Brithwin needed to be watched clandestinely. He'd have to find someone for that job whom he could trust to be loyal to him. Moving her to the adjoining room would help him keep an eye on her—although he may want to sleep with his sword.

She would be hard pressed to leave her chamber without his knowing, for he slept lightly. Royce grinned. And he would add a little something to insure he heard her should she attempt to sneak out in the night.

If Brithwin had blood on her hands, she would have to suffer the consequences. Perhaps he shouldn't have married her until he'd discovered the truth. He could have gone to the king, but Richard would not have been sympathetic to him. He'd wanted to insure peace between his lords, and marriage was one way of securing it. His gut knotted. Vows or no, he would not take her as his wife in the biblical sense until he found her innocent. He didn't want to think what he'd have to do should he find her guilty.

And how could he reconcile the possibility of her innocence with Lyndle's information of seeing Hawkwood men leaving Rosen Craig? He'd expected to find a chit with expensive jewels and fine clothes, yelling at servants that things were not done to her liking. But what he'd seen was quite the contrary. Until today, he'd never seen Brithwin in fine clothing—and he had to admit, she worked as hard as any of her servants.

He had even gone as far as going through her effects in her chamber. She had few belongings, and what she did own was of no great quality or value.

Being a good judge of someone's character was something he'd always prided himself in. He needed to find a way to prove her innocence. Otherwise, the heir that the king wanted to see would never be.

He also needed to maintain the illusion of this marriage. Should word get out that it was only a marriage in name and not been consummated, it would leave both Brithwin and him in a very vulnerable position.

Chapter 7

The kitchen echoed with talk and laughter as Royce entered. On the far wall, two large stone hearths blazed, filling the air with the savory scent of spices and herbs. Loaves of fresh bread sitting on the table bid him over with their hearty aroma. Brithwin sat at a long plank table, chattering and holding a piece of bread in her hand. A slow silence infused the room as each servant realized he'd entered. All except for Brithwin, who was explaining medicinal plants to the other ladies.

She opened her mouth but promptly shut it when Marjory stood and curtseyed. "Can I help you with something, milord?"

"Thank you, but no. I have come in search of my lady and it appears my quest is now ended." He smiled and arched one brow.

Marjory giggled. Brithwin rolled her eyes.

Royce's gaze returned to her. "Are you ready to go riding, my lady?"

"Alone?" Brithwin nibbled her bottom lip. Her body shuddered beneath his gaze.

"It will be you and me." He looked over his clothing to make sure naught was soiled or disagreeable. Was he really that repulsive to her?

She hesitated.

"The horses are saddled and the men are waiting. I have yet to meet a woman who could be punctual. Do you think you could bring your bread with you?"

"The men?" She let out a whoosh of air.

"Aye, you do not think I would take you out without guards?"

Brithwin's pinched face relaxed. Sweet mercy. What did this woman think he would do to her?

She pushed off the back of the bench and rose. Her cheeks flushed, he'd have guessed from the heat in the room if not for her gaze which bore into him. "I am ready, *my lord.*" She forced the words out between clenched teeth.

The mordant way she said his title incited a growl from her wolfhound. Royce scowled at the dog.

He contemplated giving Brithwin his arm as he led her out of the kitchen and toward the bailey but decided against it. No reason to let her believe he approved of her behavior. "I would have you show me the grounds Hawkwood possesses. Thomas suggested I take you." He snorted. "He claims you know it as well as he. I do not doubt Thomas *believes* that to be the truth."

Brithwin straightened her back and lifted her chin. "I assure you, *my lord*, Thomas speaks only the truth. I spent as much time as possible away from the castle while my father ruled. Shame that I suddenly have the same urge."

"Not without guards, I would hope. Although with your sharp tongue, 'tis possible you could draw blood."

Brithwin stomped ahead of him. If she lifted her nose any higher, she would be watching the birds fly. "Thomas always makes sure I have guards about me."

Her haughty demeanor brought on a grin, but as the words sank in, he sobered. Again, Thomas. Why had her father not seen to her safety? Even a harsh father should see to her well-being. He hadn't had a chance to speak with Thomas about Brithwin and her father, but needed to.

The bailey buzzed with morning activity. Servants bustled around with morning chores, while knights sat on low benches, honing their swords and oiling their chain mail. The men he'd chosen to accompany them on their ride stood at the ready.

The crisp morning air soon would be warmed by the sun's rays. The day promised to be good for riding. He stopped in front of a small chestnut mare and lifted Brithwin onto her seat. His hands lingered on her waist as he gazed into her stormy eyes, wishing they could have the kind of love his parents had.

What kind of magic did she weave? Royce jerked his hands away and strode to mount his warhorse.

"After you." He feigned a slight bow, fighting the spark of desire that ignited.

†††

As they made their way out the gate, Royce gave the men curt orders to stay alert. Somewhere in that charge, Brithwin was certain Royce also had given a silent command to allow them privacy, because immediately half the company separated and forged ahead while the other half dropped behind them. She guided her mare along the trail that skirted the village and headed for the eastern edge of Hawkwood's land.

"Is there anything in particular you want to see?" she asked, breaking the lingering silence.

He tipped his head toward her as if she should know the answer. "Everything."

It would take more than a day to show him everything. She'd show him the important things he needed to know.

She may not have wanted to marry him, but she wasn't foolish enough to withhold information because of it. This land and these people were still hers, and she felt responsible for them. Like it or not, she would tell him whatever he *needed* to know to keep her people safe and fed.

As they traveled, Brithwin shared information of Hawkwood's holdings. She pointed out the grazing sheep and goats on the countryside with pride. This was fertile land and coveted by many.

A goshawk swooped down in front of them from the branch of a nearby tree, close enough that she could hear the whoosh of wind beneath his wings, his talons latching onto a small rodent as the bird skimmed along the grass. Brithwin slowed to watch the magnificent hawk fly away effortlessly with his prey. Glancing over, she noticed Royce seemed taken by the gracefulness of the bird, too. Perhaps they could find something they agreed on.

The group continued on, stopping only for short stints when Royce wanted to get a closer look at something, not nearly enough time for her to get down and stretch. She would not be seen as weak—if the men didn't have to stop, neither did she.

Well into their ride, Brithwin's back ached, her thighs were rubbed raw, and every time the horse took a step, pain shot through her backside. Who would have thought the lout would keep her on her mount for five hours? With a sick father, she'd been busy running a castle the past three months, which left her precious little time to be on a horse.

The small piece of bread she'd nibbled earlier left her hungry. She shifted in her seat, trying to ease the chafing on her legs. Royce was a typical man. He gave no consideration to anyone else's discomfort—especially that of a woman.

Brithwin pointed toward the water ahead. "Hawkwood borders the river."

Royce leaned forward, stood in his stirrups, and glanced around. "Let's rest here and water the horses. We can stretch our legs and partake of the basket of food that Cook packed."

The man must have read her mind, but she was too relieved to think about it. The river gurgled past her. She drew her mount to a stop. Royce appeared next to her before she had time to attempt dismounting. Grasping her waist, he lifted her from her horse and set her feet on the ground. His grip lightened, sending her legs buckling beneath her. She let out a gasp and grasped his shoulders. His arms wrapped around her.

Supported by him, Brithwin waited for strength to return to her legs. The scent of sandalwood and leather enveloped her as she struggled to keep herself from leaning against his chest. Her legs trembled beneath her. The near presence of him didn't help her wobbly legs, and she sagged against him, causing his grip to tighten. Her breathing echoed his. The rising and falling of his chest became one with her, but his heart's rhythm threatened to be her undoing. She shoved her hands against his solid chest as she tipped her chin up.

The iron arms tightened around her again with a gentleness that belied their strength. The glimpse of concern and tenderness in his eyes made her wonder whether the man she so detested were a facade.

†††

Royce held up Brithwin's small frame and berated himself for riding so many hours without stopping. Where was his chivalry? Her head rested against his chest. The woman did strange things to him. It was hard to believe a few days ago he'd planned to make her life miserable. Heaven help him if he were to find out she had anything to do with his family's deaths.

He must not allow himself to feel anything for her until he knew the truth. Keeping a firm grasp on her shoulders, he stepped away. "Can you stand by yourself?"

"I think so." A hint of a smile played across her lips. "And thank you."

Letting his hands fall to his sides, he broke contact with her. "You need not thank me, my lady."

"No?" She eyed him with uncertainty. "I would have fallen had you not caught me."

He had much to learn about this wife of his—most would have complained an hour into the trip, demanding to stop and rest. And here she stood, thanking him for catching her. Brithwin was stronger than he credited her. His thoughts of a spoiled and coddled girl could not have been more wrong.

Royce's hands curled into fists. Admiring her strengths was a dangerous pastime.

"I believe I am fine now." She squirmed under his perusal. "Shall we water the horses and eat? I am famished."

Royce handed her the basket, grabbed the reins of both horses, and led them to the river. Waiting for the horses to finish, he glanced behind. Brithwin busied herself laying out the food. Sunlightened strands of hair escaped her plait that framed her oval face. Saints above. He need not allow his eyes to drink in her beauty. Not until he knew the truth. How many times would he have to tell himself that?

As the other men took their food and sat on rocks near the river, Royce tied the horses to a branch and made his way over to the food. He stretched out on the ground and picked up a piece of cheese. "Did you come here often?"

"Nay, 'tis too far a ride. But 'tis one of my favorite places. I savor every moment I come and try to memorize every little thing. When I was pun—when I was alone, I could come here in my mind."

Punished. She hadn't finished the word, but by the drop of her head, there was no need. Royce cocked his head. "Pray tell, my lady, why would you be punished and by whom?"

Brithwin shoved a piece of crust in her mouth and chomped vigorously.

Royce eyed her with growing suspicion. "I asked you a question, my lady."

She swallowed with a gulp. "I have no idea what you refer to."

Royce pushed up to a sitting position and scowled. "And I do not believe you. What is it you hide?"

He glimpsed the twitching of her jaw before she swung her head around. "I conceal nothing that is your right to know."

Royce grunted and got to his feet. The chit could be stubborn. He made his way to the water. Perhaps punishment was the only way her father could keep a daughter with her own mind under control.

Royce untied the horses. "We need to get back."

A straight route made the return trip much shorter. The clomping of their horses' hooves on dirt was drowned out by yells of children and the noise of workers as they entered the village. Royce adjusted in his saddle. The houses were in good shape. Several had new thatched roofs, the area around was clean, and there were no offensive smells. Not only did the castle run efficiently, but it was also obvious the villeins had expectations they had to meet.

A man, dragging a young boy by the arm, yelled out to them. Royce stopped his horse. The boy looked no older than eight or nine and squirmed like a hooked fish. The man jerked him forward, his might out powering the young lad.

He stopped upon reaching Royce. "Good eventide, milord 'n milady."

Royce pulled his steed to a stop and leaned forward, giving a quick nod with his head. "Is there a problem here?"

"Aye, that there is, milord. Me name is Peter, and I caught this here boy trying to steal one of me chickens."

Royce turned his attention to the young boy, who was looking at the ground and shuffling his feet. "Is this true, boy?"

"Peter—" Brithwin's eyes locked on the man.

Royce raised his hand to silence her. "I'm waiting for an answer, boy."

"The bird were runnin' 'cross the street." The young boy flashed a peek under his brows and returned to studying the ground.

"Where are your parents?" Perhaps they had put him up to this.

Brithwin jerked forward and lowered her voice. "His mother died a fortnight ago, *my lord.*"

The lad slowly raised his eyes to meet Royce's gaze. "My da died when I was a boy, and me ma died right before the last rain."

Royce glowered at Brithwin. "I will handle this, *my lady.*" He then turned to the lad. "What is your name, boy?"

"L-lucus."

Brithwin smiled at the small boy. "I thought you were to stay with your uncle?"

Royce swung around. "Woman, did I not make myself clear?"

The young boy stirred the dirt around with his toe. "He don't want me. Told me to leave and not come home."

Royce had heard enough. "Peter, lift the boy to me. I'll take him off your hands and determine his punishment."

Before she could raise her objection, he raised his palm to her again. "My lady, not a word."

†††

Oh, the man was insufferable. Who did he think she was? No, the question was *what* and the answer was *chattel.* She clamped her lips together. His arrogance grated on her nerves. She'd like to choke him. Now, there was a pleasant thought.

Peter tossed young Lucas up to Royce, where he was seated in front of him. The boy's eyes grew twice their size, and she was confident his awed look was for the large destrier, not fear of Royce. Lucas began asking questions about the horse, never stopping until they dismounted at Hawkwood. And to her amazement, Royce patiently answered each one in detail.

Royce towered over the young boy, who sucked in his bottom lip and lowered his eyes. Royce patted his head. "I never like to discuss business on an empty stomach, and I haven't eaten since the noon hour. Why don't you go on into the hall and find yourself a place to eat. When we are done, we will talk."

"Yes, milord!" Lucas ran toward the castle.

Brithwin studied the way a stray curl rested above Royce's brow, making him look boyish. "That was kind of you."

"The lad probably hasn't had a decent meal in days." Royce turned to his horse, tending the animal's needs.

The long ride had drained Brithwin's energy and stiffened her limbs. The return trip hadn't been as bad—they stopped regularly and stretched their legs. She ambled into the castle behind Lucas, each step causing her to wince, thankful the day's ride was over, and went directly to her room to clean up. After splashing water on her face and slipping into a clean gown, she stepped out of the portal and started down the corridor, stopping to relight a torch and return it to the wall. The shadows lengthened as light shining through the windows dimmed. She squelched the shiver that threatened. Hastening her steps, Brithwin made her way to the great hall and food.

When the evening meal was finished, Royce, still seated on the dais, summoned Lucas.

Brithwin cleared her throat and waited for Royce to turn. He gave her a warning glance before resting his eyes on the boy.

"Now, do you want to tell me why you were stealing the chicken?"

The boy looked at his feet again.

Royce scowled at the young lad. "I expect you to look at me when I talk to you, boy."

Lucas's chin quivered. "Y-yes, milord."

"Go ahead."

"He were gonna kill the bird!" he blurted out.

Royce spoke under his breath, "The boy rescued a chicken?"

Brithwin sat stunned as she witnessed Royce fighting the mirth that threatened to spill out while he attempted to sound stern.

"Still, the chicken didn't belong to you. We can't let this go unpunished." Royce rubbed his jaw. "You must like birds."

The picture of Lucas frantically trying to save a chicken meant for someone's dinner pot got the best of Brithwin, and try as she may, she could not stop the giggles that burst forth.

Lucas sneaked a glimpse and smiled.

Royce shot Brithwin a brooding look, and she clamped her hand over her mouth.

When the boy's smile withered, Royce continued. "You will work in our mews. You can labor there, keeping it clean, and maybe you can learn some things. Sleep in here and take your meals with the others. I will have someone introduce you to your duties tomorrow. You understand?"

"Yes, milord!"

"I expect you to do a good job. Run along, now."

Brithwin sat in disbelief as Royce finished speaking to Lucas. Maybe there was hope, for the man had a heart after all.

She hid her smile as Royce's head jerked around. His golden-brown eyes darkened and bore into her.

"You, my lady, need to learn your place."

Chapter 8

Brithwin remained kneeling on the floor in front of the bench long after Pater had finished praying with her. She found her heart heavy every morning of late. Pater's haunting words returned every time she prayed. *Don't let this bitterness consume you. It will not hurt your father, but it will slowly rob you of the joy in your life.* It was true. Her happiness had eluded her for a long time now. Feelings were peculiar. While he lived, she regularly suffered at his hand, yet she never had this heaviness in her soul that she now felt. She despised her father and did not want to forgive him. He didn't deserve her forgiveness, even in death. There were a thousand reasons why. Brithwin pushed Pater's words from her mind. Tears threatened as she silently begged God to hear her prayer.

Pater sat on the other side of the cool stone chapel. She knew his eyes were on her. Then, as if her slightest movement had called him, he straightened to his feet and shuffled toward her.

"Dear child, I have watched you struggle for nigh unto a fortnight, and I have been petitioning God to help you through whatever ails you. However, today I felt the Lord nudge me to you."

He knelt beside her and wrapped his arm around her shoulder. Brithwin lifted her head and choked back a sob.

The tenderness in his eyes broke loose the dam. "I have seen you struggling, my child. Will you share your burden with me?"

Brithwin swiped the tears with the back of her hand. "Pater, God does not hear my prayers."

"And how do you know that?" Compassion flooded his

voice.

Brithwin looked at the elegant crucifix that stood at the front of the room. "I do not feel His presence when I pray, and He does not answer my prayers."

"You cannot rely on feelings, my dear." Pater closed his eyes and smiled. "Do you remember when you were a child and you found that stone in the shape of a dove?"

Brithwin smiled at the memory. "Aye, I remember. I slid it under the crack in the door. I felt very sorry for you, the way my father kept you imprisoned. I thought it would cheer you up. I knew you would love the dove." Her smile broadened. "Although I didn't understand at the time it was not the bird you loved."

Pater laughed. His eyes danced with delight. "You were what kept me going every day. I looked forward to those moments you could sneak away to see me." He paused and his face clouded. "Until I learned you were punished each time your father discovered you had come to see me. But those days are behind us. When you were a child, how did you know I had the dove?"

"I gave it to you." She tipped her head sideways and waited to see what he was getting at.

"But you couldn't see it after you gave it to me, and you couldn't feel it. So how did you know I had it?"

"Because I gave it to you, and you told me you put it on your table and every time you looked at it, you thought of me."

"You trusted me. You had faith that I kept it even though you couldn't see in my room or feel it." Pater gave her a gentle squeeze. "That is the same way it is with our Lord. You do not have to feel Him for Him to be here. You know He hears your prayers because His Word tells us He hears us when we pray. You must trust Him to be true to His word."

Brithwin wiped the remains of her tears with her sleeve.

"But I feel a heaviness I have not felt before. My soul cries out for something, but I know not what. I ask, but there is no answer."

"Do you perhaps have unconfessed sin weighing on you?"

"Nay." Brithwin swallowed. She could not look at him. Pater remained silent.

"Aye," she said quietly.

A glimmer of light flickered in Pater's eyes. "You need to confess your sin, and you will find your burden lighter."

Brithwin pushed herself off her knees and slid onto the bench. "I cannot forgive my father. He was cruel up to the day he died."

Pater rose and placed his hand on her head. "Did Christ die so your sins could be forgiven?"

"Yes."

His hand skimmed down to her shoulder as Pater sat on the edge of the bench. "What did you do to deserve forgiveness?"

"Nothing." Brithwin took in a deep breath as his words sank in. "I have done nothing to deserve it."

"Still He forgives you, and now you must forgive because He tells you to. The forgiveness is not for your father, dear Brithwin. It is for you. When you forgive your father, you set yourself free from that sin." Pater smiled. "And mayhap it will change the way your heart views your husband."

Shame filled her. "How were you able to forgive, Pater? You were imprisoned for as long as I can remember."

"'Tis the fate of many Lollards. Many died for what they believed or were forced to retract their beliefs. I count myself fortunate to have lived to see you grow into the lovely lady you are today."

"Why did my father spare your life? 'Tis not as if the

man had any mercy. Did it have to do with my mother? I know you arrived here at the same time as she."

Pater pulled the collar up on his neck. "He spared my life only because I would not die, but that is a story for another day." Pater rose and moved toward the door. "And you, my child, I believe, have some business with the Lord."

††††

A month had passed since the wedding and a fortnight since Pater had encouraged her to forgive. She strolled between the rows of herbs in her garden. The anger she'd had toward her father grew less each day as Pater had assured her it would. Healing takes time, as does learning to trust, he'd told her. She supposed learning to trust helped in the healing.

Yet what of her husband? Trusting God was much easier than trusting a man she did not know or understand, a man who treated her like chattel. Brithwin made her way into the bailey.

Godwin, a man-at-arms, dropped a rock onto a pile and bent to pick up another. She hurried toward him. "What are you doing, Godwin?"

He wiped the sweat from his forehead and left a trail of blood. "Milord told me to move the rocks over yonder to here."

Brithwin stepped forward to touch his forehead. "You are bleeding!"

Godwin ducked his head. "'Tis nothing, milady. Just me hands."

"Let me see them."

He splayed his scraped hands before her.

Brithwin frowned. "You need to get those washed and salve on them before they fester."

"I still have rocks to move, milady."

"They can wait."

Godwin's gazed darted around. "'Tis punishment,

milady. For falling asleep on watch."

Brithwin forced herself to sound stern. "Godwin, you served my father, and now you serve me." She folded her arms in front of her. "I am telling you to clean the blood off your hands and put salve on them before you are unable to stand guard duty."

"Yes, milady."

"Good. Now go." Brithwin pivoted to go into her garden.

"*My lady*, what did you just do?" Royce's soft words came from behind her and the ice in his tone made her freeze.

She cringed as she slowly turned to face him. "*Someone* around here needs to care for *my* people."

Royce flexed his hands. "'Tis punishment."

Brithwin cocked her head. "He has been punished. You have drawn blood. And he now applies salve to his wounds. Do you wish to continue the punishment until he is no longer able to protect this dwelling?"

Royce stepped forward. "You undermine my authority. You take my seat to show power over me, you interfered with my punishment of the boy—and now this. I have tried to be patient, but I have had enough."

He seized her arm in a fierce grip and dragged her toward the castle. Her people stopped and stared as she struggled to keep up with his steps. Heat surged to her cheeks when chortles came from some of the men. She hoped and prayed they were Royce's men and not her own.

At the bottom of the stairs, she planted her feet and jerked her arm within his tight grasp. "I am not taking another step. Unhand me."

Royce's gaze darkened. He bent down and threw her over his shoulder.

††††

Royce grunted from the pounding of fists Brithwin

inflicted on his back as he stomped up the stairs. The little vixen had power in those hands when angry. He'd have bruises on the morrow. "Enough, Brithwin." She was causing him precious time and if the scout's sighting of Edmond proved correct, the troublesome man was escaping even now.

He'd made his way through her door when her words came grating out. "Then put me down!"

Royce took two steps and dumped her on the bed. He'd been in her room twice and both times with the same result— although the previous occasion's warm feelings now erupted in hot anger. "I have business to attend to. While I'm away, you are to occupy yourself with accepting that *I* run this castle."

Royce walked out and locked the door. A few hours of wondering when he would return should help her understand the way of things. She would learn to submit.

He made his way out of the castle and met a smiling knight in the bailey. "Ya done right, sir."

If 'twere anyone but Brithwin, he would be a laughingstock. Clearly, the vixen's ability to try a man's patience was well understood in Hawkwood. "What's your name?"

"Floyd, sir."

"You've been here long?"

The knight shifted. "Long enough."

"In two hours I want you to send a maid to unlock my lady's room." Brithwin had cost him valuable time. He didn't have minutes to track down a maid.

He clenched his teeth as memories of his last encounter with Edmond came to mind. He didn't want the man to slip through his fingers as he had when they stumbled across the small village where Edmond and his men went on a killing rampage.

"Two hours? Ah, yes, sir."

Royce walked to the stables and found Jarren and Philip, one of Royce's knights, waiting.

"Are the horses ready?"

"Saw to it myself." Jarren arched a brow. "What is eating at you?"

"'Tis that woman I married. I'd like to turn her over my knee." Royce scowled. "What are you grinning for?"

"I was remembering a conversation I had with you before you wed. I believe your words were, 'As my wife she *has to obey* and will have to answer to me.'"

Royce stalked into the stables.

†††

Locked in the chamber adjoining Royce's—the one that had been her mother's—Brithwin dangled her feet off the side of the bed and glanced at the adjoining door. She had heard him lock the hall exit. She slid from the bed and tiptoed to his door; perhaps he'd forgotten to lock it. She pulled on the latch. It didn't budge.

Brithwin stomped back and flung herself onto the bed. What terrible thing had she done for him to lock her in her room? She meant only to see to a man's welfare. Royce was like every other man in authority. Give him power and he wielded it like a weapon. He could leave her in here, for all she cared, as long as she didn't have to see him.

Brithwin stayed on her bed, listening for the sound of a key in the door as she watched the sun set in the sky. How long was he going to leave her here? If only she had not given Elspeth permission to visit her family, she would be freed by now.

With each passing hour, her anger tightened in her chest. The room grew dim, and she scooted off the bed to light a fire. Her heart raced as she knelt to stir the embers with a piece of kindling. No spark winked among the ashes. What had she been thinking, letting the fire die this far? She dropped the stick and dug through the ash with her hands. A cold chill trickled down her spine. She scanned the room for a piece of flint—nothing. Falling back on her heels, she swallowed, trying to rid herself of the constricting pain in her throat. Darkness—her father's favorite punishment.

Her heart hammered in her chest. *What have I done this time, Father? Have you reached me even from your grave?* She rushed to the window in search of light. Torches flickered, tiny pinpricks in the distance, too far away to calm her pounding heart.

When would Royce come? Or would she spend the entire night in the dark? She opened her mouth to call for help but thought better of it. She could not show such weakness. Brithwin dropped to the floor, hugging her knees to her. *Oh, God, please let the punishment end.*

Chapter 9

It was late when Royce and his men returned. Edmond had disappeared, but there was no doubt he had ridden around Hawkwood, with the amount of fresh hoof prints skimming the woods on the western border, too large for a palfrey—only a warhorse could have left them. The man was up to no good. Royce could feel it all the way to his bones.

He plodded up the stairs. The search should have taken a few hours but instead dragged on until darkness fell, slowing their progress more. He pushed open his solar door and traipsed across to his chamber. Brithwin's voice came from beyond her portal, and Royce stopped to listen. Whom was she talking to this late? Her words came fast and high, and he couldn't make sense of them. He unlocked the door and stepped into the thick darkness. Brithwin screamed and scuttled backward. He followed the sound. She shrieked at him to stay away. A crash sounded on the floor ahead of him, followed by a softer thump. Royce rushed forward. Feeling his way around the fallen table, his hands brushed over Brithwin. As he pulled her up, Brithwin's cries became more frantic, and she pounded her small fists against his chest. What game did she play?

"Let me go. Let me go!" Her voice rose to shrill panic.

Royce seized both her wrists. "Brithwin. Brithwin! Calm yourself. 'Tis me. Royce."

Her muscles relaxed as she sagged into him. She trembled like a frightened bird. Not a game, then—she truly feared something. He released her wrists and pulled her to him. Running his hands through her hair, he whispered, "'Tis well now. Shhh. All is well."

When she had calmed, he scooped her up and carried her

to his solar, where the fire burned bright, and set her in a chair. For all the fear that contorted her face, not one tear had fallen. He gave her time to calm herself.

When her breathing had slowed and the terror melted from her face, Royce knelt before her. "Did you have a nightmare?"

Brithwin shook her head.

"Are you well now?"

She drew in a shaky breath and nodded.

"Then let's get you to your room." Royce stood, trying to suppress the urge to run his hand over her hair as one would cosset a small, upset child.

"Nay! Please." Her voice came out in a frantic plea, but it was the fear and the entreaty in her eyes that gave him pause. "Will you light the fire in my room...my lord? Please."

Royce frowned. What was going on here? "Did someone hurt you while I was away?"

Brithwin shook her head and took a deep breath. She took a second deep breath and cleared her throat. "If you would light a fire in my room, I will return."

Royce stared at her. He'd not seen so much all-consuming fear, not even in the battlefield. Why did she choose to bear it alone? His gut twisted. "Aye, I will. But you will tell me why you were so upset."

Brithwin shook her head and looked at the floor. "'Tis nothing. If you would only light a fire for me, my lord." Not a hint of rancor in her murmured *my lord*.

Royce lifted her chin with his finger. "I would know what frightens you so."

Her eyes narrowed and she tipped her chin away from his hand. "I am fine." He watched in fascination as the muscle in her jaw flexed. "'Twas you, sir, who locked me up with no food nor fresh water. And *you* do not frighten me."

"I left orders for your door to be unlocked," he said softly, "my lady." Why hadn't Floyd seen to her release as he was told? A fiery gleam slowly replaced the alarm he'd seen in her eyes. Whatever had upset her had passed. Royce tipped his head and grabbed a torch from the wall as he strode into her chamber to light the hearth.

As soon as he had the fire blazing, Brithwin stomped into her room and excused him. His gaze swept over her. What had caused her such anxiety? And how could a woman so frightened become that angry in the blink of an eye?

To see his wife so full of fear tore at his heart. Royce stomped out of his room in search of Floyd. He would find out why his orders were not obeyed. He would have answers, and they had best be good ones.

Throwing open the door of the castle, Royce rushed down the stone steps and nearly ran into Floyd in the courtyard.

"Good eventide, milord." The light of torches glimmered off a toothless smile.

Royce scowled. "It was not for my wife. She has been locked in her room since I left, with no food, water, or fire. What is your excuse for disobeying my orders?"

"I—I didn't think… I thought you would be pleased that she was kept from causing trouble."

"Your first answer was correct. You did not think. I gave you an order and I expected you to heed it. A man who doesn't obey is of no use to me."

"I—I am sorry, milord." He bowed his head. "It won't happen again."

"To be sure. But to help you remember, you'll spend this night in the dungeon, with no water or light. Pity you have had your evening meal. My wife did not get hers."

Royce called to Daffydd and turned Floyd over to him.

As Daffydd led the man away, Royce called to him. "On the morrow, Floyd, you will go to my lady's garden that she loves, and you will pull weeds and line the aisles with stone."

"Milord, gardening is a woman's task. I am a warrior," Floyd argued.

"Tomorrow it is *your* task. You have caused my lady undue distress. Now you will relieve her of her duties. And don't forget to apologize for your thoughtlessness."

†††

Only a few days had passed since the ordeal of being locked in her room. The memories of that night reignited all her old fears and still haunted Brithwin. She pushed the thoughts away as she hurried to the village to check on Guy, Murielle, and their grandson, whose mind never was right, and to bring them a basket of food. Guy and Murielle had been a light in the darkness all her years growing up. She would visit them whenever she got to town, and Murielle always had a treat for her. But the years had not been kind to them, and now they needed her help. Getting to the village twice a week had become more difficult since Royce arrived. He'd disrupted her whole life. But Tuesday she'd arisen early to avoid him.

She knocked on her friends' door and heard the shuffling of feet as they drew nearer to the door.

The hinges creaked. Murielle greeted Brithwin with a toothless smile, gesturing for her to enter.

Brithwin set her basket on the rickety table and turned to Murielle's husband. "How is Guy today?"

"I am doing well enough for an old man. I expect to walk again in no time."

It was their regular dialogue. She gave him the smile she knew he waited for and sat next to him.

Brithwin rubbed her arms briskly. "'Tis chilly in here. You should burn some wood."

The old man pulled his blanket tighter around himself. "Can't use up all our wood."

"Warm weather will be here to stay in a sennight. You should keep your fire burning and your house warm until then. I will see you don't run out of wood. You do not want to catch a chill."

Time slipped away while Guy and Murielle told Brithwin all there was to know about her villeins, and Brithwin filled them in on the castle gossip. The old couple had always held a special place in her heart. When she was young, she use to slip away to the village and Murielle would have special treats for her. However, that was when Guy was well and able to work. Now they would starve if she didn't bring them food.

Brithwin's gaze searched the small cottage. "Where is Malcolm?"

"He is hiding in the loft. He ran there when you knocked." Murielle glanced in that direction.

"Will you ask him to come and fetch some wood, and I will build you a cozy fire before I take my leave?"

Brithwin set about stirring the coals while she waited for the wood. Once young Malcolm had brought the logs and the fire was crackling, she said her good-byes and began her walk back to the castle.

She'd stayed later than she'd planned. Foot traffic on the twilit road had thinned to a few stragglers who'd long disappeared. A quick glance around sent her mind abuzz—no one as far as she could see, yet she had the eerie feeling someone watched her. Gravel crunched beneath her leather sole shoes, sending an animal scampering out of a small thicket and away from her path. She glanced over her shoulder. A shiver ran through her body, causing her to quicken her step. Next time she would bring Thor.

The silhouette of stone turrets against a moon lit sky

came into view. She held up her gown and ran to the portcullis.

As she walked through the gate, a sigh escaped her lips. There was nothing like the safety of the castle walls. Brithwin made her way through the bailey and to the great hall for dinner.

†††

Royce paced the floor as he waited for Daffydd. Brithwin had left early in the morning and not returned until well after the evening meal. Had Daffydd not been following her, he would have driven himself mad with worry. A knock sounded on the door.

"Enter."

"My lord." Daffydd walked into the room, situating himself before Royce.

Royce shook his head. "There is no need for formality while we are alone. We have been through too much together." Daffydd dropped to the chair and relaxed, and Royce nodded. "My wife is late in returning. What have you learned?"

"Nothing new. Her routine is much the same from week to week." A grin broke out on Daffydd's face. "She is a busy woman."

Royce scowled. "Where was she that she missed the evening meal?"

"She went to the old couple's house and brought them a basket of food, same as every Tuesday and Friday."

Royce began his pacing again. "Have you met the grandson yet?"

Daffydd turned and followed Royce's progress. "He is as the townsmen said. I would say about sixteen but with the mind of a young child."

"You are sure?" Skepticism laced Royce's words.

"Aye, there is no doubt. He was sent outside to gather

wood for the fire, and he spent most of his time talking to the wind."

"Then she has met no one with whom she could have conspired?" Relief swept over Royce.

Daffydd folded his arms in front of him. "No, and if you were to ask me, I would say she is innocent of the charge." He cleared his throat. "She has a heart for her people. She is always giving but never takes."

Royce swung around in his pacing. "You admire her?"

"I do. You are a fortunate man, my friend. Very fortunate, indeed."

"'Tis my hope. You can go, and get Marjory to fix you something from the kitchen."

"I think I'll do that." Daffydd walked to the portal and pulled open the door.

Royce stopped him. "Daffydd, you never answered me. Why was she so late tonight?"

He stopped and looked over his shoulder. "She seems happy when she is there. Perhaps she is enjoying herself and doesn't want to return."

Royce massaged the tense muscles in his neck. "You won't need to continue to follow her. If she were going to meet with someone, she'd have done so by now."

"Glad to hear that." Daffydd swiveled to look Royce in the eyes. "Not to complain, but I'm tired of skulking around like a criminal."

Royce returned to pacing. He would soon wear a visible path on the floor if he kept this up. How could he prove her innocent if no one had seen the real murderers?

Ever since he held her in his arms on their wedding night, he'd worked like there was no tomorrow to drive her from his mind, yet she was a sickness to him—a siren with blue eyes, who wrenched his soul every time he laid eyes on her.

This couldn't continue! Proof was what he needed. He would gather a few of his men and make an excursion to Rosen Craig. Yes, he needed to talk to Lyndle again. Find out if he remembered anything else.

With his family gone, the memories of Rosen Craig were precious—more precious, yes, but more painful, too. Wasn't that why he'd chosen to stay at Hawkwood—to avoid those painful recollections? Besides, the trip would get him away from Brithwin's hold without his having to work himself to death.

†††

The unsettling sensation someone had been watching her on the road stayed with Brithwin. Since her husband seemed insensible to her safety, the least she could do was retrieve the knife she'd left in his chamber before they were married. She lay tense on her bed until she heard Royce's door close. The covers hugged her body, and she threw them off before she swung her feet to the floor. She tiptoed to the door and pressed her ear against the smooth wood surface. She bit her bottom lip—Royce paced the floor.

"Wonderful," she whispered in disgust. "He didn't leave."

The pacing stopped and she held her breath. What if he had heard her? The sound of a creaking chair and a sigh came from the room. She exhaled. Well, there was no reason to stand here the entire night. He apparently was settling in for the evening. Brithwin walked to her bed and threw herself on her covers. Her bed squeaked. That was annoying. She really needed to have someone fix that.

What to do now? She needed the knife. Someone *had* been watching her on the way home tonight—she could feel it. If she told Royce or Thomas, they might think she imagined things.

Her eating tool remained in her possession, but small,

and of no real use if attacked. Sleep would come much easier if she had a real knife under her pillow. But she would have to wait until morning to retrieve one when he was off doing whatever he could to avoid her.

Brithwin stretched out on the bed with her head pillowed on her hands. Her mind would take no respite. Who had watched her tonight? It wasn't Royce—the man couldn't get far enough away from her.

Maybe she would lock her door tonight. If Elspeth needed her, she would just have to knock. Brithwin padded to the door and bolted it. As she returned to her bed, Royce's door shut.

Remaining motionless for several minutes, she trod softly back to the door and listened for sounds coming from his solar. She cracked the door and peeked in. The room stood empty. The mistress's chamber door stood feet away from the master's, causing each to walk across the solar to reach the other's room. She slipped through her door into the solar and into her husband's chamber.

The fire lit his room with a soft glow. She glanced around. Nearly a month had passed since she had entered her old room. He had changed little in it. The wall hanging and rug she had put in the chamber remained. She hadn't the courage to ask for it. His trunk sat at the end of his bed and his hauberk and coif lay on top, looking newly oiled. In the corner, his armor lay propped against the wall, his large shield beside it. Tiptoeing around the bed, Brithwin headed for the table. The knife remained where she had left it, undisturbed. She picked it up in her hand and gently ran her thumb over it, welcoming the familiar feel. This was the one thing she had of her mother's and only because Thomas had seen to it. The knife, she'd always cherished, was finely crafted, with an engraved hawk on the handle and two small emeralds embedded for eyes.

Voices in the hallway caused her to jump. Footfalls sounded.

Brithwin's heart thundered. She had to cross the solar to get to her chamber and the footsteps came from the solar. Her heart crashed in her chest, echoing in her ears. She swung around looking for an area to hide—not a good place close by and not enough time to make it across the room. The door creaked opened. She dropped herself flat on the floor and scooted under the bed.

†††

Royce brought his goblet of ale to his room. He went and sat in front of the fire. This had become a nightly ritual, sitting and staring into the flames. Tonight was no different.

He dreaded this time because his mind would always wander to Brithwin.

He had talked to Thomas, what good that did. The man was loyal to a fault and gave him little information about her relationship with her father. Royce had merely learned her father had nothing to do with her unless it be punishment for some minor infraction. When he asked Thomas what the punishments were or why they were handed out, the man told him he had said enough and to talk to his wife if he wanted to know more. Well, she was no more cooperative than Thomas. He'd even sought out Elspeth, but she'd fled the room at a run, claiming she had forgotten her lady needed her.

Royce stretched his legs before him. Just thinking about Brithwin made his mind play tricks on him. He could swear he smelled her rose fragrance.

Tipping his cup, he finished his drink and set it down. He stood and grabbed the bottom of his tunic, hauled it over his head, folded it, and laid it on the end of the bed. The mattress sank as he let himself down. A muffled squeak came from beneath. He'd have to get that annoying dog in here to find the rodent and earn his keep. Boots and stockings removed, he tossed them to the floor. After drawing the sword from its scabbard, he placed it on the bed beside him and lay down, wishing for sleep to come swiftly.

By the rood! He must be losing his mind. The scent of Brithwin wafted around him as if she were in the room. Could he never get the blasted woman off his mind? It was too late, and he was too tired to go out and find work to keep his thoughts off her. He jerked the coverlet over him. How could he let her affect his senses this way? Never had he wanted someone to be innocent as he did her.

Getting out of Hawkwood and visiting Rosen Craig proved more important than he'd thought. He clamped his eyes shut and willed himself to sleep.

Royce woke with a start, not really sure what had disturbed his sleep, but knowing something had—a sound, a movement, something. His gut told him someone was in the room. Experience told him to continue breathing as if he were still sleeping. He silently moved his hand over the hilt of his sword. Remaining motionless, he opened his eyes and scanned the room.

A movement to his right caught his attention. He tensed, waiting for the intruder to lunge toward him. Instead, the person stepped away, rounding the end of his bed. Royce threw off the covers and lunged. His body met with a soft, womanly form. As they tumbled to the floor, the scent of roses and Brithwin filled his nostrils. His senses reeled. What was she doing in his room? Her struggle to free herself was in vain. He tightened his hold on her. She felt good in his arms. It was sweet to hold—

All thoughts fled Royce's mind as Brithwin lifted her knee into his groin. He rolled back in pain, releasing his hold, and watched as she scrambled to her feet and scampered out the door. He lifted his head to get up and let it drop back to the floor as another pain seized him. Why hadn't he remembered that knee of hers? It was a lesson he really needed to learn.

Chapter 10

Royce locked the door, staggered to the bed, and collapsed. What reason did Brithwin have to sneak into his room? He was in no condition now to chase her and find out. And it was hard to know where she would run to. She wasn't in her bed, that much he knew. Before he'd had her moved into the adjoining chamber, he'd instructed Philip to find a squeaky board and place it under her feather mattress. He heard her every time she got in or out of her bed. Not that it had done him much good tonight. She obviously had been in his room when he entered.

He'd have a look around in the morning and see if he could find what had drawn her to his chamber. Then he'd have a talk with her.

After a fitful sleep, Royce examined his room the next morning, trying to determine what had brought Brithwin within. He scanned the contents of his trunk, but nothing looked to be missing. He crouched down to peer under the bed where she must have hidden but found naught there. With his hand on the table beside the bed, he pushed himself up and glanced at where his hand rested. A vision of a knife lying there flashed through his mind. The weapon that had lain there since he began occupying the chamber had vanished. If the knife hadn't had a hawk with emerald eyes uniquely carved in its handle, he probably never would have noticed it.

Why had she not just asked him for it? Unless, of course, she still harbored anger over being locked in her room. A chill swept down his spine. The knife's blade could do serious damage to a man.

He would delay breaking his fast so he could give her

the opportunity to tell him the truth. He sat in his chair while he waited. When he heard her chamber door open, he intercepted her near the stairs.

"May I escort you to the morning meal, my lady?" Royce bit back a smile at her jumpiness—well he knew that she would rather eat alone.

Brithwin recoiled and spun to face him. "You! You are *always* about your duties at this time of morning."

He offered his arm. "Nay, not always, for I am here today. I thought to wait for you. We have much to talk about. Wouldn't you agree?"

Brithwin stiffened and raised her chin. "I am quite busy this day."

Royce started down the corridor beside her and spoke quietly in her ear. "Surely you're not too busy to spend time with your husband. I thought we might discuss yesternight."

They reached the bottom of the stairs and strolled into the hall, moving to the dais, where they took their seats. The servants rushed forward and set a bread trencher between them.

Royce stabbed a piece of meat. "Shall I serve you, my lady?"

Brithwin glowered at him. "I thank you, but I am capable of taking care of myself."

"I never doubted that." Royce popped the meat into his mouth. Her shaking hands belied the scowl on her face. Perchance it was because he was here next to her. He swallowed his food. "Is there anything you would like to do today?"

Brithwin's gaze went to her food and she began shuffling it around her trencher.

Royce raised his brows. "Is something wrong?"

"Why would you ask that?" Her voice rose on the last word.

"You haven't answered my question nor have you taken a bite of your food. You sit there shifting it around. If it does not appeal to you, I am sure the cook would be happy to get you something else."

Brithwin frowned. "I told you, I am busy this day, and you would not know my eating habits as you are never here in the morning when I break my fast."

He grinned. That had gotten her hackles up. "Yes, I have had much to do since coming here. However, I have decided to spend today with you. Therefore, you can *un*busy your day. We will spend it together."

Brithwin sniffed. "Then *you* had better hurry and eat. Pater frowns on lateness."

Brithwin's smile didn't reach her eyes. She tested him. Aye, well, she knew he avoided anything to do with God.

"We will meet when you get out." He turned back to his food and continued to eat.

"You want to spend time together, yet you will not come to prayer with me?"

"That is what I said." He placed his knife down.

The muscle in her jaw twitched, as it always did when she was agitated. "Why will you not go? If I am to spend the day going wherever you would like, I expect you at least to explain yourself."

He admired the way she stood up to him. His wife was no coward. But that did not change anything. "'Tis none of your concern. We will leave after you finish."

Brithwin slammed the cup down that she held and shoved her chair back. It teetered on its back legs before thumping down on all four. She sashayed out of the hall without a rearward glance.

An hour after prayer had ended and Pater had left, Royce still leaned against the outer wall of the church, impatiently tapping his shoe. How many prayers could one person think of? He considered himself a patient man but she'd used his up.

Tired of waiting, he bounded up the steps and slowly pulled the heavy, ornate oak door. Peeking in, he allowed his eyes to adjust. She sat with head bowed in prayer. Or maybe she slept? He closed the door and returned to his place against the wall.

Another hour later, Royce was ready to go in and haul her out, regardless of what she prayed. As he shoved away from the wall, the door opened and Brithwin stepped out.

He grunted. "Be in front of the stables in fifteen minutes. And don't keep me waiting this time."

Brithwin's blue gaze turned icy. She swung around abruptly and marched away.

Royce strode to the mews and put on the leather glove. When he held out his hand, the falcon hopped on. Lucas approached, drawing both the hawk's attention and Royce's.

"It looks like Talon is ready to go hunting." He smiled at the boy. "Do you have my lady's falcon ready?"

"Yes, sir!"

Lucas's enthusiasm made Royce chuckle. He reached out and messed the boy's hair. "Go get Lioness and bring her out for my lady."

Lucas turned and ran to the end of the building. He picked up a glove and ran back to where Brithwin's bird sat. With a grin as wide as his face, he lifted his gloved hand, and Lioness gingerly hopped on.

Lucas followed him out of the mews and strode toward the stable. "Be sure to hold tight to the tethers. I would not want her flying to my lady when she has nothing to protect her hand or arm."

Lucas nodded and ran his hand down the bird's slick feathers.

"Have you made any friends here?" Royce checked the

tethers in Lucas's hand.

Lucas nodded then shook his head and began petting the bird again.

"Well, which is it? Aye or nay? It can't be both," Royce teased.

Lucas looked up, his face pinched. "How much longer will my punishment last, milord?"

Royce's chest tightened. He knelt on one knee and rested his hand with the falcon on his leg. He searched the boy's face. "You are not happy here?"

"I am, milord."

"Then why do you concern yourself with how long you must stay?"

Lucas stared at the shoes Royce had found for him and shuffled his feet. "Old Saran from the village told me I should not make friends—that you will send me away as soon as my punishment is over."

Royce lifted the boy's chin with his fingers. "Saran is wrong. You are welcome to stay here as long as you like. I told you our falconer needed help. He has come to rely on you. You would not want to disappoint him, would you?"

A smile spread across the boy's face as Royce finished speaking. Talon raised his wings and began to flap. Royce turned to calm the bird and caught a glimpse of Brithwin scurrying away.

He sighed. She was trying to sneak away unnoticed. "Good boy," he whispered. He held his hand over the falcon's head to keep him calm. "Lady Brithwin!" he bellowed.

Brithwin froze. A threatening growl came from nearby. Royce scowled at the hound.

"You have made me wait two times for you this morn. I would not try for three." She did not disappoint him with the tilt of her chin. "And lock the dog up. He can stay here."

†††

Oh, the arrogant cad! He could send her emotions rising and falling like the waves of the sea. His obstinacy this morning left her no choice but to ride with him. Having just made up her mind of what a scoundrel she had married, what did he do? He redeemed himself by kneeling before the lad to be less intimidating and making a lowly orphan feel as if Royce needed him.

She smiled to herself. It was true, she had wanted to let him wait a wee bit longer, simply because the later they left, the less time she would have to spend with him. And perhaps, too, because she knew he loathed waiting.

The fact that he wished to discuss last eve gave her more of a reason to wish to delay. She had no desire to enter into that conversation. He was sure to ask why she'd stood by his bed, and worse yet, why she had tried to maim him. She couldn't tell him she had taken the knife, and it was doubtful he'd even noticed it on the table. Brithwin shuddered. He would have no reason to suspect she had taken it or that she now wore it strapped to her leg under her gown.

Royce's long stride ate the ground between them. "You seem to have lost your way. Let me escort you to the horses. We are taking the birds out for a hunt."

Concern for her falcon overrode the anger she felt at Royce. "Is Lioness up to flying? She has been sick."

"The falconer said it would do her good. She needs exercise."

Lucas handed her a glove. Brithwin glowered at Royce as she slid her hand into the protective leather then asked Lucas to hold the bird until she mounted.

Once settled on her horse, she reached down and took the bird onto her hand, thanking Lucas. She headed out of the bailey and toward the woods.

A smile tickled her lips as Shadowmere's hooves

pounded the ground and Royce caught up with her. He reined in slightly in front of her and looked straight ahead.

Her stomach lurched. The kindness he'd shown to Lucas hinted of another man. One she didn't know but wanted to. Yet he despised her and believed her a murderer. What other reason would there be for him not to take his husband rights? All the better for her, though. He could keep on despising her if it kept him in his own chamber at night.

But what if he went to the king with these accusations of murder, and she was deemed guilty? She would lose Hawkwood and everything dear to her. She swallowed. She could even lose her life.

Life with her father had been hard, yet Royce could make it worse. What had she done that God would send her a husband just like him in Royce?

Trust Me.

A shiver ran up Brithwin's spine. She glanced to Royce. He continued to look forward. Brithwin sighed. *I will try, God, but You will have to help.*

Stopping along the way, they flew their falcons. Talon brought in more game, but Lioness had done a fine job, adding several rabbits to the bag. The exercise did seem to perk Lioness up. Brithwin ran her hand down the sleek feathers, enjoying the smoothness against her skin.

"Brithwin." Royce drew her attention away from Lioness. "For what did you come to my room yestereve? From the way you nearly maimed me, I would say it wasn't to see me."

Her heart skipped a beat. "I'd left something in the room."

"Why did you not ask me to get it?"

"I didn't realize I'd left it until late."

"What was so important that it could not wait until morning when it has waited this long?"

Luck was on her side because no sooner had Royce asked her than a rabbit darted out from the thicket. Brithwin released Lioness. The falcon took to the air. "'Tis so good to see her soar again. She was quite sick and I feared I may lose her."

"Aye, she seems strong."

Brithwin worked hard to keep the conversation away from yestereve. When Lioness had returned with her catch, they rode on. Royce spoke of the winter preparations for the castle. Her worries that he would be angry and punish her diminished. There was kindness in every word. They continued to fly their falcons with no more mention of why she'd entered his room. In the distance, birds sang cheerful songs in the trees. A gentle breeze sent the tall, lush grass into a dance, and flowers swayed, sending up wafts of fragrance pleasing to her senses. It turned out to be a pleasant day with her husband. She enjoyed his company and was a bit sad to have to return.

Hawkwood appeared in the distance and Royce turned in his saddle, locking his gaze on her. "My lady, I would know why I found you skulking around my room yestereve. And why I frightened you so much when I tried to stop you."

Brithwin swallowed. She had convinced herself she had evaded this questioning. "I—I told you, I left something of mine. It is not as if I had much time to gather my things before you took over my chamber."

"But you would have had only to ask. I am not without compassion."

She narrowed her eyes. "I have not seen it directed at me."

"My lady, I do not wish for our whole life to be fraught with hostility. But you must accept that I am now the lord of Hawkwood, and I am the one that makes the decisions."

She was not ready to turn her people, her land, and her

will over to him. He had not proven that he would be a good and fair lord. And until he did, she would make no promises. "I am sorry if I injured you last eve."

"Well, at least you will admit to something. And since you bring it up, my lady, I would appreciate it if you would keep that knee of yours to yourself."

"Aye, *my lord.*" *Unless I ever feel threatened.*

Royce heaved a sigh and rode through the portcullis.

†††

Royce greatly enjoyed his wife's company for the view, but her lack of answers to his questions also greatly vexed him. His wife's knowledge of the land, the people, and the running of the castle amazed him. He almost laughed when his mind returned to those first days before they had met. He had expected a spoiled, simpering lord's daughter. It pleased him—and frustrated him—that he couldn't have been more wrong.

Each passing day intensified his desire for her to be innocent of the murders. Nevertheless, knowing she had taken the knife from his room nurtured the seed of doubt that had been planted.

Royce reined in as they rode into the bailey. "My lady, I wish to hear your explanation...now."

Brithwin gave him a calculating look. "Or what? You will punish me? Shall I go lock myself in my room, *my lord*?"

Would this woman ever learn her place? Royce swung from his horse and stomped to Brithwin. He should turn her over his knee. Could she not accept the kindness he tried to show her? As he lowered her to the ground, her mount sidled into her, wedging her between him and the horse. Royce stepped back and she slid down the front of him until her feet hit the ground. He held in a groan. He wanted to hold her there, run his fingers through her windblown hair. His chest tightened and he pulled her closer. Something hard jabbed his thigh. He glanced down in search of the cause. Her gown pressed against a long bump that looked suspiciously like a knife. Withdrawing his hands from her waist, he stepped away to grasp the reins and hand them to the groom.

Royce lifted the bag of rabbits. "I'll take these to Cook."

He made his way to the kitchen, his mind in search of answers. She wore the knife on her leg. If she intended to do him harm, she'd had plenty of opportunity today. He'd brought no guards as he had planned to stay in close proximity of the castle. Had she wanted to use the knife, it was the perfect time. But she had not.

If she only would have told him she'd taken the knife. He'd given her several chances, yet she evaded each opportunity.

If she felt threatened by someone, he needed to know in order to protect her. Perhaps he shouldn't have relieved Daffydd of his watch duties.

It was possible she was afraid of her husband and wore the knife merely for protection. He'd not done anything to suggest he would harm her. So why did she fear him? If he knew more of what she had endured at her father's hand, he could surely understand her better.

†††

Brithwin didn't move when Royce rushed to the kitchen as if he couldn't depart from her fast enough. Part of her wanted to run after him, wanted to feel his protective arms around her. He constantly made her angry; yet when she was in his arms, she felt so safe. She couldn't have it both ways.

His retreat reminded her how he despised her. Royce wanted nothing to do with her, and if today's questions were any indication, he still believed her his enemy.

She could see no way to prove her innocence to a man determined to find her at fault. If he deemed her guilty of this evil thing, what then? The dungeon? Death? She had hoped and prayed he would be perceptive enough to see through this veil of deception he had been given. Trusting that God would open her husband's eyes was the most difficult task she had ever faced.

Back about her daily duties, Brithwin headed to her garden.

She slowed as she neared. "Floyd?" Brithwin strained to see what he was doing in her garden.

"Yes, milady." He didn't look up but kept shoveling stone onto her walkway.

"What are you doing?"

"Following milord's orders."

"Lord Rosen Craig had you do this?"

"Aye, milady. Punishment for not letting you out of your room." He stole a quick glance and went back to throwing stone on the pathway.

"I see. Will I be in your way if I tend to my garden?"

"I have taken care of the weeding, milady."

"Did he have you do that, too?"

"Aye."

Working in her garden always helped calm her. It was kind of Royce to think of her, but now she must find something else to do. She sighed and turned to leave.

"Milady?"

"Yes, Floyd."

"'Tis sorry I am for not letting you out."

He didn't sound sorry. He sounded more like Royce had told him to apologize. She nodded and made her way into the kitchen to find something to do.

At the evening meal, she overheard Royce mention to Thomas he would be leaving for Rosen Craig soon. And though she wanted to know why he was returning to his family's estate, she wouldn't ask him. It mattered not if he left—she would have a few days relief from him. After all, wasn't that what she wanted?

She made her way up the stairs and to her room, where Elspeth awaited her. After undressing and climbing into bed, she pulled the covers tight about her shoulders, trying not to wonder about the purpose of Royce's trip to Rosen Craig.

†††

Brithwin tried to make the dream go away. But the yells of men and the horn sounding wouldn't stop. A scream—not her own—dragged her from her slumber. She threw off her covers. Dread and the acrid smell of fire jolted her awake. The horns had blown—they were under attack, or there was fire. She ran to the window. The sky glowed orange over the village.

Chapter 11

Grasping for a gown, Brithwin scrambled into the first dress that met her fingertips. Hands fumbling, she tied her sheathed knife to her leg. The light from the village raged brighter by the minute. Pungent smoke wafted through the window. How in heaven's name had the fire started?

She glanced out the window again. If her eyes didn't deceive her, it looked to be half the village aglow. Her insides twisted. Would Malcolm be safe? His grandfather, Guy, could not walk. How would Murielle get her husband out if sparks ignited the thatch on their house?

With her friend's safety in mind, Brithwin bounded down the corridor and stairs. Halfway, she remembered the basket of herbs and salves sitting next to her window. Lifting her gown, she took the stairs two at a time and returned to her room.

A moment later, clutching the basket in her hand, she fled through the door.

A quick prayer left her lips. *God, please watch over the villeins. Allow each one to escape with their lives.* Brithwin rushed across the bailey, heading for the stables, and crashed into Royce with an *oof.*

Royce grasped her shoulders. "What are you doing out here?"

"I have come to help." Brithwin twisted to free herself from his grasp. The village burned while he delayed her.

He tightened his hold. "Nay! I do not want to have to worry about you." He glanced at her basket, and some of the hardness left his face. "Go back to the castle. If any are injured, we will send them to the hall."

"Don't be a foo—"

Royce's lips pinched, and his gaze met hers in an unspoken warning.

Nay, she would not call him a fool again. "The wounded may not be able to walk to the hall."

Royce released her and folded his arms in front of him, scowling. "I'll see they arrive safely."

A quick survey told her most of the men had saddled their horses and were leaving. Lord Rosen Craig certainly wasn't going to let her go. She thrust her hands on her hips, the herb basket dangling from her arm. "I must be with my people."

"And I said *nay*. I do not have time for this, my lady. *Stay!*"

†††

He jerked away and stalked to his horse. The animal stomped and tossed its head as though scoffing at the woman's insolence. He swung his leg over his mount and glanced back. The stubborn chit remained in the same spot, with hands planted firmly on her hips and nose in the air, yet again.

With the portcullis clanking upward, the men spurred their horses to a gallop as if headed into battle. He kicked his steed's sides and joined them.

Royce rode hard to the edge of the village, where he reined in Shadowmere and swung to the ground, leaving the animal free to move. Confining his horse would put him at the mercy of the fire, should it get that far.

Even from a distance, he heard the desperate cries for help. The sounds jarred recollections—his command, his father's knights and his lack of his father's leadership couldn't stop the slaughter of the Scots. All memories he'd intentionally forced away. Now those scenes assaulted his mind with a vengeance; but he was not there now, and these people needed him. He could not let his past affect their future.

Royce sprinted for the inferno, shouting orders as he ran. "Get ladders against the houses that can be saved, and toss off the burning thatch. You, women, get water and throw it on the houses. Try to keep the fire from spreading. Anyone who is able, grab anything you can find and start beating out the flames."

Working alongside his men and the villeins, Royce heaved himself up a ladder and began throwing the blazing thatch to the ground. The heat from the flames scorched his face, and the acrid smell of singed hair assaulted his nose. Sweat rolled down his body, stinging seared skin as he worked to put out the flames of house after house.

People yelled for more water. A high-pitched wail drew his attention to a woman as two men held her from entering her home.

Royce jumped from the ladder and dashed to her side. "Who is inside?"

Smeared tears trailed through the soot on her cheeks. "My boy is in there!"

†††

As soon as Royce rode out of the gate toward the burning village, Brithwin turned in the direction of the stables. They were empty except for Fearless and an old nag. The smell of fire brought the horses on alert, and Fearless nervously threw her head about. She took the palfrey out of her stall and to a block. Not bothering with a saddle, she climbed on the horse's back and headed out of the bailey, hoping Royce had not warned the guard on duty. Holding her breath, she drew near the outer gatehouse.

The guard didn't watch who came and went. She followed his gaze, and the relief at leaving unhindered withered in the pit of her belly. The blaze looked to consume the whole village.

She squeezed her horse's flanks with her legs, and Fearless raced down the road toward the fire. The fleeting rush of hooves pounding behind her prickled her nerves, but the urgency of reaching Murielle and Guy pushed it out of her mind.

As soon as she neared the village, she tied her horse to a tree. If the fire spread too fast, she wanted Fearless far enough away to be safe. Running as fast as her feet would take her, she entered the village. Heat hit her like a furnace. Men on ladders threw off fiery thatch from roofs. Shovels beat and smothered the flames once the thatch hit the ground. People carried buckets of water from the well and the river to throw on the houses in hopes of controlling the flames.

Coughing, she fought her way through the hellish scene to find Murielle outside, bent over, gasping for air.

"Where are Guy and Malcolm?" Brithwin yelled above the chaos.

Still gasping, Murielle said, "Inside... I can't pull Guy out, and Malcolm...too frightened ...in the loft."

Brithwin ran into the house, followed by Murielle, and nearly stumbled over Guy lying near the door, his clothes smoldering. "Murielle, grab his arm and I will grab the other, and we will pull him out."

Guy's dead weight hindered their ability to move him. The crackle of dry wood burning surrounded her—the fire, hot enough to melt her skin, the smoke so thick that each breath she took strangled her, sending her into a coughing spasm and stealing a little of her strength each time. With a heavy jerk, she managed to move him a few inches.

"On the count of three, pull as hard as you can, Murielle." Brithwin choked back a round of coughing. "One, two, three, pull!"

They heaved against his weight. Guy slid halfway out the door.

"Again, Murielle."

The second pull got him out of the hut. They continued to drag him away from the glowing embers. Murielle raised her hand to her head and swayed. Brithwin reached out and grasped her arm to steady her.

"Run and get water to pour on his clothes." Brithwin glanced at the smoke billowing out the door and window. The growing flames that somehow, thankfully, had not started in the thatching licked upward. A coughing spell racked her body. She staggered toward the blazing cottage. "I will get Malcolm."

Murielle clasped hold of Brithwin's gown and followed. "You cannot go alone, milady."

Brithwin stopped and pried her garment from the old woman's hands. "Go." She gave her a firm shove. "Go, get water!" Brithwin turned and ran back into the inferno.

†††

A wall of flames engulfed the front of the house and lapped toward the back. Grabbing a shovel on his way, Royce ran around to the rear of the hovel and slammed his foot into the wall. The force of the kick jarred his teeth. The wall didn't budge. Shovel in hand, he wedged the blade between two boards and pulled on the handle. The plank's slight movement gave him hope, and he pulled harder. With a loud groan, a piece broke free, and Royce sprawled to the ground. He pushed himself up, went to the wall, and seized the next board. Bracing his feet against the base of the wall, he threw his weight backward and ripped off board after board until he'd made an opening large enough to fit through. He sucked in a breath and plunged his head into the hole to look for the child. "Boy!" He waited. "Are you in here, boy?"

Smoke stung his eyes and obscured his vision. Royce blinked and forced his eyes to stay open as he peered into the murky room. Pallets lay on the floor. He'd found their sleeping quarters. His vision blurred again. A coughing spasm gripped him, and his lungs filled with smoke. He gasped for air. The fire licked closer. Embers fell from above. He couldn't see the child.

A fiery pain bit into Royce's shoulder. Jerking his head out, he looked up to the roof and saw the flames had made it to the back of the hut and more embers showered down. To ease the pain, he rotated his arm around and glanced up again to make sure nothing else would fall. He ducked his head to lean into the hole again when someone called his name.

Jarren ran toward him, panting. "They found the boy."

Royce stumbled to the front of the cottage, a fierce ache gripping his chest. A sobbing woman hugging a young boy, not far from the burning cottage, met his sights.

Royce used his sleeve to wipe the sweat and smoke from his eyes. "Where was he?"

"He walked up to her seconds ago," Jarren replied. "Said someone sent him to get water. Apparently, his mother wasn't aware he had gotten out safely."

"I am glad he is well." Royce forced out the words and bent over in a coughing fit.

"Rosen Craig, you are bleeding!" Jarren exclaimed.

"'Tis nothing." He coughed again and his voice rasped. "An ember fell on me. Come, we have more work to do."

Jarren grabbed Royce's shoulder and pulled him upright. "Let me take a look at it. Your tunic is soaked in blood."

"It can wait." Royce rotated his arm again to show him. "There is no time to tend to a minor wound."

"Nay, that is a cut and not a small one." He stepped back and tore open the tunic. His eyes widened. "It looks like a knife wound to me."

Royce pulled away from Jarren's ministrations. "Nay, I think not. I saw no one."

Jarren eyed him questioningly.

Royce hefted a shovel and turned to go. "Enough. The village burns while we argue."

"The fire and the shouting would disguise the noise of an assailant. He probably ran when I called for you," Jarren muttered close behind him.

Royce continued back to the ladder he'd left. "These fires need be my only concern right now."

"Aye, milord."

Together they continued to put out fires. As Royce went up the ladder again and again, the rungs got slicker with blood each time he climbed. It appeared a more grievous wound than he'd first thought.

The bright flames blazed in front of him, but darkness threatened from all sides. He shook his head and grabbed the ladder as shapes shifted around him. The fire spread rapidly, giving no reprieve. His body moved in slow motion as he reached for the thatch. Tiny sparks flew upward toward the sky and then circled around him, gaining in volume and momentum. The house and ladder tilted. He leaned in the opposite direction to counter the weight. Sounds around him grew muffled, and he struggled to draw in air. Black, dense clouds engulfed him from every direction. The world began to spin, and he shook his head again, willing it to stop. He was floating—no—falling! He grabbed frantically, but his hands closed on emptiness.

†††

"Malcolm. Malcolm! Come. We must leave." Brithwin yelled for the boy.

Over the creaking of weakening wood came the howl of a frightened man-child, much like the sound of a rabbit that her hawk had chosen as prey. She ran to the ladder and grasped the hot rungs. Thick, choking, yellow smoke billowed from the opening above her. The fire had reached the thatch. She drew a deep breath and climbed.

Strong arms wrapped around her waist and pulled her from the ladder.

"Go out, milady. I will get the boy." One of Royce's men gave her a shove toward the door.

Brithwin darted back, her eyes searching for a glimpse of Malcolm as the men scaled the ladder. The thatch above her head shuddered. An orange glow worked its way toward the loft area.

"Hurry, the fire is spreading!" she shrieked as pieces of wood fell in.

The man pushed the man-boy toward the ladder and jumped off the loft. Brithwin guided Malcom as he scampered down.

Grasping Brithwin's and Malcom's arms, Royce's man pulled them from the house as the roof fell in. The three fell to the ground, coughing and struggling for air.

Brithwin crawled to where Guy still lay.

"Can you hear me, Guy?" she asked in a raspy voice.

"Aye, I hear ye, my guardian angel."

She knelt and gave him a quick hug. "Where do you hurt, Guy?"

He grasped her arm with his hand. "My legs feel like they are afire. As useless as they are, I feel pain."

Brithwin pulled back her gown to get the knife. "I need to cut the bottom of your stockings."

The trousers had burned to his legs, and she dreaded the pain it would cause Guy when she pulled off the fabric. Knowing what she had to do, she set to her task.

His valiant attempt at silence soon dissolved into screams of pain.

Her stomach roiled from the agony she caused him. Perspiration dripped down her face, and she wiped it away with her hand. With much of his skin gone from his calves, what remained was raw, angry flesh.

Finished and leaning against the horse post Guy had put there for her years ago, she closed her eyes and swallowed down the nausea. Now she needed to mix the salve.

Brithwin turned to the man who stood quietly by. "What is your name?"

"Sir Daffydd, milady."

"Thank you, Sir Daffydd." Brithwin took out the jar of salve from her basket. "We can manage. Others need your help."

"I don't think milord would approve."

Carefully she lifted the cloth cover from the jar of salve and stirred it with her finger. The heat had turned it nigh into liquid. "He will say naught."

With feet planted apart, Daffydd cleared his throat. "I am sure he would have plenty to say should harm come to you, milady. Perhaps I can be of assistance."

Brithwin lifted her head. The fire consumed the cottages, and the men worked frantically trying to save as much of the village as possible. She was selfish for feeling as she did, but she was grateful he stayed. Guy ailed and she couldn't move him alone. Murielle swayed, exhausted from the little pulling she had done. Turning her head, Brithwin looked at Malcolm—a strong boy but he'd not be gentle in his helping.

"Keep him still while I get the salve ready," Brithwin instructed Daffydd.

She turned to Murielle. "Is there any water left in the bucket?"

"Yes, milady," Murielle answered and collapsed onto the ground.

Daffydd got to Murielle first. "She has swooned."

Brithwin added more herbs to the salve while Daffydd watched over the old couple. Malcolm sat rocking back and forth hugging his knees. She took in the devastation. She needed to get the old couple to safety. Murielle was coming around now and didn't appear to have anything wrong besides a few bumps and minor burns. Exhaustion, anxiety, and too much smoke had surely caused her to faint. Brithwin turned to Daffydd. "Did you bring a horse, sir?"

"An old nag." He growled. "The only one that was left in the stables. Someone took my destrier."

"Ah, Fleetfoot."

Daffydd snorted. "You will have to ride my horse and carry Guy. Murielle can ride Fleetfoot. The boy and I will walk."

They made their way to the horses with Guy in Daffydd's arms. Guy moaned as Daffydd laid the old man over the horse's back and climbed on. Brithwin helped Murielle up and started toward the woods.

"Milady? Hawkwood is this way." Daffydd pointed toward Hawkwood.

"Aye. But I know of an abandoned crofter's cottage, not far from here."

"In the woods? 'Tis dark, milady. Do you think you can find it?" Skepticism laced Daffydd's voice. "Perhaps the castle is a better place for your friends."

"If memory serves me, the cottage is closer. The moon is full, and the path is clear most of the way."

After they had traveled for nigh onto twenty minutes, Brithwin began to doubt her choice. But to turn around now and go to the castle would only be harder on the old couple. And the castle walls would be full of her people needing a place to bed down.

They left the trail. The night sounds of owls and wild animals foraging for food replaced the yells of men and the crackling of the fire. The trees reached to the heavens, blocking out the moon's light, and darkness surrounded them. Brithwin couldn't stop the shiver overtaking her body, not from the cold but from the terror she fought to keep at bay. With not too much farther to go, she needed to keep her wits about her. She'd not remembered the cottage being so far from the village.

They slowed their pace, having lost the light of the moon. When her eyes adjusted to the dark, she scanned the woods for something familiar. *Lord, guide my steps.* The prayer barely whispered, she spotted the large tree that looked like a slingshot, a landmark which told them they headed in the right direction.

"Milady, are we close?" Daffydd asked.

"We should be there anytime now."

"I believe Hawkwood would have been closer, faster, and easier to reach, milady."

"Aye, I did not remember it being this far," Brithwin confessed. It had been some time since she'd traveled out this way, but she should have remembered. It must have been the confusion and fear that addled her mind.

As she finished speaking, she caught sight of the hut. "Thank You, Jesus," she whispered.

†††

Jarren rushed to Royce but couldn't break his fall. Kneeling, he yelled for someone to find the village healer as he ran his hands over Royce's body, probing for broken bones and feeling none. He scanned the area for a safe place to take his friend. The raging fires had spared the southern half of the village thus far. People dashed to and fro. Jarren eyed each one and remained by Royce's side, awaiting the healer.

A scratchy voice drew his attention. "Would that be our new lord?"

"Aye. Are you the healer?" He looked into the wrinkled face of an old crone.

She nodded.

"He has lost much blood from a wound in his back and now has fallen from the ladder. I have felt no broken bones."

"I be Mary. Let me look at him." The old healer knelt and carefully felt his limbs with gnarled hands. "No broken bones. Can you carry him to my cottage?"

Jarren lifted Royce into his arms with a grunt. Staggering to get his balance, he then strode toward the southern end of the village, following the healer.

As they passed the hut where Royce had been stabbed, a woman in tattered clothes ran out to him. "Sir Knight, Sir Knight! Please wait."

He slowed his pace but didn't stop. "What do you need, woman?"

She craned her neck to see. "Is milord dead?"

He pushed her out of his way and quickened his pace. "Not yet."

"Sir Knight. Wait. I found the knife that injured milord."

"Where did you find it?" Jarren stopped and turned to look at the woman.

"Right where he be when the blackguard stabbed him."

Jarren eyed her with suspicion. "And how would you know where he stood when he was stabbed?"

She crossed her arms in front of her. "I heard you talkin' to him."

"Where is the knife?"

"I gots it right here." She pulled her hand out of the fold of her tunic and held the knife out for him to see.

"Place it in my belt, and I thank you on behalf of milord," he said without looking at the knife.

"'Tis a fine knife, one that would likely bring enough food to feed me family for a year." She began replacing the knife in the folds of her skirt instead of doing his bidding.

Jarren scowled. "That was not a request. Now, place the knife in my belt, and I will tell him you found it. He can decide whether to compensate you."

"Nay, I will keep it until milord is well and then I will bring it to him. How would you find me? I cannot stay here anymore."

Jarren glared at the woman but could do nothing about her with Royce in his arms. They wasted precious time. He nodded his head and hurried on to catch the old healer, making a mental note what the woman looked like. He'd find her again.

By the time they reached the healer's house, Royce's skin bore an unhealthy pallor. Jarren laid him on the bed and stepped back. The old healer hobbled to the table that filled the middle of the room, covered with bowls full of salves and potions. The concoctions filled the air with pungent odors. She picked one up and smelled. Nodding her head, she reached for fresh leaves and set the bowl along with the handful of leaves on the stand near Royce. After swinging the arm of the pot away from the fire, she dipped out a bowl of boiling water. She grabbed a discarded cloth from the ground and shook it then returned to Royce.

She placed the leaves into the bowl of water and left them to soak. As she moved towards Royce, Jarren tensed. How loyal were these people to his lord? "Explain what you do."

"The leaves are stonecrop and will help with the pain." She wiped the blood from the wound with the rag. After squeezing the juices into the lesion, she placed the leaves over Royce's shoulder. Next, she took the other bowl, scooped out a dollop of thick salve with her fingers, and rubbed it onto the wound. "This is yarrow," she said. "It will help stop the bleeding." When she finished, the old woman tore a cloth into long thin strips and wrapped it tightly over Royce's shoulder and around his chest.

"Now, we wait." She settled her sticklike body in the

rickety old chair.

"How long before we know?" Jarren asked.

"He lost much blood. He will sleep 'til morning." She said no more as if that had answered his question.

"You rest," Jarren said, "and I will sit with Royce."

Chapter 12

Brithwin sat by Guy's still form on the ground, while Daffydd lit a fire and searched for vermin in the cottage. Since they started out, Guy had stirred only in brief coughing fits. His labored breathing was the single motion in his lifeless body. Brithwin waited by the door, clutching her basket of herbs and salves, hoping Daffydd would hurry.

A spring chill filled the night air. The chattering of teeth brought her attention behind her. Seeing Malcolm with his knees drawn to his chest, his arms wrapped around them and his head buried between his knees, caused her to forget her other concerns. She moved beside the boy, only a few years younger than her, and put her arms around him.

Brithwin spoke to him in a soothing voice. "All is well, Malcolm. Daffydd will soon have a fire ablaze, and we will be warm. I may need your help, so you must be good and do as I say. Can you do that for me?"

Malcolm raised his head and nodded, then peeked around her to see his grandfather. Murielle huddled beside Guy, stroking her husband's hair.

The boy's face tightened, and Brithwin spoke assurances. "He will mend. He needs to be tended to and get much sleep so his body can heal."

Daffydd stepped through the door. "'Tis clear inside and the fire burns, milady."

Soon after, Brithwin wearily rested near Guy's still form, warding off the chill next to the fire. Daffydd settled in across from her while the others slept. He glanced at Guy. "How long do you think he'll sleep?"

"I gave him something to aid his rest and applied salve with willow in it to help with the pain. I hope it will help him sleep through most of the night."

"How did you know this cottage lay empty, milady?"
Brithwin arched her back, trying to work out the kinks.
"The man who lived here was set upon by brigands and
killed. No one will move in. They believe if they live away
from the village, the same fate will befall them."

"But there is firewood here and a pallet for sleep."

"Aye, travelers use it when they are passing through.
They keep the firewood stocked for the next one stopping
in."

"So, on the morrow I need to replace the wood?"
Daffydd smiled.

"It would be the kindly thing to do." Brithwin yawned,
the events of the night catching up with her.

"I will rise early and chop some wood so we can return
to Hawkwood."

"Guy will be unable to travel. I will stay with him. You
may go and send back food."

"I cannot go without you. Your husband would surely
string me up in the field and use me for target practice."

"Lord Rosen Craig? He will not even notice me missing.
'Tis no secret the man avoids me, and when he does see me
he simply tolerates me." She sighed. "Besides, I overheard
him tell Sir Thomas and Sir Jarren he intends to leave for his
family's holdings. Had not the village caught fire, he would
have left in the morn. I am sure he has much on his mind
with rebuilding and his trip."

"You underestimate milord if you think that he will not
miss you."

"Nay. You needn't worry. He will think I have overslept.
He forbade me to come to the village tonight, so he will not
suspect I am here."

Daffydd let out a groan. "He forbade you? Ack! It is
worse than I thought." He closed his eyes. "I will be lucky if

I survive 'til eventide once I return you to Hawkwood. Nay, 'twould be better I die quickly."

Brithwin smirked. "Have you lost your wits? He will not punish you."

"We will see when we return." Doubt reverberated in his words.

"We should try and get some sleep while we can. It could be a long night." Her words proved to be prophetic, even though there were few hours left of nightfall. Guy awoke often, and it took both of them to keep him from thrashing around and doing more damage to his burns.

†††

Royce groaned as he shifted to his side on the narrow pallet. "I feel like I was used as a battering ram. What happened? The last thing I remember is climbing a ladder."

"Aye, you did that. You just didn't use it to come down. You should have listened to me."

Jarren had told him it would be a bad idea, hadn't he? Royce merely grunted. "The fire. How much did we lose?" His words came out hoarse.

Jarren handed him a goblet of water. "I cannot be sure, but I would say close to twenty homes burned. Some damaged, others totally lost."

"Dead?"

"I do not know. It will be today or tomorrow before we can assess the complete loss of lives and homes."

"We will start rebuilding today."

The healer tottered over, pushed Royce from his side to his stomach, and scrutinized the wound. She clucked her tongue. "There will be no rebuilding this village today for you. You must rest for a sennight and regain your strength. If you don't, you'll reopen your wound. 'Tis still possible for the fever to come upon you."

"You are the village healer?" Royce lifted his head,

surveying all the herbs hanging from the ceiling and containers sitting on a shelf.

Nodding, she busied herself with placing fresh salve and cloth strips on his wound.

Royce sucked in a breath as he sat up. "I thank you for tending to my wound and allowing me to sleep on your bed. 'Twas kind of you. However, I must get to Hawkwood."

The healer shot Jarren a glance laden with warning. Jarren heaved a sigh.

"I will go and fetch our mounts and bring you to the castle, but you must rest there." He scowled at Royce. "Yestereve I believed you would die, though I would not speak so then."

"I have warned you, milord." The healer rose abruptly. "What you do is no matter to me."

††††

Having trouble mounting his horse, Royce accepted Jarren's assistance.

Jarren frowned. "'Tis unwise. You should remain another day. Gain some strength. You cannot even climb upon your destrier without support."

Royce winced as he shifted in the saddle. "Nay, one night was enough. I am just a wee bit sore."

Jarren snorted and shook his head. He climbed on his horse and led the way to Hawkwood.

Royce tried to concentrate as Jarren told of the woman who'd found a knife. Jarren would need to check Brithwin's room for the blade when they returned. They were but a short ride. He would make it. Jarren pointed out where he'd encountered the woman as they passed the burned-out hulls, once homes. People wandered aimlessly. Royce's heart pulled at their plight. They needed him. He attempted to sit tall in the saddle as he took in the damage, though beads of perspiration trickled down his face and back. He tightened his legs on Shadowmere to keep atop the horse.

When the castle gate drew near, he sagged, grateful he had made it.

His knuckles tingled, so fierce a grip he held to the saddle, and waves of dizziness threatened to spill him from his horse. The battle-hardened muscles in his legs could no longer grasp Shadowmere's sides. By sheer, stubborn will he had not hit the ground thus far.

They reached the inner bailey and the stable. Philip rushed to them. The short excursion had turned out a major undertaking. As Royce slid off his horse, the dizziness he had fought swooped down on him like a hawk diving for its prey. His legs buckled beneath him.

Philip leaped forward and grasped his arm.

Jarren sent Royce a smug look. "Now, Rosen Craig, will you consider following the healer's advice and rest?"

Royce's glare encompassed both Philip and Jarren. "I will rest today, but on the morrow I will not remain abed."

He hobbled to his room with their help. By the rood, he felt as weak as a babe. He collapsed onto the bed.

Philip remained near the door as Royce let himself down on the bed. The knight looked exhausted. Smudges of black remained on his face and arms.

Philip cleared his throat. "'Tis surely a small matter"—he glanced at Jarren and then at Royce—"but we haven't seen milady today. She is most probably tending the injured . . . somewhere."

Royce jerked his head up, sending the room into a spin. "Find her."

His order to find Brithwin was the last thing he remembered when he awoke early the next morn to distant pounding. He wrenched himself to a sitting position. A searing pain shot through his shoulder, and he fell back, gasping. The impact of the mattress only intensified his pain.

Every muscle in his body cried out in agony. Feeling like one of the bags they used for jousting practice, he grimaced and closed his eyes. Jarren and Philip hovered nearby like anxious wet nurses.

Royce turned to them. "Have you found her yet?"

"No one has seen her since before we left for the fire." Jarren's face looked haggard, and he massaged the back of his neck with his hand. "We searched the castle and the bailey with no luck."

Royce rubbed his temple with his fingers. He'd ordered the wench to remain here. Had she used this opportunity to meet with someone—someone who had tried to kill him?

"Perhaps she tends the injured in the village," Phillip defended.

"Did anyone see her in the village during the fire? The stubborn wench insisted on going with us." Royce waited for an answer as his gaze bounced between the two men.

"We've heard nothing yet," Jarren said.

Royce scoffed at Philip. "Yet you think she may be there aiding someone, when no one has seen her."

Philip shrugged. "It is not as if we can go around knocking door to door. Twenty-four villein families lost their homes. Chaos reigns in the village. The people wander the streets like lost sheep. We are trying to gather supplies to rebuild, but 'tis difficult organizing those people. Lady Rosen Craig could be in the midst of them and no one would notice."

Royce tried to raise himself again, winced, and immediately lay back down, waiting for the pain and dizziness to subside. "This is maddening. I would get up and do for myself. "

"Marjory says 'tis the fever that keeps you weak," Jarren offered.

Philip turned his attention to Jarren. "The cook?"

"Aye, she learned healing skills from old Mary, the healer."

Royce lifted his head enough to get a good look at Jarren. "What of the woman who found the knife?"

"I looked for her while I sought out milady, and the woman with the knife was nowhere to be found. Her house is not livable, so she has most likely found somewhere to stay. I tell you the truth, Royce, 'tis hard to find anyone in the village right now."

"Have you checked Brithwin's room for the knife she took?"

"Aye. 'Tis not there. We've gone through everything twice."

It wouldn't be there. She had risked much in taking it from his room and taken it for a reason. What her purpose was, he didn't yet know—but he would find out. He *did* know she hadn't retrieved it to adorn her chamber.

"I want to see the knife this woman holds. I want to know if they are one and the same"—his voice faded to a murmur—"my lady's and this knife that stabbed me."

"Royce, don't jump to conclusions here. I doubt she is the one who stabbed you." Jarren spoke with conviction.

"How can you be so sure?" Sleep tugged at his eyes.

"The same way you could be, if you would allow yourself to really see the woman you married."

Royce closed his eyes. "I hope you are right."

"You will see I am. As I told you, the woman who found the knife will bring it here. She is hoping you will pay her for it. When she does, you will know the truth."

†††

When the sun rose, Brithwin checked on Guy. They would have to remain at the cottage for many days, even if Daffydd thought otherwise. Murielle could not care for Guy alone. Brithwin woke Daffydd and sent him for water while she threw another piece of wood on the fire, thankful the nights were no longer so cold.

After applying more soothing salve to Guy's wounded flesh, Brithwin walked around the small cottage, looking for anything useful. A cook pot sat next to the fire, and an ax rested against the wall in the corner. They would need both.

Daffydd stepped through the entrance with blood smeared on his face and tunic. Brithwin gasped. He held out the pail with a grin on his face.

Brithwin reached for the water.

"What happened to you?" Murielle squeaked.

"I brought food." He stepped out the door, bent down, and came back holding a small boar. "He is a young one but will feed us."

The three worked together preparing the food. It kept Brithwin's mind occupied and helped pass the time.

The following days Brithwin spent teaching Murielle how to care for Guy's burns. With her limited knowledge of plants, she showed her what could be used safely for pain and healing.

On the fourth day, Brithwin had to go home, for she knew not what kind of wrath she would face from Royce should he have chosen to stay at Hawkwood because of the fire. Daffydd's concern of her husband's anger did give her pause.

And she was more confident that Guy would live, though he was unable to travel as of yet. Daffydd would have to bring food until the old man healed enough to make the short journey, and then her new friend would escort them back.

After saying a prayer early in the morning for Guy's healing, they readied to leave. A smile touched her lips when Daffydd asked her to pray Royce would show him mercy, but quickly faded when she considered he was serious. Both horses needed to remain with Murielle. If Guy worsened, they would be able to reach Brithwin quicker…she hoped. She left Murielle her knife—it was all she would have for protection. The two traveled to Hawkwood in relative silence. She imagined he was as nervous as she to face Royce. She prayed Royce went on to Rosen Craig, but Daffydd's lack of faith that her husband had caused her to worry.

Even as much as Royce avoided her, by now he would have noticed her absence. Elspeth would have covered for her the first day, maybe two, but far too much time had passed. Her maid was probably beside herself with worry. She prayed again that Royce would have mercy on both Daffydd and her.

The portcullis stood open. Brithwin and Daffydd passed under it and into the outer bailey.

Brithwin looked at the old gown she had thrown on the night of the fire. She doubted mending it would make it suitable to wear again. Thinking about a hot bath and clean clothes, she quickened her step. When she finished bathing, she would go and get fresh, warm bread and a slice of cheese. The thought caused her stomach to rumble.

Stepping through the unmanned gate that led into the inner bailey, Brithwin turned to Daffydd. "What will you do now we have returned?"

"The old couple needs food, so I will head to the kitchen and gather enough food for a few days. Then I plan to deliver it to them." He smiled.

"'Tis good of you to look after them. They have always been dear to me."

"I am pleased to be of service." He bowed. "It has been an honor getting to know you, milady. Lord Rosen Craig is a fortunate man." He turned and walked toward the kitchen. As he left, she heard him mutter, "Even if he's too much a fool to realize it."

That made her smile. But she needed to tell him never to allow Royce to hear him use fool in the same sentence with her husband's name.

As Daffydd disappeared into the castle, she turned and was beset upon by rough hands and dragged away.

†††

A tumult coming from the bailey jolted Royce awake. The position of the sun's rays on the chamber wall told him it was late morning. Straining to lift his head brought on a fiery pain in his shoulder, a grim reminder of his wound—and his weakness. He dropped his head back to the bed. He had slept fitfully through the night, each time waking with Brithwin on his mind. A fog enveloped his thoughts, making it hard to think and separate dreams from reality. It was the fever making him feel that way. He'd had it before.

Marjory sat on a stool next to his bed and wiped his forehead with a cool, wet cloth. "'Tis quite a commotion out there and sorry I am it woke you."

"Do you know what is happening?" His voice came out raspy from disuse.

The sounds of boots came rushing up the stairs and then a loud rapping on the door. It flew open and one of his knights burst in the room. "We have Lady Rosen Craig! She walked into the bailey disguised as a peasant." He paused to catch his breath. "I knew you would be anxious to hear, milord. We have heard she is the one you seek for your wound."

Royce battled the haze that clouded his thinking. "Is she?" He was unsure, but didn't he want to find her for some reason?

"Aye, milord, she is," the knight said with confidence.

Royce shook his head, trying to clear it, but that caused

the room to spin. The man standing there looked self-assured. Marjory appeared alarmed.

"Shall I bring her to you?" the knight asked.

"Nay!" Marjory sprang to her feet. "You need rest, milord."

The knight puffed up. "We can lock her up until you wish to see her."

He seemed pleased to have brought this news. Darkness closed in. Royce struggled to stay awake. "I need to be the first to speak with her." Royce mumbled his words.

The knight turned to leave the room, but Marjory's angry words brought him to a halt. "Where are you taking her?"

"To the dungeon." The knight gave a malicious smile. "Where else would I put a murderer? She did try to kill our lord."

"You cannot put milady in the dungeon! He will not allow it."

Indeed, he wouldn't, if he could form the words through the dark fog that held him captive. His eyes grew heavier.

The knight smiled arrogantly. "You heard him. Lord Rosen Craig wants to be the first to speak with her. Obviously, he is unable to do that right now. I am ensuring his wishes are carried out."

With a humorless laugh, he turned abruptly and left the room.

Chapter 13

"Milady, come to the door. I have brought you a torch for light." Marjory paused as heavy footsteps sounded behind her, "Someone is coming. I shall talk to Sir Thomas. He will get you out."

"Why is he doing this to me?" Brithwin raised her head to peer out the small window, her voice raw.

Marjory stood and looked over her shoulder. The guard bore toward her. She whispered, "Lord Rosen Craig does not think clearly. 'Tis the fe—"

The booming voice of the man pulling her away from the door drowned her out.

"No one is to speak to her before Laird Rosen Craig. Now off with ye," he pushed her away from the door, "before I throw ye in for aiding the enemy."

Brithwin called to his retreating back. "Please tell me why he put me in here. What does he think I have done?"

His laugh sent icy fingers of fear down her back. "Ye will find out soon enough, *milady*."

†††

The combination of the damp, musty cell and the pungent odor of rotting varmints caused Brithwin's stomach to roil. Even in the dim light, she was able to make out a dead rat. She scrambled closer to the door and hugged her knees to her chest.

Dampness from the ground seeped into her chemise, as if to flee the bone-chilling cold. Her teeth chattered. The scampering of small, clawed feet, all too familiar to her ears, beat a maddening, irregular rhythm. At least the sliver of light—her beacon—helped hold the burning in her belly at bay and gave some comfort. She wiped at the perspiration beading on her forehead despite the chill, and tried to make sense out of what had just happened. They'd stripped her to her chemise, looking for her knife. She wore nothing now but her thin undergarment. Her body quaked at the memory. The men who'd shredded her clothes had enjoyed her discomfort, sneering and laughing at each other's vulgar observations, then leering at her as if she were a criminal. Their lewd and mordant remarks seared into her mind.

She rubbed at her body, trying to rid herself of their filthy touch and wishing she had soap and water to expunge the way they made her feel.

How could her husband allow such manhandling of her? And why did Marjory say Royce didn't think clearly?

Royce was no different than her father, sending her to her own nightmare. Nothing could cause her insides to quake like this dungeon. She laid her head on her knees as her energy bled from her.

A wicked chuckle sounded outside her door, then a soft scrape of wood against stone. Her sliver of light vanished, plunging her back into dark terror.

†††

It was early morning. Thomas lingered in the kitchen talking in a hushed voice with Marjory while Elspeth waited silently. Three days had passed since Brithwin's imprisonment. It was time they made their move. "You have stayed away from all of Lord Rosen Craig's men?"

"Aye, I did just as you told me. I have not left the kitchen since we have talked. I have even made a pallet to sleep on." She pointed to a bed lying at the side of the fire.

"We cannot give them any reason to think we are up to something. I have met with many of Hawkwood's men, and they will get the word to the others. Tonight we will get milady out, and I need your help. Are you still willing?"

Marjory's eyes drew to a squint. "You know I will do anything for milady."

"Good. Now listen close." Thomas's voice dropped low. "We cannot afford mistakes. When Lord Rosen Craig's men are all sleeping, I need you to make a sleeping tonic for milady's guard. Elspeth will take it down to him. After he has fallen asleep, I will rescue milady. I want you to depart to her old room and wait for her there."

"But Elspeth?" Marjory began shaking her head. "She is a lady's maid."

Thomas straightened and looked down at her. "I will not take chances on milady's life. We do not know whom we can trust, and Elspeth has agreed to help."

"I can go in her place. You do not know what you ask of her." Marjory's eyes shifted quickly to Elspeth and back to Thomas before she lowered her voice to a whisper. "The girl can swoon at a cross word."

"'Tis too late to change plans. It stays as is. Do you understand what is expected of you, Marjory?"

"I understand. But how am I to get milady's things to take with us?"

Thomas folded his arms. "We are not leaving. This is Lady Brithwin's home. Where could she go and remain safe?"

"But she will not be safe here. Not until Lord Rosen Craig…" The color drained from Marjory's face. "Thomas, I did not even think." She shook her head. "I have been sending up a sleeping draught for milord every day. Sir Jarren had requested it so milord could rest and heal."

Thomas lifted his hand and stroked his chin. "Hmm, I could have misjudged Sir Jarren. Do you believe he is keeping Lord Rosen Craig asleep to keep milady confined?"

"I do not know who to trust or what to believe." Marjory's voice quavered.

"No one speaks of her confinement. I have told my men not to talk on it and raise suspicions. However, Lord Rosen Craig's men have not said anything, either. Hence, I do not know who is aware of it and who is not. 'Tis very troubling. We must be careful."

"Aye, very careful." Marjory replied.

Thomas' gaze locked with Elspeth's. "I will bring milady there straight away. If something goes awry, all of you must stay there where you will be safe. Our men will be lying in the midst of Lord Rosen Craig's men tonight. Should an alarm sound, they will be ready with their swords."

Elspeth rung her hands. "What happens after you get her out? Something will have to be done, or we will all be in grave trouble."

"Once milady is safely in her room, I intend to confront Lord Rosen Craig. Something is amiss. A knight stands guard over milord."

"What of milord's friend?" Elspeth rubbed her arms. "Do you think he is responsible for milady's plight?"

"Jarren has been down to the village every day, and I have not seen him go up to see Lord Rosen Craig. But we cannot know for sure."

Marjory dug through her basket of herbs. "Shall I send a sleeping draught to milord's guard also?"

"Aye, I would like to restrain from any bloodshed this night. Do not put any more in Lord Rosen Craig's drink, but continue to send the drink up as you always do. I need to speak to him. I cannot believe it has come to this. I pray I do not have to turn on Milord. There is no honor in that, but milady is like a daughter and I will do what I must." Thomas nodded and withdrew from the kitchen.

†††

Jarren stood with his hands on his hips, facing Philip and Marjory in the kitchen.

Marjory busied herself wiping the crumbs from the table to the floor. "I tell you, I will not do it! If you want him to drink it, you take it to him. I have done enough in making it." She hoped she did not shake outwardly, for her insides quaked. She had not spoken to Sir Jarren since her lord's fever had broken and he'd ordered the draught. It was just her luck to have him come to her now that Thomas had warned her to stay away from them.

Philip smiled. "It was your idea, Jarren, and you are his closest friend. He will take it better coming from you."

"When he finds out *we* have kept him sleeping for several days I don't think he will take it well from anyone," Jarren grumbled.

"It has only been three days thus far, the other four his fever kept him a-bed." Philip gave a lopsided grin.

Jarren took the goblet that Marjory held with trembling hands and headed for Rosen Craig's chamber. Before he could mount the stairs, Daffydd intercepted him. Leaning in and keeping his voice low, Daffydd spoke. "We need to meet privately."

"I will meet you later. I am bringing this up to our lord." Jarren lifted the drink for Daffydd to see and stepped around him. Daffydd grasped his arm in a firm grip.

"We need to talk. Now." Urgency rang in Daffydd's voice.

Jarren followed him to the outer bailey where Daffydd glanced around. Frowning, Jarren folded his arms, the drink dangling from his fingers. "What is so secretive that you must drag me out here?"

"There are things going on that I do not like. Do you know where Lady Rosen Craig is?"

Jarren looked at him with impatience. "I have been too busy overseeing the rebuilding at the village to watch after Lady Rosen Craig. Is there a problem?"

Daffydd let out whoosh of air. "You do not know then."

"Know what? I have no time for this."

"Lady Rosen Craig languishes in the dungeon as we speak."

Jarren had heard enough nonsense. "Have you been listening to gossipmongers? If that were so, I would know and I have heard no such thing."

Daffydd flashed a glance around. "'Tis true. I heard two of the men holding her there talking. They have imprisoned her to await our lord's punishment. The one knight said he heard Lord Rosen Craig say she is guilty of trying to murder him."

"'Tis ridiculous. Royce does not believe that."

Daffydd shrugged. "That is not all."

Jarren's stomach twisted. "What else must I know?"

"No one is talking about milady, not our men or Hawkwood's men. I know that many have been working at the village, but I am telling you, I can feel the tension. I fear we could have a battle between knights of Hawkwood and knights of Rosen Craig if we don't move quickly."

Daffydd leaned close to Jarren. "Something is amiss."

Jarren took a deep breath and wiped his hand down over his face. What a mess. He had kept Rosen Craig sleeping knowing it would help him heal and, in doing so, had possibly caused this. "I am going down to get milady out. Find Philip and apprise him."

Jarren rushed to the dungeon and came face-to-face with Lachlan, a brawny Scotsman who had joined up with Royce on the return trip from the border skirmish. "I've come to see milady."

"Sorry, me friend, but ye won't be seeing the lass today. I got me orders, ye know."

"And where do these orders come from?"

Lachlan cocked his head. "Well, now, they be comin

from da laird."

"So Rosen Craig spoke to you personally?" This man was aware of the friendship between him and Royce. Surely he would listen to him.

"Now, I not be sayin dat. But me orders came from him nonetheless."

"I am here on Rosen Craig's behalf. If he'd wanted his wife down here, I would know about it. Now step aside." He swung his body to walk past and felt the cold steel blade of a sword against his neck.

"As I was sayin, only the laird be changing the orders."

It wasn't the blade of steel at his neck that made Jarren back down, but the concern for milady and Royce. He didn't dare set off a catalyst of events that would put them in danger.

Jarren spun on his heel and ascended the stairs, leaving the dungeon. He walked across the bailey and toward the great hall, taking the stairs two at a time, and turned toward Rosen Craig's chamber. Seeing the guard posted at his door, he nodded and walked past. What was going on? There was only one man he knew he could trust. Jarren headed to the back stairs in search of Hawkwood's guard at arms.

Jarren found Thomas on the practice field, bent over, his hands resting on his knees, and dripping with sweat while his opponent did the same. Thomas straightened and greeted Jarren.

"If you have come to challenge me, you are too late. I have no more energy for another bout."

Jarren glanced at the men watching. "Nay, I was wondering if you could come with me over to the stables and have a look at my horse."

Thomas raised his eyebrow and pushed his sword into its sheath. They reached the edge of the practice field before Jarren used the same approach that Daffydd had used on him.

"Do you know where Lady Rosen Craig is, Thomas?"

Thomas eyed Jarren suspiciously. No one knew whom to trust.

"I can see by your reaction, you do."

"Aye," he said slowly.

Jarren rubbed his neck where Lachlan's blade had rested. "I have just come from the dungeon and Rosen Craig's room. Both have guards."

Thomas's brows narrowed. "When did you hear of milady's plight?"

"Only minutes ago. Lord Rosen Craig had been concerned that his wife did not feel safe, so he, unbeknownst to Lady Rosen Craig, sent Daffydd to keep watch over her."

"I see." Skepticism filled Thomas's voice.

The man apparently wasn't going to offer anything. "Do you know how many men are involved in this?"

"'Tis hard to say. We have tried to determine that ourselves and have decided not to trust any of your men."

"I understand, but I can assure you, neither Philip nor I was previously aware of this. I know you will not stand by and do nothing while milady is held prisoner."

Thomas placed his hand on the hilt of his sword. "Very well, but if you betray us, I will run you through and throw your body to the wild animals."

Jarren met his gaze. "Fair enough."

††††

"Ye won't be goin' nowhere or seein' no one until me laird tells me so." Brithwin jumped when the booming voice broke the silence of the room a few minutes after she'd heard Jarren speak to the guard.

"When will that be?" She struggled to keep a steady voice.

"Sorry, lass, but I got me orders. No one is to talk to you

and that includes me." He snickered as his footsteps faded.

Brithwin slid down the wall to the cold stone floor of her cubicle and drew her arms tight about her knees. Iron claws gripped her chest, stealing her breath. The cold had seeped into her bones, stiffening her joints. Water dripped down the walls, leaving a slimy black sheen where the mysterious light hit. Pungent odors filled the room and seemed to draw the rats, mice, and insects. She wasn't sure who was eating whom, but the rats were hungry. They grew braver with every passing day, waking her by gnawing on her feet. The food and water came in small portions, should she get any at all. Weakness invaded her body.

She thanked God for the light, which now sat on the wall beyond her door. Who had placed it there, she didn't know, but it stayed there and remained lit. She didn't know how, but she knew whom to thank.

With no window to the outdoors and inconsistent meals, she was not sure how much time had passed. Enough to nurture the growing anger she felt toward Royce. He was no different from her father, the man who'd delighted in her misery. How many times had he sent her here, and left her in the darkness? Royce must have been born with the same vile nature. She had done nothing to him to deserve his accusations.

She rocked back and forth, trying to bring warmth to her body. It was unfair. She did not deserve this. Holding the tears at bay, she refused to let them fall. If she did, he would win.

Why, God? Why are you allowing this? I have tried to live by all Pater has taught me about you. What did I do to deserve this?

She pushed the heels of her hands against her eyes to stop the flow. Then, as she sat in the silence that surrounded her, she heard a still small voice which was silent yet so clear.

Do you trust me, Brithwin?

Lowering her hands from her eyes, she slowly lifted her head. The words Pater had spoken so many times floated across her mind. *Trust in the Lord with all thine heart; and lean not unto thine own understanding. In all thy ways acknowledge Him, and He shall direct thy paths.*

Her voice caught in her throat from lack of water and use. It came out a whisper. "I am trying to trust You, Lord. I want to trust You, but I don't understand why I must endure this."

I am with you always, unto the end of time.

Brithwin felt the arms of God wrap around her like a blanket warmed before a fire. His presence surrounded her, pushing away the damp chill of her cell and her heart. The torch flared brighter, illuminating the dank room. Peace poured into her, filling her heart, and for the first time since she entered her prison, she wasn't afraid.

✝✝✝

An unexpected backdraft from the large stone fireplace sent up a thick grey haze of smoke. It fit Jarren's mood. The evening repast progressed in hushed restraint. Thomas and Jarren sat next to their lord's and lady's empty seats on the dais. Jarren fidgeted, not knowing how the night would end.

He looked out upon the mixed group of men. "It is an unsettling feeling, watching these men, not knowing who is a part of this scheme."

Thomas joined Jarren's morose gaze and stared out in front of him. "Let's pray tonight goes as planned. If it does, we will find out the truth."

Jarren continued searching the men's faces, turmoil building within him. "These are men with whom Royce and I fought side by side in many a battle. 'Tis hard to believe any have betrayed him."

"Only God knows a man's heart. Some men are masters at hiding their true nature."

While the men began moving the tables to the side making room to bed down for the night, Jarren and Thomas quietly went over the strategy for later and then split up to await word of the rescues.

Jarren and Philip went to Brithwin's old chamber and were met by Marjory and Elspeth. Jarren paced the floor. Philip leaned against the wall with his arms crossed. "Your pacing puts me on edge."

"'Tis making me nervous, too." Elspeth sat on a stool. "How much longer must we wait?"

"Not much longer. It has been quiet in the hall for a while."

He stepped over and stirred the fire for something to do. Thor raised his head slightly and looked at him. "Where were you, you useless old hound?"

"Don't take it out on him," Elspeth defended. "Milady locked him in her chamber when she left to prevent his getting in the way."

Philip pushed away from the wall. "I'm off to see if the guard at Lord Rosen Craig's door is sleeping yet."

He returned soon after with a smirk on his face. "The guard won't be waking any time soon. How much did you put in his drink, Marjory? I shoved him with my boot, and he didn't stir. You didn't kill him, did you?"

She scowled. "I know what I do. I did not wish to take a chance on him waking."

Jarren headed to the door and turned. "Lock the door behind us, and do not open it for anyone but us."

Elspeth ran to the door and clutched his sleeve. "What will happen to Brithwin if things go wrong?"

Jarren pulled from her grasp. "Thomas will guard her with his life."

Elspeth balled her hands into fists. "She could die." Her words shook as they tumbled out. "We all could die. This is not good. Not good, I tell yo—"

Jarren's voice thundered as he took hold of Elspeth's shoulders and shook her. "Elspeth! Milady is counting on your courage. It is up to us to rescue her. Can she rely on you?"

Elspeth's face drained of color. She nodded.

His voice softened, as well as his touch. "All will turn out well. Remember, your lady needs you." Jarren dropped his hands from her shoulders and slipped out the door.

Both men crept down the dark hall with their hands on the hilts of their swords, listening for sounds of the traitors. The sleeping guard lay sprawled on the floor blocking the entrance. Jarren rolled the guard over, slowly opened the door, and peered inside. Looking back, he nodded. He and Philip pulled the guard into the room and shut the door.

†††

Royce fought the darkness to open his eyes, but the need for sleep kept pulling him back to his dream. He was in Scotland with his men and stood in the middle of a village. The Scots swarmed out of their homes with weapons drawn. A battle cry went up amongst the throng of angry sheep farmers. His men drew their swords. The Scots descended from every direction, dressed in all manner of clothing.

They were no match for Royce's trained knights. They fell like babes. Blood soaked the ground. A second bevy pressed forward. He wanted to stop his men. These weren't men—mercy—they were mere boys. He called a halt, but the roar of voices and the clank of steel against steel drowned out his voice. A flash from the sun's light bounced off a blade, drawing his attention to the terrified face of a woman as her loved one fell to the sword. She bent and clasped the mighty weapon and turned on the offender. A scream of anguish flew from her lips. His knight swung in an arc to defend himself, but she pressed on. Royce yelled and tried to run, to save her from her own folly, but the screams and clanging metal again drowned out his words. He needed to run, but stones strapped to his feet kept him firm. Someone grabbed him from behind, pinioned his arms, and shook him. He struggled to break free. He had to help the woman, but strength abandoned him. Someone called his name from far away. He couldn't see them. The familiar voice was worried. He moved toward the voice and the frightened woman began to fade. He needed to help her, to save her. He had to go back. The voice beckoned with urgency and he followed.

"Rosen Craig! Rosen Craig! You have to wake up." Jarren's forceful voice jarred Royce's head. Was the infernal man trying to shake his teeth loose?

"I thought Marjory was told not to put anything in Royce's drink," Philip said.

"She didn't," Jarren countered.

Royce struggled to open his eyes. Two anxious sets of eyes scoured him. "You can stop shaking me." His reprimand came out a pathetic, raspy plea.

Philip grinned. "For a minute I worried Marjory put you to an eternal sleep."

He handed Royce a goblet of water. "How do you feel?"

"I can lift my head and breathe at the same time if that counts for something." His lips cracked as he spoke, leaving a metallic taste in his mouth.

"I suppose it does." Philip's smile broadened.

Jarren stepped forward to help. "Can you sit?"

Royce sat up, swinging his feet over the side of the bed while trying to grasp his jumbled memories. "How long have I been abed?"

Jarren cleared his throat. "Near to eight days now."

"My mind is a haze. I remember naught." The fire, being

stabbed, the old healer's home, near falling from his horse, but not much more.

Jarren shot an inscrutable glance at Philip then pulled a chair up and sat. "There is much to tell while we wait."

†††

"Who goes there?" the guard roared.

Brithwin put her ear to the barred window.

"'Tis Elspeth. I bring your meal," her voice quivered.

"Ah, Elspeth, such a lovely name. Did you come to keep me company?" Brithwin envisioned the smirk on the guard's face. Elspeth should not have come down alone.

"N-no, I brought your food."

"I should rather have your company."

Brithwin held her breath. Elspeth's gasp echoed on the stone walls. Her body quaked for her friend. "Run, Elspeth. Leave while you can," Brithwin whispered.

"Come, now. You don't have to be shy around me. There's no one here to interrupt us." The guard's smooth voice sent shivers down Brithwin's spine.

"Your food will get cold." Elspeth's words came out so low Brithwin could barely make them out.

"'Tis food. I have eaten it cold many a time. Now come here, wench."

Elspeth screamed. Something thudded. "I shall go get you more," Elspeth's voice warbled.

"It can wait. Right now, I am hungry for something else."

Poor Elspeth. Brithwin's stomach convulsed for her friend.

A muffled scream rent the air. Brithwin could only imagine that the man forced himself on Elspeth as she listened.

He chuckled. "I like 'em feisty. Give me another kiss."

Fabric ripped. Brithwin thought she might be sick. She

banged on the metal door, screaming at the guard to let Elspeth go.

"Don't worry your pretty little head, milady. Your turn yet comes."

Chapter 14

The shuffle of boots rushing down the stone stairs echoed like a distant thunder through the dungeon. A loud crash, Elspeth's squeal, and a resounding thud were nearly Brithwin's undoing. "Elspeth. Elspeth!"

"Stand down." Thomas's warning sent a wave of relief through Brithwin.

She peered out the small window of her cell, waiting silently, her aching hands gripping the metal window bars. If only she could stick her head out the door and see if her friend was uninjured. She closed her eyes and leaned her head against the door.

Father, please protect our rescuer.

Metal on metal resonated through the air. She recognized the chiming of swords. But this time it was no mock battle the men fought. This was real. More clanging of metal reverberated down the hall—then a groan. Heavy footfalls thumped on the ground, growing louder as they drew nearer to her. Panic snaked up from the pit of her belly.

I will not doubt God. He has already won this battle for me.

Brithwin moved back as the footsteps stopped in front of her door. She couldn't see the man's face as he stood before her window, but she recognized the stained tunic of the guard. The same guard who'd promised she'd be next. Her stomach convulsed. The metal bolt slid against the door that slowly swung open. The guard fell in—injured.

The figure standing behind him made Brithwin want to weep. Her champion rushed in with concern filling his eyes. She fell into Thomas's open arms, swallowing a sob.

He wrapped his arms around her and leaned down. "We

must hurry and get you to safety, milady."

They had reached the stairs when a movement to Brithwin's left caught her attention. A cry escaped her lips, and she stumbled to Elspeth, who huddled on the floor with her knees drawn up and head buried in her legs. Drained of strength, Brithwin dropped to the floor beside her maid and pulled the girl to herself.

Taking in her torn dress, Brithwin wiped away the tears—thoughts for herself gone. "Did he hurt you?"

Elspeth raised her head. Her chin quivered as she answered. "Nay, he did not hurt me." Elspeth burst into tears. "'Twas terrible, milady. I thought . . . I thought . . ."

"Hush, now, dear one." She stroked Elspeth's hair. "All is well."

Thomas cleared his throat. "Milady, we must hurry and get you to safety. We do not know what else has happened while we were down here."

"Of course. Can you stand, Elspeth?" Brithwin looked at her with sympathy. She couldn't help her, and she questioned if she had the strength to rise herself.

Thomas stepped forward. "If you will allow me?"

Brithwin fell back. Daffydd came down the steps and around the corner with sword drawn.

Thomas lifted Elspeth into his arms and looked to Daffydd. "How does it look above?"

"So far, everything is going as planned."

"Good. We must hurry." Thomas started up the steps with Elspeth.

Brithwin glanced back toward the cell with the injured guard. "We must send someone to tend to the guard.'"

You are soft-hearted, Brithwin." Thomas spoke as he climbed the stairs. "When this is over..."

Daffydd sneered. "Wouldn't want him to die before Royce has a chance to pass judgment on him."

Brithwin shivered at the promise in those words. The guard would pay dearly. She hurried up the stairs behind Thomas. Nearing the top, a torch threw light on Thomas's leg, revealing a glistening red slash.

Brithwin gasped. "Thomas, you are injured."

"I will be fine, milady. We must not talk until we have you to safety."

Daffydd came up the steps from behind and slipped past them into the lead. Keeping to the shadows to avoid the guards walking the ramparts, they walked in silence. Daffydd held up his hand for them to wait then slipped into the castle. A minute later, he signaled all was clear. They crept up the stairs and into Brithwin's room to find Marjory pacing the floor. She ran to Brithwin and embraced her.

Marjory guided her to a chair. "Come, sit before you fall down."

Brithwin acquiesced but frowned at her injured rescuer. "Thomas, let me look at your wound."

"'Tis a scratch. Nothing for you to worry about."

Brithwin's gaze passed over each of the dear faces now assembled in her old room but stopped on Elspeth. Her maid remained where Thomas had set her down, clutching her gown together. Brithwin went to her chest and pulled out her cloak, wrapping it around Elspeth. As she did so, Thomas and Daffydd slipped from the room, mumbling something about seeing how Jarren fared.

Elspeth dipped her head shyly. "Thank you, milady."

Brithwin sank down on a chair. "It is I who should thank you. You have risked much and done me a great service this day. I will not forget it."

†††

Royce sat before the fire as Thomas entered his room. Jarren waited quietly by, after telling him a number of acts committed by his household—acts bordering on treachery.

Tension permeated the chamber. Trust once taken for granted now teetered on a precipice which could easily crumble.

Thomas moved forward. "I'd like to hear what you have to say about milady," the man growled like an angry father. He stood with feet apart, his arms folded, and braced for battle. His leg bore a gash in need of attention, confirming the unrest of the castle.

"I am told she was in the dungeon. Jarren filled me in as you arrived. How is my lady?" Royce hadn't felt this low since he discovered his family murdered. He was supposed to be Brithwin's protector, but instead he lay in bed, weak as a new born babe.

Thomas gave him a guarded look. "She fares better than you would expect. She tended to Elspeth when we left. Milady is strong, and her faith once again sustains her."

Royce dragged a hand through his hair. "This should not have happened." He sent a harsh look to Jarren. "Some men have forgotten their place."

"Did you not accuse her of stabbing you? They stripped her to her chemise looking for her knife."

Royce frowned. "I would not accuse her without proof." Yet he had accused her—accused her of the murder of his family.

Jarren cleared his throat and shifted. "Rosen Craig, from what I am told, when you had the fever, you did not defend her. When others blamed her."

Royce let out a groan and dropped his head into his hands. He'd like to strangle Jarren right now. If the man hadn't laced his drink with a sleeping draught, this never would have happened.

Jarren looked at him soberly. "There is more."

Royce glared at him. "More?"

Drawing in a deep breath, Jarren rubbed his neck. "Aye, there is.

"Let's go to my solar where we can sit. I want to hear the whole of this mess."

Several hours later, the men left, and Royce returned to his chamber. He had put two of Hawkwood's knights to guard Brithwin's door and keep her safe. His gut twisted every time he envisioned Brithwin locked in the dank cell. She was a woman he could admire. The ordeal would have broken most. He thought about the last time he'd seen her, standing with her hands on her hips, frowning at him as he rode to fight the fire. A clipped laugh escaped. He had believed she would obey him. She just waited for him to leave so she could defy him. The woman could drive him mad. She was beautiful, brave, and stubborn. One minute she could make him smile, and in the next, infuriate him. He desired her as a husband does a wife, yet guilt for feeling that way toward his parent's possible murderer tempered the desire.

Daffydd's story of all she had done, how she had risked her life for an old peasant and a feebleminded boy, made him see her in a different light. She came nowhere near the spoiled wench he imagined. How many women would have stayed in a run-down hut, with little food, and cared for the old man? Thank the saints he had sent Daffydd to watch her.

On the morrow he would speak with her. He settled onto his bed and glimpsed the faint light breaking up the night sky. He would not have long to wait, for morning had arrived.

†††

Brithwin had risen as dawn streaked the sky with pale light. Along with the bathwater Elspeth had seen to, she delivered a message from Royce—he wished to see her. Steam from the heated water in the wooden tub ascended in a foggy mist. The water caressed her body as she lowered herself into it. The scent of roses tickled her nose. Leaning her head back, she closed her eyes and tried to block out the nightmare she'd just lived. To lie in the water all day and forget what had happened would be heaven. The heat soothed her sore muscles and aching joints. She slid down and dipped her head under the water to wet her hair. Every part of the filthy cell she would wash from her body.

Elspeth cleaned her with gentle fingers, kneaded her scalp, and scrubbed her hair until every trace of the pungent smell disappeared. As the bath cooled, Brithwin continued to luxuriate in the tepid water. She sighed from the pure pleasure of it.

"I would imagine you will not be so anxious to go pray with Pater." Elspeth dried her hands on the cloth next to her.

"Of course I will. I have much to be thankful for."

"How can you say that, after what you have gone through? After what I went through? It was horrible enough for me. And to think about you down there in that devil's den." Elspeth shuddered.

Brithwin smiled at her. "'Tis God who saw me through it, not put me there. I tell you true, there was no one around, just a whisper, then a sliver of light shone through my door. Day and night, the torch stayed lit, yet I never saw anyone light or replace it. The Lord was with me. I felt His presence, and He kept my fear from overtaking me."

Elspeth merely looked away, and Brithwin finally stepped out of the tub, leaving little round droplets of water seeping into the wooden floor. After drying, she dressed in a clean chemise and sat before the fire, combing her fingers through her hair. The morning grew late while she lounged in her chair, nibbling on the bread and cheese brought to break her fast. She pushed aside the last piece of bread. The time had come to face Royce. She could not delay much longer. He was not a man to be put off.

The lovely gown Thomas had given her for her wedding

beckoned to her. The more contrast she could get from her prison clothes the better, but the memories from her wedding dress were not pleasant, either. Indecision gave way. She chose a gown saved for special occasions. Elspeth had dressed her hair to hang down in a plait, brushing her waist. Now all she had left to do was wait for his lordship.

Elspeth had barely stepped out when there was a strong rap on the door.

"'Tis Royce." Brithwin whispered to herself as she quickly sat. "You may enter." Her insides twisted. Would he blame her yet again for things she hadn't done?

Royce stepped through the portal. His clothing hung loose on his thinned frame. Brithwin's breath hitched. She turned her head, hoping he had not noticed her surprise. Why should she care if he'd been ill, when he had left her in the dungeon with little food and nothing but her chemise to wear?

†††

The smell of roses pervading the room sent Royce's senses reeling. "I hope you are feeling well, my lady."

Brithwin folded her arms across her chest. The small window appeared to have attracted her interest, for she didn't turn from it. "It is as you say, *my lord.*"

The mockery in her voice made Royce wince. It was obvious they had followed his orders and no one had spoken to her about her confinement. "Could you look at me, Brithwin?"

She turned slowly. "Yes, *my lord.*"

Royce frowned at her continued derision. "I am glad you were not harmed, my lady."

Brithwin's eyes bore into his. "'Tis no thanks to you, but that is no matter. The Lord took care of me and kept me."

"And you blame me?" He knew she did.

She tipped her chin and pulled back her shoulders. "You,

my lord, are the one who gives the orders here, are you not?" Brithwin's statement caught him off guard. They were the same words he had used to condemn her of Hawkwood's part in his family's deaths. He raised his eyebrows and took a step toward her. "You believe me guilty of this? Have I ever given you cause to think I am capable of such a thing?"

Brithwin's eyes were the color of angry blue flames as she narrowed them on him. "From the day of your arrival, you have despised me. You look at me with distaste and impatience. You accuse me of murder. You avoid me or ignore me. Need I go on, *my lord?*"

Royce could not take his eyes off her. She was even more beautiful full of righteous anger. He took three more steps, halting before her. She lifted her chin a little higher. He bit back a smile. She was proud and would not be intimidated. He slowly raised his hand and rubbed the backs of his fingers across her cheek, savoring the smoothness of petal soft skin. She didn't balk, but continued to hold his stare. That gave him hope, and he ran a finger down her neck and over the throbbing vein there. Was it from fear? Nay, she braved a week in the dungeon—the lady was fearless. Was it anger, then? Or dare he hope she felt what he did?

Passion and desire rose within him, quickening his own pulse at the smallest of touches. He yearned to pull her into his arms and to kiss the remaining stubbornness into submission. A mental shake brought him around.

To cover his discomfiture, he stepped away. "I'm not ignoring you now, am I?"

Every nerve in his body alerted him to her nearness. The woman drew him in just as in the stories about the sirens of old. She was a lure to him, beckoning him to come, drawing him to his demise; and, as in those stories, he could not resist her temptation. She did not have to open her mouth to tempt him; she needed merely to stand before him, alone, and in her chamber.

He plunged his hands through his hair. "What do you do to me?"

She tilted her head to the side. "I have done nothing to you. If you remember, it is you who has done this evil thing to me."

Royce wasn't sure whether she truly misunderstood him, but he was glad for it. He needed to draw the conversation to an end and remove himself from her presence before he did something he regretted.

"Brithwin, I spent the last week in my room with a fever and dosed with a sleeping draught. I knew nothing of your imprisonment."

"How convenient for you, *my lord*."

"There was nothing convenient about a knife wound. I give you surety of that."

Her eyes narrowed, and her face flushed. "So that is why they stripped me to my chemise, looking for my knife? They left me for days in a cold stone tomb, with water trickling down the walls, in nothing but a thin piece of cotton. And you want me to believe you were not responsible?"

Royce wanted to grab her and shake some sense into her. "I have given you no reason to doubt my word. A man is only as good as his word. I would not dishonor myself so."

Brithwin turned away and swung back, eyes ablaze. "You give me many reasons! You do not trust me. Do you think *I* would dishonor myself? Yet still you think I am guilty of your family's death. Trust works both ways, *my lord*."

Royce paced across the room, taking several deep breaths before returning to stop in front of her. He ground his teeth together. She used his title, but she made sure he heard her disparaging tone. She deliberately irritated him. He shrugged it off, braced his feet apart, and folded his arms. "I give you my word. You can trust it. And I am declaring my innocence, something you still have failed to do."

The emotions washed over her. Oh, she was easy to read. At least she was when she did not have time to think about putting on a mask. The fury melted away like water on snow, and uncertainty replaced it. She searched his face as if to discern the truth.

She scowled at him. "Then let me avow today that I had no hand in your family's deaths." She lifted her chin, a habit she seemed to save for him. "Now let us see who is willing to trust."

Chapter 15

Did Royce toy with her? Thomas believed he was a man of his word. Brithwin couldn't tell, and suddenly she needed to escape his overwhelming presence. She moved to the door.

He growled her name. "Brithwin, we have not finished." She stopped. "I intend to break my fast, *my lord.*"

"Very well. If you wish to continue this in the great hall rather than in private, 'tis all the same to me." He stepped forward and offered her his arm. "Shall we, then?"

Brithwin wanted to stomp her foot. He knew she would not wish to feed the gossip mongers with juicy meat. "What else do you wish to discuss?" Her shoulders dropped as she turned back into the room.

He smirked. "Let's move to my solar where we can both sit."

In the solar, Brithwin collapsed into the chair. He looked so smug—a man who had proved he would get what he wanted. "It is unseemly to speak of private matters before a room full of servants and men-at-arms."

"'Tis of little concern to me."

Brithwin rolled her eyes. "Aye, that is the truth of it."

He continued to stand, arms folded, glaring at her. "First I seek an answer to my question. I would know why you do not take my word as the truth?"

She averted her gaze, mulling her answer. "'Tis as I said. You give the orders, and the only man who ever wanted to hurt me that way is dead."

"Your mind must be addled to believe this. I tell you on my honor as a knight, I was unaware and had no part in it."

She tried to decipher the truth in his words. His jaw clenched as he swore on his honor, something she could tell he loathed to do. He wanted her to take him at his word, yet he would not do the same for her. "I will pray for the Lord to reveal the truth to me. That is all I can offer."

"*If* He answers you, you will know my hands are clean— although, I wouldn't be putting all my bread in that basket."

"If that is all, *my lord*, I would like to break my fast and go to morning prayer."

Royce picked up a plate of food which sat on a chair inside the solar door and placed it on her lap. "I thought as much, so I had something brought up. You can eat here. Prayer will wait for you, as you are well aware, for there is one other item I wish to inquire about."

He sank into a nearby chair and tented his fingers together, his gaze on her unwavering. She sat motionless and refused to give in to the urge to shift under his perusal.

Silence engulfed the room while time deceived her. Had she sat under his scrutiny for only a few minutes? A loud *crack* from the fire disrupted the quiet. She jerked. A slight smile hinted at the corner of his lips. It would seem he had been waiting for a chink in her armor.

"Do you recall the eventide before the fire, Brithwin?"

She eyed him wearily. "A sennight has passed and many an unpleasant night, so 'tis hard to say which is which."

"Perhaps if I were to assist your memory it would help. You went to the village and did not return until well after the evening meal. Upon your arrival here, you went to your chamber and waited for me to leave my solar. Once all was quiet, you slipped into my room; however, I returned sooner than you expected."

Brithwin gave in to the urge to shift in her chair. Did he know how things had happened or was he guessing? A cold trickle crept down her spine.

He lowered his hands and leaned forward. His eyes sparkled with assurance. "What you do not know, and would not know because we have yet to spend a night together, is I am a light sleeper."

Brithwin's throat went dry and she tried to swallow. Heat climbed to her face. Dread lay in her stomach. Would he punish her now? She set the plate of roasted meat and cheese on the table, the aroma suddenly disagreeable.

"I was awakened to see what I believed was a common thief sneaking about my chamber. Imagine my surprise when I attacked the intruder and discovered him to be my wife. I had to ask myself, why would you be in here in the middle of the night? My questions had to wait 'til morning." His look turned dark. "Of course, you would know why that was."

Brithwin could sit still no longer. She shot from her chair. "I only defended myself."

"I thought that might help your recollection." Royce's eyes bore into her as she began pacing the room. "By all means, continue. I am nothing but ears."

Her plait fell over her shoulder and down the front of her gown. Picking it up, she ran her hand over the neat weave of her hair. She didn't know where to begin and certainly didn't want to reveal more than she had to. "'Tis true, I did come here to get something that was mine. Elspeth forgot it when she gathered my things from this room." She turned and glared at him. "I was given no notice I would be vacating my chamber so quickly." He remained silent and inscrutable, apparently waiting for more. "'Twas my mother's knife. It is all I have that was hers."

He frowned. "Why not just ask me for it? Did you think I would deny you something of your mother's?"

"I—I did not know."

"Do I seem without honor?" Exasperation filled his voice.

"Nay. Aye. Oh, I do not know!"

Royce chuckled. "I would have given it to you."

Why did he laugh at her? She could find no humor in the conversation or in the way her insides twisted.

"So you say, and yet all I see is a man who has no trust in me. If I had asked and you denied me, I would have had no chance of retrieving it from your chamber."

"Why could you not tell me this when I asked? How many times did I give you opportunity to tell me you had taken the knife?"

"Because I did not know what you would do." She shrugged.

"I knew what you had taken, for I saw it missing. I only wanted to hear you tell me with your own lips."

She lowered her eyes. "I tell the truth."

"Perhaps, but not all. There is more."

Brithwin crossed her arms in front of her. There was more but none he needed to know.

"Until I hear the whole of it, we will not leave." His tone brooked no argument this time.

He settled back in the chair. She was certain he would hold her here for months. It was obvious he was used to getting his way.

"Oh, very well. I was followed the eventide I had returned late to the castle." She begrudged telling him the whole of it. "I wanted my knife for protection. Up until then I had no need for it and had not thought about where I had left it."

Royce raised his eyebrows. "Why did you not tell Thomas?"

"Thomas would have made me stay in the safety of the grounds or made me take a knight with me."

Royce grimaced. "Had you but mentioned this to me, I could have told you that you were being guarded."

Fire darted through her veins. "You did not see fit to tell me of this?"

His golden brown eyes locked with hers. "There is much I do not tell you."

"You had no—" Brithwin shoved her hands on her hips and glowered at him. "Am I still to be followed?"

He smiled. "Aye."

"Why? Is there something else you have failed to tell me? Perchance you have enemies who would do me harm? Or could it be *you* still do not trust *me*?"

"He is there for protection, my lady. I have enemies."

Was that a flicker of guilt? "Is there anything else you would like to know, *my lord*? I have wasted enough time here."

"I marvel at your stubbornness, my lady." With a sigh, he nodded his head. "You are dismissed."

†††

For a week after the confrontation with his wife, Royce had attempted to show more kindness and understanding toward Brithwin. To hear her say she had no blood on her hands when it came to his family's deaths gave him some comfort even if he still had no proof.

Here he stood, staring at the garden where Brithwin worked, holding in his hand the bouquet of wild flowers he'd picked outside the castles walls. It was a silly idea to bring her wildflowers when she worked in the middle of beautiful blooms. She'd probably think him an imbecile. He wiped the sweat off his forehead. He was as nervous as a young squire at his first battle. The hope to please his wife by bringing her flowers wilted like the blooms he'd already plucked from the bouquet and tossed aside.

The decision to lob the rest of the flowers on the ground almost won when Brithwin lifted her head and put her hand up to shade her eyes. She gave a timid wave. Royce tried to swallow, his throat suddenly dry. He forced himself to walk.

Her head was cocked, her cheeks flushed, and her

wimple had fallen from her head, leaving her hair free to escape the plait.

He stopped in front of her. "You look beautiful, my lady." The wide-eyed shocked stare she gave him reminded him that he'd not given her such a compliment before. "I have thought it from the first time I set my eyes on you."

"Th-thank you, my lord. 'Tis kind of you to say." Her gaze fell to the flowers in his hands.

He held them out. "For you. Not nearly as lovely as you, but I thought you might enjoy them."

"They are beautiful. 'Twas kind of you to think of me, my lord."

"I know you grow more beautiful blooms here in your own garden. I…I just wanted you to know I was thinking of you today."

Britwin's eyes turned glassy and she swallowed. "They are more beautiful because no one tended them but our Lord. I weed and water my flowers to make them look as they do. But these," she lifted them to her nose and breathed in, "these did not have as easy a time." Her lashes fluttered. "And they are special because you picked them for me."

"Rosen Craig!" Jarren yelled from the court yard.

Royce bowed. "I am glad they please you, my lady." He sighed. "It appears I am needed. Shall I see you later at the evening meal?"

She curtseyed. "Aye, my lord."

†††

Brithwin stood at a loom in the weaver's room while the rhythmic clicking of shuttles lulled her. Plunging into work had helped her put the nightmare of the dungeon behind her. She knew not whether her imprisonment or her argument with Royce had changed his view on her, he now seemed so different. He not only spoke to her with respect, but when he'd brought her the flowers, he'd almost seemed nervous, as if courting her.

Perhaps they could live in some sort of harmony.

Heaven knows she was ready for it. Each day with her father had held enough turmoil for a lifetime. If she and Royce could at least work well together and speak civilly to each other, she would try to be content.

Elspeth's chatter interrupted her thoughts. Her friend always wished to speak of the latest castle gossip, and it routinely grated on Brithwin's nerves.

Elspeth leaned toward her. "Don't you think it would be so romantic to have a knight defend your honor?"

Brithwin glanced over. "What do you speak of?"

Elspeth huffed. "Have you not heard a word I said? The scullery maid said this happened to her."

Brithwin passed her shuttle through the warp threads of the tapestry she was weaving. "Thomas defended you."

Elspeth snorted. "He is old."

Brithwin fought a grin. "Thomas is not old. And you should not believe all you hear anyway. 'Tis meaningless talk, that is all."

"But you have heard the stories the troubadours tell, of chivalry, honor, and love. I have heard you speak of it yourself." Elspeth gave her a smug look.

"'Tis true." Brithwin sighed and looked down at the loom. "But I have discovered there is no man who cares for a woman enough to put her before his own needs and desires. 'Tis purely dreams of a foolish woman."

Elspeth's shoulders sagged. "Milady, please do not tell me you have given up on love."

"I am afraid it is so. A woman is nothing more than chattel, a mere possession. The sooner you realize that, the better off you will be. I have made my peace with it and you should, too. If I could leave here, knowing my people would be treated fairly, it would be tempting to go." The memory of

Royce handing her the flowers danced before her mind's eye. Did she really want to leave now that something was changing between them?

"Go?" Elspeth gave an unladylike snort. "Where would you go?"

Brithwin thought for a moment. "I have aunts and uncles in Scotland. My mother's family. Blood is a thick bond even if we have not met. Aye, that is what I would do. I would go to them." But if she did, would she always wonder what might have been?

"You have never spoken of them. I did not know."

"I know nothing of them. As you well know, I could not ask my father. When I was a young girl, I asked Sir Thomas about mother. He told me she was from Scotland. She and a group of travelers, which included Pater, stopped by for shelter on a stormy night. Neither she nor Pater ever left but the others in their group did. I went to my father because I desired to know more about her. He punished me."

"Scotland? You would travel that far?" She directed the subject away from Brithwin's father, like so many times before.

"Hmm . . . I would. To be free of these restraints would be wonderful." But what if her restraints came with love and affection? Could she be happy with them, then? And even if she went to Scotland, she would be expected to marry. It would be no different she supposed.

Elspeth tamped down the threads from the piece she worked on. "Surely you would not leave and travel a long distance in your condition." She turned her head to look at Brithwin.

Brithwin sniffed. "What is wrong with my condition? I am in excellent health. Even the dungeon did not make me ill for long."

"'Tis not what I imply. I have heard it is not a good time

for you to travel."

Brithwin jerked the beater down to the weave. "The weather has been fair. I see no reason I could not travel should I wish to." The woman could exasperate her at times. "I am not leaving, Elspeth. My people are *my* responsibility. I was only saying—"

"'Tis not that." Elspeth leaned closer. A secretive smile played on her lips. "I have heard it could harm the babe."

"Whose babe?" Brithwin leaned back and eyed her suspiciously.

"Why, yours. Are you not with child?"

"Nay!" Brithwin returned to her weaving, not caring the fabric design rapidly grew uneven. "Why would you ask that?"

"'Tis been more than a month since your wedding night." Elspeth snickered.

"It is not possible for me to be with child, so you need not worry about it."

"What do you mean? I saw how late Lord Rosen Craig left your room on your wedding night." Elspeth stood with folded arms. "And you have been ill."

Brithwin's faced flushed, and she glanced around to see if everyone continued at their work. She leaned near Elspeth's ear and whispered, "You must trust me on this. I am not with child."

"Then why were you sick?"

"The dungeon has always done that to me. You should know that."

The excitement left Elspeth's face. "Then we should not be expecting a babe?"

The smile continued to fade from Elspeth's lips and Brithwin was sorry to see it leave. "Nay, I am afraid not."

"Everyone will be so disappointed," she murmured.

Brithwin's brows shot up. "What do you mean

everyone?"

"Well, of course, I don't mean everyone. 'Twas mostly the kitchen workers and perhaps a knight or two."

Brithwin sagged into the nearest chair with a groan and dropped her head in her hands. Why did things like this happen to her? She lifted her head up. "Please see the gossip is stopped. I have enough on my mind without worrying about that, too."

At her first chance, Brithwin slipped out and left Elspeth with the weavers. Her chamber would give her solace.

The quiet of her chamber was a welcome respite as she pulled her knees to her chest and leaned back in the chair. Closing her eyes, she listened to the clamor in the courtyard. Children laughed and called to Thor. The large dog's great bark sounded like thunder. Imagining them chasing the wolfhound around the bailey, she smiled. Royce was out in the practice field with his men. Swords clanged and men cheered each other on.

She opened her eyes and stared at the wall. What would Royce say if this gossip reached his ears? He would know she couldn't be with child. Unless he believed she had been unfaithful. Brithwin quivered at the thought. She did not need any more problems between her and Royce. They had more than their share.

The wedding night—Elspeth had said she'd seen Royce leave late. Brithwin raised her head and drew in a deep breath. That was what Royce was up to when he took a nap in the chair. He'd saved her from humiliation and kept the gossips from thinking he was displeased with her or worse. Royce had protected her honor, though some might consider a woman's honor unimportant. He knew it was of great consequence to her how her people viewed her. She had finally determined what kind of a man he was, and again she discovered another layer to him.

What had she just told Elspeth about men? They were all the same, caring simply about themselves. Then here he does something, upsetting what she believed. Would a man who cared nothing for her save her from humiliation? Pick her flowers? He must care for her in some way. The ice in her veins began to thaw like a sheet of snow sliding off a sunlit roof. No! She needed to stay angry with him. Her heart was safer that way. The man didn't trust her. It seemed there was no middle ground for her and Lord Rosen Craig—she was either furious with him or falling under his charms.

Brithwin slipped from the chair and onto her knees.

"Lord, guide me. I feel myself pulled in different directions. Please help me to remain indifferent to Lord Rosen Craig." A cool breeze blew in through the uncovered window, and she lifted her head. "Do you hear me, Lord? I cannot bear rejection again. Harden my heart toward him."

You ask Me to guide you, but you want your own will. It cannot be both. You must trust I know what is best for you.

Brithwin dropped her head. The Lord had safely kept her while she waited in the dungeon. Surely, she could trust Him in this.

The Lord's words which she had read came to her memory. "Cast all your care upon Him, for He careth for you." With determination she rose from her knees.

††

Royce leaned against a tree near the practice field, sweat dripping down his back as he gasped for air. His mind drifted from his men. He could not stop thinking about their conversation in those early morning hours—or her claim to innocence. It was time to reconcile with himself. He believed her. Deep within, he had known all along she was not responsible for his family's deaths.

Something was different about her. He saw it in her eyes and in her actions. It spoke of her innocence without words.

Yes, he knew she was, so why did he fight it?
A chill passed over him. *Because you are not good
enough for her.* Royce shook off the thought.
He was tired of denying what he felt. Brithwin was
beautiful, intelligent, and caring, and he called her wife. The
time had come to make their marriage more than a word. He
wasn't good enough for her, but if she were willing to start
anew, he intended to try. Would she be agreeable to forget
the past? Did she care for him at all? She no longer spat *my
lord* like the taste was bitter on her tongue. He chuckled.
That was one tone he hoped never to hear come from those
beautiful lips again.

Treating her with respect had affected her attitude in a
very positive way. But was there anything more than
tolerance for him? He had seen interest in those eyes before,
but had he waited too long? He wanted her to be his wife in
every way. He wanted her to love him and for them to have a
relationship like his parents'. One built on trust. He would
hope that he hadn't waited too long.

He needed a plan—one that would confirm his words to
her. He couldn't continue in this fashion, longing for her
from such close proximity, and keep his sanity.

Royce spent the next few days formulating his plan. He
wished he could pray for its success, but alas, it would do
him no good. God was not on his side.

†††

Brithwin sat on her heels, pulling weeds from her
garden. She loved being in her garden. The birdsong, the
sunshine—God's handiwork shone all around. Lifting a
handful of dirt to breathe in its earthy scent, she smiled. How
many people liked the smell of dirt?

Thor, lying by her feet, pricked his ears.

"Now, that is a sight I could get used to seeing."

Brithwin popped her head up. She had not heard Royce's

approach. Thor lifted his head as Royce drew near. "And what is that, my lord?"

"You need not address me as my lord. I would like you to call me Royce."

Brithwin eyed him suspiciously. "'Tis not what I remember."

Royce sighed, meeting her gaze. "I spent much time pondering our situation." He gave her a crooked grin. "Besides, surrender is so much sweeter when offered willingly."

What was he about now? She lowered her head and continued working. "What is it you want?"

"A little of your time."

She glanced at Thor. He rested his head on his paws without a growl. She ran her hand through his wiry fur. "Do you not feel well, boy?"

Royce cleared his throat.

She shifted her gaze to him. "You wish me to do something for you?"

"Do you still blame me?"

"Nay, I do not. I can see you were a victim as much as I." She grinned. "And Thomas told me the whole of it."

"Would you go riding with me, my lady? Shadowmere and Fearless could use a good run."

Trust. She must trust the Lord. He would direct her path. She must follow the path God had laid out for her. This was her husband, their marriage ordained by God. She paused, taking in his hair curled haphazardly around his face. Her hands itched to reach up and smooth the stray strand away from his eyes. A hesitant smile etched his face.

Fighting the anxiety which built in her, she answered. "As you are aware, I left my horse with Murielle."

Royce shrugged. "I will have another mare saddled for you."

She rose, brushing the soil from her hands and her skirt. "I will go. I am sure the horses will enjoy the exercise."

He ran a hand through his hair, a gesture she'd grown accustomed to. "I had hoped *you* would enjoy it, my lady."

"I guess we shall have to see, then." Brithwin gave him a sassy smirk.

A grin crept across his face.

Hoping his good humor would make him generous, she plunged in. "Thor has not had much time out either."

He gave a pained sigh. "Whatever my lady wishes."

Within half an hour, they were riding out the gate. Royce led as he guided his horse around the castle walls and away from the village. He stopped as they reached an open meadow.

"Would you like to race to the other side of the field?" A challenge rang in his voice.

Reaching behind her saddle, she lifted the cloth bag which held their lunch and handed it to Royce. "It will hardly be a fair race with your great war horse's muscled body against this young mare, which has yet to fill out."

When his hand let go of the reins to take hold of the bag, Brithwin tossed it to him, slapped her mare, and yelled, "Ya."

Flattening her body against the horse and resting her head against its neck, she urged the mare on. A glance behind her told her Royce had realized what she was about and encouraged Shadowmere into a gallop.

With her eyes closed, she took in the th-thump of hooves hitting the ground. Her body relaxed, and she and the horse moved as one. The wind worked her hair out of its plait, whipping it to and fro, stinging her skin and all the while cooling her body from the sun's warm rays. The sweet aroma of the green grass beneath the horse's pounding hooves rose around her like perfume. She drank it in until a second set of hoofbeats caught her attention. Opening her eyes, she could see the outstretched legs of Shadowmere digging up the ground and closing her lead.

"Faster girl, faster!" She laughed as Thor barked in protest and fell behind. Royce moved beside her, but she refused to look at him, keeping her body flat, looking straight ahead to the edge of the meadow and victory.

Feeling her triumph, Brithwin raised her body to see Royce overtake her and cross the edge of the field with a sparkle in his eyes and a grin on his face.

He pulled his horse to a stop. Shadowmere lifted his feet and danced around. Once he brought the large destrier under control, he turned to Brithwin in mock astonishment. "I cannot believe you would cheat."

Brithwin laughed, enjoying the moment. "When I am at such a disadvantage, I must do all I can to impede my rival and benefit myself."

His easy smile let her know he saw through her words.

They reached the stream and Royce dismounted, helping Brithwin from her horse. They guided their mounts to the water for a drink.

Sitting near the stream, Brithwin spread her gown around her. She had enjoyed the run with Royce. It was turning into a fine day. She smiled as she let out a long sigh.

Royce grabbed the cloth bag containing their lunch and pulled out a loaf of bread and lump of cheese. "Did you work up an appetite?"

"I feel as if I have not eaten all day." Her stomach rumbled in agreement and Royce laughed.

After they finished their meal and drank water from the stream, Royce stretched out on the grass, lacing his fingers behind his head.

Brithwin broke the lingering silence. "You have changed."

Rolling on to his side, he propped his head on his hand.

Brithwin fidgeted "It is just that, you seem—"

His gaze devoured her with eyes piercing through any armor. "I am deciding how to answer you. Nothing has changed, and yet much has changed. I have found myself drawn to you. You are to be admired." He winked. "Even by those who think they are your enemy. You are beautiful. Then as I watched you, I was able to see you are every bit as beautiful within. You are kind to others, even those below your station. You have great forgiveness and always look for the best in people. You are different, Brithwin, from any woman I have ever known. I can no longer keep up this pretense. You have broken down my resistance. I do not wish to continue this indifference anymore."

Royce gently pulled Brithwin beside him and cupped her chin with his hand. "I want you as my wife," he whispered. "I want to take care of you and to protect you. I want you in all ways."

Brithwin could not speak for fear it was a devilish trick.

"My lady, I cannot continue like this." Desperation twisted his features. "I would be your husband in every way or not at all. 'Tis for you to choose."

†††

He bent down and brushed his lips over hers, pausing to see if she would protest. When she didn't, he returned, deepening the kiss, and drew her to him. Brithwin's fingers wove through his hair and he stifled a moan. Her touch set him afire and he battled the desires within.

With difficulty, he pulled back. "Milady, your answer. I beg you."

A brief struggle flashed across her face then disappeared, leaving a sweet light shining in her eyes. "Yes, my lord."

He kissed her again. Nearby, Thor growled low in his throat. The ill-tempered beast needed to learn his place.

As the kiss lingered, Royce became aware of the silence.

The hair on the back of his neck lifted. Stillness had enveloped the woods. Not an animal moved nor a bird chirped. Listening intently, Royce tilted his head as if to continue the kiss and in an almost inaudible voice whispered, "Do not move. We are being watched."

Chapter 16

Royce tensed while shielding Brithwin with his body. How many men lurked out there? Perhaps a few, for if more roamed, he'd have heard them—as would Brithwin's miserable beast of a dog. But then perhaps that was why he growled. The creature had skulked away and was now nowhere to be seen, when he could finally be of use.

With Brithwin beside him, he couldn't circle around and surprise the attackers and leave Brithwin unprotected. How could he have been so careless as to come out alone? His own desires had caused him to be reckless.

"I will summon my horse. When I tell you, I want you to rise, and I will put you on him. You are to ride quickly, without looking back." Royce kept his voice low but stern enough to brook no argument. "Do not stop until you reach Hawkwood."

When Brithwin opened her mouth to protest, he leaned down and covered her lips with his. Royce feared the ruse would not succeed but desperately hoped it would. Tension reigned in her unspoken objection, but he would not allow her to have a say in this. "My love," he breathed, "if you trust me, do not question what I ask of you."

Speaking loud enough, he hoped, for the intruder's ears, he lifted his head and gazed into Brithwin's widened eyes. "Come love, let us get water to drink."

She rose at his bidding, and he gave a low whistle. Shadowmere lifted his head and drew near to them. Royce's hands encompassed her waist, and he lifted her onto his horse. She gripped the reins.

The crunch of a broken twig came from behind him. At Brithwin's gasp, he swung around and faced two men with drawn swords. "Now, Brithwin!" He slapped the horse's rump. Shadowmere bolted toward an opening in the woods. As his wife and horse drew near the opening and safety, another sword-wielding man stepped into their path.

Fear jolted through his veins, shooting pain to his head. He sprinted toward her as his horse's abrupt stop threw Brithwin from her seat. She flew through the air and crumpled to the ground. Two of the knights hemmed Royce in, and he fended them off, desperate to aid Brithwin. The other man lunged toward her. He couldn't reach her.

In a stolen second between thrust and parry, he loosed a high-pitched whistle. Shadowmere reared up and lashed out at the attackers with his murderous front hooves.

Royce fought for their lives. Steel clanged. With his adversaries taking turns to wear him out, he could do little but defend himself. The taller, burly knight pressed Royce, forcing him away from Brithwin. In hopes of throwing his opponent, he spun around, swinging his sword as he went. The knight lost his footing, giving Royce an opening. With a strong, swift plunge of Royce's sword, his enemy crumpled to the ground, leaving two men remaining.

Now this was an even match. He quickly dispatched the second smaller knight and turned to the third.

From the corner of his eye, he glimpsed Brithwin push herself to a sitting position. He shoved his adversary back, watching and moving toward Brithwin. She attempted to stand and collapsed to the ground. His gut clenched. The man continued to attempt to reach her, while staying out of Shadowmere's reach. She scrambled toward the horse.

That's my girl! Stay close to Shadowmere.

The knight circled behind Brithwin and wrapped his beefy arms around her. She twisted and kicked her feet at him, though her soft shoes would do little damage. The brute caught hold of her arm and wrenched it behind her back. She whimpered. The man sneered at Royce, filling him with rage. He would force him to lay down his sword. Only a miracle could save them now—if God would grant one to a man such as he. Royce moved closer to Brithwin and her attacker.

An unearthly growl brought his attention around. Brithwin's assailant cowered, staring into the face of an angry wolfhound. Thor pounced on the attacker, latched onto his leg, and gave a shake, forcing the man to release Brithwin as he fell to the ground, freeing his bloody leg from the wolfhound's jaws. The man scrambled to his feet and fled into the woods.

Feet pounded the ground and disappeared further into the woods. Royce fought the urge to give chase. He could overtake the man, but that would leave his wife vulnerable should there be anyone else lurking in the woods. Royce scanned the trees and undergrowth for more men. Thor sneezed and trotted into the undergrowth.

Royce ran to Brithwin and knelt beside her. "Are you hurt?" Alert for sounds of further attack, he felt her limbs for broken bones.

"I am fine, Royce." Her lips trembled. "I just wish to return to Hawkwood."

"That we shall, my lady."

Thor silently emerged from the forest and returned to Brithwin's side, blood smeared on the hair around his mouth. He gazed at Royce and lowered his head a finger's breadth. Royce dropped his hand and cautiously patted the wolfhound's head. "Brave dog. I am relieved you found me to your liking today."

The mare grazed placidly nearby, unaffected by all the ruckus. Royce gathered both horses. Lifting Brithwin, he brushed his lips across her brow, placed her on Shadowmere, and swung up behind her. He secured the mare's tether to his mount and looked around at the clearing where he had hoped to begin the mending process of his marriage. Two knights lay dead, the other man's fate unknown. A shudder went through his body. How close he had come to losing Brithwin. He firmly curled his arm about her. She sat with her back straight, head held high. This day he could add brave to the list of her attributes. Daffydd was right—he was a lucky man.

He tapped the horse's sides, and they headed home. Brithwin tipped her head and looked at him. "I could have ridden my horse, Royce. I told you I am uninjured."

"At least one man escaped, but I believe I heard another in the woods. 'Tis easier for me to keep you out of harm's way like this."

Brithwin made a silent, "Oh," and settled against Royce's chest. Her soft body molded against him, tantalizing his senses. He closed his eyes and drew in a deep breath, reminding himself of her innocence.

She glanced back at him. "What are you smiling for? We were nearly killed."

"I like that."

Brithwin's eyebrows rose. "You may enjoy a fight, but I most certainly do not!" She jerked back around.

He chuckled. "That is not what I speak of. You called me Royce." His heart thrilled as he recalled the way his name rolled off her tongue. "I like the sound of my name on your lips."

She shifted. "You have trained your horse well."

He chuckled. "Are you changing the subject?"

"Perhaps, *Royce*."

"In battle, a well-trained horse can mean life or death. I trained Shadowmere afore I went to my first battle."

"Where was that battle?"

"Scotland." He'd fought too many battles with the Scots. He shook off the recent memory.

"Scotland?" She twisted to see him. "My mother's family comes from Scotland. Pater, mother, and a group of travelers were traveling from there when they stopped by Hawkwood."

Royce swallowed hard. He prayed none of the people he'd fought were her family. "'Tis a lot of land up there, highlands and lowlands. Where in Scotland did she hail from?"

She settled back against him. "Pater never told me. He may not have known, although I get the feeling mother and he were friends."

"What is the story on Pater?" He wanted to keep her talking, keep her mind off what had happened, and keep her relaxed body melded next to his.

Her body immediately stiffened and she pulled forward, sitting up straight.

He sighed. That was the wrong question to ask.

"There is nothing to tell." Even her words were stiff.

"I sense there is, my lady."

"I do not wish to talk on it." She sat rigidly before him, resisting his gentle tug back to him.

"My lady, Brithwin," he whispered in her ear. "You must share this with me. I would never harm someone who is so precious to you."

"'Tis nothing you need to know, my lord."

"But I want to know. I have given my word no harm will come to him."

She glanced over her shoulder. "You promise me no harm will come to him?"

"Unless he has done something to harm you or Hawkwood, he has my protection, and you have my word." He tugged her to lean against his chest again.

She relented and relaxed. "Pater suffered much at my father's hand. More than I, truthfully."

"Why did your father dislike him? Did Pater betray him?" If the man betrayed her father for Brithwin's safety, he could understand.

"Nay." She quickly peeked over her shoulder, and he got the feeling she was weighing what she would tell him. "Pater is a follower of John Wycliffe."

For some reason the announcement did not surprise him. "A Lollard."

She sucked in a breath.

"Do not trouble yourself, my lady. I gave you my word. But I will have you know that I agree with their stand on indulgences. I do not believe any amount of money can buy you free of your sin."

"'Tis more than that." Brithwin pushed the wisps of hair away from her face and tucked them behind her ears. "He wanted the bible to get to the common man because God's word is the true authority where we find our salvation."

Royce writhed in his saddle. He could never have that. For all the good he had done, he had committed evil that wiped it out. His fate was sealed.

When the castle walls came into view, Royce leaned forward and whispered in her ear. "I am sorry those blackguards spoiled our day. 'Twas careless, taking you outside of Hawkwood without guards. I put your life in danger, and there is no excuse."

Brithwin twisted and tipped her head. "You did not know brigands were on Hawkwood land."

Royce shook his head. "I will not be so rash in the future. This has played havoc with what I had planned today."

Her eyes widened. "And what was that?"

"I had hoped we would have time to talk. I wish to begin our marriage anew. We have gotten off to an unpleasant start. I would ask for your forgiveness, my lady. I wish to be a

good husband to you and treat you fairly."
Brithwin sucked in a breath as she gazed at Royce. With
what appeared reservation, she touched his cheek. "I never
thought I would hear those words from your lips. God has
been faithful, just as His word tells us. I only needed to trust
him. Now here you are offering me something I never
dreamed possible."

†††

Brithwin had bathwater sent to her chamber as soon as
they arrived. She slipped into the water, leaning her head
back and draping her limp arms over the sides of the tub.
"Why are you smiling like that?" Elspeth asked.
"Like what?"
"Oh, you know what, like you have a secret! Out with it.
I will not let you rest until you tell me."
"Mmm, 'tis nothing. No, that is not true. It is
something…something wonderful."
Elspeth knelt next to the tub. "Tell me what is so
wonderful."
Brithwin leaned her head sideways to see her maid.
"Lord Rosen Craig has asked my forgiveness, and I have
given it. We shall begin our marriage anew with all forgotten.
I can hardly believe it."
"So you will finally have a real marriage?"
Brithwin ran her finger over her lips, remembering
Royce's kiss. "'Tis hard to believe, but aye. I do not know
why I find it so hard to believe—God can do anything, and
Pater tells me not a bird falls from the sky that God does not
know. I have put my trust in Him, and He has not failed me."
Elspeth looked at her with skepticism. "What if my lord
had not changed his mind, would that mean God failed you?"
"Elspeth you are always negative. Why can you not see
God as He truly is? God will not fail me, regardless. We must
put our trust in Him, and He will see us through as He did me

with my father."

"Aye, milady." Elspeth handed Brithwin the rose scented soap.

When she finished bathing, Brithwin put on her knitted hose and fine chemise. She sat in front of the fire, drying her hair and trying to decide what gown to wear.

"Elspeth, bring me my blue gown, the one Thomas gave me for my wedding. I want to show Lord Rosen Craig I am willing to start at the beginning of our marriage."

Brithwin stepped into the gown and sighed. She never believed she'd know such contentment. The gown slid down her skin, clinging to the curves of her body. She fastened the gold belt and let it drape over her hips, then slid on her slippers. Elspeth laced up the gown. Brithwin made her way to a chair while her lady's maid fixed her hair.

Finished, Elspeth moved back. "You look beautiful, milady."

Brithwin couldn't help but smile, remembering Royce telling her the same thing. "Thank you, and you may go. I will wait for Lord Rosen Craig."

A light knock sounded at the entrance between their chambers, and she bid him enter. Royce opened the door and paused, keeping it open and eyes locked on her. A tangle of emotions knotted in her. Could she do this? Was this what she wanted?

He smiled. "Stay there. I will return." Disappearing out of the room, he returned before she had time to wonder why he'd left. Royce knelt before her chair, pulled out a small cloth bag from his pocket, and placed it in her hand. "This was my mother's and is my wedding gift to you."

Brithwin opened the bag and tipped it into her palm. She gasped. "They are lovely. I have never seen anything more exquisite." She ran her fingers over the smooth string of pearls, all brilliant white and matched in size that he'd just given her.

"They do not do you justice. You are far more beautiful, my Brithwin."

Heat surged to her face.

"Is that a blush I see?" He fastened the strand about her throat, letting his fingers linger for a moment on her collarbone then placed a kiss where his hand had been. "I have embarrassed you?"

"No man has ever spoken to me thus." Her voice caught, and she finished in a whisper. "You are kind."

"I only tell you the truth. Come, let us go and eat." Winking at her, he presented his arm. "I am anxious to show off my beautiful wife."

Brithwin strolled into the great hall on Royce's arm. A slow hush overcame the room as heads turned and looks fell on them. Tipping his head down, he whispered for her ears alone. "It would appear I am not the only one who cannot take their eyes from you. You have left them speechless, which is quite a feat."

She glanced around the hall at the people who filled it. Her heart sang. How proud she was of the man who walked beside her, her husband, and he had earned the respect of not only the knights, but the villeins and servants. God had indeed blessed her.

The servants filled the tables with trenchers. The meal, a feast once again befitting a king. Spread out before them and displayed with great beauty lay a wide variety of meats, sauces, cheese, fish, nuts, sweet meats, and fresh breads.

"How did you have all this prepared so quickly?"

"They have been working on this for days now. Preparing it was not the hard part, they tell me, but keeping it from you." He chuckled as he pulled out her chair and then took his seat.

Brithwin giggled, thinking how wonderful it was to see

his eyes sparkle with amusement. A more handsome man she had never seen. His dark wavy hair remained damp from his bath. He'd donned an elegant blue tunic over a white shirt made of the finest linen.

Marjory's cooking and Royce's healthy appetite had put meat back on his bones. It was evident in the way his muscles again pulled at the seams of his garments. He had shaved, leaving no stubble on his face. Her hands ached to run over the smooth, firm skin of his jaw.

Royce stabbed a fig with his dagger. He turned to her and raised one eyebrow.

Looking down, she pretended to be engrossed in her meal.

Royce slipped a finger under her chin and lifted it until he gazed into her eyes. "You were staring at me. Could that mean you see something in me you like?"

Brithwin opened her mouth to answer, but instead he held out the fig, enticing her with it. Taking a bite, she closed her eyes for a moment to savor it. "It is wonderful."

"Aye, that it is, much like you." Royce sobered and his voice turned gravelly. "You are too good for me. I do not deserve you."

"How can you say such a thing? I am no better than you. We both have fallen short, but God loves us regardless of what we have done."

His jaw hardened. "You do not know the sin I carry. But this is not the time to talk of these things. This is a celebration. Look, the troubadour and jugglers come out to entertain us now."

The rest of the evening continued with merriment. However, Brithwin couldn't stop the sadness that came upon her. She put on a mask and struggled to keep up the pretense. Her mind strayed, and try as she may, it kept coming back to the same question. What could Royce have done to make him feel unworthy of her, and was this why he shunned God?

Between her concern for Royce and the worry of what the night might bring, the evening crept by. On the few occasions her father had allowed her to hear the tales of chivalry and honor the troubadours told, she fell under their spell. They filled her with longing, but tonight she could not concentrate. Her husband's feelings of unworthiness consumed her mind. How could she make him see he was precious to the Lord?

Never could she have survived the years with her father's brutality without the Lord's strength to lean on. How many times did she run to the wooden door in the tower and complain to Pater about it, and he always sent her to the Lord.

But Royce was a man who relied on himself. Was it possible for him to see the importance of turning everything over to God—giving Him control of his life, past and future?

Royce leaned and whispered to Brithwin, "'Tis time to go to our chamber."

Brithwin's preoccupations scattered away as she arose with Royce. Elspeth rose and made her way toward the stairs. "Elspeth," Royce's voice stopped her, "Lady Rosen Craig will not need your assistance this night."

God help me, Brithwin sent a silent plea. If only she could melt into the floor. Elspeth's oh-so-knowing smile gave her the courage to lift her head and square her shoulders as she took to the stairs.

Royce opened the door to the solar. His smoldering gaze nearly sent her scampering away. She had to remind herself she liked his kisses—she liked them very much.

She stepped through the entrance and into Royce's embrace. A shiver ran up her spine, and she drew in a deep breath to steady herself.

Chapter 17

Brithwin's insides quivered as Royce closed the door behind him and leaned against it. His gaze swept over her. Turning away to break her uneasiness, she glanced around the room. He had changed it. Beautiful tapestries hung on the walls. One portrayed scenes of battle, another an afternoon hunt, and a third, the king's court. However, they were not the ones that drew her interest. She gravitated toward the vivid image hanging above the side table. An array of brightly colored flowers surrounded a woman much her size and of similar shape and coloring. Kneeling before her was a knight in full armor, offering her a flower.

Royce's voice, a low rumble, broke the silence. "'Tis peculiar how much she looks like you, aye?"

"Aye, it is." She reached out to run her fingers along the smooth tapestry. "'Tis a beautiful wall hanging."

Royce's gaze fell to the floor. "I purchased these as a gift for my mother. I never had the chance to give them to her."

"I am sorry for your loss, Royce. I do not believe I told you, but I am. I cannot imagine losing someone you hold so dear. I never knew my mother, and my father loathed me, so there was no grief when he died. Thomas and Pater are the only people who have truly cared for me. They are dear to me. They would remain by my side if I were a poor serf. What I am or have matters not to them."

Royce pushed away from the door and walked toward her. "If Thomas and Pater were younger men, I would be jealous."

"They are the only fathers I have ever known. Thomas looked after me, keeping me safe, and Pater cared for my spirit."

"And Elspeth? She cares for you."

"Aye. Elspeth cares for me, to be sure. I did not realize how much until she risked her life for me."

Brithwin stroked the lustrous wall hanging once more and turned to face Royce. He laid his hands on her shoulders, his gentle voice seeping in and warming every part of her. "I have wronged you many times over, and still you forgive me. I would like to be one of those people who will stay by your side, Brithwin. I desire to have a marriage that is strong in trust and caring."

"I—I, too, desire this," Brithwin's voice quivered.

"Do you? Then come, and sit, and let me take the plaits from your hair. I will be your maid for the night."

Her heart raced, sending blood pounding in her ears. She lifted another silent prayer, *Dear Lord in heaven, please do not let my trust in him be unfounded.* She sat in the chair Royce had walked her to. Fear and anticipation swirled inside her.

Trust him, beloved.

He lifted the gold ring that sat on her head and laid it on the oak chest. Gently, he ran his fingers through the plaits, letting her hair fall on her shoulders and down her back. Brithwin closed her eyes and bit her lip to keep from quivering. She must trust him. Had he not already shown himself different from her father?

Royce whispered over her shoulder, "Did I tell you how pleased I am you wore the dress I bought you?"

Brithwin turned her head to see him. "You bought my dress? I thought Thomas . . ."

"Nay, my sweet Brithwin. When I discovered you did not have a wedding dress, I could not let my beautiful wife marry in rags."

"But why did you not tell me?"

He ran his hand down her arm, making her shiver. "I feared you would not accept it if you knew it came from me."

Brithwin opened her mouth to protest and closed it. It would be a lie to say she would have worn it when well she knew she would not have. After all, had she not told Thomas she wished to wear her black mourning clothes? His hand skimmed back up her arm. She drew in a deep breath and released it. "I thank you kindly for my gown. 'Tis the most beautiful thing I own."

Royce pulled her from the chair and captured her lips with his own. His fingers tangled in her hip length hair. Royce drew her closer—his ragged breath brushed against her ear. For some reason it was pleasing to know she affected him thus.

He pulled back and drew in a deep breath. "Are you ready for this part of our marriage, Brithwin? I want you to come willingly. If you are not ready—I will wait."

Brithwin suspected what those last three words had cost him. How could she deny him his marriage right? It was ordained by God, she told herself again. Certainty arose within her.

"Aye, I am ready."

He scooped her up and carried her to the marriage bed.

††††

Brithwin stretched and let out a light sigh.

"Good morn."

At the sound of the deep voice beside her, her eyes popped open.

Royce stood next to the bed. His eyes twinkled and a smile spread across his face.

"Good—good morn to you." Brithwin rested on her side.

With a caress, Royce coaxed her head back. "Did you know you are very beautiful when you sleep?"

"It would be hard for me to know, for I am sleeping,"

she said impishly.

"I see you are in good humor." He stroked her cheek. "It is time to get up and break our fast. The day wastes."

Brithwin lifted her head to get a better look at him. "You are dressed and ready to start the day?"

"Aye, I have already given my men their orders." He pulled his hand from behind his back. "I have a gift for you."

She rolled to her back and ran her hand over the cloth he revealed in his hand. "Oh, how lovely."

"It is from the East. Make something for yourself, Brithwin. I will look forward to seeing you in it."

Brithwin continued to stroke the fabric. "'Tis so beautiful, I do not want to cut it."

"It is not much good if you do not." He smiled at her. "Elspeth waits outside the door to assist you. If you are ready, I will send her in."

She wanted to lie on the bed and relive each and every moment, to remember the tender and passionate words he had spoken, the gentleness in his touch, and the longing in his caress, but he was right, the day wasted. She bid him to send Elspeth in to her. The wish to languish in her room quickly diminished after enduring a torrent of pointed questions and giggled insinuations from Elspeth. Brithwin was happy to escape to the great hall.

†††

In an attempt to get the rest of the tenants into their homes, Royce spent another day at the village. There were two more cottages to conclude work on before the village would be set to rights. But for how long? He spoke with the village people as he walked through—the crofters assured him the fire could not have started from their carelessness. With Jarren's help, they scoured the edge of the village and into the woods, searching for evidence to indicate whether it had been set deliberately. From what they could surmise, it was no accident. It appeared someone had taken a torch and walked along the backside of the huts, setting fire to each one. Perhaps once the work was finished and the cottages completed, they should temporarily post a few guards around at night to make sure no more mischief occurred.

He would be glad to have the tenants in their homes so he could get back to his regular duties around the castle. Spending morning 'til evening at the village every day left little time for him to see his new wife.

Ah, the innocence of her. He smiled to himself. The look on her face—wide-eyed shock— had spoken more than words of how she thought his suggestion of her moving into his chamber was scandalous. Yet still she moved her belongings in at his bidding. She was more than he deserved as a wife.

Royce stood between the two cottages, inspecting their work. They had tied the timbers together, applied wattle to the walls, and finally, finished daubing the twigs with mud. The new construction pleased him, quite an improvement from the old buildings.

He had snatched an armful of thatch to haul up to the men finishing the roof when one gave a yell. A horse and cart barreled toward him. The whites of the horse's eyes glared against the animal's sweaty hide. The wide cart bumped and bounced against the sides of the two new cottages as the beast sped down the narrow passageway.

Royce turned to run when Jarren shouted from the edge of the roof. Royce glanced up to see Jarren lay down, arms over the edge, reaching for him. Dropping the thatch, he sprang up and gripped his friend's hands, all the while hoping the roof did not give way under the weight of two men. Drawing his legs to his chest, Royce tightened his grasp as the runaway horse and cart careened by. The lingering draft whispered of a near brush with death.

Royce let go of his friend's hands and dropped to the ground.

Jarren leaped off the roof, his feet hitting the ground with a thud. "That was close. Where did it come from?"

Royce looked up and down the narrow pathway. "It was as if it appeared out of nowhere."

Jarren's brows pinched together. "I wonder what spooked the beast."

"Hard to say. Let's get these finished up. I am ready to get home." Royce gathered the fallen thatch.

Jarren crossed his arms in front of his chest, his feet spread. "I don't think it was an accident, Rosen Craig. Send someone to find the horse and see who owns it. Perhaps they can find out what frightened the animal."

Royce couldn't keep the smirk from his face. "You can be worse than a mother hen at times, my friend."

"Someone has to look out for you."

Royce slapped Jarren on the shoulder and carried his bundle of thatch toward the fallen ladder. "You worry overmuch."

"Where would I go if I did not keep you in one piece?" Jarren chuckled. "I have grown fond of Hawkwood."

Dusk had fallen upon them by the time they mounted their horses for the return ride. Royce stayed later than planned, but it was worth the extra time, for they had finished. Urging his horse forward, he looked back as his men fell in around him. Villeins gathered out in front of their new cottages, silhouettes in the fading light, yelling words of thanks to the men.

Jarren and a young knight moved their horses beside him. His friend gestured with his hand for the man beside him to speak.

Arthur cleared his throat. "I found the horse and cart's owner. It would seem, milord, a man he knew not approached him and offered him coin to borrow the pair. The coin was more than the animal's value."

Royce swiveled in his saddle to look at the man. "What of the horse? Did you find out what spooked it?"

He took a deep breath and launched into his tale. "The cart got wedged between two trees. The animal's whole body trembled as I approached it, though I could not see anything amiss. I checked the horse from head to hooves and found nothing. When I began to detach it from the cart, I leaned on the saddle as I worked with the straps. The horse went wild, thrashing and throwing itself around. I then removed the saddle and found a handful of burrs beneath it. Knowing a crofter could not afford one, I asked him about it. He claims the horse has never had one on its back. It was no accident, milord—someone sent that horse to kill you."

Chapter 18

Edmond Cuthbrid stood in a meadow bordering Hawkwood's lands, sneering at the man cowering before him. "Idiot. How could you fumble such an easy task?" He paced away then turned to glance behind him as the fool straightened. "I won't suffer incompetence." He smiled coldly as he turned and walked in front of the idiot again. The man braced himself. Edmond slammed his fist into his cowardly face with a satisfying, bone-shattering *crunch*. Shaking his hand, Edmond grimaced and the man crumpled to the ground.

A cooper, raggedly clad, stepped forward. "What ye want us to do with em, sir?"

Edmond tossed the words over his shoulder as he turned away. "Tie him to a tree and whip him until he begs for mercy or dies. He needs to be an example."

He strode across the clearing and dropped himself on the log. Robert, his most reliable man and the closest thing he had to a friend, followed.

Edmond ran his hand down the scar on his face. "Thrice now the attempts on Royce's life have failed. I am beginning to believe the man is charmed. How often does a second son inherit his father's estate—the one that should have been mine—and then marry an heiress with an equally impressive fortune?"

"Aye, the man must be charmed," Robert nodded and spit into the bushes.

Edmond leaped up and paced to ease his nervous energy. "Royce will be watchful now. We will not have it so easy next time. We must take him off guard."

Robert sat where Edmond vacated. "Do you have

something in mind?"

"Do you trust the new man?"

"Montfort?" He shrugged. "He is as trustworthy as any of them, I suppose. What of him?"

Edmond rubbed the wrinkled flesh on his face. "We need a man inside Hawkwood. He didn't fight with us in Northumberland thus he has never met Royce."

"'Tis unlikely he will be willing to go, after what happened to his friends."

"He will go or he will die." Edmond's voice rose, but he willed it under control. "His friends were fools. I sent four men against one man and a feeble wench."

Robert picked a twig from the ground and broke it into small pieces. "Will not Lord Rosen Craig be suspicious of a stranger?"

"I told you not to call him that!" Edmond seethed. "The name is rightfully mine, but that is the beauty of this plan. I will use Royce's goodness against him."

"How is that?"

"We will have a little fun with Montfort, throw him on the road where he will be found beaten by brigands. Royce will see to his mending. Then Montfort, out of gratitude, will offer to serve him. Of course, Royce will accept. It cannot fail."

Robert's forehead wrinkled. "What if Montfort resents the beating and betrays you?"

Edmond curled his hands into fists. "You said he was trustworthy. If he is not, then it will be your neck as well as his."

Robert dropped the broken sticks and wiped his hand over his beard. "I said he is as trustworthy as the rest. I will not stand behind Montfort. I trust none of these men enough to put my life in their hands."

"Then we will have to assure him of a long and painful

death if he fails me."

"That may work." Robert pushed himself up and grinned.

Edmond folded his arms. "Summon the men. I want them to know what will await them should they decide to betray me. I will have my revenge on Royce." He gave a bitter chuckle. "I will see the man dead if it is the last thing I do."

†††

Brithwin stepped through the gate of the outer bailey and dashed along the castle wall until she was out of sight of the gatekeeper. Thor bounded behind her, tail wagging, waiting for her to throw the stick she held in her hand. Upon his demanding bark, she hurled the stick with all her strength then leaned against the wall and waited, paying no attention to Thor loping down the hill. She set down the cloth sack of food and waited. Within a few minutes, the reward for her patience arrived.

Brithwin grinned inwardly. "Good afternoon, Sir Daffydd."

"And to you, milady."

"Where are you off to today?"

Daffydd glanced up at the sky. "Well, it is a fine day. I— I thought I would step out of the bailey for a bit."

Brithwin fought the smile that threatened. "Then I will leave you be and go on my way."

"I would be happy to accompany you, milady."

"Nay, I am sure you have other things to see to. I do not want to trouble you."

Daffydd shuffled his feet. "Truly, it would be no inconvenience. I ha—"

Brithwin giggled. "'Tis all right, Daffydd. I know Sir Royce has sent you to guard me. I was having a little fun at your expense. Will you forgive me?"

Daffydd smiled, the stiffness melting from his body. "Aye, milady."

"I am headed to help Guy, Murielle, and their grandson move back to their cottage. Would you like to come along?"

"Aye, milady, I would be most relieved to escort you." Brithwin picked up the sack and handed it to Daffydd. They headed toward the village, kicking up mud from the rain-soaked road as they went. The sun hit its peak, warming the air—spring would soon turn to summer. Walking silently, Brithwin listened to the birdsong in the trees. She knew a moment of alarm when Thor scampered out of the woods as if an enemy were at his heels. She laughed lightly at his antics when he stopped, suddenly spinning around to catch his tail.

"'Tis a dangerous animal you have there, milady." A grin teased one side of his mouth.

Brithwin raised her eyebrows. "Do not let his cheerful mood fool you. He can be formidable when he feels threatened or thinks I am in danger, as I am sure you have heard."

Daffydd's gaze cut toward Thor. "I hope he knows I am your friend."

Brithwin shuddered at the memory of blood smeared on Thor's mouth. "Aye, I think he knows you would do me no harm."

Daffydd lowered his eyes. "I am sorry, milady, I did not mean anything improper. 'Tis not my place to call you a friend. I am a knight in your service. I beg you forgive me."

"No harm is done, Sir Daffydd. I am honored to call you my friend. I do not have many."

He grinned. "You may count me as one, milady."

When they reached the entrance to the village and she laid eyes on the newly built cottages, she could not believe her eyes. "They have worked a miracle here. It is impossible to tell there was ever a fire!"

"Milord had given orders for the rebuilding of the village homes before he became ill." Daffydd, too, looked around with satisfaction as he set the sack on the ground by his feet. "Jarren had the men-at-arms that could be spared working down here, and he put the village people to work. Jarren is very good at organizing—'twas a sight to see, I tell you. By the time Lord Rosen Craig healed, the village was well on its way to being set aright."

Brithwin took in the huts in wonderment. "My lord said the men worked hard."

"'Twas a lot of work, milady."

"Oh, aye, I doubt not. I am pleased Guy and Murielle's cottage is completed and that you came along, for you will make my task much easier. I hope they have fared well along with our horses."

Daffydd grabbed the sack and with long strides headed into the woods. "I brought food three days ago, and they were doing well and ready to return to their home."

Brithwin quickened her pace to catch up. "I am anxious to see them."

Stepping off the road, they made their way through the woods and toward the cottage. She hurried along, sticks and briars snagging her gown as she went. Getting the couple and their grandson back to the village, where checking on them would be easier, would be a relief.

As the landmark tree came into view, Daffydd turned to Brithwin. "'Tis hard to believe Lord Rosen Craig allowed you to come out here alone."

Brithwin chuckled. "Not alone. Well I knew you would come."

Daffydd stopped walking and gave her a stern look. "Milady, does milord know you are coming here?"

Brithwin slowed her pace but kept moving. "Nay, he was

busy holding court. But we are still on Hawkwood land, and I bring a knight, so I did not think it necessary to tell him."

"We must return, milady. 'Tis not safe for you out here. Brigands pay no heed to boundaries."

Brithwin pointed ahead. "But the cottage lies just beyond this tree. We are here."

"Lord Rosen Craig will not be pleased, I assure you." Daffydd's voice gave stern warning.

"If my lord did not wish me to go anywhere, why would he give me a guard? Surely he would allow me to see my friends when I was careful to wait for you before leaving the safety of the castles walls."

"Perhaps you do not understand the enemy we battle. Lord Rosen Craig only wishes to protect his wife." He let out a defeated sigh. "But, aye, I see we have nearly arrived. Let us quickly get the couple and go to the castle, where I can return you to safety, and then I will take them to their home."

"Aye, we will hurry. I am sorry if I have caused trouble for you. I will speak with my lord and tell him it was my foolishness."

They had made good time with the sunny day and keeping to the seldom-used trail. Brithwin lifted her gown and dashed forward through the copse of trees, bringing the cottage into view.

Daffydd dashed past her with lengthened strides. "Wait here, milady, while I make sure all is safe."

Brithwin grinned. "Goodness, Daffydd, you overly worry."

With hand on hilt, he pushed on the door. The hinges creaked in protest. The old place needed work. "'Tis good news we bri—" The words caught in his throat and he whirled around, reaching out to stop Brithwin from entering.

†††

Leaning his head back in his chair on the dais, Royce

looked over the crowded room. Oh, to have Solomon's or his own father's wisdom right now. How could so many people have grievances against their neighbors? He had put down judgments for hours now, and still the room remained full with peasants who had come to court. It was amazing they could not get along and learn to work out their differences amongst themselves. Growing up, he had always avoided the great hall when his father had to sit and listen to the complaints of his subjects. It was one of the few things he counted as a blessing in being a second son.

Royce stared wearily at the two men bickering before him. How many cows out there trampled gardens? He had heard at least three of these complaints. A simple solution, and yet they could not come to an agreement without his help. Shaking his head, he ordered the owner of the cow to compensate the loss of food and sent them on their way.

Hours later, Royce unfolded himself from the chair and stretched as he scanned the room again for Brithwin. He had not seen her since morning—although, she probably avoided the room just as he had once, as a lad. The room had emptied. He was ready to sentence the men who had imprisoned Brithwin. He had hoped she would be here for this because they did not agree on the punishment. She was far too forgiving. He would have them drawn and quartered for what they did to her, but she cried for mercy.

Motioning for his men to bring the prisoners in, he returned to retake his seat.

The five men approached the dais. The stench of them pervaded the room. Filth covered their clothes and unwashed bodies. Fire burned through Royce's veins at their approach. Halting before him, the men kept their eyes downcast.

Royce slammed his fist on the table. "Look at me! I want to see the faces of the men who tormented my wife and thought to make decisions for me."

They jerked their heads up in unison as if puppets pulled by strings. Royce snarled and leaned forward. "What is your defense?"

The shortest of the group stepped forward. "My lord, I heard you accuse your wife of stabbing you. I only wished to protect you."

Royce took a deep breath in an attempt to hold his fury. "What is your name?"

"John."

"There are many problems here, John. The first is you didn't think. The second is you wish to protect me from *my* wife. Third and last, you threw a helpless woman into the dungeon. Do I understand this correct?"

"Aye, my lord." His voice faded.

Royce turned his gaze to the other men. "What say the rest of you? What is your reason for such poor treatment to Lady Rosen Craig?"

They shuffled their feet, shook their heads, and mumbled apologies. His eyes stopped on a burly man with his head bowed. Narrowing his eyes, Royce was about to speak when John's voice stopped him.

"My lord, if I may speak."

He clenched his teeth and nodded.

"I gave the orders these men followed. 'Tis I who should be punished."

"Nay!" The Scot yelled out. "Ye will not be takin' me blame. I take me own punishment."

Royce glared at the men as a murmur of agreement rolled through the other three. "You are right there. A man takes his own punishment." Royce was drawn back to the man with his head still down. "I said look at me, man."

The knight lifted his head. A fury to match his own burned in the man's eyes.

Royce spread his hands on the wood table and pushed

himself up. His brows drew together. He leaned forward and rested his weight on his hands. "Do you have something to say for yourself?"

"Nothin'," the man spat.

Royce flared his nostrils. "Your name!"

"Samuel," he sneered.

Royce raked his gaze over the men, lingering on each one and letting them squirm under his perusal. "You can each be thankful I have a wife who believes in mercy. My first choice was to have each of you drawn and quartered." Someone sucked in a breath. "However, my lady, the woman you treated so poorly, begged me to be lenient. My second choice was to have you hung from the parapets and let the birds pick at your dead carcasses. Again, the woman you mistreated came to your aid. I have reached a compromise, not because I think you deserve a lesser punishment, but because I will not cause my wife more grief. Therefore, your punishment will be a month in the same dungeon you subjected her to. Your food will be bread and water. When you finish your punishment, you will kneel before my wife in front of the entire castle holding and swear fealty to her." He shifted his gaze to Samuel. "Except for you, Samuel. When your time in my dungeon is through, I will have you escorted off Hawkwood property which you will never be allowed back on. Do I make myself clear?"

Samuel's eyes burned with hostility. Royce had to fight to remember Brithwin's request of leniency. Then again, for Brithwin's sake perhaps he should not let this man go.

Samuel scoffed. "I would *never* swear fealty to a woman."

Royce slammed his fist on the table again. "Get them out of here before I change my mind."

After the guards took the prisoners to the dungeon, Royce drew in a long breath, slowly releasing it. Glad he was to get that task behind him. The day grew late and he still had things to do, the first of which was to find Brithwin. As he rose from his chair, a peasant woman pushed past one of his knights.

"Milord! Milord! A word with you, please."

Royce dropped back in his chair. What was one more? "Come forward. What is your complaint?"

She stopped and made an awkward curtsey. "Nay, nothin' to the likes of that, milord."

"What do you want?" He was tired and ready to be done.

"'Tis I who have something ye might want." She pulled a knife from the folds of her tunic. "I told yer knight I would be back."

Royce was awake now. He leaned forward. "May I see it?"

"Aye, milord." She handed him the knife.

Royce took the blade from her hands. "Where did you find this?"

"Right where ye were when ye were stabbed." She wrung her hands.

"And how is it you know where I was?"

"I overheard you and your knight speakin'. So I went back there to have meself a look, I did."

"I thank you for this." Royce lifted his gaze to the woman in front of him and his memory flooded back. "Is your boy well?"

Her eyes opened wide. "Ye remember? Aye, he is fine, milord."

"Where is your husband?"

"He died, milord. 'Tis only me son and meself."

"I see." Royce summoned Jarren to the front of the hall. "See this woman is paid more than a fair price for the knife."

Royce studied the knife he held in his hands as the

woman walked away. The intricate detail, the jewels imbedded in the handle—there was no mistaking it. It was Edmond's. The day Edmond had taken the knife was clear. Royce could still hear the cry for mercy. The look of horror on the man's face as Edmond ran him through with his sword, and the metallic smell of his blood that flowed freely, remained a vivid memory.

He curled his hand around the hilt of the weapon. Edmond wanted him dead. Aye, he knew this day would come. And as fate would have it, the time came when he had finally found happiness with Brithwin.

Brithwin...he'd not seen Brithwin all day. He'd seen her maid, but not a glimpse of his wife. Surely, she would not leave the castle grounds without his knowledge. His eyes shot around the hall in search of her. By the rood! If she had, her very life could be in danger.

Chapter 19

Guy lay sprawled before Brithwin, clutching the wound at his chest. His lifeless eyes stared at the thatched roof. Blood had seeped from beneath his body and pooled around him, soaking into the dirt floor. Brithwin fell across the man she had grown to care for, feeling the cold from his body that had penetrated his thin cotton shirt. She swallowed a sob, glancing up at Daffydd. He held a finger to his lips as he peered around the room. Silently drawing his sword from its sheath, he stepped outside. Twigs cracked as he walked around the small cottage. Thor remained in the doorway, baring his teeth in a low, menacing growl, the hair on his neck standing in attention.

Brithwin swallowed. "We are too late, Thor," she whispered.

She forced herself up and walked to where Murielle lay face down on the floor in her own blood. Falling again to her knees, she rolled the supple body over. The warmth of Murielle's blood soaked Brithwin's hand, and she whimpered with hope.

Without thought, Brithwin tore a strip of fabric from her gown and pressed it against the wound in Murielle's abdomen. The blood pumped into the cloth. Brithwin held her friend, increasing the pressure against the wound and fighting the tremors racking her own body.

Tears rolled down her face. She swiped them with her shoulder. "Please do not die. I need you."

A faint moan came from Murielle's throat. Her eyelids fluttered.

"No, Murielle, wake up. Please come back to me! Don't die, do you hear me?"

Daffydd returned, appearing just inside the doorway. "Is there something I can get for you, milady?"

Brithwin wrenched her head around. "She is still alive. We must get her back to Hawkwood where I can care for her."

Murielle raised her hand and touched Brithwin's cheek. "You need not bother," she murmured. "You know as well as I that I do not have much time." Her voice came out a near whisper.

Tears welled and Brithwin fought them. The blood continued to ooze despite the pressure. "I can save you if we bring you back to the castle. I have herbs. They will help."

Murielle's voice weakened. Brithwin leaned down close to Murielle's lips. "No one can save me, save the Lord, and I think He has determined it is time for me to go home."

Brithwin drew in a shaky breath and let it out. "Nay, I will not let you go."

"You have no say, my dear. Promise me you will find the boy." Murielle's voice faded in and out. "He ran when they came. I am thankful he got away."

Brithwin brought Murielle's hand to her cheek. "I will find him."

"I know it is much to ask of you, milady, but I need you to find someone who will look after him and be good to him."

"I will."

Daffydd cleared his voice. "Milady, I am sorry, but may I ask her a few questions?"

Murielle's gaze shifted to Daffydd.

"Do you know who did this?"

Murielle's face contorted with pain at the slight shake of her head, and she gasped. "Thieves. They took milady's knife." She turned her attention back to Brithwin with sorrowful eyes.

Brithwin's voice cracked. "Do not concern yourself with me."

Daffydd moved closer. "Can you tell me anything unusual about any of them? Did they say anything that might help us? Where they were going? What about their clothes, their horses?"

Murielle coughed and blood trickled from her mouth. "I—I didn't see their horses."

"Do you remember anything?" Daffydd's voice pleaded.

Again, a slight shake of her head.

Daffydd turned to go back outside when Murielle garnered her strength and called out in weak voice, "Wait."

Fearful he didn't hear her, Brithwin called to him, "Daffydd."

He came and squatted by her side. "You remember something?"

"The leader—a scar."

"A scar?" Something between dismay and anger sounded in Daffydd's voice.

"His face." She gulped in air. "And neck."

"Thank you. We will find them."

Murielle closed her eyes and drifted into unconsciousness. They lifted her onto the same pallet Guy had spent so much time on a sennight ago.

Brithwin's body continued to tremble. She drew in a ragged breath. "I have already failed to keep them safe. I should never have brought them here. 'Tis my fault this has happened." Brithwin spun around, facing toward the door. "The boy! You need to search for Malcolm. He must be scared near unto death. It is hard to say how far he has gone in all this time."

Daffydd gently squeezed her arm. "I have found the boy."

His sympathetic gaze caused Brithwin's breath to hitch.

She staggered back. Tears filled her eyes. Her knees buckled beneath her, his grip on her arm the only thing holding her up. "Nay. I promised. I promised."

"I am sorry, milady."

Bile rose in Brithwin's throat and she tried to swallow. She jumped to her feet and ran out the door, emptying her stomach onto the ground. She stumbled back in and sank to the floor beside Murielle, robbed of her strength.

Daffydd left the cottage with a blanket and returned with a blanket-covered body. He gently laid the man-boy beside his grandfather. Raising the cloth, he covered Guy's body, too.

"Milady we must go. 'Tis not safe for you."

"Please. Just a few minutes." She caressed Murielle's wrinkled cheeks.

"I cannot allow you much time."

Murielle's breathing had grown shallow. Brithwin remained beside her until she took her last breath. Leaning forward, Brithwin kissed her and rose to her feet. An ache she could not explain gnawed at her heart. She lifted burning eyes to Daffydd. "'Tis time."

They left the cottage, and three precious people, behind. Brithwin clenched her teeth and fisted her hands. With each step she took, her muscles grew tauter. Her grief and her anger snarled together. How could a loving God allow this to happen? An innocent family dead. Did He not care?

Thor followed close at her heels. Daffydd's glance shifted from side to side as they trudged through brush and around trees, avoiding the main trail. They continued in silence, which was good, for she felt not like speaking, so black was her mood.

Daffydd stopped. His gaze swung around to encompass the forest. Brithwin stilled, narrowing her eyes and searching for what he sought. "What—"

His strong hand clamped over her mouth and he whispered in her ear. "Horses."

He pushed her to the ground and drew his sword before hunching beside her. Brithwin sucked in a breath and held it as the sound of pounding hooves drew nearer. Were these her friends' murderers?

Daffydd's breath blew over her face, its warmth mingling with the scent of cool, moist earth. "Where is Thor?"

Brithwin's eyes widened and she shook her head. Heaven save them. Would Thor lead these men straight to them?

The outline of horses became visible. Fighting the urge to flee, she gripped the small branches of the bush before her, its thorny ends biting into her hands. Daffydd's arm remained securely around her shoulders as if to impart courage and protection. The mounted men advanced and began passing by no farther than the length of two jousting sticks. Her heart thundered in her chest. Daffydd's arm tightened. She peeked through the bush. One of the men had broken away from the group and approached.

Thor's bark sounded in the distance. A cry went up and the men spurred their horses to a gallop. Brithwin let out a sigh when again Daffydd's fingers dug into her arm. She shifted her gaze to see the man who had broken away slide from his horse. Muttering, he walked to a tree to relieve himself, and Brithwin dropped her head. When he turned around to mount his horse, he would see them.

Brithwin squeezed her eyes shut for a moment and prayed. *Lord, please do not let him see us.* She swallowed. After what she had thought, how dare she pray? Why would God answer?

As if the Lord sought to show His forgiveness, the horse turned and cantered in the opposite direction. The brigand spun around, eyes locked on his retreating horse. He dashed after his mount, bellowing as he went. The more he roared the faster the horse ran. God surely proved He was in control. As the man faded into the woods, Daffydd let his arm drop from her shoulder.

He grasped her hand and plucked her to her feet. "Come, we must hurry. When they see someone has been at the cottage, they will return."

†††

Laughter and friendly banter accompanied the evening meal, well under way, but Royce could not shrug off the mantle of restlessness that weighed on him. A thin haze of smoke hung about the room, and bodies in bad need of washing saturated the stagnant air and tainted the smell of fresh-cooked food. Royce wished more men would pick up the habit of bathing. It wasn't so bad once one became accustomed to it. Jarren sat beside him, devouring a chunk of boar haunch and regaling the knights with the tale of the hunt. Grunting in acknowledgment to Jarren's rambling, Royce took another bite and glanced once more toward the door.

Jarren leaned toward Royce. "Watching the door will not bring her in any sooner."

With his hand hovering to pick up his cup, Royce snapped his head toward Jarren. "Why think you I wait on her?"

Jarren's eyes opened wide and the corner of his mouth quivered upward. "Perhaps the fact you have glanced at the entrance a dozen times since we sat down."

Royce took a swallow of his drink and slammed the goblet down. "So, what now. You keep track of how often I lift my head?"

Jarren sopped the gravy with a piece of bread and stuffed it in his mouth before answering. "No, but it is distracting, for it draws my gaze and interferes with me enjoying my food."

"She is late." Royce spoke the words more to himself. "Did you not send her maid to find her? Hawkwood is no small castle."

"Aye, but if she were here someone would have seen her. I will wait no longer. My gut tells me she is in danger." He pushed himself from the table. "Gather the men. We go and search for her."

Jarren shoved his trencher away and leaned back. "Did you not say Daffydd was to watch her?"

Royce looked at his friend with annoyance. "Aye, and he is not here either. If she were within the castle walls, he would be eating with us."

Royce moved toward the exit with haste as Jarren gathered the men. Minutes later, they rode out of the gates.

Jarren brought his mount beside Royce's. "Where do we start? The village?"

Royce wrapped the reins around his hand. "Nay. We go to the old couple in the woods."

"Milady would not go there without telling you."

Turning in his saddle, Royce raised his eyebrows and fixed his gaze on Jarren. "Surely you jest?"

Jarren clamped his mouth shut, riding on in silence. They veered to the left and followed the path that led to the old crofter's cottage. Not far down the trail, Royce caught sight of riders. He spurred Shadowmere into a run. The oncoming riders sent their horses off the trail and into the heavy woods. His men's horses pounded the ground behind him. As he reached the area where the riders had turned off the trail, Royce slowed his horse and eased his way into the woods. There had been a dozen or more riders, but to his relief none rode double. Brithwin was not among them, but they were on his land, running from him, which meant they planned mischief. He would see they left, if nothing else. The pursuit dragged on, twisting and turning. Royce ducked as he approached a low branch. The brigands gained ground and looked to know the lay of the land better than he. The sun lowered in the sky. Pulling on the reins, he turned to Jarren as his horse stopped. "Let them go. We lose light and I must find Brithwin."

They circled around and headed toward the cottage. Dusk was nigh upon them when two figures slid behind a group of yew bushes. He nudged his horse forward cautiously. His heart thundered in his chest. *Please let this be Brithwin.*

Royce reined in his mount several feet back. "Show yourselves."

A gasp came from the brush then a man stepped out. "Lord Rosen Craig, is that you?"

"Aye, it is me. Do you have milady?"

Brithwin emerged beside Daffydd. "I am here."

Her voice was thick. He longed to see her face. He dismounted, and his long stride ate up the ground between them. Every step that drew him closer revealed more of the distress her posture conveyed. Her haggard face and despondent eyes coming into view whispered something was amiss. Beside her stood an equally downcast Daffydd. Even the haze of dusk could not hide her lowered head tilted to one side and the slump of her shoulders. Royce drew her to him, enfolding her in his arms.

Her bottom lip quivered against his chest. He scooped her up and carried her to his horse, mounting behind her. Jarren leaned down, offered his hand to Daffydd, and pulled him up behind him.

Daffydd cleared his throat. "When we return, we must speak."

"The old couple?" Royce asked. Daffydd met his gaze, and from the turmoil reflected there, Royce knew the news would not be good. He nodded his head and nudged Shadowmere toward Hawkwood.

When they arrived in the bailey, Royce slid from his horse and lifted Brithwin into his arms. She leaned her head against his chest as he made his way to the manor and up the steps. Jarren ran ahead and pulled the door. Torches hanging from rings on the walls lit up the entrance. He lowered his eyes and choked as he glimpsed her bloodstained gown. His gaze shot to her face. The blank stare she gave him sent chills through his body.

Daffydd came up behind him. "The blood is not hers."

Royce gave a quick nod. "Have a bath brought to our chamber, and send Elspeth with it. I will speak to you in my solar after Elspeth arrives."

Royce took to the steps with Brithwin still in his arms. With great care, he lowered her into a chair and squatted before her. "Can you tell me what happened today?"

Her vacant eyes looked past him, causing a tremor of alarm to lace through him. This was not the fire-spitting Brithwin he knew. Never had he seen her so meek. Whatever she had experienced had surely been vile. She belonged to him—her safety was his responsibility, and he had failed her.

He scooped her up, dropped himself in the chair, and nestled her on his lap. With arms wrapped around her, he gently kissed her forehead and pulled her tightly to his chest. If he could remove this suffering from her, he would gladly take it upon himself. Never again would he allow someone to hurt her like this. He would protect her at any cost, even to his own death. This oath he made.

†††

A rap on the door brought Royce's head up, and he bid Elspeth and the servants enter with Brithwin's bathwater.

Leaning forward, he tenderly brushed his lips over hers then stood and sat her in the chair. He caressed her cheek with his finger. "I must go speak with Daffydd. Elspeth will take care of you. If you want me, send a servant, and I will come."

Royce stepped through the door and into his solar to see Daffydd looking out the window. He strode across the room. Daffydd tore his gaze from outside. "How is she?"

"She is distressed." Royce advanced on Daffydd, and grasped the man's collar. "What happened? I trusted you to protect her!" He shoved him back and plunged both hands through his hair. He had barely finished the motion when he thrust his fist into the wall, leaving an indentation of his passion in the soft wood. Pain shot up his arm, bringing coherence back to his thoughts.

Daffydd's eyes rounded. "She did not tell you?"

"I couldn't get any words from her. I have never seen her so distraught. Was she—attacked?" He could not bring himself to ask the question that seared his heart.

"Nothing like that, Royce."

Royce let out a whoosh of air and with it some of the anger. "Sit and tell me what has taken place."

Daffydd gave an account of the events from the time he had stepped outside Hawkwood's bailey and met Brithwin. He told him in detail what they walked into and her reaction from the moment they had entered the cottage.

Royce clenched his teeth. Brithwin was too innocent to witness this gruesome scene. He had indeed failed her.

The men he had chased were very well the same who had murdered her friends—and he had given up the pursuit. His gut twisted. He had let them slip through his fingers. He should have pressed onward and apprehended them.

Daffydd's silence drew his attention. Royce's eyes narrowed as he stared back.

"There is one more thing." Daffydd shifted in his chair.

"Before Murielle died, she described one of her attackers. 'Twas Edmond."

Chapter 20

Royce bolted out of his chair. "Edmond!" He had been within his grasp. If he'd only known, he would have finished the chase. Ended it then and there.

He glared at Daffydd. "You should have returned immediately and told me."

Daffydd drew himself up. "I could not leave milady, for fear of their return, and I could not take her from Murielle's side until she died."

Royce rubbed his jaw, weighing Daffydd's words. "Aye, you did right. 'Tis the frustration of knowing I nearly had Edmond." He turned. "You may take your leave."

Royce paced the floor. How could he look Brithwin in the eye and tell her he'd let those murderers escape? He pushed open the door to their room and to where Brithwin sat wrapped in a blanket, staring at the floor.

"You may go, Elspeth." Royce knelt before Brithwin's chair and gently took her hands, bringing them to his lips. Anguish twisted his heart as he crouched before her. What he would give to take her pain. With his lips pressed against her skin, he lifted his gaze to meet with hers. Pain and sorrow etched every feature.

He raised one hand and stroked her cheek. "Ah, love, is there nothing I can do to help you with this ache?"

He wished she would cry. The simple act would free her and help release her pain.

She drew in a deep breath and shuddered as she let it out. "Will you hold me?" A tear slipped down her cheek and she brushed it away.

Royce lifted her and laid her on the bed. Lowering himself next to her, he enfolded her in his arms, crooning words of comfort. Running his hands through her silky chestnut hair, he continued to whisper until she drifted to sleep. He lay there, waiting for her breathing to steady. His mind would not rest. He could think of nothing but the cause of her anguish—and bringing Edmond to justice. Slipping his arm from under her, he slid off the bed.

"Please don't leave me," Brithwin's voice broke the silence of the night.

The pleading tone in her voice drew him back. Sinking next to her, he pulled her close. "I am here, love. I won't go anywhere."

As dawn broke the next morning, Royce remained beside the bed gazing at Brithwin while she slept. Her suffering tore at his heart. She needed him, and he would be here for her. Bending over, he brushed the hair from her face then gently kissed her forehead. He would send his men to retrieve the bodies from the crofter's cottage.

"I love you," he whispered and strode from the room, attempting to keep his boots from clunking on the floor and waking her.

†††

The small room adjoining the great hall held the injured man. Royce gazed out the window as Marjory tended her patient. His men had found the man lying on the ground near the crofter's cottage a few hours earlier while retrieving the bodies. He'd taken a beating, but it was obvious his attackers hadn't planned to kill him. Something didn't feel right.

Jarren stepped inside the room and glanced around. "How does he fare?"

Royce spun around and waited, with Jarren, for Marjory's response.

She pulled the blanket around the man's chest and raised her head. "He has not stirred. No broken bones, but it looks as if someone hit him over the head and not gently. I would guess it is what ended the fight."

Royce waited as Marjory let herself out of the room then made his way to the bed. "Humph. A fight?" He picked up the man's hand, which dangled off the side, and examined it. Laying it down, he frowned and picked up the other hand to inspect.

Jarren leaned forward. "Something amiss?"

Royce rubbed his neck. His gut, along with his eyes, cautioned him something wasn't right. "What think you of a man who has taken this type of beating yet does not have a scratch on his hands?"

Jarren frowned. "No defense wounds? You mean to say, he did not attempt to protect himself?"

"I checked both hands. They are about the only parts of him that are not black and blue. Few men would not fight back."

Jarren shrugged. "It is possible they held him while they beat him."

"Aye, possible, but there was no bruising to indicate that nor signs his wrists had been tied. Think you he would get one or two swings in somehow. If luck be on my side, he will recover quickly enough that I can get answers on the morrow."

A light thumping sounded on the door.

"Enter." Royce moved away from the bed.

Pater leaned his head in. "Is the man conscious that I may pray with him?"

Royce glanced at the sleeping man. "Nay, he is not."

Pater nodded and pulled the heavy wood door shut.

Jarren scratched his jaw while eyeing the door. "Why does he not leave Hawkwood? Does he have no family or place to go?"

"I don't know why he stays. Perhaps because there is still persecution of Lollards, but I have a feeling it is something more than that."

Royce and Jarren left the patient's room. The light shone through the windows in the great hall. He doused the torch next to the room. Today the man needed rest, but on the morrow he would get answers.

†††

Brithwin woke with the rays of sunshine slicing across her covers. She rolled to her side and placed her palm on the bed where Royce's head had lain. It was cold. Staring at her hand, she recalled the sweet words of comfort Royce had spoken to her yestereve. The reason for those words flooded her mind. She rolled to her back, throwing her arm over her eyes.

A light tapping on the door brought her out of her morose thoughts. "You may enter."

Elspeth stepped in. "Milady, are you ready to break your fast?"

"Nay, I cannot eat, but you may help me dress."

"My lord left instructions to see that you ate. He knew you would not wish to. You must keep your strength up."

Brithwin lowered her arm from her eyes and squinted. "I will be fine."

Elspeth's gown rustled as she moved forward. "You are under much stress, and he does not want you to fall ill."

"I truly do not feel like eating." She swung her feet off the bed and onto the floor.

"My lord worries and had planned to come himself, but his men returned with an injured man. He sent me in his stead. Maybe you can eat a little and keep me out of trouble?"

Brithwin slapped her hand over her mouth and ran to the chamber pot. Beads of perspiration formed on her forehead as her stomach convulsed and heaved. Rolling back on her heels, she panted, waiting for the dizziness to subside.

Elspeth rushed forward and brushed Brithwin's face with a cloth that she kept with her wash basin. "I thought you just made excuses, but I see you do not feel well." She helped her to her feet. "Come, get back to your bed."

Brithwin shook her head. The room spun and she clasped hold of Elspeth. "Help me to the chair. I am sure this will pass in a moment. 'Tis all that has happened has my belly upset. I need to sit quiet."

"I will fetch you bread. That is good to settle the belly." Elspeth disappeared out the door.

Brithwin's stomach settled shortly after nibbling a few bites of bread. She moved to the table, leaned over the bowl, and splashed water on her face. The cold air hit her wet skin, refreshing her. She dabbed her face dry. Elspeth helped her dress, and then Brithwin sought her garden.

Strolling down the path, she took note of the new growth. The rain had given the plants firm roots. She longed to see her flowers in full color. Murielle had cherished the blooms she took to her each summer.

"Excuse me, milady." Thomas's voice brought her from her thoughts.

She launched herself into his arms. Thomas patted her back. "There, there, Lady Brithwin. This sadness will pass."

Brithwin squeezed her eyes shut. "It will never be the same."

Pater's voice came from beyond Thomas. "You must lean on the Lord."

Brithwin swung around to see Pater saunter forward. She drew herself upright and dabbed at her eyes with her fingers. "'Tis so hard at times. It makes me angry, Pater. He took people away from me that I cared for."

Pater stopped in front of her. "We live in the world, and evil is about us. 'Tis not the Lord who took your friends from you. You must not blame God. His Word tells us,' It is appointed unto man once to die and then the judgment.' No one escapes death."

"Why a horrible death, though? Why did God allow that?" She leaned her head against Thomas's chest again, and his arms tightened around her.

Pater moved to her side, gesturing with his palms up. "I do not pretend to know the mind of God, my child. You must accept it and know they are in a better place, for they loved the Lord and served Him well."

Thomas stepped away and glanced from Pater to Brithwin. "I came to speak with you about burying Guy, Murielle, and Malcolm." He cleared his throat. "They dig their graves as we speak. Lord Rosen Craig would have them buried on the morrow."

Brithwin didn't want the day to end. Placing her friends in the ground put finality to their death and the promise she would never see them again. But the day wore on, evening fell, and before she was ready, morning had come.

It was early when they lowered her beloved friends in the ground. She leaned against Royce for support. Pinpricks burned her eyes, the tears begging release. With determination, she swallowed and shut her eyes. Tears would accomplish nothing, and she willed them away. Finally able to open her eyes and keep control, she looked beyond the graves to the trees budding, giving new life. A new life, just as her dear friends now had.

✝✝✝

Edmond kicked the dirt with his boot. Royce would be on alert. He would have to be careful to stay off Hawkwood land for a few days. "You would have stopped me?"

Robert glared at him. "That was a foolish thing to do."

Edmond shoved him backward. "Do not gainsay me again if you wish to live another day. Ye are overconfident if you think to tell me what I can and cannot do."

"I did not like the way you sent Montfort to Lor—to Royce in the first place, but now you have given him more reason to question things. *Your overconfidence* will only increase his anger. 'Tis like you provoke him deliberately. What were you thinking, having Montfort feed him information?"

Edmond spat on the ground. "You are not the one who had his life snatched from him. Rosen Craig should have been mine! I will never forget what our worthless king stole from my family. That estate should be mine, not Royce's, had it not been ripped from my father's hand by Richard. And the title of Earl would be mine, now, instead of Royce's. My father lost everything, including my mother. She could not endure the hardships she faced. She became ill and never recovered. My father killed himself trying to gain favor with the king."

Edmond swung his fist up and thrust his thumb to his chest. "I vowed, when my father died, I would make them pay for what they had denied him and me. Royce grew up with everything that should have been mine. I was born in that castle. Do you have any idea what it feels like to have all you have known ripped from you—knowing every day someone else is living your life?"

Robert frowned. "I don't see what this has to do with Montfort."

"I have a plan to obtain Rosen Craig, and I have a means to achieve it. Important news has come to me, and I intend to use it to its fullest."

"What is this information?"

Edmond narrowed his eyes and punched his finger into Robert's chest. "I will tell you this much—everything of Royce's will be mine, including his wife."

Chapter 21

Royce wrapped his arm around Brithwin's shoulders and pulled her close. Tremors racked her body as they lowered her friends into the ground. Wrinkles creased her forehead even as she had slept this morning. He gave a gentle squeeze on her shoulder. She raised her head to meet his gaze. She was pale as a frog's belly. Dark circles surrounded her lusterless blue eyes, and sorrow etched her face with thin lines. His gut twisted—she looked sick. He lightly kissed her forehead. Heaven knew how much he loved this woman.

Her eyes filled with tears before she managed to conquer what he was sure she saw as a weakness. A hot flood surged through him. Edmond had caused her this pain. He would pay for every tear she withheld.

They returned to the manor after the last shovel of dirt fell on the graves. Brithwin spoke not a word, and now, as they sat before their midday meal, she continued her silence.

Royce looked at her untouched food. "You are not eating."

Brithwin pushed her trencher away. "The very sight of food causes my belly to rebel."

Royce moved her food back. "You look tired. You must eat and keep up your strength."

Brithwin turned away from her meal. "Has the man you found spoken of why Edmond did this?"

"Nay. He still sleeps. However, I have dealt with Edmond nigh on to as many years as you are old. He has a strong hatred for me, and it seems because of it other people suffer."

"God gives each of us free choice—you cannot blame yourself for what another does." Brithwin shuddered. "I do not understand why he would do this horrible thing to an old couple and a simple man."

Royce's fists tightened, his nails digging into his palms. "He murdered people on my land, people I am responsible for, to send a message to me. Edmond understands me well enough to know I will not sit idly by although he could not have known how deeply this would affect me and mine. The time has come to put a stop to his machinations."

†††

Royce sat opposite a chess board from Jarren, his hand on his bishop. "Would you like me to make this quick and painless?"

Jarren tapped his fingers on the table. "Make your move."

Royce pushed his piece to its new square and leaned back in his chair. "I'm ready to get answers from our guest."

"So, that is what we are calling him?" Jarren moved his knight to protect his king and threaten Royce's queen.

"For the time being." Royce slid his rook across the board.

Jarren stared at the chess pieces. "You sure you want to do that?"

"Aye."

Jarren shrugged, swiped up Royce's queen, and placed his knight on the square. "When do we talk to our *guest?*"

Royce's gaze rose from the table, and he smiled as he moved his pawn up a space. "Now. I believe that is checkmate."

Jarren blinked and shook his head. "Finished off by a lowly pawn."

Standing from his chair, Royce let his smile fade. "A lesson I learned early in life. Even those things that look innocent cannot always be trusted."

Jarren followed him to the patient's room. He entered to

find Marjory tending the injured man.

Royce sauntered to the bed. "Is there any improvement?"

"He woke during the night from thirst. He has yet to rouse this morning."

As if her words bid him to wake, the knight opened his eyes. His voice cracked. "Water."

She scurried over and held a cup to his lips. He gulped the liquid then fell back from the effort.

Jarren moved to the wall and leaned against it.

Royce handed Marjory her basket of herbs. "You may leave."

When the door closed behind her, Royce turned to the beaten knight. "What is your name?"

"Montfort," his voice rasped.

"Montfort, what are you doing on my land?"

Wariness shone in the man's eyes. He surveyed both Royce and Jarren. "I was only passing through."

Royce leaned down and scowled. "To where are you traveling?"

The knight turned his head away and winced. "I have no destination."

"You mean you wander aimlessly, or perhaps you are a brigand looking to prey on my people?"

"Nay!" He rolled his head toward Royce. "I am a knight."

Royce straightened and crossed the room, closing the distance. "You are a mercenary?"

"I look for honest work as a knight."

"Do you know who did this to you?"

Montfort moaned as he pushed himself onto his elbows. "His name was Edmond. I am to give a message to Royce. Are you him?"

Royce eyed him for deception. "I am. What is this message?"

"He said to tell you, Rosen Craig will soon be his, including all you hold dear. He will do the same to anyone who gets in his way as he did to the old couple in the cottage."

Royce ground his teeth together and a knot formed in his gut. He drew in a deep breath and let it out slowly to keep control. "Where is Edmond?"

Montfort shook his head and flinched. "That is not all. He said to ask if you missed your family, and to tell you that you will be joining them soon. As to where he is, I know not. It was not long after our discussion that I lost consciousness."

Royce walked out of the small room with every muscle tense and on fire. Jarren came out after him.

"What think you, Royce?"

"Edmond goads me. He wants me to come after him."

Jarren narrowed his eyes. "Then you believe Montfort?"

"I have no doubt he speaks the truth, but I trust him not. He has no anger. If someone left me beaten on a road and gave me a message to give another, I would want to know what that man did to warrant my beating in order to deliver a message. He also did not seem curious as to why I would miss my family and why I would be meeting them again soon. Methinks he accepts his plight too easily. If he is not one of Edmond's men, then he has been paid well to deliver the message—and I wager he knows more than he tells."

"What do we do with him when he recovers? He is a knight. We cannot imprison him without cause."

Royce flexed his hands. "We will set a guard on him. If Edmond plans something, 'tis important for me to see my defense is strong and my people safe. We need to travel to Rosen Craig."

Soft footsteps padded behind him. Royce turned. Brithwin's weary smile greeted him. His heart twisted at leaving her.

She drew near, and he laid his hand on her arm. "Brithwin, love, I have to go to Rosen Craig and see to the defenses."

She raised her eyes to his. "When do we leave?"

"'Tis I that must go. You will remain here."

"I wish to go with you."

Heads turned their way, and he lowered his voice. "I would take you, but Edmond has made threats to all I care for, and I would see you remain safe within Hawkwood walls."

Brithwin grasped his hand. "I will be safe with you, Royce. You will protect me."

"Your innocence still amazes me. However, we will be riding through areas where I expect an ambush. 'Tis true I would do all I could to protect you, but I am merely a man. I will not jeopardize your safety."

"You give me no choice?"

"Nay, you will stay. I ask a boon of you, my lady—that you do not step outside the walls of Hawkwood until I return. I know not what Edmond plans, but as long as you remain inside this edifice I know Thomas can protect you."

Brithwin's eyes turned glassy, and Royce's resolve almost melted, sympathy stirring deep within him.

"I will grant you your boon, my lord, but in return I ask one of you."

"If it is possible, I will do it." Royce's voice was thick.

"Keep yourself safe and come to me with haste."

"I will do all in my power to grant your wish." He pulled her into his arms. The smell of roses wafted to his nose. Her scent. He ran his finger across her smooth cheek. "If the weather holds, we will leave on the morrow."

Royce turned to Jarren. "Montfort troubles me. Perhaps you should remain here to look after things."

"You need me to watch *your* back. I am sure Thomas is

capable of looking after Hawkwood. The guard you put on Montfort's room is sufficient. Moreover, he will not be getting around any too soon."

Brithwin grasped Royce's arm. "You must take Jarren. If you wish me to stay within these walls, it is only fair you take precautions as well. Thomas has looked after Hawkwood and me for all my years. 'Twould offend him to think you did not have faith in him."

††††

Brithwin leaned her head against Royce's chest in the garden, seeking a brief reprieve from her sorrow. Somehow his embrace helped ease the ache in her heart. It was as if through his caring he helped carry her load. She may not see him for a fortnight or longer—a long time to be apart. She'd persuaded him to spend the day with her, but convincing him to take her riding proved much more difficult. He refused to take her out of Hawkwood—for her safety, he'd said. She leaned back in his arms and glanced around the garden.

His brown eyes softened. "What troubles you?"

"'Twas not long ago I would come here to hide from my father. My life has changed so much in a short period of time."

The heat from his body seeped into her. Her heart raced. She could never get enough of this man.

He stroked her hair. "That troubles you? I would like our life to give you pleasure."

"'Tis not you or us. Just remembering things I ought not to, I suppose."

"Tell me of your father."

She didn't want to dredge up those memories. She just wanted to remain where she was, secure in his arms, enjoying her garden. She would not allow her father to steal her joy in death. "He was a cruel man."

His lips brushed over her ear. "And . . ."

Brithwin drew in a shaky breath. "I know 'tis a terrible thing to say of one's sire, but 'tis the truth. My mother died giving birth to me. He never forgave me. Whenever he could find a reason to punish me, he did." She swallowed, willing herself to go on. "The more I feared him, the more he enjoyed punishing me. 'Twas not until I realized my terror fed his hunger for cruelty that I found some reprieve."

His arms tightened around her. "I wish I could change what you had to endure."

She lifted her gaze to his. "What I went through has made me who I am today. I hated my father for a long time for what he did to me. I was able to overcome everything, except what my father called my special room. He would mention it so he could see my fear, and he thrived on that." She leaned into him, trying to chase away the chill. Even held in his embrace, she couldn't still the shiver which ran down her spine. Royce ran his hands briskly over her arms, sending welcome warmth.

Brithwin closed her eyes to get the courage to continue. She wanted him to know her deepest secret and to be able to trust him with it. "I cannot be alone in the dark without a fear so great it consumes me. Not until after my father's death and much soul searching could I forgive him for the things he did to me. Pater helped me to see my bitterness did not hurt my father but rather harmed my relationship with the Lord."

"'Tis good your father is dead, for I think I would take his life for what he has done, and I need no more black marks on my soul. I know not how a man could treat his daughter as he did you. He was not a man, but a beast."

Brithwin studied Royce. "You have spoken often of your sin. What have you done that you think God cannot forgive?"

Royce shook his head. "What I have witnessed, what I have done, are not for innocent ears to hear."

"I have seen much in my years. My father made sure of

that. You will not shock me, Royce."

Royce's voice deepened with regret. "You may think you have, but I vow you have never seen the likes of what tortures my soul, and I will not be the one to sully your mind."

Brithwin brushed the lock of hair off his forehead. "You need not tell me, then, but I tell you true—God is bigger than anything you have done. He sent His Son to die for our sins—for all our sins. You need to let God forgive you so you can forgive yourself. Only then will you be truly happy. I know this because I, too, have struggled with letting go of my sin."

"That may be so, however, there is a wide chasm between what you have done and what I have done. This"— he lifted her chin with his finger—"is not how I want to spend the rest of our day together. Let us talk of something pleasant."

"Let me leave you with one thing to think on."

Royce smiled. "Do I have a choice?"

Brithwin brushed off invisible dirt from her gown. "My father's cruelty caused me to distrust most men. But through God and your kindness, I have overcome this fear. My reluctance to become your wife in all ways was not conquered our first night together, but God listened to my prayers and allowed me to see you differently than at first. Talk to God, and listen to what He has to say to you."

He leaned forward and brushed his lips over hers. "I am glad you have come to trust me. If it will ease your mind, I will think about what you have said. But God will not speak to me."

"Pater tells me God wants to talk to us. The problem is we usually do not want to listen."

Brithwin nuzzled closer, and silently she added, *And I will pray God will ease your burden.*

The next morn she rose early to bid farewell to her husband as the sun peeked above the horizon, casting an orange and yellow haze low in the sky. Royce remained next to Shadowmere who anxiously pawed the ground. His men had mounted and sat waiting for his command to ride out.

Royce cupped Brithwin's chin. "I wish you would let me leave Jarren here with you. It would put my mind to ease."

She shook her head and willed her eyes to stay dry for his sake. "But then what of mine? I would worry for you, and remember, I am within the safety of Hawkwood's walls. You will be out there." She gestured with a sweeping motion of her hand. "With nothing between you and trouble, should it seek you out."

Pulling a knife from his belt, he held it out to her. "It was Edmond's. Until I retrieve yours, it's fitting you should have his."

She pulled her hands behind her. "'Tis the knife that almost killed you."

"'Tis not the knife but the man behind it that does the killing, sweet Brithwin. I know 'tis larger and not your mother's, but 'tis protection."

His lips covered hers and lingered. The men behind him chuckled. He whispered in her ear, "You are a stubborn wench." He slid the knife into the belt of her gown. Turning, he yelled to his men. "What are you tittering about? Have you not seen a man kiss his wife good-bye?"

He threw himself onto his horse.

She grasped his hand as if to keep him there. "Be careful, and God go with you."

"We will be safe. Remember your vow to me. I will send word to you and let you know how long before I return." Royce nudged his horse forward, and their hands parted, leaving Brithwin's heart in his safekeeping.

Chapter 22

After a hard day's ride, Royce guided Shadowmere across Rosen Craig's bailey and stopped near two stable boys. He and Jarren dismounted and handed their reins to the lads. Not waiting for the rest of his party, they strode toward the manor.

The memory of riding out Hawkwood's gate haunted him. When he'd turned in his saddle to wave at Brithwin, he'd caught movement in the lower manor window as Montfort dropped the curtain. He'd stopped long enough to reinforce his distrust of the man with Thomas, but it was as if a dark cloud now followed him.

Royce pulled open the heavy wooden door of Rosen Craig and listened to the familiar creak of its hinges. Memories flooded back. Wretchedness gripped his soul and twisted. His steps faltered.

Jarren glanced around. "Is something amiss?"

Royce shook himself. "Nay, a long day in the saddle with little sleep is all."

The aroma of cinnamon apple tarts drew them to the great hall where servants served the evening meal.

Lyndle glanced up from his seat on the dais. He stood abruptly, sending his chair teetering. Swinging around to grab it, he knocked his cup, spilling his drink. A young servant girl scurried forward and mopped up the mess. Lyndle righted the chair.

"Royce, my lord, I knew not of your return." With shaking hand, he gestured to him. "Come, eat."

Royce stepped to the table and eyed Lyndle as he shuffled his plate from the lord's place, relinquishing it to Royce. Royce sat with a sigh, closing his eyes. It was strange to sit in his father's seat.

"Hello, Lord Rosen Craig," a voice purred. "You have grown into quite a man."

Royce turned. "Clarice." He rose and took her offered hand, kissing it. "I apologize. I didn't see you. I am sorry for the loss of your betrothed." And he was sorry for his loss of his brother. He missed Bryce.

"You mean I am so plain I fit right in with these men?" She pouted.

It hadn't slipped by Royce that she'd not acknowledged his brother's death. "'Tis my mistake. We are weary." What was Bryce's betrothed doing at Rosen Craig?

Plates were placed before him and his men.

A trill of laughter rang out. "So you *are* saying I blend in."

"N-nay."

"Oh, my lord, I only tease you." She smiled and laid her hand over his. "As long as it does not happen again." She batted her lashes.

The warmth from her hand seeped into his. Suddenly he yearned to see Brithwin. He detached his hand from hers and began to eat. The woman didn't act as if she'd just lost her betrothed. But then the two had been promised since childhood it was entirely possible she did not hold deep feelings for his brother.

She frowned as he pulled away. "I have not seen you for many years. You were just a boy."

Royce snorted. "I am merely a year younger than Bryce and several years older than you."

"I guess you seemed much younger." Her gaze swooped over him. "You surely have turned out well. I venture to say you could put most men to shame."

He cared not for her forward ways. He turned to Lyndle. "Is all well?"

"Aye." His voice was curt.

"I feared Edmond would appear, causing trouble."

"Edmond? I have not seen him since afore your family's deaths."

Royce swallowed a bite of meat and reached for his goblet to wash it down. "I want to examine the defenses of the keep, among other things, while I am here. I will meet you on the morrow for the morning meal, and we can discuss these things."

Lyndle shrugged. "As you wish, Lord Rosen Craig. Not much has changed."

Royce finished his meal and pushed his chair back to stand. "It has been a long day. I think I will retire to my chamber. Is Bryce's room unused?"

"Aye. No one will use it for fear his spirit still lingers there."

He scowled. "One would think grown men would not be so superstitious. My brother does not haunt this castle."

Royce called out to Jarren who leaned against a chair's back, watching a game of dice. "I will show you to your chamber."

Jarren followed to Bryce's room. Royce bid him good night and strode to his old room. He pulled off his tunic and chausses and lay on his bed. Hands clasped behind his head, he stared out the small window. Visions passed before his eyes as if he were still in the borderland of Scotland. He shook his head to rid his mind of them, but they clung on with persistence. The death of so many rested on his soul.

They'd taken the village. His men were filled with blood lust. They went on a rampage, killing the innocent for sport. The screams of young girls, as knights brutally assaulted them, rang in his ears. He closed his eyes and the bile burned in his throat.

God would never forgive him. He wished Brithwin were

right, but she knew not what he had seen, what he had done, or what he had failed to do. How could a man find forgiveness whose hesitation caused such depravity? A leader who could not control and stop the blood lust of his own men? He was a condemned man.

And now, his gut twisted anew for the loss of his family. It was God's punishment. He wished he could pray—ask God not to take Brithwin, too. If he had to distance himself from her to keep her safe from his punishment, he would. Perhaps if he could bring Edmond to justice he could earn some forgiveness.

He fell into a fitful sleep, fighting the demons that plagued him, tossing and turning throughout the night. He awoke as tired as when he'd closed his eyes.

The next several days were filled riding Rosen Craig's estate, visiting the villeins and freemen, discussing the problems that had arisen in their crops, and making suggestions to increase their yield. He set men to work, reinforcing the stone walls to protect Rosen Craig. Trying to improve his understanding of Rosen Craig, he spoke with the servants and learned each of their duties. A great appreciation grew for his father's wisdom.

At last he had seen to everything, finally, except the accounts. Royce met with Lyndle, after the noon meal, to look them over. Hours later, they still sat, going over the purchases.

Lyndle fidgeted in his seat. "There are things I need to see to before I retire for the night, if you do not need me anymore."

Royce looked up from the figures. The light of the candle danced erratically before him. "One question before you retire. While speaking with the cook today, I learned we have no healer. I would like to know why a castle as great as Rosen Craig does not have a healer. I remember there being

one when I was a young boy. I know my father did not like
Mother to carry the full responsibility."

Lyndle tapped a finger against his chin. "'Tis strange.
The healer and her husband disappeared without a word the
day after the deaths of milord and lady." His eyes narrowed
and wrinkles creased his brow. "Now that I think on it, 'tis
troubling they left without a word."

"They are freemen?" Royce raised his brows and waited.
Lyndle glanced to where Royce sat. "Hmm, oh, aye, they
are freemen."

"I'm surprised they didn't speak with you about their
departure. Are you certain they did not take a part in my
family's death?"

"Aye. I have told you who I saw. 'Twas not the healer."
He nodded. It was odd that they left, but the violent
deaths may have scared them away. "We need one."

"Clarice is well versed in the art of healing."

"I have been meaning to ask, why *is* she here?" Royce
didn't bother to look up from the numbers.

"Bryce was her betrothed."

Royce put his finger by an entry and met Lyndle's smug
gaze. "Aye, he *was*. Seems odd she would come here when
her betrothed is no longer alive."

"I think she comes to escape her brother and his cruelty.
Now, if that is all you need from me, I'd like to see to my
other responsibilities."

Royce waved him on. "I will see you on the morrow,
then."

Working through the evening meal and well into the wee
hours, Royce finally finished the accounts. The candle had
burned down to a nub. He blew out the flickering flame and
went to his room.

The next morning, Royce awoke with his skin drenched
in sweat and his gut in a knot. He sat on the edge of his bed

with his head in his hands. He could not continue like this. Foreboding haunted him. Each day his trepidations grew. Robbed of his family, he would not allow Brithwin to be next.

He dragged himself to the morning meal. The room was full. He had lingered in his room longer than usual.

Clarice's smooth voice drifted across the hall. "Good morn. I am pleased you choose to join us this day. You are usually gone before I rise." She gave him a coy smile. "I begin to think you avoid me."

Royce took his seat. "There is much to learn. I am busy from dawn to dusk."

"I was in hope you would take me out for a ride. My palfrey needs exercise, and 'tis so boring riding with any of these men." She swept her hand out, gesturing to the knights and men-at-arms eating.

Royce bristled at her rudeness. "Get Lyndle to take you after I speak with him. I have no time to go riding today."

"Then I will wait until the morrow." She stuck out her bottom lip. "I want *you* to take me. I miss your brother and have been left alone to grieve all these months."

Royce stood and picked up his bread and cheese. He turned to Lyndle. "When you finish breaking your fast, come to my solar."

Clarice continued to pout. "Can you not take time to eat with us?"

The woman had been dealt a harsh blow. After years of waiting on the arranged marriage, she loses her betrothed just months before their wedding. He softened his tone. "Nay, I wish to finish with this and get back to my wife." While he longed to see Brithwin, this was not a total truth—he could not dismiss the fear that his return would endanger her.

Clarice clamped her mouth shut and looked away.

Royce made his way to the solitude of his solar. It was

not long before Lyndle walked in without knocking. "You wish to speak to me?"

"Yes, there are questions I have in the accounts. What is this expenditure?" He pointed to a line on the paper and waited while Lyndle made his way to him.

He bent over and examined where Royce pointed.

""'Twas for iron and new tools for the blacksmith."

"So large an amount? Why did you not put it down as such? You have done so on all the others."

"I must have laid it aside and forgotten to finish when I came back." He straightened. "As to the cost, tools and iron are expensive, as you will learn."

His condescending tone scored like claws on Royce's ears. "You may leave."

Lyndle strode out. Royce continued looking at the accounts after he left. Something was amiss. The best way to resolve it was to speak to the blacksmith.

The next morning, Royce made his way to the forge on the far side of the bailey. Heat and the strong spicy scent of wood smoke rolled out to meet him as he entered. The blacksmith lifted his head. His smile revealed a full set of teeth in a soot-covered face. Leathery hands covered in scars gave witness to the years of toiling in the trade.

He quickly set down his tools and wiped an arm across his brow. "Good day to you, m'lord. Is there something I can do for you?"

Royce eyed the fine dagger on his anvil. "I came to discuss inventory."

"M'lord?"

"It concerns the new tools and iron."

The blacksmith gave a blank stare.

Royce nodded toward the spread out tools. "Your new tools, the ones for working your trade?"

"But I have no new tools. These have served me well for

many years and continue to do so." He picked up pincers to show him. "I have no need for new. Truth to tell, I have grown partial to these and have made adjustments to them so they are just as I like them."

Uneasiness settled in Royce's stomach. "What of the iron? The last price seemed high."

"Nay, m'lord, the price has not changed. 'Tis the same as it has always been."

"I won't keep you from your work." Royce hesitated. "Do you mind?" He nodded toward the dagger the man had been working on.

"'Tis cooled." He handed it to Royce.

Royce ran his fingers over the dull blade. The workmanship surpassed most.

"'Twill be a fine sword."

The blacksmith smiled. "Thank ye. Perhaps fine enough for a lord?"

Royce grinned. "I look forward to knowing." He stepped away from the heat of the forge and into the sunlight. A cool breeze blew on his sweat-drenched skin. He lingered, motionless, facing the wind, allowing it to dry the dampness from his body. What went on here? Lyndle and the blacksmith were not in agreement, and he saw no reason for the blacksmith to lie.

†††

Brithwin walked in the courtyard, craving activity to ease her nerves. Eight days had passed since Royce departed for Rosen Craig, and her heart ached for his return. Hawkwood alone was no longer enough to keep her content. Royce had changed all that.

She smiled and touched a hand to her abdomen. Things were much different now. She was not certain, but she suspected she was with child. This would be her secret until she knew for certain. She couldn't trust Elspeth with it. Not after the last time when Elspeth just *thought* she was with child and spread the gossip through the castle. A shudder went through her body at the memory. There would be no doubts before Brithwin told anyone, including Royce.

Montfort passed in front of her followed by a sentry. Thomas would not tell her whether he was a guest or a prisoner. She guessed the latter. The man was never out alone and a set sentry stood at his door each night. The man seemed most pleasant, despite his treatment, and always spoke kindly to her. Speaking to the workers and the knights both, he walked about the bailey visiting.

Thomas was never far away, with his hawk-like sight bearing down on the man as if he were prey. It was obvious to her Thomas neither liked nor trusted him. She would avoid the man until Royce came home. From her husband's missive, it could be weeks before he was able to return to her. His assurance that he knew she was more than capable to oversee the castle was of little consolation, but she had to admit his confidence in her did please her.

She stopped in front of the mews. Lucas stepped out the door.

"Good day to you, Lucas," she said cheerfully.

"And to you, milady."

"Are you learning much about our hawks?"

His eyes sparkled as he told her all he had learned.

A cat screeched, and Thor bounded between her and Lucas, bumping into Brithwin in chase of the cat. Twisting to catch her balance, she stepped on the hem of her gown and began to fall. Two strong hands caught her arms and stopped her decent. Lifting her head, she peered into the cool grey eyes of Montfort. An icy chill trickled down her spine. Once she had her footing, she straightened and attempted to step away. His firm grip continued to hold her arms.

She jerked herself from his grasp. Thomas's deep voice

brought her head around. He glared at the man. "You forget yourself, sir."

Montfort's face remained emotionless. "The hound bolted into the lady. I meant only to keep her from falling."

"Aye, I know what you *meant*." Thomas flexed his fingers into fists. "Now, understand me well. You stay away from milady."

Montfort bowed and walked away.

Thomas turned his frown on her. "Milady, I would appreciate it if you would avoid that man. I do not trust him."

"In my defense, Thomas, he was walking a different direction when I came here to speak to Lucas."

"Be careful, milady, even inside our gates." Thomas held her gaze for a moment then strode toward the practice field.

"I don't like that man." Vehemence sounded in Lucas's voice.

Brithwin turned to see Lucas watching Montfort's retreat. "Why do you say such a thing?"

"Because he is a bad man."

†††

The days passed, each one slower than the one before. Brithwin found herself on the parapets daily, searching the horizon, waiting for Royce. What kept him from returning to her? No more missives had arrived from him explaining his delay. Could this separation have caused his feelings for her to change? *Not that*, she prayed. Especially now that she may be with child.

Exhausted, she dragged herself to her chamber and slipped out of her gown. Orange coals flickered in the fireplace. Tossing a log on, she gently blew on the coals until a warm fire took hold. She curled up in the large empty bed and drifted asleep.

When she woke, the fire had died, the torch out, and her room was dark. A hand clamped over her mouth, and a man leaned over her. Tossing her head from side to side, she attempted to pull free and call for help. She tore at his hand and thrashed her legs as she fought to get away. He pressed against her, stopping her twisting.

The low thunder of Thor's growl echoed in the silence. The man stilled. Brithwin wrenched her head away and let out a scream. Thor lunged toward the bed. The blackguard released her and fled toward the door. As he slipped out, Thor sank his teeth into flesh. The man gasped and slammed the door. Thor scratched frantically on the wood, letting out low growls. Brithwin ran to the door and called for Thomas. Thor slipped out the opening. The torches shone light on the escaping brigand. Brithwin gasped as Montfort disappeared from sight.

✝✝✝

Lyndle glanced across the empty hall before swinging around to face Clarice. "It is disgraceful the way you throw yourself at him."

"I want to spend time with him. He is the lord of Rosen Craig, and I wish to be mistress of Rosen Craig."

"'Twas not long ago you wished to spend time with me."

Clarice flitted her hand. "That was before I knew Lord Rosen Craig was still alive. I want what is rightfully mine."

Lyndle's mouth pinched. "His name is Royce not Bryce. This castle is not rightfully yours. You never married Bryce, might I remind you."

"But I *will* marry Lord Rosen Craig. Nothing has changed."

He snorted. "My lord is married and does not appear to be interested in you."

Clarice ran her finger along the chair. "Give him time. He has forgotten me, that is all. He loved me once. The king made him marry, did he not? It wasn't to my lord's choosing."

Lyndle's brow tightened. "Lord Rosen Craig never loved you."

"He did! He was my betrothed."

"You are mad, woman! Royce was not your betrothed." Clarice frowned, leaving tiny lines etched on her forehead. "N-nay. Lord Rosen Craig is my betrothed." She shook her head. "I will have him."

"Royce is honorable and will not set his wife aside. You do not know him if you think he will."

"Bryce tells me I am beautiful. He will still want me. Men oft tell me there is no beauty to match mine. I can win him back to me."

"Bryce is dead. There is no winning him back. You are mad."

"Do not call me that!" A glimmer shone in her eyes. "Lord Rosen Craig's wife could die."

He pointed his finger at her. "You threaten milady's life? What makes you think I would stand by and let you do such a thing?"

"I merely make an observation. But remember—I know *your* secrets."

Chapter 23

Royce ran up the steps to his solar and closed the door with a sigh. Clarice clung to him and demanded too much of his time. The woman would not leave him alone. A twinge of guilt niggled him. She had lost her betrothed and her father within a short span of each other. Her mother died when she was young, and her brother was a greedy scoundrel. It was no wonder she did not want to return to her home. It was admirable how she tried to be cheerful and to put up a good front for everyone.

A knock sounded on the door, breaking into his thoughts.

"Yes?" *Please, not Clarice.*

A servant peeked his head in. "Milord, there is a messenger below who wishes to speak to you. He said he is to give no one but you the message."

Irritation nudged Royce. "Where is he from?"

"He is one of the village lads."

Royce grimaced. "Send him up."

A moment later, the servant pushed the door open, admitting a boy who could not have seen eight years, his eyes wide as a frightened deer. The way he shuffled his feet on the floor, the lad reminded him of Lucas. Smiling, he called the boy in.

Royce looked to the servant. "Bring us something to drink, and see if you can find something sweet for this young lad."

A beam of pleasure covered the boy's face.

"What do they call you?"

The boy swept a lock of red hair out of his eyes. "Aldrid, sir."

"What is it you have been sent to tell me, Aldrid?"
The excitement drained from his face and he dropped his head. He peered through strands of dirty hair and Royce motioned him to sit. He would not get the full message if the boy were frightened speechless. One thing was for sure, if what the boy had to tell him was important, he needed him at ease.

"While we wait for our food, tell me, do you like horses?"
The lad nodded vigorously.
"Well, we have mighty fine ones here. Let me tell you about them." Royce talked about Shadowmere until the servant returned with their treats, calming the boy's nerves.

As Aldrid shoved in another bite of bread and honey, Royce leaned forward. "Can you tell me who sent the message?"
The boy nodded again, licking his fingers. "He was a knight." He frowned. "He looked mean."
Royce nodded and smiled. "Can you tell me what he looked like?"
He stopped cleaning his fingers with his tongue, but continued to hold his hand near his mouth. "He had a scar on his face."
Royce struggled to show no emotion. "Tell me the message."
Tears welled in the boy's eyes.
"Do not be afraid. I know of whom you speak, and he is not a good man. You will not be punished for bringing me his message."
Aldrid swallowed. "But you have been nice to me, and I do not want to tell you bad things."
Royce's heart skipped. Could Edmond have gotten to Brithwin? "I must know what he said, and you are the only one who can tell me."

"He said your parents died greffen . . . grevven?"

"Grieving?" His hands dug into the arms of the chair as he waited. He must withhold his furry and not frighten the child more.

Aldrid dropped his sticky hands into his lap and stared at them. "Aye, he said your parents died grieving for your death." He slowly lifted his head. "Does that mean you are going to die?"

"Nay, go on." Royce battled the urge to stand and pace the room.

The boy's gaze returned to his lap. "He said he liked watching their faces when he told them you were dead, and it was too bad they could not have suffered more before they died."

"Is that everything?" It was like pulling teeth, simply getting the answer he asked for.

He shook his head again. "He said you have a pretty wife."

Royce felt like someone had dumped ice water on him. "When did he give you this message?"

"Yesterday, when I was out fetching firewood."

By the rood! A day had passed since Edmond was on Rosen Craig land. "Why did you wait to come see me?"

Aldrid cowered back in his chair. "He told me if I did not do exactly as he said, he would hurt Mama. Are . . . are you angry at me?"

Royce launched himself from his chair. "Nay! It is not you who angers me. You have done well. Take the rest of the sweets, and get on home to your mother before she worries about you."

The boy pushed from his chair and scuttled away.

Royce waited for the door to shut and gave in to the urge to pace. Brithwin would suffer alongside him, now that he loved her. He couldn't change their being married, but he could distance himself from her. His gut roiled. To be unable to run his fingers through her hair, caress her cheek, or kiss her soft lips tore at his soul. He should stay away, but would his heart let him?

Royce plunged his hands through his hair. What had he done? He had married her but never planned to fall in love. Now, because of his love she was in danger. Why did God not strike him down if He was so angry with him? Why would He allow a woman with so much forgiveness in her heart, and so much faith in Him, to suffer for someone else's sins?

You bring pain to anyone who cares for you. You have failed God, just as you failed your family, and you will fail Brithwin.

Royce spun around at the wall and rubbed his face. What had Brithwin told him to think about? God would forgive him, but he had to forgive himself. He wished he could believe her words. They would be like a balm to his soul. Brithwin's goodness blinded her to the evil in him. She could not see that God looked at her much differently than He looked at him.

Royce stopped his pacing. Edmond had killed his parents. He was sure of it now, and to make it worse, Edmond had lied to his parents, telling them of their second son's death. The vile man had wanted them to suffer before he took their lives from them.

But now the question was, did Edmond remain here or return to Hawkwood?

Royce flung the door open, banging it against the wall, and stomped down the stairs bellowing for Jarren. He found him on the practice field, dripping wet.

"Jarren!"

His friend handed his practice sword to another knight and trudged to Royce. "What is wrong?"

"We must talk."

They headed back to the castle where Royce and Jarren spent the next several hours holed up in his solar while he explained all he had discovered about Lyndle and about Edmond's message.

Royce's mind drifted to Brithwin. He never would have believed *he* would miss a woman. "Let the men know we leave in the morning."

Jarren stretched out in his chair and folded his hands behind his head. "Are you sure you do not wish me to stay and keep an eye on Lyndle?"

"From what I can tell, that is the only discrepancy thus far. I would not have begrudged him extra money, had he asked." Royce stood and rubbed the sore muscles in his neck. "However, that is the least of my worries now. I only wish to get to Brithwin and Hawkwood."

Jarren pushed himself up and followed Royce out of the room. "I'll give you, Edmond is a threat. He has proven that. However, I am not sure the man is smart enough to be responsible for your family's murders."

"Yes, 'tis possible he uses the circumstances to goad me. When I capture him, and I assure you I will, then we will know for sure." Royce moved swiftly down the stone steps.

Jarren headed out to the bailey, and Royce went in search of Lyndle.

Royce came around the corner and nearly trampled Clarice. "I apologize, Clarice. I was not paying attention."

Clarice laid her hand on his sleeve. "Where are you off to in such a hurry, my lord? I have been looking for you for hours." Her fingers gently stroked his arm. "I wanted to ask you to take me hawking today."

"I am looking for Lyndle." He glanced down at the circling caress and thought of Brithwin. He grasped her fingers in his to cease the sensations threatening to awaken at the feminine touch.

"Lyndle went to the village. I'm sure he'll return quite late. So"—she dragged out the word—"will you take me hawking?"

He cast her hand away. "I cannot. We leave on the morrow, and I have things I must see to."

She folded her arms with a pout. "Where are you going?"

"I am returning to Hawkwood."

"You cannot leave me here," she whined.

Royce took in a deep breath and slowly let it out. "I have responsibilities at Hawkwood as well. If you do not wish to remain here, I am sure your brother will welcome you home."

"I will not go back there. He will marry me to a man thrice my age." Tears filled her eyes.

Royce groaned. Why did women do that? He could not stand to see a woman cry. That was one of the things he loved about Brithwin—she never used tears to control him. Truth was, he had never seen her weep.

A sniffle brought him back to the problem at hand. "You are welcome to stay here as long as you like."

"'Tis depressing here by myself. Everywhere I look are memories." Her eyes grew wide with excitement. "I could go with you. Your wife and I are sure to have much in common. 'Twould be a blessing to have a friend."

Maybe this was an answer to his problem. If Brithwin stayed occupied with Clarice, perhaps his absence from her would go unnoticed. For Brithwin's protection, he had resolved to put distance between them.

Brithwin would be a good influence on Clarice, the way she always put others before herself. It was a good match, if the chit didn't drive Brithwin mad. Women's ways were a mystery to him. "We leave by dawn's light. We will not dally, and if you are not ready, we will leave without you."

"I will be ready and waiting." She squeezed his arm and danced away.

†††

Lyndle scanned the silent village as he wove his way to the small cottage. Flickering lights shone in a few tenants' windows, the ones fortunate enough to have the means for candles and torches. Slinking inside the dark hut, he discovered Edmond already there.

"What do you want?" he hissed.

Edmond grinned, a sliver of moonlight casting a cold gleam on his face. "Now, now, let's not be too impatient."

Lyndle narrowed his eyes. "Get on with it."

Edmond pointed to a chair. "Sit. We have much to go over."

"Don't be giving me orders." He didn't move toward the chair. "Remember who outranks whom."

Edmond snickered. "That may change. I have had plenty of time to think about this, and 'tis the perfect time to make my move. I have designs on Rosen Craig and I need your help. As you know, it should have been mine to begin with."

"Nay, I will not help you." Lyndle's lips curled in a sneer. "The king will not allow you to be lord of that demesne."

"I will persuade him." Edmond leaned back in the chair and gazed at him. "You, however, have no choice in the matter. I would hate to have to share your ugly secret."

Lyndle glared at Edmond.

"I wouldn't want it ever to be said I am unfair." Edmond raised his brows. "To make this tempting for you, I will see to it you acquire Hawkwood and the lovely Brithwin. I had hoped to see her dead, but there is no need as long as Royce believes she is."

Lyndle gave Edmond a scathing look. "What makes you

think I would want her?"

"Don't act so high and mighty. I know you have had designs on her for, what, two years now? It is amazing what a bird will sing with a little torture." His smile didn't reach his eyes.

"What plans do you have for Lord Rosen Craig?"

Edmond met his eyes. "His name is Royce! He doesn't deserve his title, and he will have to go the way of his family."

Lyndle's eyes narrowed under Edmond's scrutiny. "What do you want from me?"

"I need access to Brithwin so I can steal her from Hawkwood." Edmond picked at the dirt under his nails.

Lyndle hesitated. "There is a way, but we would need to bring someone else into this."

"I will not risk this getting back to Royce."

"Her name is Clarice." Lyndle lowered himself into the chair. "She traveled to Hawkwood with Royce. Everyone knows she has designs on him. Except for maybe Royce." And Clarice at times. The woman seemed to be losing her mind, thinking Royce was Bryce.

Leaning forward, Edmond rested his arms on his legs and clasped his hands together. "Why would she help me kill Royce?"

Lyndle rolled his eyes. "You could not tell her that. But if she believes she is getting his wife out of the way, Clarice would do whatever you ask."

Edmond snorted. "How do I speak with her?"

"I think you will remember Clarice. You could not take your eyes off her the night you told Royce's family of his unfortunate demise."

A smile crept across his face. "Ah, the fair wench betrothed to Bryce."

He nodded. "That is the one. You could send a message

to her giving her a little of the information. If she thinks she stands to gain, she will come."

"When this is through, there will be much I can offer her."

Lyndle rose. "Do not muddle this, Edmond. I go along with you because I choose to. Royce may not have proof of your guilt—yet—but he already believes you guilty of his family's murders. If you cross me, I will suddenly remember things and confirm his suspicions." He strode to the door, opened it, and left.

He could feel Edmond's eyes on him as he crept out into the darkness and disappeared. He would let the fool believe he went along with things, as long as they were to his benefit. When they no longer were—Edmond was expendable.

✝✝✝

Brithwin sat in her garden, gathering herbs. The clopping of hooves grabbed her attention, and she looked up to see Royce ride into the bailey. She dropped the herbs from her hands and rushed out to the courtyard, her heart singing. He was home! Royce scanned the bailey and his eyes stopped on her. A smile spread over his face and he jumped from his horse. She flew into his arms and they wrapped around her like a warm blanket protecting her from the winter's cold. She laid her head on his chest—and his body became rigid. He stepped back.

Brithwin glanced past him. A woman sitting on a palfrey kept her gaze on Royce. Even with the scowl on her face, she was beautiful. Brithwin looked down at her gown and its usual state of disarray. She forced an uncertain smile to her lips. "'Tis good to have you home, husband."

The joy and relief in his eyes vanished, and she looked into the eyes of a man still fighting his demons. "'Tis good to be home. I have someone I wish you to meet." He walked to the beautiful woman, still sitting on her horse, and lifted her down. She smiled brightly, and he returned the smile. "Lady Rosen Craig, this is Clarice Coble. She was Bryce's betrothed."

Jealousy ripped through Brithwin. She suddenly felt like she needed to protect what was hers. This was Bryce's betrothed? She certainly wasn't looking at Royce like she grieved the loss of his brother. It was silly to feel like this, but the woman did not look at him as if he were family, at least not *that* kind of family.

They greeted each other as two she-wolves would— staking their claim. Royce excused himself, leaving the two. Brithwin narrowed her brows and lifted her chin as she turned from Clarice to call a servant. "Show Miss Coble to the guest room in the west wing." She turned back to Clarice. "I am sure you would like to clean up before the evening meal." Brithwin spun on her heel and headed to her own room to do the same.

Bryce's betrothed had ridden a horse all day and looked better than she did. Brithwin sent Elspeth for fresh water as she chose one of her nicer gowns. The joy that had filled her with Royce's return churned to something dark that she didn't like. She would take extra time to look nice for her husband.

A clamor of voices came from the great hall as she hurried through the corridor—the meal had started. Midway down the steps, Brithwin caught sight of Royce speaking to Clarice, who sat next to him at table. She stopped. He lowered his head in an intimate way, for Clarice's ears only. Clarice's hand covered his and she tilted her head and smiled. Brithwin bristled at the familiarity between the two. She glided the rest of the way down and feigned a smile.

"I am sorry I am late, dearling. I took longer than I thought," she said with contrived cheerfulness.

Royce jerked his hand back and rose. He reached for his

goblet. "We were just speaking of you." He waited for her to take her seat.

"Hmm." She would not give Clarice the satisfaction of thinking she was the least bit curious.

"What have you been doing in my absence? It looks as though you have been busy around here. Everything is in fine order," he said as he retook his seat.

"Nothing exciting." She took a bite of cheese.

Thomas cleared his throat, and all heads turned to him. "Milady, I have kept my part of the bargain, now you must keep yours."

She glowered at him. "'Tis nothing, Thomas. Leave be." She did not want to give Royce this news in front of *her*.

Thomas's brows shot up. "Why do you not let Lord Rosen Craig make that decision?"

"Yes, why not let me?" Royce cocked a brow.

Brithwin shot an irritated look at Royce.

Clarice leaned into Royce. "It is something she obviously wishes to keep from you."

That was enough. Brithwin had lived a secluded life in many ways, but she understood a threat when she saw it as Clarice leaned into Royce. She would not allow the woman to get away with suggesting she had done anything wrong.

Brithwin lifted her chin. "I assume Thomas did tell you Montfort took his leave of here. I hate to say *escape* because you never said he was a prisoner."

Royce nodded. "Yes, he informed me."

She smiled and tilted her head to the side. "It would seem he desired my company."

Thomas choked. "Don't make light of this, milady. The man came to either harm you or kidnap you. And while you slept."

Brithwin shrugged. "I suppose. Thor once again saved me. 'Tis hard to say what would have happened had he not been sleeping next to my bed."

Royce threw back his wooden chair. Placing his hands on the table, he leaned forward, eyeing Thomas. "Why did you not tell me this when we arrived?"

"Because I asked him not to." Brithwin's words came out a little more forceful than she'd wished. The great hall quieted and all eyes turned to watch the commotion on the dais.

Thomas appeared unconcerned with the stares. "I will speak for myself, milady." Turning to Royce, he rose from his chair. "I have protected milady since the day she came from her mother's womb. Think you that I would ever do anything to jeopardize her? I would die for her. She asked me to allow her to tell her husband, and I granted the request. I have served her for near one score years, and I will not lightly turn away one of her requests if it is reasonable. Had you learned of this a few hours ago, 'twould change nothing."

Royce closed his eyes and drew in several breaths. "It is not you I am angry with. I knew the man was not to be trusted and should have taken stronger precautions."

Clarice interrupted, drawing the men's attention. "See, everything turned out fine."

"Nay." Royce turned to Brithwin. "It is not over. I have put you in harm's way just by our association as husband and wife." His gaze pleaded with her. "I am sorry, Brithwin. You do not deserve this."

Brithwin's heart skipped a beat. The sorrow in those beautiful golden brown eyes was for her. She was still the woman he cared for. She smiled and felt the joy return all the way to her toes. "'Tis fine, my lord, for I know you will keep me safe."

Pride covered his face when the words left her lips. But it faded and what replaced it she could not name but knew she did not like, for with the look came determination. "You are not to leave Hawkwood without me, my lady." She jumped at Royce's sharp tone. "Until Montfort and Edmond are apprehended, you are not safe." Clarice popped her head up. "Who is Edmond?" Royce tapped his eating knife on the table. "A man who would go to great lengths to do me harm." "Well, it is good I have come! We will become best of friends, you and I, my lady." Royce's eyes lit up. "That is kind of you, Clarice. I am sure you two will get along well. You were almost sisters by marriage." "I doubt Clarice wants to stay here locked inside. She was just being kind." Brithwin forced a smile and glanced at Clarice. "Not at all. I have never had the company of a sister or someone my age. So, you see, I am a little selfish." Royce's gaze bounced from Brithwin to Clarice. "Then it is settled. You will stay here as long as you like." Brithwin chewed her bottom lip as Clarice looked at her smugly. He had just played into Clarice's hand. Royce had given this woman an open invitation. Was he blind to her purpose? That purpose, Brithwin was certain, had nothing to do with being her friend.

Chapter 24

Brithwin paced her room. Clarice's visit wore on her. They would never be friends. "How can a man be so blind? 'Tis obvious she has her designs on him."

Elspeth looked up from her embroidery. "Mayhap he is just being kind."

She paused as Elspeth pulled another stitch. "Nay, he is blind. I can see it in his eyes."

Elspeth chuckled.

Brithwin crossed her arms and scowled. "What do you find so humorous?"

"Nothing. I was just . . . oh, never mind."

"He ignores me in favor of her." She ran her hands down the front of her gown.

"Get his attention." Elspeth took another stitch. She poked herself and yelped then stuck her finger in her mouth.

"That is a good idea." Brithwin walked to the window, placed her hands on the frame, and peered out. "It has been a sennight since her arrival, and she has stolen every moment she could with him. He comes to his chamber long after I have retired and rises before I wake. I do not even get *that* time with him! I must do something to turn the tide."

Aye, she would not sit by idle, waiting to discover her fate. She would fight for her husband. God had given him to her. She would not allow another woman to steal him. An inspiration came to mind and with it a grin. She pivoted around.

Elspeth popped her head up. "I see you have thought of something. What do you intend to do?"

She spun around and spoke with glee in her voice. "I will tell him I am with child!"

"Oh! A baby! 'Tis wonderful news." Elspeth squealed and launched herself from her chair then paused. "'Tis true, is it not?"

Brithwin stopped and snatched hold of the chair back to steady herself. "Of course, 'tis true. I would not lie to him."

"Why did you not tell me?" Hurt filled Elspeth's voice.

"I wanted to be sure, after the last rumors flew around here."

Elspeth blushed. "I will not say a word to anyone until you tell me I can."

"Thank you." Brithwin let go of the chair and swung around to sit in it. "Now, help me make a plan."

†††

Brithwin set her basket on the small table in their solar and sighed. They had put the plan in motion. She paused to send up a prayer all would go as hoped.

"Do you think he will come before he eats?" Elspeth gazed at her intently.

She lifted the cloth off the basket. "If you have done as I asked, he will be here. Help me finish putting the food out."

"I told Lucas to tell Philip to tell milord he was needed in his solar, and I told him to be sure it was before the dinner hour." Elspeth giggled. "I hope he can keep it straight. Just thinking about it confuses me."

"He is a smart boy. He will say it precisely as you told him to." Brithwin placed the cups on the table and sighed. "I wish we could lock the door from the outside so when Royce enters he cannot escape before I have a chance to tell him."

Elspeth pulled out the bread and cheese and laid it in the center of the table. "Do you wish me to wait in your chamber should you need something?"

"Nay, go and enjoy your meal. I will be fine." As Elspeth closed the door, Brithwin called out to her. "Do say a prayer for me."

A few minutes later, shoes clunked on the stairs. Waiting for the door to open, Brithwin's heart pounded. Royce pushed the door open and stepped in. His gaze swept the room, settling on her. "I was told I was needed here. You who need me?"

"'Aye. I have not seen you unaccompanied since your return, and I wished for time alone with my husband." She waved her hand before the food in a simple gesture. "I have had our food brought to our solar to allow us time by ourselves."

Royce's hesitation drew out, leaving an uncomfortable silence.

"That was thoughtful of you. However, do you not think it would be rude if we fail to show for the evening meal?"

"Oh, aye, very rude indeed!" She grinned. "That is why I asked Thomas to make our excuses."

"I see." He slowly walked to the table.

"Sit and we can eat and talk in private."

They took their seats and Brithwin chattered, trying to draw Royce out. His lack of response to her attempts at light conversation weighed heavily on her fleeting certainty that this was a good idea.

She pushed her trencher away and took in a deep breath before plunging in. "I miss the time we had together before you left for Rosen Craig. You have changed . . . distanced yourself from me. Have I done something wrong?"

Royce tapped his eating utensil lightly on the table. "Nay, you have not. People are out there who will harm you because of me, as you have already discovered. Next time, we may not be so lucky."

"There was no luck involved." Reaching across the table, Brithwin clasped his hands. "God protected me and kept me safe. Nothing will happen to me He does not allow. You have to trust Him."

Royce drew his hands back and shook his head. "I know this is what you believe, but what if the punishment for my sins hurts you?"

"Your sins have already been paid for. Christ paid for them when He died on the cross. God is not punishing you for them." She straightened and slid her hands onto her lap, missing the warmth of his skin. "Aye, there are consequences to our sins, but the punishment is paid. You need only accept forgiveness. I wish I could make you see."

"You do not know how much I desire to believe that, my lady." Royce unfolded himself from the chair and lingered a moment as if undecided what he would say. "I have enjoyed this eve with you. However, I must get down and speak with Jarren."

A bolt of urgency shot through her. "Wait!" She bolted to her feet.

Royce paused.

"I have one more thing I must tell you. I hope you will consider it good news. It pleases me."

Royce smiled. "You sound more frightened than happy."

Brithwin looked at her hands as she smoothed invisible wrinkles out of the cloth covering the table. "I do not know how you will . . . feel about it. We have not discussed it thus far."

Royce shifted his weight then cocked his head. "You have me intrigued."

"I am with child." The words melded together as she blurted them out.

Royce blinked. "Did you say you are to have a babe?"

Her eyes locked on to his. "Aye, *we* are."

"I am to have an heir." A smile spread across his face, lighting his eyes, bringing her joy.

"You mean *we* will have an heir," she corrected.

"When is the child due?"

Brithwin grinned. "I am thinking eight months."

"Oh, aye, eight months and I am to be a father." He smiled and then quickly added, "And you will be a mother." He strode toward the door, and with each step her insides twisted a little more. She needed to know his feelings. "You are pleased, then?"

Reaching for the handle, he turned. "I am very pleased." He disappeared into the hall. She wanted to scream. *He was very pleased.* Indeed! She was still grumbling when the roar of applause came from the great hall.

"I cannot believe he walked out of here and told everyone in the great hall. You would think I have no part in this."

Elspeth peeked her head in. "Who are you talking to?"

Brithwin sighed and let her shoulders drop. "To myself."

"My lord is in the great hall boasting about his heir." She stepped into the room. "You have made him a happy man."

She crossed her arms and tapped her toe. "Have I? He did not stay around long enough for me to find out."

"Clarice did not seem pleased with the news. Between her pinched face and her puckered lips, she looked as if she just kissed a pig." Elspeth covered her mouth, hiding her snicker.

That made Brithwin smile. "Well, mayhap it will all work out. I need to listen to my own words. I told Lord Rosen Craig he must trust the Lord, but sometimes I forget it myself."

Elspeth scooped the basket from the floor and began clearing the table. "Clarice will have a hard time winning milord's attentions now."

"I do not plan to hide in here now that he has gone down. Let us go meet the well-wishers."

†††

Royce halted to observe Brithwin in her garden. She was

unhappy, but he could not help that *and* keep her safe. Right now, keeping her out of harm's way was more important. Now he had two with whom to concern himself.

"Where have you been, my lord? I have looked everywhere for you."

Royce turned at the silky sound of Clarice's voice. He sighed inwardly. "I have been here."

She glanced around as if she sought his interest. "Ah, you are watching your wife. You are concerned about her, also."

His eyebrows drew together. "Why are you concerned for my wife?"

"She is very unhappy." Clarice's face fell. "Especially since she found out she is with child. She worries you will not find her attractive and when the child comes you will give it all your attention."

Royce's blood heated. "She has told you this?"

Clarice's eyes grew wide. "Oh! You must not tell her I said anything, my lord. She would never speak to me again."

"Nay, my lady is too forgiving."

Clarice laid her hand on his arm. "Then she has changed. Please keep what I have said between us. If you were to confront her with it, she would not speak freely to me anymore."

How could Brithwin be unhappy about an heir? She didn't seem so when he'd left her in the solar to share his good fortune with everyone. Perhaps he should have remained a little longer and sought out her real feelings.

He studied Clarice. She looked sincere. "I will say nothing to her."

Clarice let out her breath. "Thank you. I do not wish to harm our friendship, but as her husband, I felt you should know."

He excused himself to get on with his duties. He didn't

enjoy Clarice's company and he needed time to think.

††††

Royce hadn't heard nor seen anything of Montfort as the days passed by quietly. Perhaps the man had moved on to easier pickings. Edmond must have holed up somewhere off Hawkwood land. He had sent out regular patrols, and there were no signs of him. Mayhap his distancing himself from Brithwin had appeased God's desire to punish him through her, and he could relax. At least part of his life was falling into some sort of order.

He had seen little of Brithwin, but what he did see, he didn't like. She'd lost weight, her face appeared drawn, and she ate little. It was hard at first to believe Clarice's words that Brithwin was not happy about the child. However, he began to, for she rarely smiled and the sparkle had left her eyes. It was as if her joy had left her, and she trudged through life because she had no other choice.

The flash of a memory burned him—Brithwin as she entered the great hall after the discovery of her friends' brutal murders. Her eyes lacked the vibrancy he had come to expect in her. Much like now. It tore at his heart. He loved her yet could not tell her. He longed to hold her and console her, but to do so would undermine his own attempts at keeping her safe. The yearning for her laughter, to witness the glow on her face, tugged at him, but he would have to content himself with their few memories, for the time being.

He trotted to the practice field. It was always a good liberation for stress.

Royce threw himself into the mock battle. The second man fell. A young knight faced him, his gaze wavering between Royce and the man he'd just sent to his knees, gasping for air.

Royce goaded, "You will never win a battle standing there, and your friend will obviously be no help."

Royce raised his sword, and the battle began. He swung and parried, lunged and sidestepped. The sweat dripped down his face, stinging his eyes. Battle hardened muscles complained, and his breathing strained. His foe stumbled. Royce grinned. Time to go in for the kill. The blunted practice blade touched the throat of his opponent.

"Do you yield to me?" Royce gasped.

"Mercy, milord, mercy!" the young knight cried.

Royce moved away and let him fall to the ground panting. A slap hit his shoulder.

"I see you haven't lost your touch, old boy. What was that, three? And all younger than you." Jarren's eyes danced with amusement. "You won't have to worry about them challenging your position."

Royce grabbed his shirt from the ground and wiped his face. "They seem to come from nowhere when I pick up a blunted sword."

"They want bragging rights to say they beat their lord."

"I detest the day that comes." He pulled the shirt over his head. "And here I thought they fought me only to learn from my skills." He chuckled.

"They learn from you. Each time, they take a little more with them in hopes the next time you will be the one begging for mercy." Jarren pulled off his shirt and picked up the practice sword.

Royce glanced at the men circled around waiting for action. The young men were no match for Jarren, either.

"I can see you men need some excitement. Perhaps a boar hunt is warranted."

Backslapping and good-natured jesting ensued.

Royce headed toward the manor, parched. As he made his way, laughter and boasting of previous hunts floated through the air.

The young knight's words returned to him. *Mercy,*

milord, mercy. He shuddered. Would he someday stand before his Lord crying, "Mercy, Lord, mercy"? The words sent a dark cloud over him, for he would find none. Of late, his mind wandered more and more to those dark thoughts. If he could only banish them.

Clarice moved quickly toward him as he made his way to the castle. "My lord, I need to speak to you." Her breathless voice raised the hairs on his arms.

"Aye?"

"First, I want you to know my lady is fine." She grasped his arm. "But she took a fall down the stairs. Lord Rosen Craig, I would not tell you this, but I worry for her. She did not trip. I saw her throw herself down the steps. I think she tries to lose the child. When I spoke to her about it, she got angry with me."

"Where is she?"

"She is in her bed. I insisted she rest. Please do not be angry with her. She is very upset."

Royce turned and met her gaze. "You are a true friend, Clarice. Brithwin is lucky to have you."

She smiled at him. The smile didn't reach her eyes, but it must be due to her concern for his wife.

Royce ran, his long strides taking up the distance between him and the manor. He flung the door open and marched up the stairs and into Brithwin's room. "How is the babe?"

Elspeth dropped the goblet she held in her hands and scuttled after it.

"You may leave, Elspeth." Royce ground out the words. "I will call you when I leave."

Elspeth rushed to the door and disappeared as Brithwin pushed herself onto her elbows. "Is something wrong?"

"Is something wrong?" His voice rose with his temper. "Of course, something is wrong. You could have lost the babe."

She laid back and, placing her hand on her belly and stared dully at the ceiling. "But I did not."

Royce snorted. "Until it happens again."

Did he know this woman? They had never discussed children. How was he supposed to know she wouldn't want a babe? Most women were pleased to be with child.

Brithwin frowned. "What mean you?"

He clenched his teeth and glared at her, but she didn't flinch. "Did you try to lose the child?"

Brithwin's mouth dropped open and quickly closed. "Your guest, Clarice, pushed me, and I could not stop the fall!"

Royce took two quick strides to the bed and brought his hands down on it. He lowered his face to hers. "You accuse her? She rushed to tell me you had fallen, worrying about you, telling me not to be angry with you, and you lay blame on her?"

"Get out. Get out!" She fell back.

He straightened and strode to the door. He paused and scowled over his shoulder at her. "That is my child, too. Have a care."

Royce stomped down the stairs and out into the fresh air. Did he truly believe Brithwin could harm their unborn child, or was this a way he could drive a wedge between them? He told himself it mattered not, for it achieved his purpose. She would remain safe.

††††

Brithwin stared at the door Royce had walked out. She swallowed the lump in her throat, but it would not leave. "I will not cry. It does not accomplish anything. 'Tis weakness." Her voice threatened to betray her. Closing her eyes, she pushed the heels of her hands against them, drawing on her inner strength. She would not let one tear fall.

They were useless.

How could he believe Clarice over her? Worse yet, how could he think such a wretched thing about her? *God has forsaken you, Brithwin. 'Tis time to give up. Your husband believes another woman. He cares naught for you. Did he ask about you? Nay, he only inquired on the unborn child. If God really cared, would He make you go through these trials your whole life?*

Brithwin lay on her bed—a hole gaped where her heart once beat. She had lost her chance at happiness. Royce no longer cared for her nor desired her as his wife. Now that he believed she had tried to end their child's life, he would never want her.

Sleep beckoned to her. Someone entered her chamber, but exhaustion won out and she drifted off.

When she opened her eyes, Elspeth sat beside her bed. Disquiet creased her brow. "Can I get you anything?"

Brithwin shook her head. She wasn't sure she trusted her voice to be strong.

"You have been sleeping for a long while. I had become concerned."

Brithwin swallowed. "Distress has likely worn me out."

Elspeth, with her haggard face, red eyes, and pinched brows truly cared for her. God had sent this friend in her hour of need, one who had always been there and one that she needed to appreciate more.

The despair lifted. God had not left her. The enemy planted seeds of doubt, and she allowed them to grow. She must remember who she belonged to and where to put her trust.

Brithwin lifted her hand and placed it on Elspeth's. "You are a true friend."

Tears gathered in Elspeth's eyes and trailed down her cheeks. "You have never called me friend."

Brithwin smiled. "I have not, and I have been remiss in not doing so."

†††

Montfort slipped through the trees silently. He couldn't get anywhere near Pater. Temporarily giving up, he sought Edmond off Royce's land. Luckily, he had evaded Hawkwood men thus far. Their daily patrols had become a nuisance. He squatted and peered over the lush green underbrush. The site where Edmond and his men slept remained quiet. He wished he had come up with a plan to his advantage. If he were to hand the information of Pater to Edmond, he would get naught for his part in it. He had to figure out a way to make Edmond pay for it.

Cold steel pressed against the side of Montfort's neck and he stiffened. He dare not flinch. He liked his neck.

"What are you doing here, lurking about?" Edmond's gruff voice came from behind him.

"If you take the blade from my throat, I will answer you."

The blade dropped away and he spun around. "You could have killed me."

Edmond lifted the knife and pressed the tip into the skin over Montfort's heart. The steel point stung his flesh, and a drop of blood penetrated the cloth. "You would deserve it for skulking around, not making yourself known. What are you doing here? Did I not give you orders to find a place at Hawkwood?"

He jerked back and pushed away the knife. "Aye, after you beat me near unconscious."

Edmond shrugged. "I see you survived. Now, tell me why you are here and not there."

Montfort leaned against the nearest tree and folded his arms. "Royce did not believe the farce. I had my own personal guard, even when I could barely pull my body from

Debbie Lynne Costello

the bed."

"Did you do something to make him doubt you?" Edmond's eyes narrowed.

"Nay, you did. 'Twas a mistake to leave me in the same place you killed the family. Insisting I give him a message added to his distrust. 'Twas not a good tactical move."

"How did you escape?"

"I took advantage of a lapse of their judgment. Once out of the gates, I have continued to elude the patrols sent out from Hawkwood. However, I heard rumor of a large group departing in a few days to boar hunt. I decided to move on, lest I be spotted."

"Your story sounds false. Do you work for Royce now?" Edmond lifted his sword.

"I work for myself. I come with information." He hesitated. "To sell."

"Fair enough. Tell me what you know."

Montfort studied Edmond's face. "What will you give me for it?"

Edmond grinned. "Your life, of course."

Montfort peered into the ice-cold eyes of Edmond and flinched. He had made an error in trying to bargain with Edmond. "How do I know you will let me live if I give it to you?"

Edmond smirked at him. "You don't. It depends on how valuable I think your information is. What you do know is, if you don't tell me, I will end your life, here, and now."

If he had been able to retrieve a sword before he escaped, this could be a fair fight. Without a weapon, he stood no chance. Edmond had no honor.

"'Tis about a man they call Pater."

Edmond fingered the hilt of his sword. "Go on."

When he finished speaking, Edmond smiled.

"'Tis good news for you, my friend. This information

could help me obtain Rosen Craig with the king's blessing." He slapped him on the back. "Let us celebrate with a drink, and we can make plans on how we will acquire this Pater."

Chapter 25

Royce rode his warhorse, with Lucas sitting behind him. The men wove their way through the trees and brush, following the game trail. Twilight approached, and they had the boar nearly worn down from the chase. The woods and evening air carried the bantering and laughter of his men, meant to hone the animal's fear and keep it running on its familiar trail.

"Get him cornered," a knight yelled. "'Tis getting late."

Voices rang out simultaneously. "Aye."

The men surrounded the exhausted animal and dismounted from their horses with thuds. As they drew their pikes and lances, the beast pawed the ground.

Royce remained on his horse, talking with Jarren. The men's antics would normally be entertaining, but despite ensuring Brithwin's safety within the bailey, he itched to get back and see for himself all was well there. As if sensing his discomfort, the horse flicked his ears and sidestepped.

Lucas leaned around Royce's body and peered up at him. "Milord, can I get down and see?"

"Aye, but stay out of the men's way and the boar's."

"He reminds me of myself when I was his age." Jarren's gaze was on the boy as he walked away. "Full of energy and too curious for my own good."

Royce chuckled. "I am afraid that is a trait many of us can lay claim to."

"I am surprised he wished to come with us, knowing he rescued the chicken." Jarren grinned and shook his head.

"They got 'im, they got 'im! Come see!" Lucas jumped up and down, waving his arms in a wild gesture.

Jarren faced Royce, amusement glimmering in his eyes.

"I believe you have been summoned."

"I think that was for both of us." Royce smirked.

Royce threw his leg off Shadowmere when a burning jolt knocked him to the ground. Jarren shouted, and before Royce could lift himself off the forest floor, his men surrounded him with swords drawn; another shout came then horses running into the woods. Royce examined the arrow that had sliced through his shoulder. "Break it and pull it out."

"Should you wait until we get to Hawkwood? We can take better care of it there," Jarren suggested while probing the place of penetration.

Royce held his saddle for stability. "I am not riding into Hawkwood with an arrow protruding from my shoulder. If you do not want to pull it out, I will do it myself."

Jarren broke the tip from the arrow, tossing it to the ground, and went to his horse where he pulled a piece of cloth from his pack. He returned to Royce and handed the cloth to him. "Hold this." He grasped the arrow. "'Twill be quick." As he spoke, he jerked the arrow out.

Royce hissed and pressed the cloth against the wound.

Minutes later, the men on horseback returned.

One of them approached. "Whoever it was is gone."

"Did you see any tracks?" Jarren looked the men over.

"We found one set but lost them along the river."

Royce pressed harder against the small round opening to stanch the flow of blood. "'Tis time to head home."

They mounted and set out for Hawkwood, with Lucas riding behind Jarren this time. The men encircled Royce, making a human shield.

On Royce's orders, the portcullis remained closed until their return. Jarren sent a man ahead, and it stood open by the time they reached the gate. The horses thundered through the opening and into the busy courtyard.

Within minutes, Royce slumped in his chair with

Marjory clucking her tongue while she tended to his injury. "You should not have pulled the arrow out, milord. It does more damage."

Royce humphed.

The heavy wooden solar door creaked open and light footsteps padded to his chair. He didn't have to turn to know who approached.

†††

Brithwin gasped when she reached her husband. His shirt lay on the floor covered in blood, and a metallic odor filled her nose. Marjory leaned over him with a bloody rag.

He didn't turn to acknowledge her. "Looks worse than 'tis, my lady."

Her heart nearly beat out of her chest. "You would tell me that if you were on your deathbed."

Marjory's hand stilled on Royce's bare chest and she gazed up at her. "He tells the truth."

Legs still weak, Brithwin dropped to her knees and lifted his hand to her cheek. "What happened?"

"I was hit with an arrow. I will be fine."

His assurance of his well-being did no good as another tremor coursed through her body. "Who did this?"

His body stiffened. "You know I have enemies. People who would like to see me dead."

She laid her head on his lap, still clutching his hand to her cheek. How she wished he would touch her, but at least he was not pushing her away. "I am sorry," she whispered.

"Don't be." His voice was harsh. "'Tis not the first scar I have sustained and will not be my last."

The door swung open, and Clarice rushed into the solar.

"Oh, Lord Rosen Craig, you poor man." Her voice warbled as she crossed the room. "Can I do anything to help you? I am good in healing."

She glanced at Brithwin with a smug look and hastened

around to situate herself before Royce. Sniffling, she made a display of wiping the tears from her face. Brithwin rolled her eyes with disgust and sat up.

Royce's tone softened. "Do not cry, Clarice. Marjory is doing a fine job taking care of me."

"But you must be in pain. I cannot endure the thought of you suffering." Her coddling tone sent sharp needles into Brithwin's nerves.

The woman was a fraud. Why couldn't Royce see that? Did he not see the bright red pinch marks on her cheeks to bring the false tears? His lack of discernment irritated her even more. "Did you not hear him? He said the ministration Marjory gives him is sufficient. You are not needed here."

Clarice rose and flounced from the room.

"Lady Rosen Craig," Royce chastised, "that was uncalled for. The poor woman has been through much with the loss of Bryce and her father. You should be kinder to her."

Brithwin choked. Kinder to her! She wanted to scream and stomp her feet. It was childish, but she felt certain it would make her feel better. She took a deep breath, released his hand, and rose.

She lifted her chin. "I can see you are in too much pain to think clearly. I will leave and allow Marjory to tend to you." She marched from the room, wishing she could make her husband see the truth in that woman.

✝✝✝

Three days passed since the removal of the arrow, and Royce remained free of fever. Brithwin knelt in the chapel. *Thank You, Lord, for keeping him safe and well.* She had spent many hours here on her knees, lifting her husband up and praying for guidance. Ready to leave, she tugged open the door and stepped out of the chapel into the warm sunshine. She strolled across the bailey, kicking up dust as she went. Grey, it fit her mood. The bright sun did nothing to lift her spirits.

How Clarice's deception could take in an intelligent man like her husband baffled her. The woman followed Royce around more than Thor trailed Brithwin. It was obvious she would like to replace her as Royce's wife. Was she the only one who could see what Clarice wanted? Nay, Marjory and Elspeth both saw it. It was the men who were blinded by Clarice's beauty.

Nothing had been the same since Royce brought the woman home with him. He had distanced himself from her, and Clarice took advantage of it, vying for his attention.

She could not get through this on her own. God would have to give her the strength to weather this storm, and the wisdom to know how to handle it. Why were things so hard for her? She would climb one hill to see she had a steeper one ahead. Now, more than ever, doubt poked its ugly head up, trying to persuade her God didn't care. It was a daily battle.

She would do what she must to make Royce happy, and if it meant befriending Clarice, she would do it. But she should use caution. If Clarice truly did mean to push her down the stairs, she was capable of doing anything. The good thing about it was, if Clarice stayed with her, she could not be with Royce.

Brithwin had finished walking the interior of the courtyard when she came upon Royce showing Clarice the mews.

She forced a smile. "I have been looking for you, Clarice."

"You have?" Clarice glanced at Royce.

"I thought we could spend time together, get to know each other. 'Tis Royce's wish. Is that not right, dearling?"

Royce lifted one eyebrow. "Aye."

"I could finish showing her the mews. You have been busy of late. I am sure you have much to do, husband."

"My lord, I did not mean to take so much of your time." Clarice's whine reminded Brithwin of the high-pitched wail of a cat with its tail caught.

The thought made her lips twitch. She bit the inside of her mouth to stifle the smile.

Brithwin stepped around the clawed-up wooden perch and ran her hand down Talon's smooth feathers. "Dearling, you go attend to your work. Clarice and I shall become best of friends, inseparable. After all, we were practically sisters by marriage, isn't that what you said?"

Royce gave a slight bow. "Aye. I am pleased to hear. Then I will take my leave of you ladies and your new friendship."

When Royce disappeared, Clarice pounced on Brithwin like their terrier on rats. "The mews have suddenly lost interest to me," she snarled at her and stomped away.

Quickening her pace, Brithwin caught her. She would not let her off so easy. "What would you like to do then?"

Clarice stopped and swung around. "Nothing with you."

Brithwin opened her eyes wide in mock surprise. "You do not wish to be my friend? What else could keep you here?"

"I do not wish to go home and bear my brother's vindictiveness. If I am not there, he forgets I exist." Clarice threw the words over her shoulder as she started walking again. "Why do you not go about your own business? You have accomplished what you came to do."

"I told Royce I would be your companion, and that is what I intend to do. I am a woman of my word." The conviction in her voice belied the twisting of her insides. She would make herself spend time with Clarice. What if she was wrong about her? Brithwin could understand Clarice wanting to get away from a cruel brother.

She had lived her whole life waking up and wondering what kind of brutality her father had in store for her. She'd tried to stay out of her father's sight so he wouldn't think about her. Perhaps Clarice and she were more alike than she thought. But didn't Clarice push her down the stairs? She had denied it from the beginning. Could Clarice have bumped her and not realized it?

Clarice sniffed. "*As am I a lady of my word.* What could you possibly do that would interest me?"

"I told Marjory I would fix a draught for a young boy in the village."

Despite the scowl Clarice shot her, Brithwin explained the symptoms of the cough ailing the child and what Marjory had asked her to prepare.

Once they entered the kitchen, Brithwin set to work. Clarice stayed back as Brithwin dug through baskets of herbs, searching for what she needed. It wasn't long before Clarice inched her way up, making suggestions of a salve to rub on the boy's chest.

Clarice's understanding of the different herbs and their uses surprised her. The woman seemed too much about herself to be interested in healing potions for others. As much as she did not want to admit it, Clarice's knowledge far surpassed her own in the uses of herbs. Only because she cared more for the boy than for her pride did Brithwin ask for her opinion and take her advice.

They had been working together for most of the day before Brithwin allowed herself to relax. She listened intently as Clarice explained some of the less-known attributes of the different herbs. When they had finished what Marjory had asked of her, plus the salve, they went out to the garden, where Clarice continued to explain to her the simple and more complex herbs a healer uses.

The next few days, Brithwin went out with Clarice to the garden, where she taught her a vast amount of information, even so much as drawing pictures of plants that could be found outside the castle walls that would be wise to keep on hand. She learned things she'd always desired to know but never had anyone take the time to show her. She loved to learn and sought to know all of Clarice's expertise.

As the days passed, she began having doubts as to whether she had misjudged Clarice. She'd been so upset when she'd fallen, it was possible she remembered it wrong. Perhaps Royce was right. He was her husband, and she should trust his opinion. Clarice hadn't given her any reason of late to believe she was scheming to steal him from her.

In the evenings, if they were not busy sewing, Brithwin taught Clarice to play chess.

"Does my lord play chess much?" Clarice wrapped a long strand of hair around her finger.

"Aye, he likes to relax and play a game in the evenings, when he is able." Brithwin raised her head but kept her fingers on her knight.

"I never see him play."

"He has been busy." Brithwin scanned the board before letting go of her chess piece and completing her move. "He doesn't usually play with dice."

Clarice frowned. "Then why did you teach me with dice?"

"'Tis the easiest way to play."

"But I wish to learn how to play like my lord." Clarice's voice came out in her cat-like whine.

Brithwin tensed and drew her brows together. "You play with me, so why should it matter?"

Clarice stared at the pieces on the board. She picked one up and eyed Brithwin, twirling it in her fingers. "I meant nothing by it. I thought, if my lord plays without dice, then most men would play the same way, and I might want to play chess with a man sometime."

The request seemed reasonable. Brithwin relaxed. "When you have mastered chess with the dice, I will teach you how to play without them."

Clarice smiled. "Thank you."

†††

Brithwin sat next to Pater in the chapel the following day. So unlike him, he fidgeted as she waited for him to speak—to tell her why he had summoned her here. His eyes, so kind and gentle, held the familiar pain she'd known her whole life.

His smile faltered. "I have been burdened with this since"—he paused as if unsure of his next words—"your father died."

Laying her hand on his, she squeezed. "What has troubled you?"

His gaze wandered from their hands to the front of the chapel, where a large metal cross rested on a table. "I fear you will not forgive me."

Brithwin smiled though he did not see. "I cannot imagine anything that I would ever have to forgive you for. You have always been so good to me—like a father." She stroked his wrinkled hand. "What is it you wish to tell me?"

Pater turned to gaze into her eyes. "Do you remember when you asked me why your father kept me here? I told you the story was for another day?"

Her insides quivered at the thought of what he would tell her, but she didn't know why. She nodded. "I remember."

He let out a breath. "Your mother and I traveled north together. She went to visit her family in Scotland. We met not long before she planned to depart on her trip. I had stopped in her village to share God's word with the people living there."

He dropped his head. "I was weak and fell in love with your mother. She had great inner beauty as well as outer. We married quickly so I could take the journey with her as her husband. I thought to travel to Scotland and share the bible there, as the Lollards had not reached so far north."

Brithwin's jaw quivered. "Y-you were married to my mother? Then how—"

Pater's eyes turned glassy. "When we arrived here for shelter and rest, the Lord of Hawkwood took one look at your mother and wanted her. Your mother was ill, so we stayed longer than planned. We hoped she would recover quickly so we could get on our way.

But before we could leave, your father discovered I was a follower of John Wycliffe. A hundred questions raced through her mind, but only one came out. "Why?"

"Why did he really want me dead?" A sad smile lingered on his lips. "So he could marry your mother."

She tried to grasp all he told her, but things did not make sense. "I know Lollards were killed, so why did my father spare you if he wanted your wife?"

Pater pulled up the collar of his tunic and held his hand on his neck. "He attempted to have me killed."

Brithwin's eyes widened. "Attempted how?"

Pater's hand tightened. "He hung me."

"Yet you are still here." Her eyes dropped to where his hand rested on his neck.

"Aye, the rope snapped—a perfectly good rope. When that happened, your father feared God's hand on me and His wrath should he take my life, so he imprisoned me instead with little food and hoped I would die of sickness as many do."

Brithwin searched Pater's eyes. "Why would he think that my mother would marry him?"

"I cannot answer that, child. I do not know the madness

that went through that man's head."

Brithwin's mind raced. Things did not make sense. "I don't understand."

He looked away. "Have you never wondered why your father hated you so?"

"It was because my mother died giving birth..."

He turned back to her and their gazes met. "Aye. I am your father."

Brithwin's heart galloped inside her, stealing her breath and her voice. All these years, nay it could not be. The pounding in her ears matched the galloping of her heart. Strength seeped from her, and she was thankful she was sitting.

"She died giving birth to you. He hated you, and he hated me because we kept him from what he wanted most. Punishing you, he hurt me as well. He always had me informed of your punishments."

"I—I did not know," she whispered.

"I longed to tell you, but for your safety I could not. He forbade us to spend time together—my punishment. That is why whenever he found out you'd come to see me, you were punished.

It was too much. She couldn't sit and listen anymore. The fact that the blood of the man she thought was her father did not run through her veins should make her happy, but instead she wanted to cry and yell. She'd been cheated. Cheated out of a kind and loving father. "I have to go." She rose on shaky legs.

Pater stood beside her. "I know this is hard, but I have always loved you, Brithwin. When your father forbade me to see you, I told the one man I hoped I could trust—Thomas. I asked him to look after you."

Brithwin stumbled back. "Thomas knew. Both of you kept this from me? You allowed me to despise the vile blood that flowed through my veins when all the while you knew 'twas not so?" She turned and fled out of the chapel.

†††

Brithwin woke with her head pounding. She had wept late into the night, wishing Royce's arms were there to comfort her. It was morning and she had slept through the evening meal yestereve, and no one had come to wake her. She rolled to her side and sat up. With the same urgency of the last week, she bolted for the chamber pot. Once again, her stomach rebelled. After pausing to gain her strength, she stood and walked to the bowl sitting on the table to splash water on her face.

Her conversation with Pater came tumbling back. She glanced at her wrinkled clothes, pulled down a gown hanging on a nail, and changed before heading down to the hall. Royce needed to know what she had learned. He would help her sort through it.

Brithwin came down the steps into a mass of confusion. Before her were knights aplenty with Royce pushing his way through them. More accurately, he was seething and throwing them out of the way.

"How can a man find out anything with you packed around like mother hens?" Royce growled.

Brithwin backed up a few steps for a better view over the men's heads—in the center of them stood a freeman, battered and bleeding. She recognized him as the man who came to the castle daily to see one of the young servant girls.

Royce approached the man and motioned for him to sit. "Get the man a drink." He pulled a chair next to him.

His words were weak and scratchy. "Thank you, milord."

"I see you have my men in an uproar. What tale do you tell?"

The man cleared his throat. "The truth, milord."

"Which is?" Royce tapped his hand on the arm of the chair.

"I was working in the field when I heard someone yell for help. I ran to the road and saw a man accosting Pater. I tried to help him. That was when someone hit me from behind. The last I saw, a man hauled Pater off as the others turned their fury on me."

"Do you know in which direction they took him?"

"East, milord."

Brithwin's knees weakened. She swayed, her hands seeking the cool smooth stone of the wall for support. The voices faded and blackness encroached around her.

She woke, what could only have been moments later. Strong arms held her, and she opened her eyes.

Daffydd stared down at her with his brow furrowed. "You and those stairs do not get along."

She swallowed the rising bile. "I must have swooned. Pray, forgive me. I am not accustomed to doing so."

He shifted her in his arms. "It is my pleasure, milady, I assure you. I am pleased I was here, and you did not meet the ground."

A throat cleared. Brithwin turned.

Royce glared at Daffydd. "My wife."

"Daffydd, please put me down." Her voice came out strangled. "I need to speak to Lord Rosen Craig."

Royce reached to take her. "I will carry you. Are you ill? Do you need to lie down?"

"Nay. I can stand. Daffydd put me down."

"If you are sure, milady." He glanced to Royce than did her bidding.

She swayed when her feet touched the ground. She reached out and grasped Royce's arm. "I need to speak with you privately--someplace where we can be alone." Urgency built inside her 'til she thought she'd burst.

Royce wrapped his arm around her and held her close to his body. "Daffydd, go find out what you can while I take my lady to her chamber."

His spurs clicked ominously on each of the wooden steps, his face unreadable. He pushed open the door and helped her to the bed. He let himself down beside her. The bed sank under his weight.

"Now what is this about, my lady?"

Brithwin wrapped her arms around herself to quell the shiver that stole over her as she imagined Pater, kidnapped and beaten. She opened her mouth to speak, but her throat was so dry it stuck together. She tried to swallow. Royce grabbed a cup from the table and handed it to her. She gulped the water and lowered the cup to her lap.

Her hands shook as well as her insides. "You must find Pater and bring him home. He is my father."

Brithwin searched Royce's face. He cocked his head and his brow wrinkled. "Your father?"

"Aye. He told me yestereve."

Royce plunged his hand through his hair. "By the rood! What kind of tale do you tell?"

"Not a tale but the truth. You must find him, for I fear his life is in danger."

Chapter 26

Clarice studied the hastily scribbled note the lad had handed her. Dare she trust this Edmond? This was the man for whom Lord Rosen Craig searched, or one of his minions. His note was succinct—meet him where the river forks. It would benefit them both, and she was to come now. She smiled. She cared not a whit if it helped him, as long as it was a means for her to procure Lord Rosen Craig, her betrothed—at least he would have been her betrothed if not for Brithwin.

"Tell him I will be along in short order. I must make some excuses here."

The boy nodded and turned toward the gate.

"Wait." She grabbed his arm. "How do I find this fork in the river?"

When the boy had finished giving her directions, she rushed to the castle. She found Brithwin where she had left her, still mending a shirt for Lord Rosen Craig.

Brithwin looked up from where she sat. "I hope the messenger did not bring bad news."

"'Tis my brother trying to make my life miserable. Even from afar." She came in and returned to her seat.

Brithwin pulled up the last stitch and tied it off, breaking the thread with her teeth. "I am truly sorry. I understand how hard it is to live with cruel guardians."

"Aye, 'tis hard, and receiving a missive from him has worn me out. I believe I shall go and lie down for a short while."

Brithwin rose and shook out the shirt to inspect it. "I will make sure no one disturbs you."

Clarice smiled. "You are so kind."

Peeking out the door, Clarice made sure no one was around. She slipped out the door and took the back staircase, making her way to the rendezvous. "This had better be worth it," she muttered to herself minutes later when her gown caught on a bush.

Edmond parted the branches and stepped through. "Oh, it will be. You have my promise."

Clarice swallowed a scream. "Are you trying to put me in my grave, scaring me like that? I thought I was to meet you at the river."

Edmond gave a courtly bow. "'Tis an honor to meet you, Clarice. We *were* to meet at the river. However, you were so noisy that anyone in the vicinity of Hawkwood could have heard you coming. I decided to save you the trip, lest you give us away."

Clarice gave an unladylike snort. "A man with any chivalry at all never would have asked me to meet him in this forsaken place."

"I never claimed any chivalry. I came so I could get what I want."

What had she done? Here she stood alone in the woods with a strange man who had no honor and not a soul knew she was there. Knots coiled in her belly. She wiped the perspiration beading on her forehead with the back of her hand and squared her shoulders. It was best to not let him see her apprehension.

She narrowed her eyes and shoved her fists on her hips, hoping her voice would not quiver. "I don't have much time. Why did you wish to speak with me?"

"Ah, yes, let's get right to it." He leaned his shoulder against the nearest tree. "I have it on good authority you want to be Royce's wife."

Clarice frowned. "Aye, Lord Rosen Craig, my betrothed. I have long waited for this day."

Edmond's eyes clouded over and his brows drew down. "I thought Bryce was your betrothed."

Clarice frowned. "Lord Rosen Craig is my betrothed."

"Aye, if that is what you say. Help me get rid of Brithwin and I could make you Lady of Rosen Craig."

Lady Rosen Craig. The title she'd been born to have. "What do you want from me?"

"Bring Brithwin to me. I'm good at making people disappear. And that my dear will leave the way open for you."

Clarice shifted her feet. "What do you want to do with her?" Brithwin had become her friend. She didn't want her harmed. She just needed her to go away.

He examined his fingernails. "'Tis no concern of yours."

"Then I cannot help you."

"I would think again." He pushed away from the tree.

"Why? What good does it do me? Only her death will free him."

He shrugged. "I can take care of that."

Clarice brought her hand to her throat. "You would kill her? I could not have her blood on my hands."

Edmond frowned. "Are you mad?"

"Don't say that!" Clarice brought her fisted hand to her mouth. "I—I'm not mad. I want what is rightly mine."

All her life she'd known she would be Lady Rosen Craig. She would marry Bryce...no, Royce. She brought her hands up and clutched her head. She was so confused. Royce was Lord Rosen Craig. He was the man she had to marry to be Lady Rosen Craig. Why did he marry when it was supposed to be her?

Brithwin had befriended her. How could she turn her over to this man? *She only pretends to be your friend because she knows you can take what she has.*

No. Brithwin cared for her. They were friends.

If you don't marry Lord Rosen Craig, your brother will marry you off to a man thrice your age and crueler than him. Clarice tried to push away the voice in her head. *You don't have a choice. Besides she took what was rightfully yours. You were born to be Lady Rosen Craig. She needs to die.*
"No, no!"

"What is wrong with you, wench?" Edmond sneered.

She lowered her hands from her head. "Nothing is wrong with me."

"Then who were you talking to?" His perusal lingered on her. "Forget that question. Just tell me if you are willing to help."

It is either you or Brithwin. There can only be one Lady Rosen Craig.

"What do you need from me?"

He picked up a stick then pulled a knife from his boot. He whittled fine shavings from the wood, watching them flutter to the ground. "Bring her out here, and I will take her with me."

Clarice's gaze fastened on the weapon. "My lord will not let her leave the castle gate. I have heard him tell her as much."

He took a threatening step toward her. "Then you will need to be persuasive."

Everything in her wanted to recoil, but Clarice refused to show fear. "I will do what I can. Lord Rosen Craig has gone searching." She hesitated. "I think, perhaps, for you."

He sneered, again. "That is why we meet now. My men and I left a trail in the wrong direction." His laugh sent an icy chill down her spine. "It will be a few days of searching before Royce returns. Bring Brithwin here on the morrow."

"I will see if I can convince her. After we break our fast."

"Then I shall see you on the morrow. Be careful in your

return. I would not want anything foul to befall you." With
the chill of those words settling around her heart he
disappeared into the woods.

Clarice hurried back to the castle and sought out her
chamber to think. When she entered her room, her maid sat
on the chair waiting for Clarice's return. "Did anyone come
by while I was away?"

The maid stood and curtsied. "Nay, miss. 'Twas just me
here."

"Very good, you may leave. However, if anyone asks
about me, do not say I was gone. If you do, things will go
badly for you."

"Aye, miss. You were here all along." Her voice
quivered. She curtsied again took her leave.

Clarice paced within the confines of her room. Brithwin
would not walk out of Hawkwood, not when Lord Rosen
Craig had forbidden her to. She slowed her pace as an idea
unfolded. A smile crept across her face.

†††

Brithwin said a prayer for Royce's safety as she entered
the kitchen from her garden. She had never seen him as
determined as she had when he left in search of Edmond.
Unjustified guilt had weighed heavy on him. She strode
across the kitchen and into the great hall to see Elspeth
mending in one of the chairs by the fire. Brithwin gathered
thread, needle, and a shirt and sat across from her. Brows knit
in a frown, Elspeth worked at her sewing without
acknowledging her.

Brithwin touched her friend's arm. "Is something
troubling you?"

She glanced up. "You would tell me it is none of my
concern."

"After all you have done for me, I would not say such a
thing."

Elspeth paused with needle still in her hand. "You seem to have become fast friends with Miss Coble. I do not trust her."

Brithwin put the thread through the needle and knotted it. "I begin to think I was wrong in judging Clarice so harshly."

"I would not be so quick to change your opinion of her." Elspeth picked the shirt up and stabbed the needle through the fabric. "You have spent a mere few weeks with her. Methinks she is cunning and has hoodwinked you, mayhap as part of a devious plan."

Brithwin giggled. "You make her sound as if she were a brigand. I do not think she deceives me. Since I have spent time with her, I have come to know and understand her better. Royce was right. I was not fair to her."

Elspeth jerked the thread tight and then jabbed it back into the cloth. "Must I remind you that she pushed you down the stairs? You were right not to trust her."

Brithwin shifted in the chair. "What if I was wrong and she bumped me innocently? She claims not to be aware she did. I begin to wonder if I overreacted."

"I do not trust her. You must take precautions. There is the babe now." Elspeth tied the thread and bit it in two. "She is up to something, befriending you."

"Nay, you are wrong there. Life has not been easy for her. When she was young, her mother died. Her father and her betrothed both died this year. I am told her brother is a scoundrel, cares only for himself, and treats her poorly." Brithwin examined the shirt for other holes. "She has no one who cares for her, no friends. I believe she knows Royce is honorable and she can trust him. It is natural for her to be drawn to him. He is her betrothed's brother."

"You are too kindhearted, milady. You are nothing like her."

Brithwin smiled at her. "But Clarice has no one. I have always had you, Thomas, and Pater."

"Tell me you will heed my words, and I will leave you alone." Elspeth gave her a pointed look.

Brithwin tilted her head. "I shall be careful."

She turned her attention to her work and her mind to Pater and her husband. She missed Royce and she worried for Pat . . . her father. Her heart twisted when she recalled the last time she saw him. Her refusing to continue the discussion then rushing out must have hurt him. She hadn't considered his feelings. All she could think about at the time was how it had affected her. Tears stung her eyes and one spilled out and fell onto the cloth. She swiped her lashes with her sleeve. Now she may never have the chance to tell him how happy she was to call him father or to tell him she loved him.

With the mending done, Brithwin knelt and placed Royce's mended shirt in the trunk at the end of his bed. She smiled, recalling the night she'd hidden under this bed and how he had frightened her. He appeared so large, stern, and unforgiving. She sighed. In truth, he was a kind man, but his inability to forgive himself kept him feeling unworthy and in constant turmoil. She got to her feet and closed the top of the trunk.

Running her hand along the covers, she walked around the bed. His gentle embrace still burned in her memory, as well as his kiss. She picked up the beautiful fabric he'd given her. It truly was like nothing she'd ever seen. Rubbing the cloth against her cheek, she caught the lingering scent of Royce. He had, in all probability, packed it with his belongings for the trip to Hawkwood. Hugging it to her chest, she turned and went to her room.

She needed to busy herself to keep from worrying about her father and missing her husband. Already, she'd seen to the thorough cleaning of the manor yet her hands itched for another task.

Laying the cloth on the floor, she knelt beside it and used the gown Royce had given her for a wedding dress as a guide, she took out her scissors and cut the fabric.

Hours later, she fell onto the bed, exhausted, back aching, but the dress was ready to begin sewing. On the morrow she'd enlist Elspeth's help. Perhaps Clarice would come out of her room and help, too.

When she opened her eyes, the sky held a hint of grey as it readied to welcome the morning sun. Brithwin rubbed her eyes and blinked in the dimness. A flash of heat knotted her insides, and she took a deep breath to ward off the old fear—light would soon fill the room.

Sitting up, she waited to see if her stomach would rebel. It didn't. Perhaps she was past the sickness. The thought cheered her. She would break her fast, for the cook would be in the kitchen seeing to the day's meals—she would sneak down and get something to eat before the hall filled with hungry men.

Brithwin quickly dressed and ran her hands down the silky green gown, smoothing out the wrinkles. Royce had made her give many of her plainer dresses away, insisting he did not want her looking like one of the villeins. He'd sent to London for her new gowns. He'd been so attentive. She sighed. But that was before he evaded her at every turn. If only she could make him see the truth of God's forgiveness.

There was naught she could do to change that today, though. It could be another day before he returned. Sewing would keep her hands busy and help time move along while she waited.

As Brithwin neared the kitchen, Marjory scolded a servant for allowing the fire to die. Brithwin peeked in the room as Marjory continued to give orders to Kenneth.

Brithwin stepped in. "Good morn to you."

The young boy's head poked up from behind the wood in his arms. "Good morn to you, milady."

Marjory turned to Kenneth. "Throw the logs on the fire and begone with you. The hens are waiting for you to come gather their eggs."

He shot Brithwin a quick glance. "'Tis more like they cannot wait to peck my hands."

"Go, go!" Marjory shooed him with her hands. "And make sure you get them all."

When the lad had departed, she motioned for Brithwin to sit. "What has you up so early, milady?"

Brithwin lowered herself to the bench. "I fell asleep early, and when I woke, the room was dark. I did not desire to return to my slumber. Do you have any cheese and yesterday's bread?"

Marjory walked over, picked up the food wrapped in two separate cloths, and set them before Brithwin. "'Tis not my place to say this, milady, and 'tis only because I worry for you. But I wish to speak freely."

"You know you can speak freely with me. What troubles you?" Brithwin unwrapped the cheese, broke off a piece, and popped it into her mouth.

Wrinkles appeared on Marjory's brow. "I think you are too trusting when it comes to the likes of Miss Coble."

Brithwin twirled her wedding ring around on her finger. "She has befriended me. I was wrong in my first judgment of her. She has been nothing but kind and helpful. The healing potion she helped me make may very well have saved the young boy from the village."

"Ha!" Marjory rolled her eyes. "Mayhap the fall down the stairs addled your brain."

Brithwin winced at the remark. She had said speak freely. "You have spoken your mind, and I have listened.

However, I am afraid this time we do not agree."

The lines on Marjorie's brows deepened. "I would say this, and you can do with me as you wish, but hear this, milady: she is like a snake in the grass waiting to strike. I see it in her eyes." Marjory turned and stomped away.

Chapter 27

A light breeze blew through the solar window. Brithwin stretched and pressed her hands to her back. "I am pleased with our progress."

Elspeth, bent over the sleeve she sewed, scrunched her eyes and pulled another stitch through the fabric. "Aye, milady, 'tis coming right along."

Brithwin returned to her sewing. She shifted in her seat. Marjory's fierce conviction about Clarice continued to gnaw at her, and she could not force the thoughts from her mind. Elspeth's warning about Clarice rang in her ears. Mayhap she should ask Elspeth if she thought any differently now that she had spent more time around Clarice.

A light rapping on the door broke into her thoughts. Clarice stuck her head in as if Brithwin's thoughts had conjured her up. Brithwin quickly sent a prayer of thanks for not voicing her question to Elspeth.

Clarice stepped into the room. "I have been looking for you."

Brithwin paused, the needle halfway through the fabric. "I am here, working diligently, trying to pass the time until my lord returns."

Glancing at Elspeth, Clarice hesitated. "Do you have time to walk with me in the garden?"

Brithwin stood and set the gown in the chair she'd vacated. "Fresh air would be a welcome change. I could use a good stretch, as my back aches from bending."

Elspeth looked from her work. "Would you have me continue, milady?"

"If you do not need a rest yourself." Brithwin moved to the door and stopped. Elspeth was a devoted friend. "Thank you." She smiled at her and stepped out the door.

They had strolled through the garden but a brief while when Clarice curled her lip. "I cannot believe you thank your servants for doing their jobs."

Brithwin raised her brows. "'Tis true I expect them to do as I ask, but a thank-you lets them know I appreciate them."

"If I were lady of the castle, they would learn to show me their appreciation." Clarice brought her hand to her chest. "If I wanted to, I could send them on their way and find others to take their place."

Brithwin shook her head. "My people work hard for me."

"Oh, well." Clarice flitted her hands in the air. "'Tis not the reason I asked you out here. I have good news."

Brithwin meandered to the roses and leaned over to smell their delicate fragrance. "I thought we came for fresh air."

"You came for fresh air. I came to give you news."

She straightened and considered the feverish glitter in Clarice's eyes. "And what, pray tell, is that?"

Clarice moved to stand by her. "Lord Rosen Craig returns—not an hour's ride from here.

"He comes home?" Brithwin's insides quivered with excitement. "How did you find this out?"

"A traveler saw them." She crossed her arms and smiled smugly.

Brithwin sucked in a breath. "I should go and see to a fine meal."

"Wait. 'Tis why I told you out here. Let us ride and meet them."

She stepped away from Clarice, shaking her head. "Nay, my lord forbade me to leave Hawkwood."

"Would it not be a fine surprise? He is not far out by now. Surely he would not mind. He is nearly here, and it is safe for us."

Brithwin chewed her bottom lip. She would love to meet him, but she did not want to risk his displeasure. Much had happened lately to draw his ire.

"I have not asked much of you, my lady. I wish to get out of this stuffy place, away from the smells of animals and unwashed bodies. Whoever has tried to harm you and Lord Rosen Craig is far away from here by now. They would know he is looking for them."

Brithwin's resistance began to waver. "Mayhap if we take a few guards with us."

Clarice stomped her foot. "Nay!" She hesitated then smiled. "What kind of welcome is it if we ride up with a small army? Besides, he gets closer as we speak, and think how long it would take to gather men. I go with or without you."

"'Tis not safe for you to go alone. You are sure he is not far?"

Clarice grabbed her hand and hurried toward the stables. "You have my word."

Two horses stood saddled and ready. Brithwin stopped and stared at the palfreys. "You readied the horses?"

Clarice shrugged. "I did not want to waste time, and I knew you would decide to go."

The words Marjory had spoken earlier returned. *But hear this, milady, she is like a snake in the grass waiting to strike. I see it in her eyes.* Brithwin shrugged them off. She missed Royce fiercely, and though Clarice was her friend, she would not have Clarice welcoming her husband home without her. And if she truly trusts Clarice, she needs to act upon that trust.

One of the stable men came out to assist them onto their mounts. When they reached the portcullis, the gatekeeper stopped them.

"Good day, milady, Miss Coble. 'Tis a beautiful—"

"We are in a hurry. So if you please," Clarice cut in.

The gatekeeper looked at Brithwin with raised brows. "I understood milord asked you not to leave the safety of Hawkwood."

That was a kind way of putting it. To be precise, he'd *commanded* her to remain. Brithwin forced a smile and hoped she didn't look as guilty as she felt.

Clarice glared at the man. "You dare to question her?"

He cleared his throat. "I am following milord's orders."

Brithwin's smile wobbled. "'Tis all right. We are on our way to meet my lord."

The gatekeeper tipped his head and looked at Brithwin. "I have not heard any word as to his return."

"You question your lady again?" Clarice straightened in her saddle and glared at him. "I will speak to Lord Rosen Craig about your disrespect."

Disregarding Clarice, he continued to meet Brithwin's gaze. "I mean no disrespect, milady."

Brithwin brushed a strand of hair from her eyes. "I understand, but we have had word he is not far, and we go to meet him." And as much as she didn't wish to disobey Royce, she wanted to show faith in her friend.

His gaze quickly slid to Clarice and then returned to Brithwin. "Are you certain, milady? I do not want to feel milord's wrath."

"I will take all responsibility for leaving." She hoped the assurance would put his mind at ease.

Clarice nudged her horse forward. "Come, my lady. If we do not hurry, he will be here before we leave."

A few minutes later, as Brithwin looked over her shoulder at the protection of the walls falling further behind them, doubt crept in. Remembering Royce's words that there were places good for an ambush, she scanned the area in front of them as they approached a copse of trees.

A chill crept up her spine. "Perhaps we should turn back. I do not feel good about this."

Clarice smiled. "Let us ride a little farther, and if we do not see him, we will return."

Brithwin's belly knotted. She wanted to return but did not want to leave Clarice. "Not much farther."

They had ridden halfway through the cluster of trees when there was a thunder of hooves hitting the ground and a snapping of branches. Her stomach vaulted. She had made a grave error. How she knew the horses were not her husband and his men, she did not know, but she was certain.

She reined her horse around as a rider broke through the trees in front of her. Pulling the reins to the right, she urged her horse on. Another rider plunged toward her and she refused to relinquish her mind to the panic that wanted to take over. She yanked her palfrey to spin around in the other direction. To her horror, men crashed through the woods from every side.

Her horse sidled to the right, and she fought to keep him under control. A large warhorse barreled down on her, and its rider reached for her reins. White rimmed her horse's eyes before he reared up. Brithwin grabbed at his mane but caught air.

The ground slammed into her back. She could draw no breath. When she opened her eyes, the trees and sky spun above her, and the yells of men around her faded.

†††

Brithwin's body went limp, and Clarice screamed.

Edmond jerked his horse toward her. "Shut up, you witless wench."

"Is she—is she dead?" she whimpered.

"I said, keep quiet," Edmond growled. "She lives."

Clarice, still upon her horse, glanced down at Brithwin

lying on the ground. "Are you sure?"

He dismounted and hunkered next to Brithwin. "I am certain."

"Then I will be on my way back to Hawkwood." She nudged her horse with her heels.

A burly man snatched the reins, halting the animal.

Edmond grinned. "Sorry, but that won't be possible."

Clarice's knees weakened. "What treachery is this?"

"No treachery. I will not have you going to Hawkwood and letting them know Brithwin is missing." Edmond slipped his hands under Brithwin and lifted her effortlessly. "You must remain here until the sun sets. Once darkness falls, 'tis nearly impossible to follow."

"I will not stay here alone." Clarice shuddered. "'Tis dangerous to remain by myself."

The men chuckled and exchanged lascivious glances.

"Your friend might say it is not safe with us." Edmond smiled.

Clarice shifted her gaze to Brithwin's still body. Her heart stuttered. A good person would not commit such a terrible act of betrayal up on a friend. "We had an agreement." She couldn't prevent her eyes from returning to Brithwin. What had she done?

"You will stay." His voice brooked no argument.

"I will depart once you do, I assure you. I owe you nothing," she sniffed.

Edmond addressed the knight holding her reins. "Stay with her. You can let her go on her way just before dusk, and come meet up with us at Rosen Craig."

The knight sat on his warhorse and nodded.

"Nay! You cannot leave me here with this—" Clarice looked into the man's eyes devouring her and was unable to finish. A chill ran down her spine.

"Be careful, milady." Edmond's slow words resonated

with warning. "This man is the only person here to tend to your safety."

"How am I to know if I can trust him to be honorable?" Clarice's gaze shifted from Edmond to the burly knight who nearly drooled.

The knight let out a loud guffaw. "No one ever called me that."

Edmond looked at the man and frowned. "We need her cooperation, so mind your hands, if you want to keep them."

Her guard gave a loud humph.

Edmond handed Brithwin to a mounted man and climbed on his horse. After retrieving Brithwin, he turned to Clarice. "If you stay here and do as you're told, Sir Honorable Knight here will not trouble you. However, if you try to flee, you are at his mercy."

"But I have no food, no drink. How can I stay here all day?" Clarice argued.

Edmond jerked his head toward the knight holding her horse's reins. "He has food in his bag."

Edmond disappeared with Brithwin into the brush and trees. Clarice slid from her horse. She stepped away from her mount and whirled around. "Did you hear that?"

"Hear what?"

"I heard something coming from there." She pointed in the opposite direction that Edmond had left.

"Nay, probably an animal spooked from the horses." He dismounted from his horse and stretched.

"Could someone be watching us?" Her voice faltered.

"Nay. 'Tis just you, me, and the animals out here." He smirked.

†††

Thomas pushed his horse until its sides heaved. A single rider broke through the trees, and no other followed. His gut coiled. The gatekeeper had said both Miss Coble and

Brithwin had ridden out of the castle gates on mounts. He hastened to meet the rider, praying it would be Brithwin.

The men surrounded Clarice, and Thomas reined in beside her. "Where is my lady?"

"I do not know."

"What do you mean? You left with her, did you not?"

She cowered as his voice thundered. "Brigands attacked us. They separated us. I do not know where they took her."

"Which direction did they go?"

"I do not know. I was frightened and only worried about getting away."

"Do you remember anything? A fallen tree? A creek? Anything at all that can help?" Thomas longed to spur his destrier on in search of Brithwin, but he needed to know anything this woman could remember.

"Nay. I saw nothing unusual. Just trees," Clarice whimpered.

Thomas shifted his attention to Philip. "Take the lady back to Hawkwood while the rest of us fan out to search for milady."

Darkness was nearly on them, but Thomas couldn't give up so easily, even though he knew a search with a cloudy sky and no light would be fruitless. They broke into the line of trees, and the small amount of light they had disappeared. Slowing their horses, they rode into the woods a short way when Thomas had them stop. They sat silently, the only sounds the heavy breathing of the animals they sat upon. Thomas strained to hear riders in the distance, but not a sound reached his ears. He glanced around, but there was no way to see tracks or evidence of the party that had taken Brithwin.

He'd failed her. Royce had trusted him to keep her safe. He'd failed them both. The men all looked to him for direction. But he could see in each of their faces the doubts they had of their mission.

"We can see nothing to guide us. We return to Hawkwood and leave by dawn to search again."

Back at the castle, Thomas summoned Clarice from her room. She slumped in the chair before him.

He narrowed his eyes on her. "Why did Brithwin leave the castle grounds when she was given orders to stay within the walls?"

Clarice stared at her hands. "We went out to meet Lord Rosen Craig."

A knot formed in his gut. "Who told you Lord Rosen Craig was on Hawkwood land?" It took all of his power not to shake the woman to get quicker answers.

Clarice leaned back with a sigh. "I do not know what you are asking."

"Answer my question." He stood in front of her chair. "What made you think my lord and his men were on Hawkwood land?"

"A messenger came by and told me."

"Who is this messenger?" He glared at her. "No one else has seen him."

"Well, I did." She glanced up and turned away. "He came in early and gave me the news."

Thomas folded his arms in front of him. "The gatekeeper saw no one enter whom he did not know."

Clarice frowned. "You doubt my word? You would believe a servant over me?"

"He is not a servant but a knight, and *he* has no reason to lie."

"Are you suggesting I do?" Her voice rose.

He didn't trust this woman. Something about her sent up warnings. "You tell me, Miss Coble. How is it you managed to escape and not her?"

"I will not sit here and listen to this." Clarice stood,

nearly bumping into him. "When Lord Rosen Craig returns, I
will tell him of your treatment of his guests."

"Sit down!" Thomas bellowed.

Clarice fell onto the chair as if her legs had given out.

Thomas leaned forward, resting his hands and weight on
the chair's arms. "You will not leave until I have my
answers. Now, did the boy Lucas go with you?"

Clarice looked genuinely puzzled. "No. Just Lady Rosen
Craig and I went out. Why do you ask?"

He straightened back up. "He is missing also."

She shifted in her seat. "Oh."

"Did you recognize any of the men who took milady?"

Clarice clasped her hands in her lap. "No."

Thomas frowned. "How is it you escaped and not
Brithwin?"

"They separated us. All but one man went with her. That
man guarded me and would not let me leave. They said they
didn't want me alerting anyone that she'd been taken."

"The messenger. You said he told you. Why would a
messenger go to you and not milady?"

"I was frightened. Perhaps I misspoke. The boy
addressed my lady, and I heard him." She yawned. "I am
very tired. I wish to retire for the night."

Thomas frowned. "Aye, you may go." He did not
believe further interrogation would get anything helpful out
of the woman anyway.

Clarice had no sooner walked up the stairs when the
gatekeeper strode in.

"Sir Thomas, may we speak?" The gatekeeper glanced to
where Clarice had exited.

"What is it?" Thomas was glad to see the man, for he
had questions to ask.

"I am not remiss in my job. I saw no messenger arrive,
Sir Thomas. But milady's friend, Miss Coble, was very

insistent they go. When I tried to stop milady, Miss Coble became angry."

"Milady—did she go willingly?"

"Aye. I would have stopped her if she did not. She appeared to be hesitant, and Miss Coble did most of the talking."

"And you are certain there was no messenger?" Thomas was sure of what the answer would be, but he needed to hear it one more time.

"Aye. But Miss Coble did receive a message yesterday and then went out of the gates shortly thereafter." The gatekeeper brushed his curly hair out of his eyes.

"Is there any more you can tell me?" Thomas was ready to break down Clarice's door to get answers.

"Nay."

"You may go." Thomas didn't wait for the gatekeeper to leave before he headed up the steps, two at a time.

He pounded on Clarice's door. "I need to speak with you Miss Coble."

"I am to bed."

Thomas didn't care a whit. He burst through the door and she let out a gasp. He could barely contain his fury. "You will answer my questions with the truth this time. I am told no messengers came today, but I understand you had a messenger deliver you a missive yesterday. What was it?"

Clarice pulled the covers up to her neck. "'Twas a missive from my brother. He has found another old man to marry me off to. But I will not do it."

"Why did you leave shortly after?"

"I forgot to have the boy relay something to my brother."

He didn't trust the woman, but he did know from Royce that her brother was cruel. Thomas closed the door without saying any more.

†††

Fog surrounded Brithwin's mind. Where was she that steady bouncing pummeled her? Every muscle in her body screamed out. She pried her eyes open. Forest trees, bushes, and ground moved beneath her. It all came back—going to meet Royce; the attackers; trying to flee; falling from the horse. She closed her eyes. She did not know these men. Whoever they were, they intended no good will toward her.

Clarice. Did they have her, too?

She must ensure they continued to believe her unconscious. At least until she could decide what to do. She listened for the lilt of a female voice among the low rumble of men's conversations ahead and horses' hooves crunching on leaves beneath. No sounds came from behind her. With luck they pulled up the rear. Perhaps being in back would work to her advantage. The knife Royce had given her, she carried tied to her calf.

If she could reach her knife, she could wound her captor, push him from the horse, turn the beast around, and flee. It was her only hope. Her chances of success were not good against a band of men, but she would not go with them willingly. Not knowing their destination, she had better act soon—she may never have another chance.

Planning her escape, she remained slumped sidesaddle in front of her captor with her hands dangling beside her legs. His arm clamped around her, keeping her from tumbling to the ground.

Slowly, she slid her hand to her leg and the concealed knife. The weapon pulled out effortlessly. Hiding it in the folds of her gown, she took a deep breath. Her heart thundered so violently, her ears pulsed with the sound. She tightened her grip on the knife. Thomas said her self-preservation had kept her alive all these years. She would use it now, for she was not a simpering female who would surrender in the face of danger—especially not when happiness was almost within her grasp.

Royce was a good man and she carried his babe in her womb, and a strong, fierce love grew within her daily for them both. She had the father she'd always wanted in Pater, who loved her. She would not let these brigands take away those things without a fight.

Lifting her body to an upright position, she slid the knife along her leg, keeping it hidden in the fold of her gown.

"You are awake." He loosened his grip around her waist.

"Where do you take me?" She would not turn and look at him. It was best not to see the face of the man she would stab.

"No crying or swooning?"

She straightened her back. "I asked you a question. I would like an answer."

He laughed. "Very well. I take you to Rosen Craig."

She headed to Royce's family castle. His men must have rescued her while she lay unconscious. "Is Royce coming there also?"

"I suspect he will show shortly."

She closed her eyes and relaxed. "How did you find me?"

He leaned forward and she could smell his foul breath. "Clarice brought you to us."

"She did? Then why do we go to Rosen Craig?"

"Where else would we go?" He whispered in her ear.

"Back to Hawkwood."

He harrumphed. "I do not wish an early death—for me anyway."

She turned to look at him. "Who are you?"

"Why, milady, I thought you knew. I am Edmond," he grinned at her, "at your service."

She gasped when his name rolled off his lips. He had taken Pater. A foreboding shiver crept up her spine. Now he took her to lure Royce into a trap.

Fire surged through her body. She jerked the knife from beneath her gown and plunged it into his thigh. He grunted, and before he could move, she wrenched the knife out and thrust it into his arm.

Knowing she had but one chance to escape, she shoved her hands against his chest. He didn't budge. Her stomach lurched—she had underestimated his strength. A murderous look shone from his eyes. He raised his hand and brought it crashing on to the side of her head. Arrows of pain dug into her senses. The knife fell from her hand. A second blow landed. She could taste blood, and then blackness crept in.

Chapter 28

Two days of hard riding and searching turned up nothing. Royce had covered every trail and road, spoken to anyone in a field he passed by, and no one had seen any sign of Pater. Had Edmond sent them on a false trail? Royce began to believe that was the truth of things, and he and his men had lost valuable time because of it. With no other leads, they pressed onward.

If only there was a way around telling Brithwin. The news would crush her. She often kept a facade of bravery, but he saw through it. Sometimes he wished he didn't. But this time was different. When she'd discovered Pater had been taken, the sadness, anxiety, and fear he'd witnessed in her tore at his heart. He wanted to wrap her tightly in his arms and comfort her. She had faced so much of late.

Royce would do anything to take away the pain she tried to hide. Anything but tell her how he felt. If he could simply harden his heart to her—but it was too late for that. He loved her. He would give his life for Brithwin, yet he couldn't tell her. The sorrow she now faced lay on his shoulders. The risk to her was too great, and he could not bear it if the same fate fell upon her as had fallen upon his family. No, he could never tell her how he felt. It was something he would take to his grave to keep her safe. By denying himself, perhaps he could appease an angry God.

Feeling eyes on him, he glanced over at Jarren riding beside him, watching him.

Jarren raised his brows. "You look deep in thought."

"There is much to think about. You have said nothing to me, but I know you, Jarren. You have come to the same conclusion I have."

"Ah, you mean they have led us on a merry chase?"

Royce nodded his head. "They are gone now to wherever they had planned to go. And we have no way of knowing where."

Jarren stood in his stirrups and stretched. "Methinks you are right."

"It is time to put our heads together." Royce met his gaze. "And catch Edmond at his own game."

Jarren dropped back in his saddle. "How is it you think to catch him when we do not know where he is?"

"I do not know…yet." He shrugged. "But I will find him, and we will flush him out."

Royce and his friend again fell silent. They continued their ride until the sun lowered in the sky.

"'Tis getting late, Royce. We would do well to find a place to spend the night."

"We passed a stream in these woods our first time through here. 'Tis not far." He looked up at the sky. "Looks like fair weather."

"And I am thankful."

When they reached the stream, the men watered their horses and set up camp. Royce yanked out a handful of grass and rubbed down Shadowmere.

Jarren had finished assigning the watches for the night and walked over. "It's meager provisions we have left, and 'tis too late to hunt."

Royce tossed down the grass and sat on a fallen log. "We will be home on the morrow. What we have will get us by."

When they had finished eating the hard meat and stale bread, Royce made his bed near a tree where the grass was soft. The dew had fallen, leaving his clothes damp. Lacing his hands behind his head, he listened to the low murmur of the men. An owl hooted in a nearby tree, and the crickets chirped their evening songs. In the distance, the haunting sound of a wolf reached his ears. The flames from the fire danced and flickered to the night breeze that brought the acrid smoke to his nostrils. He closed his eyes. He needed sleep tonight.

Royce woke long before the sun rose with such an urgency to return that he awakened the men and hurried on to Hawkwood. The weather continued in their favor, and just as the sun peeked over the horizon, they entered the gates.

"We've made good time." Royce glanced over as Jarren pulled up beside him.

"Aye, I just wish we returned with good news."

Royce nudged his horse into a canter, Jarren's words sobering him. The news would be hard for Brithwin.

As he entered the bailey, utter chaos surrounded him. The men looked ready to do battle. The turmoil affected even Shadowmere, who danced nervously, pawing the ground.

"'Tis all right." Royce patted his neck.

"Thank God, you are here." Dark shadows circled beneath Thomas's eyes.

"What is amiss? It looks as if we are ready to meet the enemy."

"Come into the castle where it is quiet, and we can talk." Thomas walked away without waiting.

Royce dismounted and threw the reins to a knight. Hurrying up the steps and into the hall, he found Thomas pacing.

"Why the uproar?"

Worry lines etched Thomas's brow. He stood tense, his hands balled into fists. "Milady's been kidnapped."

"What!" Royce bellowed. "Who has her?" He knew the answer to that. "How and when did they get to her?"

Royce approached Thomas like a lion to its prey.

Thomas stood his ground. "She was taken yesterday. We

do not know who, but we know from where."

Royce pinned Thomas against the wall, nose to nose. "She has been gone for a day and you are just going out to find her? What kind of knight are you?" He drove his fist into Thomas's jaw with a sickening, satisfying thud.

Thomas shoved him away and wiped the blood from his mouth. "Clarice and my lady left around the noon hour. When we realized they were not inside the castle walls, we went looking for them. We found Clarice, but they had separated the women, and when we went into the woods in search of milady, we could see nothing. We returned to Hawkwood so we could leave this morning before sunrise."

Royce spun around and slammed his fist into the table sending a heavy thud through the room. He shook his aching fist. "It was Edmond, and it is me he wants. He gets to me through Brithwin." He grabbed a goblet from the table and flung it against the wall. Wood splintered and the liquid drained down. Servants scurried to clean up the mess. "We must go now. I will make Edmond pay for what he has done."

Returning to his men, he cleared his throat and stood. "If any have not yet heard, the Lady of Rosen Craig has been taken. We depart now to bring my lady home."

They had not traveled far when Royce put up his hand to stop the men. A horse and rider barreled across the field toward them. The rider appeared young, a boy perhaps. He continued to observe the rider as he drew near and recognized Lucas.

The boy pulled on the reins, and the lathered horse skidded to a stop.

What was Lucas doing on a horse? He didn't have time to deal with the boy, but he did need to stop him from ruining a good animal. "You trying to kill that horse, boy?"

"Nay, milord." He gasped for air. "They took milady."

"We are looking for her now." Royce nudged his horse to move forward.

"But milord"—Lucas gasped again—"I know where they took her."

Royce pulled on Shadowmere's reins to stop him. The horse danced to the side in protest. "How do you know where she is?"

"I heard 'em talkin'." Lucas's hand shook as he wiped the sweat off his face. "I was in the woods when they took her. I saw 'em."

"Why did you not give this information yesternight?" He was beginning to think the boy told a tale.

"I thought she were dead when she fell off her horse, but she woke up." Lucas's voice trembled. "When they took milady, I followed them."

Royce groaned. She may be hurt, and what of the babe? A fall could cause her to lose it, and she could die herself. "Where did they take her?"

"To Rosen Craig."

Rosen Craig. They must have overpowered Lyndle, and now they held the castle. Royce took in the young lad's weary appearance and sought to gain control over the bolts of fire shooting through his body. "Did the man have a scar on his face?"

Lucas's eyes got big. "How did you know?"

"He is an old foe. Can you tell me anything else?"

Lucas shook his head.

"You go on to Hawkwood." Royce slapped Lucas on the leg. "You have done well. Just be sure to see to your mount before you see to your own needs."

Royce turned to go, but another rider barreled toward them. Skirts billowed back from the sidesaddle. He groaned. Clarice. What was the woman about? He waited for her to reach them, anxious to get on his way but wondering if she had news.

"Lord Rosen Craig, I am glad I caught you." Clarice smiled as if all were well.

"What are you doing out of the Hawkwood gates?" Royce fought to keep from raising his voice.

"I am going with you."

Royce turned to Patrick. "Take the boy and Clarice back to Hawkwood."

"Nay!" Her response came out in a high-pitched scream. "I am not going back there."

"I do not have time for this, Clarice. We know not what we go into. It could very well put you in danger. You will go back to the castle with the boy and Patrick."

Her face reddened. "Nay! I can make my own decisions."

Royce lashed back at her. "When you chose to stay at my demesne, you became my responsibility."

Still on her horse, Clarice leaned over and grabbed his arm. "What of my lady? If she is hurt, I can help her. I am good with healing."

Thomas raised his brows. "Does not a castle as large as Rosen Craig have a healer?"

"Lyndle did say Rosen Craig's healer left when my family died." Royce weighed the complication of bringing her against needing her skills.

Thomas leaned over and spoke for Royce's ears only. "It would not hurt, my lord. She can be kept away until we know what is what."

Royce shifted in his saddle. "Patrick, she is your responsibility. If she cannot keep the pace, stay with her. Lucas, return to Hawkwood, and have a care with the horse."

Turning his attention to Jarren and Thomas, he lowered his voice. "I expect Pater is also held there. I am thinking Edmond has kidnapped Pater to use as a bribe for Rosen

Craig."

Thomas frowned. "What is this you speak?"

Royce glanced around him then locked his eyes on Thomas. "I know the truth of Pater. Let us hope Edmond does not and he only took him to draw me there. He wishes to take my life. With Rosen Craig already in his possession, when he approaches the king, he would simply need King Richard's blessing for the transfer of ownership. Who knows what lies he would tell our king to acquire this castle."

"The king would never give Edmond Rosen Craig," Jarren argued.

"Edmond may have found a way to use Pater to his advantage, one that would please the king."

Thomas frowned. "Why take Brithwin, then?"

"Edmond wants me dead. If he succeeds in that and marries her, he gives the king more reason to agree to his plan. I imagine he is covering every area he possibly can." He gestured for the men to move out. "Remember, men, our enemy does not fight fair. Expect an ambush along the way."

†††

The horses were lathered and tired. They couldn't push them any farther. They needed rest. Royce rode to a small stream to water his animal. He dismounted and motioned for Jarren and Thomas to follow.

Royce leaned against a tree and folded his arms. "Rosen Craig is less than an hour's ride."

Thomas looked him in the eye. "What do you plan?"

Royce glanced at the two men. "I know the place they will choose to ambush us."

Jarren pulled out his dagger, sliced a piece of cheese he had pulled from a bag, and popped the morsel in his mouth. "'Twould be safest if you stayed here while we took care of things."

Royce let out his breath in disgust. "You insult me.

Think you I would let you go without me?"

Jarren sliced another piece from the wedge. "Nay, but I do not wish you to take unnecessary chances."

"I will rescue my wife."

Jarren grunted. "That is my concern—that you will worry for your wife and not yourself."

Brithwin flashed through Royce's mind's eye—the last eve they had spent together as husband and wife, her unbound hair flowing to her waist, and the warmth of her soft skin against his hands.

He shook his head. Distractions at a time like this could get him killed and his men with him.

†††

Royce held up his hand before they came to the spot he felt sure the ambush would take place. "Be alert. We enter the devil's den."

His men answered in nods. The sky was clear, allowing the moon to shine a dim light on their path. If he hadn't expected the attack they would be easy targets in the calmness of the night. The faint smell of smoke wafted through the air as a breeze ruffled the leaves. Edmond was foolish to have built a fire. In the distant a wolf howled. Frogs chirped, sending out a mating call from a nearby creek. A horse nickered. Chain mail clinked and leather creaked as the men moved restlessly in their saddles, waiting on an assault. Royce flexed his hand inside the smooth leather glove as he gripped the hilt of his sword. Heavy breathing filled the air as each man awaited his fate.

A horse kicked a stone and it was as if it had been a call to battle. Branches snapped and men filled the opening before them. Metal struck metal, resounding through the encroaching darkness. The occasional thud from the broadside of a sword hitting chainmail echoed in their midst. Shouts of battle and cries of the wounded rent the air.

He searched through the melee, his gaze stopping on Edmond. This would be the night that settled all—one of them would not return home.

He dug his spurs into his destrier's flanks, and with a roar, charged toward Edmond. Shadowmere dug up the ground between them. The sounds around him faded except for steady hooves beating against the ground. He tightened his grip on the hilt of his sword.

They collided with a crash of swords that jolted his body. Edmond thrust and Royce parried, their blades connecting with equal force. For every swing and thrust of Royce's sword, Edmond parried and swung back. The battle, begun long ago, raged on between them.

Fatigued muscles burned as Royce swung his weapon, looking for Edmond's weakness. He clenched exhausted legs against Shadowmere's flanks to guide the horse to do his bidding. Edmond's sword swung lower and with less speed.

They were equals in strength and skill. The difference was, Royce had more to lose. Brithwin's image drove him. He heaved his sword up, and with a desperate shout, dislodged Edmond's weapon from his hand. The blade rose in the air then clunked to the ground.

Edmond snarled and spun his horse around. Before Royce could land the final blow, Edmond spurred his horse into a gallop for the woods.

Royce pursued. This must end here and now. Reaching the edge of the woods, he leaned his body next to his horse. The branches tore at his skin and battered his mount. Ignoring the assault, he urged Shadowmere on, racing through the woods, narrowing the gap between them. Ahead, a low tree limb overhung the path. Royce pressed himself lower to his horse's neck.

From behind where the fighting raged on, someone ululated with a war cry.

Edmond glanced over his shoulder. His head connected with the stout branch, hurling him from his horse. He landed headfirst, sending forth a muffled crack. His body went limp, crumpling in an unnatural position on the ground.

Royce ducked under the branch, slowed his horse, and dismounted. The chiming of swords faded as he walked over and nudged Edmond with his foot. The man's head flopped at a sickening angle.

Edmond's horse ambled back to stand by his dead master. Royce took the dangling reins, and as he turned to go, a flicker of green caught his eyes. Stones set in the handle of a knife. He squatted and pulled the blade from the belt of Edmond's hauberk.

Holding it in his hand, he ran his thumb over the hawk that embellished the handle. Carved to look elegant yet strong. The bird's tiny emerald eyes stared at him, not so different from Edmond's—no anger, no hatred, but void of emotion.

Royce gripped the small slender weapon that belonged to Brithwin's mother. He slid the blade beneath his belt, tied Edmond's horse's reins to his saddle, then hefted Edmond up and threw him over his horse. As much as he loathed the man he deserved a burial. He wound his way back through the woods, taking it slow so as to keep Edmond on his horse.

Reaching the edge of the woods, the men had put down their swords. Some tended others' wounds, some their own, and others walked around checking for dead. Royce took a steadying breath, thankful that those he could make out were his men. They had won this skirmish. The metallic smell of blood filled the air as he stepped into the battle's aftermath. He could only hope he didn't lose any men. Now the part he loathed—finding who survived and who did not.

It was much like this day when he'd lost his squire in battle—the dead littered the ground. And once again, it was at Edmond's hand. However, today Edmond did not fare as well. Battle-hardened though he was, remembering the sound of Edmond's skull whacking into the tree branch made Royce's stomach twist.

"Rosen Craig." Jarren stood in the clearing, the last of the evenings light fading behind him, his voice beckoning his attention. Dirt and blood smudged his friend's face as he leaned his weight on his sword. A gash oozed blood on his hand.

Royce dismounted. "'Tis glad I am to see you still standing."

"And you, my friend. When you disappeared into the woods, I thought to follow but had my hands full. However, I see you did not need me."

"Nay, I did not. Edmond saw to his own demise. Hitting a low branch, he broke his neck when he fell."

Jarren rubbed his neck. "I would not wish to die that way—fleeing from battle."

Royce shrugged. "I am relieved he will trouble me no longer." He turned to one of his knights, who weaved his way between bodies. "John. Come give your report."

John strode to them. "Good news, sir. We have lost no man thus far. Five men in immediate need of a healer while others with only cuts, needing mending."

"What of Edmond's men?" Royce's gaze skimmed the battlefield.

"Of those that did not die or flee, two live, but I believe one will not make it off this field."

Royce's eyes stopped on a still body. "Montfort. Is he of the living?"

John shook his head. "He is not, sir."

"I had hoped to talk to him." Frustration twisted in Royce's gut. He'd wanted to ask the man some questions.

John's eyes lit up. "The man who does live is Sir Robert,

Edmond's confidant."

A glimmer of hope stirred in Royce. "Take me to him. Mayhap I will get my answers."

†††

Brithwin woke and opened her eyes. Ominous darkness surrounded her. She rubbed her eyes and opened them again. Her head pounded, and everything remained black. A jolt of cold spiraled through her veins. Her breath caught. The last thing she remembered was the blow she had received. Was she blind? She waved her hand before her face and the air passed by, but her eyes caught no hint of movement. Was she back in her personal prison at Hawkwood? Her hands quickly went to the floor. Her palms slapped against wood, not the wet dirt of her prison. This was not Hawkwood. Mayhap she *was* blind. The thought sent a bolt of fear searing through her.

She stood and steadied herself, taking one step, then another, while running her hands along the walls, feeling for a door. The room was small—a pantry or buttery, perhaps. A whoosh of air then a shaky laugh escaped her lips. Such a room would have no windows, no light. Her hands bumped the door frame and her fingers skimmed around it. It was impossible to open from the inside. She banged on the door and called out until her hands were bruised. Either no one could hear her or no one cared. She continued to trace along the wall until she reached the back of the room. Once there, she slowly slid to the floor.

The perpetual darkness battered her, dredging up memories she held inside. She drew her legs to her chest and wrapped her arms around them. Leaning her head against the wall, she closed her eyes. It was a cruel man who had punished her in the dungeon, a man who was not her father. Her true father was a kind and loving man. The thudding of her heart lessened as she kept her eyes closed and thought of

312

Pater—her father.

She drew in a breath and held it before letting it out. With her head still pounding, she tried to put her thoughts in order. Edmond had used her to draw Royce here—to Rosen Craig. Of that much she felt certain. Had Clarice escaped and returned to Hawkwood to inform them, or was she a part of this scheme as he had tried to make her believe? Either way, Royce would be searching for her by now and would walk into a trap, and she had no way to warn him.

Lord, I ask you to put a hedge of protection around Royce. Give him insight and wisdom as he comes in search of me. Keep him safe.

††††

Brithwin woke to footfalls. When had she dozed off? Keeping her back to the wall, she pushed herself up. The footsteps stopped outside the door. Her legs trembled. She held her breath. The door creaked open, and light filtered in until it flooded the room. She raised her hand to shield her eyes, waiting for them to adjust and reveal who stood before her.

A man stepped into the room. "I see Edmond has hurt you."

Squinting, she tried to see who stood before her as her eyes adjusted to the light. She didn't recognize the voice. He knew that Edmond had brought her. Brithwin touched her swollen eye as the man came into focus. "Do I know you?" She didn't like the way he looked at her.

The man grinned. "I am Lyndle."

Chapter 29

A sense of dread filled Brithwin. She blinked, trying to force her eyes to stay focused.

"Do you know who I am?" Lyndle cocked his head. His eyes bore into her.

She wanted to writhe under his stare. "You are Royce's uncle and the steward of Rosen Craig."

"I am that." His eyes didn't waver from their grip. "Does the name mean nothing else to you?" He wore his tawny hair cut short, so unlike Royce's brown hair, which brushed his collar. A dark birthmark marred his temple. Some believed the blemish to be the mark of the devil.

"Nay, should it?" She had seen babies abandoned because of such a mark.

His brows rose. "Your father never mentioned me?"

Brithwin flattened herself against the wall. "Should he have?" His age and thin frame gave her hope she could overpower him.

His eyes bore into her again. "Did he not tell you I asked for your hand?"

She shook her head. It wasn't the birthmark that made her feel ill at ease. There was something truly dark about him.

"No. No, I don't suppose he did. You see, it was a perfect match." He sidled closer and touched her cheek. She jerked away. He let his hand fall to his side. "Your father had no heir, I had no castle, and the woman I loved was married to my brother."

"You loved Royce's mother?" The words flew out before she could stop them. She could not have heard him correctly.

"You and I would have gotten along fine. However, your father laughed at my request." Lyndle's hands balled into fists, fury burned in his eyes. "He laughed and told me you were too good for me. That I was a spawn of the devil. Then he bid me to leave." He touched the mark on his face. "He did not have the courtesy to invite me to stay the night but sent me out after darkness had fallen. So I returned to Rosen Craig, but I did not forget what he said to me—how he humiliated me."

Brithwin remained pressed against the wall. She did not want the anger she saw in his eyes directed at her. She needed a way out. "I am sorry for my father's cruel words. He was not a kind man—even to his daughter."

His shoulders dropped and a hint of compassion softened the hard lines scored on his face. "I had heard that but wondered if it were true."

Her heart battered the inside of her chest. She clutched her gown in sweaty fists as her mind sought a plan of escape. "Can we go out of this room to talk?"

He frowned at her and moved toward the door. "You will stay here until all has played out."

She had to keep him in the room. "Where is Miss Coble?"

"Clarice? I would guess she is on her way here." He stood blocking the door. "Did you know she was Bryce's betrothed?"

"Yes, she has told me."

A wicked smile crept over his face. "I would wager she did not tell you she was here when Bryce died."

Brithwin shook her head.

"You see, she wanted to be Lady of Rosen Craig." He shook his head and glanced down. "However, she was impatient and didn't want to wait for Bryce's father to grow old and die. 'Twas quite a dilemma for her."

"I don't understand." She didn't but was beginning to. If he spoke the truth, she'd been naïve in trusting Clarice and not heeding her maid's and cook's warnings.

"Bryce was always busy and never had time for Clarice, so I befriended her. She was knowledgeable in healing herbs." The oily smile was back. "One day, I asked her to give me hemlock."

Brithwin shivered and hugged her arms to herself. He was an evil man, but he was her solitary hope to escape. "For what reason did you need hemlock?"

His smile broadened. "You will thank me for this. I brought your father dates laced with it." His eyes glittered as he began the story. "Your father, being the selfish man he was, wouldn't share them. Did you think he died from natural causes? Oh, no." His lips twitched into a smirk. "It was my revenge."

Brithwin choked. "Y-you killed my father?"

"Does it please you? You see"—he raised his hands and splayed them open before him—"where I made my mistake was, one of the dates had remained in my bag. When I returned home and laid the bag down, the one date I had missed rolled out and fell to the floor." He looked at the floor as if expecting to see it there. "I was not fast enough, and my brother's terrier pounced on it and ate it. The dog died. My brother had seen enough poison in his day and knew what it was."

"You poisoned him?" Brithwin's fingers bit into her arms as she tightened them, trying to still the quiver.

"'Twas an accident." He shrugged.

Brithwin did not correct him that she still spoke of her father, not the dog.

"Unfortunately, my brother knew I had asked your father for your hand and had been turned down. He also knew I hated your father for it. A few days later, when my brother heard of the death of your father, he discerned that I was the one who poisoned him."

Brithwin's stomach churned, but she had to know the truth. "He knew you killed my father, yet he did nothing?" Could Royce's father be so dishonorable?

Lyndle folded his arms in front of him. "My noble brother could not let me go unpunished but did not want to soil the family name. Oh, the dilemma of honor! While he was deciding what to do with me, he kept me locked in my room and told no one of my shame."

Another chill slid down her spine when he tipped his head.

"I was amazed the poisoning had been kept quiet. Not even you were aware, were you?"

Brithwin forced out a whisper. "Nay, I did not know."

"When Clarice heard the rumor of your father's death, she knew. She came to see me regularly after my brother locked me up."

"D-did she know what you planned to do when she gave you the hemlock?" Brithwin closed her eyes as she waited for the reply.

"She did not know with whom I sought to even the score, if that is what you ask."

Why was he telling her this? And what would he do to her now that she knew?

He glanced down and scuffed the floor with his boot. "When Edmond came to Rosen Craig and told of Royce's alleged death, I had an inspiration. Clarice was just the person I needed to help. The whole castle was in mourning for the beloved son. Three days later, she gave a sleeping draught in the meat at the evening meal then came to let me out after all had fallen into a deep sleep."

He paused and looked off as if reliving it. "When I killed my brother, his wife awoke and she began to scream." His voice wavered. "Lady Isobel, so beautiful. Did I tell you I loved her? It broke my heart, for apparently she had not eaten the meat. I tried to silence her, but she struggled and I—I broke her neck. 'Twas an accident. I would never have killed the woman I loved."

Brithwin flattened herself against the wall and took a step, eyeing the opening behind Royce's uncle.

For a fleeting moment, his feral eyes filled with pain.

"I went down and killed Bryce. The gatekeeper had not eaten the meat either. He rushed in when he heard Royce's mother scream. I met him coming into the castle. I sent him back to the gate, explaining Lady Isobel had had a bad dream."

"How could you kill your brother and nephew?" Brithwin sucked in her breath. He would not let her live now he had told her these things. The knot in her stomach gave another twist, shooting spears of fear through her veins.

"How else would I become Lord of Rosen Craig? I decided my last vengeance against your father would be to sully the name of Hawkwood by accusing them of the murders." He sniggered. "Then, to my surprise, Royce returns days later very much alive. Imagine my shock when I found out he was betrothed to you—and after I had named your father's castle as the party responsible for his family's death."

Brithwin clenched her fists. His callous attitude taunted her. He stepped back and out of the room.

"Wait!" Brithwin pushed away from the wall.

He stopped. She feared all was lost if she could not escape. She had to delay him.

She stepped forward. "What about the gatekeeper? He would know you lied."

"I went back and killed him too." He said it so casually, she could not stop the shiver this time. "Unfortunately, one of

Edmond's men had gotten sick and remained at Rosen Craig.
He was outside emptying his gut and saw me kill the guard."
He sighed and glanced toward the door. "Edmond has since
made demands on me."

She slowly edged her way forward. "Why did you not
kill Edmond's man so he could not tell?"

He looked at her as if she were witless. "Because I did
not know the man was there."

She edged closer to where he stood. "What did Edmond
want from you?"

"At first he wanted money. Then, he wanted me to help
him get retribution on Royce. He thought he could take
Rosen Craig and leave me Hawkwood and I would be happy.
He is a fool. So he devised a plan to kill my nephew."

She inched forward. "I do not understand. *You* would be
lord of Rosen Craig if Royce died without an heir." Her hand
went to her abdomen.

His gaze followed her hand and he frowned. "Edmond
thinks he can blackmail me into giving him Rosen Craig to
run as his own. Why should I give him anything, when I can
have it all, including you?" He paused and dragged his eyes
from where her hand lay to meet her gaze. "By now, Edmond
has ambushed and killed Lord Rosen Craig. When he returns
to claim this castle, I will tell Rosen Craig's knights what he
has done. They will dispatch him for the murder of my
nephew without my even bloodying my hands. Then I will
become Lord Rosen Craig."

Voices rang out from somewhere inside the castle. He
turned.

Brithwin lunged forward and darted out the door. She
caught a glimpse of freedom before Lyndle jerked her back
into the room.

He shoved her to the floor. Her body jolted as it hit the
hard surface, sending shards of pain through her hip and her

arm.

He narrowed his brows. "That was foolish. I must go speak with Edmond. He has returned from taking care of Royce."

As he pulled the door closed and darkness enveloped her once more, he snickered softly. "I shall return soon for you, my pet."

†††

Royce reached the top of the steps of the castle well ahead of his men and in time to glimpse Lyndle creeping from the shadows.

His uncle's jaw dropped. "My lord! What are you doing here?"

Royce studied Lyndle for a moment before the sword hanging at the older man's side caught his attention. "I did not know you wore a sword, Uncle."

Lyndle glanced down at the blade and slid it out. "'Tis beautiful, isn't it?"

The gems in the sword were well cut and costly. Royce recognized his father's sword. Looking up, he met Lyndle's smug smile.

"I noticed my father's sword missing. I assumed his murderer took it." Royce's gut twisted. He wanted to believe it wasn't true.

"You do not seem surprised." Lyndle's smile faded.

Royce flexed his hands. "One of Edmond's men was happy to share the information with me."

"Ah, yes, Edmond. He did not do his job." He ran his finger down the side of the sword. "Did you kill him?"

Royce nodded. His feet remained planted apart as he examined his uncle's behavior. "His men are dead, except one."

"Such a pity. I would have preferred to turn Edmond over to be killed. I am not made for all this bloodshed, but since he died rather than you, there is no choice, is there?" Lyndle lifted his weapon.

Fire blazed through Royce's veins. His knuckles burned where he gripped the hilt of his sword. His strength returned and, with the speed of a striking snake, Royce smacked his uncle's head with the flat of his sword. The man collapsed in a heap at the top of the stairs. A trickle of blood traced a path around his birthmark as if his own blood believed the lie of the superstition and was fearful of the mark.

Leaving Lyndle for his men to deal with, Royce turned and ran through the castle, looking for Brithwin. He rushed down the corridors, throwing open doors and calling out her name. With each empty room, his hope faded.

Where was she? He flung open the last door to find the room likewise empty. His heart lurched in his chest. He had to find her. Royce dashed back down the corridor, glancing in each room as he passed. He slowed, as muffled crying came from somewhere ahead of him. He stepped through the entrance of the next room and made a quick assessment—vacant. He reminded himself he'd never seen Brithwin cry. He was losing his mind. He turned to go, but again a quiet sob reached his ears. *That* was not in his mind. He turned. A narrow door in the wall held an old storage room that he'd forgotten about. Royce yanked it open, and light filled the tiny, dark cell. Brithwin lay curled in a ball on the floor.

He approached her. "Brithwin, love."

She remained curled up, sobbing.

Royce came down on his haunches, reached out, and gently laid his hand on her back. "Brithwin, my love, it is me."

Brithwin sat and launched herself against Royce's body. "You came. You live!"

"Aye, I am back." He gazed on a swollen cheek and eye. "Who did this?" He caressed her skin with the back of his finger.

She covered his hand with hers. "Edmond hit me after I—I stabbed him."

Still squatting, Royce pulled her into his arms, gently brushing his lips across the bruised skin. "If he were not already dead . . ."

"He is dead?" Her voice trembled.

"Aye, he will not bother us again." Royce stood and offered his hand. "Come."

He pulled her up. Brithwin threw her arms around him. Tears trickled down her cheek. "I thought I would never see you again. I thought I would never be able to tell you I love you."

Royce grasped her shoulders and squeezed. "You love me?"

She wrenched free and screamed as she swung herself between Royce and the door. He turned just as Lyndle brought down his sword.

Brithwin crumpled to the floor. Royce let out a howl. Lifting his sword, he warded off the second blow Lyndle intended for him. The small room held a disadvantage for both of them. Metal met metal, again and again.

The swords locked and Royce gazed down at the blood surrounding Brithwin—her chest lay still, breathless. Though exhausted from battle, Royce drew on his anger for strength. Lyndle staggered then braced himself against the wall. Royce hacked at Lyndle, putting him on the defensive. Lyndle pulled himself up, returning driving blows.

Lyndle lunged forward and swung his sword in an arc. Royce raised his weapon to block the blow. His uncle's foot slipped in Brithwin's blood, throwing him into Royce's blade as he fell. The sharp edge sliced through his tunic and into his chest before he tumbled to the floor with a thud. Crimson pumped from the wound onto his tunic. He didn't move.

Royce knelt. He still breathed. At least he didn't have another death at his hands.

Numbness filled his soul. He had lost. Without Brithwin, his life was worth nothing to him. He returned to his wife, pins pricking the back of his eyes. He had failed her.

She had told him she loved him, and he never had the chance to tell her. He slumped to the ground and pulled her in his lap. Her head dangled over his arm. Pushing her cheek against his chest, he drew her close. Tears broke free and fell unchecked.

He leaned against the wall. Closing his eyes, he drew his arms tightly around her limp body as a sob escaped him. She loved him.

†††

Commotion came from down the hall as he rocked Brithwin and stroked her hair. Jarren dashed into the small room. Lyndle's unconscious body lay in a pool of Brithwin's blood.

Jarren grunted and stepped over the body. "He dead?"

Royce shook his head.

Jarren squatted. "My lady?"

Royce swallowed the lump. "Aye. She saved me. The blade was meant for me."

Jarren leaned forward and grasped Royce's arm. "Come. At least let us take her away from here."

As Royce stood, Brithwin let out a soft gurgle. His breath caught in his throat. "She is not dead!"

"Nay. I heard her, too."

"Please, God, do not let her die." Royce's voice shook as he said his first prayer in two years. The words flowed out. He did not think about his sin, for in his desperation there was no place else to turn.

Yelling orders as he went, he rushed to the master's chamber with Brithwin in his arms and laid her on the bed.

"Jarren!"

Jarren stood in the doorway. "I am here."

"Quickly. Go and see if Clarice has arrived."

Jarren hastened out the door and down the stairs. When he returned a few minutes later, the cook, Nog, followed him. "She is not here, Royce. The cook said she has learned some in the art of healing."

Royce moved out of the way to allow the old woman room to tend to Brithwin. "Will she live?"

She opened a small cloth bag and pulled out two bowls. "I do not know, milord. She appears to have lost much blood. But I will do all I know to save her." She placed the bowls on the table next to the bed and crumbled leaves into the first one. The second bowl contained a salve. The old woman looked around the room.

Royce was anxious to have the bleeding stopped. "What do you look for?"

"I need water, milord. For the leaves."

Jarren had already rushed out of the room. By the time Royce turned to give orders, Jarren returned with a bucket of water and a cloth.

The old cook poured water on the leaves and left them to soak. Turning her attention to Brithwin, she dipped the cloth in the water and wiped the blood from Brithwin's wound. She picked up the soaking leaves and let the water drip into the gash.

Royce leaned forward. "What is that?"

"'Tis stonecrop, milord. The leaves should help her with the pain.

"She is unconscious. She feels no pain. You need to stop the bleeding." His voice came out harsh. He didn't care.

"Aye, milord." She picked up the salve and spread it around. Then she took a cloth and placed it on the wound, holding it securely with her hand.

Royce frowned. "What else can you do for her?"

"'Tis all I know to do, milord." The cook's voice quivered.

"I will hold the cloth."

"Aye, milord." She stood, shuffled to the door, and hesitated. "'Tis sorry I am about your lady." She disappeared out the door.

Royce glanced at Jarren, still standing on alert next to the portal. "She uses the same herbs Brithwin used on me when I was stabbed."

Jarren nodded.

With his other hand, Royce brushed her hair away from her face. She was pale. His chest tightened. "Have you found Pater?"

"Aye, he was found locked in a room. He has been beaten but he will live."

Royce swallowed to steady his voice. "It will mean much to Brithwin."

†††

Royce raised Brithwin's hand and kissed it. He lifted his lips enough to whisper a promise. "My lady, I shall not leave your side until you recover." Again, he brushed his mouth over her soft skin.

A knock sounded on the door and without hesitation, Jarren entered.

"Your uncle is awake in the holding and asks for you."

His uncle. If he had tied Lyndle up when he first knocked him out, Brithwin would not be lying here. "I will not see him until I know Brithwin lives." It was best for both of them.

"I understand." Jarren set down a trencher and goblet on the table. "I brought you food and something to drink."

"I am not hungry." He continued to stroke her hand.

Jarren sat and stretched out his legs. "You need to keep

your strength. You fought hard today."

"I cannot think about eating right now. All I know is I cannot lose her." Royce took a deep breath to conquer his emotions.

"You can do nothing more for her, Royce. You should eat and get some sleep." Jarren held out the trencher.

Royce pushed it away. "Thank you, my friend. Your concern is appreciated."

Jarren frowned and strolled out of the room. Royce gingerly climbed onto the bed with Brithwin. He slipped his arms around her and drew himself to her. If he could will her to live, he would. With a sigh, he closed his eyes and waited for sleep to come.

He woke with a start. The candle had burned down, giving only a flicker of light. His clothes were damp, and Brithwin thrashed in his arms.

She burned with fever.

Chapter 30

Royce carefully pulled his arms from around his wife's raging hot skin and sprang to the floor. Within two strides, he was at the door, bellowing for Nog.

"I am here, milord," she said from within the chamber. Royce turned as the woman rose from a pallet on the floor.

"She has the fever." His voice sounded strained even to himself. He could not lose Brithwin. He could not.

"'Tis what I feared." She pushed past him and shuffled to the bed. "We must keep her cool by wiping her down with a cold cloth. How long has she been like this?"

Royce shook his head. "I do not know. Her clothes are wet, her body hot, and she thrashes like she is tormented by demons."

He spent the remainder of the night bathing her with cool water and whispering his love to her. He allowed no one to minister to her, taking care of her needs himself.

When morning arrived, the sun streaked across the bed and shrouded Brithwin's quiet body. Even in sickness, she was beautiful. The thrashing had stopped just before dawn, but her lack of movement sent whispers of torture to his mind. Her chest rose and fell but her breathing was ever so shallow. Afraid to take his eyes away for fear her breaths would stop, he gently brushed her hair away from her face. The fever remained an insidious enemy that was slowly stealing her from him. He dipped the cloth and bathed her face again.

†††

A light tapping on the door brought Royce's head around. "Enter." Three days he had sat vigil tending to

Brithwin in an attempt to keep her fever down. He'd
expected Pater to walk through the door for the daily prayer
over his wife. If God would listen to anyone, it would be a
man like Pater.

Clarice poked her head in the door. "My lord, I have
come to see if I can be of any assistance."

"Come in." Exhaustion racked his body, but he forced a
smile. She was good to check regularly on Brithwin.

Clarice stepped into the room. "How is she today?"

"For days she has fought this fever. You know some
healing. Tell me she will get better." Would the fever
continue to draw out until it took every bit of her life?

"I wish I could tell you, my lord, but it is out of our
control." She placed her hand on his shoulder. "You look
tired. I can take this vigil for you."

"Aye, I am that." He handed her the wet cloth then
walked around and lay on the bed.

"You should go to another room where you will not be
disturbed so you can get rest." She smiled at him as she sat
next to Brithwin.

Royce closed his eyes and threw his arm over them to
block out the sunlight. "I have given her my vow. I will
remain by her side until she is well."

Clarice raised her eyebrows. "She has woken, then?"

Royce lifted his arm and peeked at Clarice. "Nay, but
that matters not. I have made the vow. I will stay."

He had not left her side since he brought her in. He
feared if he were to leave, when he returned she would be
dead. It was a foolish thought but real enough to make him
promise to stay with her. He closed his eyes again. Brithwin
was strong. She had to be because she could not die. He
would not allow it. He would will her to live.

By eventide, Brithwin again tossed and turned in her
sleep. The fever rose, leaving her skin hot to the touch. Once

again alone with her, Royce spent the night bathing her body in the cool water. The lack of sleep had taken its toll on him. His mind clouded over with the repetitive motions, as he wiped, dipped, and wrung out water.

When morning arrived, Clarice tiptoed into the chamber. "How is Brithwin?"

Royce grinned. "Her fever broke with dawn."

Clarice halted. "So she will live?" Shock filled her voice.

"'Tis a glorious day, I tell you. With the fever gone, 'tis only a matter of time before she wakes."

"I am sure you are right." Clarice glided over to the bed. "She is a fortunate woman to have a man like you."

Royce caressed Brithwin's cheek with the back of his finger. "Nay, I am the fortunate one."

Clarice ran her hand down his arm. "Now she is well, would you like me to stay with her for a bit?"

He leaned back in his chair and yawned. "I do not need to leave, but you have my thanks."

When Clarice shut the door, Royce went and lay beside Brithwin. He scooted next to her and pressed his lips to her forehead. She remained cool. She would live. He was certain. A sigh escaped him as he drifted off to sleep.

Royce woke to more tapping at the door.

Clarice sailed into the room with a goblet in hand. "Royce, I have brought an herb drink for Brithwin."

His hackles prickled that she had entered their room without invitation. "What is this?" Royce sat, took the goblet from her, and smelled it.

"'Tis herbs used for healing." She took the herb mix back. "Can you help me get this in her?"

"What is it for?" He moved behind Brithwin, holding her, while Clarice forced the liquid down her throat.

"She needs to gain her strength. This will help."

Brithwin choked. Royce frowned. "Have a care. She

knows not she is supposed to swallow."

"Aye, my lord." Clarice's chin flew up and her lips tightened.

He wiped the liquid off Brithwin's face and neck with the bedsheet. A young servant knocked and poked her head in the open door. Royce waved her in. She quietly came in and set a tray on the table beside him before scurrying out of the room.

Clarice narrowed her eyes. "Your people would like to see you take meals with them in the hall. It would give them a feeling all is well."

Royce threw the cloth into the pan of water. "Brithwin is the one I concern myself with now."

"Of course, my lord." She went to the door and turned. "I will bring her more of the healing herbs on the morrow. She should be taking the drink twice a day."

"Thank you, Clarice. We will see she doesn't miss any of her doses. My lady is fortunate in having you for a friend."

†††

Royce stared at Brithwin. What had gone wrong? Three days had passed since her fever broke. Yet her health continued to decline. She lay on the bed, delirious and vomiting. The broth they fed her came up almost as quickly as it went down. Immediately after her fever broke, she'd become sick. She awoke, but her ramblings made no sense, she kept no food down, and from what he could tell, her vision had deteriorated. He witnessed her slipping away a little more each day and could do nothing to prevent it. He'd not had a chance to tell her he loved her, and he would not say so until she could hear and understand the words that would leave his lips.

Brithwin moaned and wrapped her arms around her belly. Her eyes fluttered open but the lack of recognition told him the delirium remained.

Royce picked up a goblet. "Here, drink some water." Clarice sailed in the room with the herb drink in hand. "Nay, my lord. She has not had her herbs today. It is important she drinks this and gets nourishment."

Clarice placed the goblet to Brithwin's lips. Brithwin pushed the goblet away.

"You must drink this if you are to get better." Clarice's voice was stern.

Brithwin slapped at the goblet, and it spilled down the front of her and onto the bed. She opened her mouth, but no words came out.

Clarice growled and shoved her fists onto her hips. "Look what you have done. Now I will have to make more." She jerked her head up and met Royce's glare. "I am sorry, Lord Rosen Craig. It is the worry that frustrates me."

Royce searched Brithwin's face. Her eyes were wide and glassy. Was that alarm? Nay, it was terror in her eyes. She must be confused again. Her illness continued to rip his heart out. He wanted to assure her she would be fine. "You may leave, Clarice. I will see to my wife."

Brithwin again tried to speak, but no sound left her throat. Royce put his finger to her lips. "Shh. All is well. I will take care of you. Do you want water?"

Brithwin nodded her head.

He put the goblet to her lips, and she took small sips.

"You must rest and get well. Let me get you in dry clothes and bedding."

By the time he had finished making her comfortable, Brithwin had fallen asleep. Royce turned to the sound of sniffling.

The old cook stood peeking in the door. "She is dying, milord."

"Do not speak those words!" Royce would not consider her death. Not when she'd come this far.

"You have to know this, milord." Nog backed up. "Prepare yourself."

"Nay! Go!" Royce's words spewed forth in a roar.

She spun around and scurried out of the room. Her whimpers faded with the tapping of her footsteps. He should not have yelled at her. She spoke the truth. Brithwin was dying. Everyone knew it but was afraid to speak it and feel his wrath. Nog took the risk because she cared.

Royce summoned Pater to his chamber, anxious for him to come and not wanting to wait for the man to show up on his own.

Minutes later, Brithwin's father moved quietly into the room. "You wish to see me, my lord?"

Royce leaned over Brithwin's body on the bed. "Brithwin is—dying. I wish for you to pray for her to live."

Pater raised anguished eyes. "You know I pray for my daughter daily, my lord. Do you pray for her?"

Royce shook his head without taking his eyes off Brithwin. "I cannot, as you are well aware."

Pater straightened and lifted his chin. "Cannot or will not?"

Royce closed his eyes. "Must we go through this again? You do not understand."

"I have come here every day since Brithwin has been sick. I ache inside also, son. I have not had so much as an hour with her as my daughter. But I have hope in the Lord. What I see in you is a man tormented by his past. Tell me about it. I am here to help."

Royce slumped down to the chair in silence, his gaze fixed on Brithwin. If it were only so simple. He would do anything to spare Brithwin's life, including give his own.

Pater moved closer. "Do you love her?"

Royce's voice caught. "More than life itself."

"Did you tell her?"

"There has not been any time." His throat thickened. He pinched his eyes shut to keep the tears at bay.

Pater placed his hand on Royce's shoulder and leaned over. "Then show her. She wanted you to forgive yourself and find forgiveness with God. 'Twas her greatest desire."

Royce pushed Pater's hand from him and stood. "We are back to that. You do not know what I have done. There is no forgiveness for someone like me. I am beyond absolution."

"Do you believe that?"

Royce took a deep breath. "I not only believe it, but I know it to be true."

"If I could prove to you God forgives you"—Pater cocked his head and eyed Royce—"could you then forgive yourself?"

Royce scoffed at him. "Who am I to not forgive if God can?"

Pater walked over and sat. "Come, pull over a chair, and sit with me so we can talk."

Royce dropped on the chair and leaned forward, putting his head in his hands. He did not want to talk about his past; since he returned from the uprising, his life had been nothing but heartache.

"Tell me what you have done that you believe God will not forgive."

His heart banged like a battering ram in his chest so that the roar of blood filled his ears. Just thinking of his past caused a knot in his stomach. The memories tormented him. How could he tell a godly man like Pater what he had done?

Understanding showed in Pater's eyes. "Do not believe me above sin, my son. God tells us, all have sinned and fallen short of the glory of God. What you have done will not shock me."

Did this man read minds? If he did, then he already knew his secrets. Royce clenched his hands into fists and cleared his throat as he lifted his head. "'Twas the day we rode into the small village in Scotland. We weren't aware that Edmond had taunted the people, raping some, killing others, and promising to return. The people were angry. Having heard of an uprising but not knowing the cause, my father sent me to squelch it."

Royce shook his head. "It all happened so fast. The men came rushing out to defend their land and families, but we just saw a rebellion. We were seasoned warriors. They died. Then the young boys came out and many of my men had *the fever* and began slaying…" He choked. "They were only children. I tried to stop them, but too many had gone wild. They went after the women. I could not control my men."

"I understand you had to kill your own men to stop the bloodshed."

Royce swallowed. "I had no choice. But now, their blood, too, is on my hands. I hesitated in my orders. I was the leader. By doing nothing, I condoned their actions. I should have taken my sword against them before the first boy fell."

"You are only a man, son." Pater's voice softened. "You had a hard decision to make, and you did what you had to do. It is no wonder you hesitated making that judgment."

Royce shook his head as the memories of slaughter burned through his mind.

Brithwin's father leaned forward. "We all have sinned, son, even David, the man after God's own heart. He committed adultery and then had the woman's husband murdered, and yet God still loved him."

Royce shoved his hands through his hair and glanced at the ceiling. He didn't know a lot about the bible, but he did know David was special to God—called a man after God's own heart. And he, Royce, meant nothing to God. "But how many more could I have saved if I had not delayed?"

"God will forgive you this." Pater smiled. "He has

forgiven other men far more."

Why couldn't this man understand that just because you wish it to be so does not make it so? "And how do you know he has forgiven more? Perhaps these men simply are not bothered by their sin."

"I know because God's word tells us of such men. There is Paul, the man who wrote much of the New Testament. He persecuted the Christians. Had them put to death and even held the clothes of Steven as they stoned him, yet God forgave him and used him in a mighty way to reach the gentiles for Christ."

Royce looked into the eyes of this godly man. Their love and warmth gave him hope. "I would have this forgiveness if I could."

Pater bent forward. "You can. It is for every man. It is a gift. You need only accept it."

Royce stood and walked away. Pater was a godly man and he had deep respect for him. The man would not lie to him or give him false hope. But how could God who knows no sin forgive him? The possibility gave him hope and joy, but also fear. Fear that Pater could be wrong.

Royce thought about Paul and all the deaths that blotted his soul. If God could truly forgive Paul, maybe, just maybe his sin wasn't too great for God. He crossed the room and bowed his head. Pouring out his heart to God, he laid his sin, guilt, and pain before Him. He gave the Lord his pride and fear of not measuring up. He had tried to remain distant to Brithwin and to God so he didn't have to be found lacking, and because of it, he had kept himself from receiving the things he wanted the most. The burden lifted from his soul like the sun shining through the clouds on a gloomy day. The darkness that had hovered over him for so long disappeared. Peace settled on him and wrapped around him like a cloak. When he lifted his head, he was a forgiven man.

His gaze met Pater's.

Pater smiled. "You have found forgiveness?"

"Aye."

"Now, my son, you go and pray for your wife." Pater stood and walked out of the room.

For the rest of the day, Royce remained with Brithwin, praying God would spare her life.

The following day, Brithwin lost the babe.

His heart was heavy for the precious life he and his wife had lost. His shoulders held the weight of a castle stone. Would he bury his wife, too? Even in his grief, he found comfort in knowing that if he never had another moment with her here on earth, he would see her in heaven.

Time passed, but he no longer kept track. When he was not praying, he would climb into the bed, slip his arms around Brithwin, and hold her close.

Light filtered in through the window. A knock sounded, and then Jarren opened the chamber door. "How is she this morning?"

Royce sat beside her, holding her hand. "There has been no change. She is weak. I do not know how she hangs on." His heart ached, for he truly did not know how much longer she would cling to life.

Jarren leaned against the door frame. "Marjory and Elspeth have come to see her. They traveled back with Philip after he took your message to Hawkwood."

"Tell them they may come up."

Moments later, Royce bid them to enter and moved to sit on the other side of the bed. Elspeth gasped as her gaze fell on Brithwin. She slapped her hand over her mouth, choked on a sob, and fled from the room. Royce knew then how bad she looked. He'd spent every day with her, but to these women who had last seen her healthy and full of life, the sight came as a shock.

Marjory sat on the edge of the bed and lifted Brithwin's hand to her cheek. Tears filled the old woman's eyes.

Clarice walked in with Brithwin's herbal drink, drawing Royce's attention to her. "Set it on the table. I will give it to her later."

Clarice nodded and left the room.

Marjory's eyes narrowed and her brows furrowed. "What is that?"

"'Tis an herb drink Clarice makes, to give her nourishment other than the broth we give her."

"And how long has she taken this mixture?"

Royce ran his hand over his face. "Since the day her fever broke."

"I would like to see this drink." Marjory got off the bed and walked to the table. She picked it up and smelled it.

"Is something amiss?" Royce frowned.

"I am not sure. A faint smell, could be foxglove. 'Tis hard to know. Oh, there is one way to know for sure." Marjory tipped the goblet and drank.

Royce sat with eyes fixed on Marjory. Could it be possible that Clarice had betrayed him and Brithwin? Could he have been so worried about his wife that he didn't see her deception? "If you believe it poisoned, why did you drink it?"

Marjory smiled. "If it is, it is not enough to kill me. Just make me sick. Did you not say Brithwin has drunk it since the fever left her over a sennight ago?"

Royce didn't take his eyes from Marjory. He should have drunk the mixture if there was a chance it was tainted. He was young and healthy. "Aye. How long before we will know?"

Marjory moved to the chair. "Within the hour." She leaned back in the chair, resting her hands in her lap as if she waited for nothing more than a bite to eat.

He could not believe this of Clarice. She had taken the time every day to make this healing drink for Brithwin. She had sat with his wife and bathed her feverish body. "If Clarice had meant to poison her, do you not think she would give her enough to kill her, not just make her sick?" How could he forgive himself if he had helped give her the poison every day?

Marjory's brows furrowed. "She gives her a small amount so you believe she is sick, and when she gives her the fatal dose, you will not suspect anything."

"But you speak as if you have no doubt."

Marjory stood, flew to the chamber pot, and emptied her stomach.

She turned around and looked Royce in the eyes. "Aye, I know." Then she doubled over.

Royce was at her side, lifting her in his arms. He laid her on the bed beside Brithwin.

"'Twas foolish, Marjory. How do you know this was not the fatal dose?" Royce chided. Now he would have to worry for both their lives.

Marjorie groaned. "Nay, the smell was too faint. It was not strong enough to take my life."

Royce made his way to the portal, and opening it, he roared for Clarice.

Clarice padded up the stairs and into the chamber. She wrinkled her nose as she stepped in the room. Royce shut the door.

"You sound angry, my lord. Would you like me to remove this servant?" She motioned toward Marjory on the bed.

"Nay. She can stay for the time being."

Marjory moaned.

Clarice turned. "What is wrong with her?"

Royce's face burned. He flexed his hands. He had never

hit a woman, but he burned to strike this one. "She drank Brithwin's herb drink."

The color drained from Clarice's face, and she stepped back. "Wh—what are you saying?"

He moved toward her. "I think you know, Clarice. You have been poisoning my wife."

"Nay, 'tis not true!" Clarice took another step backward. He glared at her. "Aye, and with foxglove. Marjory caught a faint hint of it, and that is why she drank it."

Clarice continued inching toward the door. When she bumped into it, she turned, opened the door, and fled.

Royce strode out after her to the edge of the stairs. Clarice had gone down two steps and stared below her. He looked around her to see what held her attention. His eyes caught sight of the knight at the bottom of the stairs the same time Clarice went limp and fell forward. He was powerless to reach her before she tumbled.

Royce's legs weakened. He grabbed hold of the wall for support.

Bryce, his dead brother, stared up at him.

Chapter 31

Royce's brother, Bryce, put his ear to Clarice's chest. Royce rushed down the stairs, ready to call Nog. Bryce slowly raised his head and tucked a strand of hair behind Clarice's ear. His pinched mouth and furrowed brow gave Royce his answer.

"I could not catch her." Bryce choked his words out as he scooped her in his arms and sat on the step.

"Nor could I. I am sorry, Brother." Royce wanted to throw his arms around this dead brother who'd come back to life—and to ask him where he had been.

"My return shocked her—caused her to fall." Bryce's hand trembled as he rocked her.

She probably had realized she'd thrown everything away and for nothing. Clarice would have been lady of the castle after all. His brother cradled Clarice's lifeless body, caressing her cheek.

Instead of the anger Royce experienced moments earlier when he'd confronted her about poisoning his wife, he felt pity for her. She'd died searching for happiness.

"Nay, there is much more to it than the shock of seeing you." He rubbed his brother's shoulder.

With Clarice still in his arms, Bryce stood.

Jarren came around the corner, with Elspeth on his heels, and nearly tripped. His wide-eyed stare told Royce that Jarren was seeing Bryce for the first time.

Royce turned to Elspeth. "Go tend to Brithwin and Marjory."

Elspeth's gaze swept over them, landing on Clarice, and then bouncing up to Bryce. There was a strong resemblance between him and his brother, and it was obvious she'd seen it. "Aye, my lord." She skirted around Bryce and headed up the stairs and turned. "Marjory, my lord?"

"Aye. She is not feeling well."

Royce turned his gaze back to his brother, his chest filling nearly to bursting. He loved this man. "Come, Brother, we have much to discuss."

Bryce took a step, with Clarice still in his arms, and Royce stopped. A crowd of curious servants had begun to gather. Royce called two of his men to take care of Clarice's body.

"Nay." Bryce hugged her to him—his face contorting.

Royce knew well how Bryce felt. But Royce's anguish had only been temporary when he'd discovered Brithwin lived. Bryce would not be so fortunate.

He grasped his brother's arm. "I will explain." Royce gently squeezed his arm as they took Clarice's body.

Bryce followed him to the solar. His brother's homecoming had been tarnished by Clarice's death, but Royce could not contain the joy within him. When he closed the door, he threw his arms around Bryce and thumped him soundly on the back before holding him at arm's length and looking him over. He had lost weight. "I had thought you dead— killed by Lyndle."

Bryce's brows drew together. "Lyndle?"

Royce glanced at the door as footfalls passed. He held up his finger until they were alone again. He did not wish to be disturbed. "Aye, 'twas our uncle behind the attempt on your life."

Bryce scrubbed his hands down his face. "I do not understand. You say Lyndle attempted to kill me?"

Royce wished there were words to comfort his brother but knew only God and time could do that. He had so many questions, but Bryce needed time to grieve. And would need answers himself. One thing he had to know. "Mother and father, were they rescued also?" A glimmer of hope flickered in his soul as he awaited his brother's reply.

Bryce stared off. "I lay near death for weeks. Much of the first weeks, I have no recollection. All I know is what the healer has told me. She and her husband prepared Mother's and Father's bodies, but when they came to mine, they saw I still lived—though barely. They buried the carcass of a deer in my place. Then, in the night, they slipped me out through the bolt-hole."

Royce led him to a chair, his hope for his parents gone. "Why? Did they know it was Lyndle?"

Bryce leaned back and stretched out his legs. "Nay, they did not know whom to trust. They took me away until I was well enough to travel and could decide for myself what to do."

"So you came to confront our uncle?" Royce leaned forward, anxious to hear Bryce's reply and still not believing he sat before him.

Bryce's pale complexion and sunken eyes gave witness to how close to death he had been, and eerily reminded him of Brithwin. "Truly, I was not sure if what I remembered was real or one of my nightmares."

Royce shook his head slowly. "I do not know how the old couple carried your hulking body out of here. God must have given them Samson's strength." Although that same body had withered to much less.

"Something like that." Bryce attempted a smile. "They brought their sons to help. But you? Last we'd heard, you were killed in battle. How is it you sit before me?"

"That was just one of Edmond's lies." Royce shifted in his chair. He would have to tell him about Clarice. He hated to add to his pain. Royce cleared his throat. "Did you love Clarice?"

"'Twas a marriage of convenience." Bryce shrugged.

"You know we were betrothed as children."

Royce could see through Bryce's armor. "I remember, but you have not answered my question." He studied his brother closely.

"Aye, I grew to love her." His words caught in his throat.

Royce wanted to comfort him, but what he must tell him would only add to his grieving spirit. 'Twould be easier if Bryce had not loved her. "I do not think it was just the shock of seeing you that caused her to fall, although that was a great one." Grief rose afresh on his brother's face, and he wished there were a less painful way to tell him. "Marjory and I had just discovered Clarice was poisoning Brithwin, and I confronted her. She fled the room and that is when she saw you."

Royce could see the disbelief in his brother's eyes. "Who are Marjory and Brithwin? And why would Clarice try to poison anyone?"

Royce pushed himself out of the chair and paced. "Brithwin is my wife." He suddenly realized his brother knew nothing of his new life. "She was given to me in marriage by the king. I received the missive as I left for the north to put down the rebellion. She is the heir of Hawkwood. Marjory is the healer there." He paused and turned.

Bryce stood and folded his arms in front of him. "Why would Clarice try to kill her?"

"She wanted to be lady of Rosen Craig. I am sure this is hard to believe—her a murderer. I think she felt Rosen Craig was rightfully hers." Royce stopped and took a deep breath, trying to give his brother time to absorb what he was hearing. "I wish I did not have such grievous news for you—"

Bryce raised his hands to stop him from speaking. "I cannot believe this. Clarice is not like that."

"Truthfully, I did not believe she harbored any ill will toward my wife until today. She did not deny it when I confronted her. She ran."

Bryce rubbed his hand over his short beard. "'Tis hard to take in."

Royce met his brother's troubled gaze. "I will give you time alone. I need to be up with my wife. She is not faring well."

Giving his brother privacy to come to terms with Clarice's betrayal, Royce returned to his chamber. Brithwin slept but Marjory clutched her belly and moaned.

"I hate to disturb you, Marjory, but I must know something. Will Brithwin live? For she no longer takes the poison."

"She is weak, my lord. I cannot tell you that answer. Only God knows whether your wife will survive."

Royce called Jarren and had him take Marjory to another room so she could rest without being disturbed. He sat on the bed next to Brithwin. Right now, he wanted to be alone with his wife. If this was to be her last day, he didn't want to share it with anyone. He pushed her hair away so he could better see her face and stroked the side of her cheek. Even in sickness, her skin was as soft as a rose petal.

Putting his trust in God proved hard at a time like this. To believe whatever God chose was for the best—and to accept it—he questioned that he had strong enough faith.

He leaned over and kissed each of Brithwin's eyelids. "You must get well, love, and teach me how to have a stronger faith. I do not wish to do this alone."

Royce climbed onto the bed and encompassed her in his arms, the same as he had done every day. He buried his head into her hair and beckoned sleep to take him.

†††

Over a fortnight had passed since Brithwin fell ill, and

three days since she had drank her last dose of foxglove. Marjory sat in the chair next to Royce—her face etched in worry.

Royce wanted some sort of explanation he could understand. "You have been well for two days. Why does she not come around?"

"Truth to tell, I do not know. I would say it is all her body has gone through. She had much more poison in her than I did along with the fever. She lost much blood from the wound and she also lost the babe. She has been through much."

"But she will live."

"As I said, she was wounded, poisoned, then lost a babe. 'Tis a miracle she is still alive, milord."

"How much longer, do you think?" He left the question open to her interpretation.

Marjory glanced at her folded hands and then at Royce. "If she does not come out of it soon, I am concerned she never will. She weakens daily without more nourishment than broth."

She left the room, and Royce slid to his knees and prayed. He prayed through the noon and evening meals, stopping only to see to Brithwin's needs. He lit several candles around the room and returned to his vigil. The candles burned to mere nubs, and he continued to beseech the Lord to spare Brithwin's life.

†††

Brithwin opened her eyes to find Royce kneeling on the floor with red-rimmed eyes, his voice so full of pain—she shut her eyes and opened them again. Did she dream? He remained on his knees. Praying. He prayed, and for her. She tried to swallow, but her parched throat would not allow it.

She lifted her hand—so heavy—it took all her strength to raise it. She let it fall on Royce's shoulder. His muscle tightened under her palm. He raised his head, his eyes full of uncertainty.

She smiled at him. "Water." Her voice came out barely a rasp. How long had she slept?

"Thank you, Lord!" Royce wrapped his arms around her and kissed her tenderly. "I thought I would lose you. There was precious little hope."

"Water." If she did not get water soon, she surely *would* die.

Royce grabbed the goblet from the table and helped her drink from it. "Slowly, you do not want to make yourself sick."

The cool liquid running down her throat was pure delight. She lifted her eyes, looking over the goblet at a man at peace.

She took another swallow and pushed the goblet away. "You have changed."

A smile spread across his face and his eyes twinkled. "Aye, I have found forgiveness."

She tried to smile and winced as her lips cracked. "'Tis a glorious thing, forgiveness."

Royce's smile faded, and he gazed on her with longing. "I love you. When I thought you would die, I had a glimpse of how empty my life would be without you."

She touched a tear as it slid down his face. "You do not know how I have longed to hear those words come from your lips."

He laughed, and a mischievous gleam shone in his eyes. "I think I fell in love with you the day you walked in on me while I took a bath."

Brithwin licked her lips and smiled at the memory. "You mean, while you were taking *my bath*," she whispered.

Royce threw his head back and laughed. "'Twas your bath. Aye."

"I am glad you admit that now."

"And you, my lady…when did you know?"

"When Guy, Murielle, and Malcolm were murdered and you held me. 'Twas then I knew, but I think I began to fall in love with you when you gave Lucas a home instead of punishment."

Royce ran his hand across his chin. "Hmm, that reminds me. I need to talk to the boy. I would like to know what he was doing out in the woods alone, and with a horse at that."

Her eyes grew heavy and she gave in to a yawn. There were so many questions she had, but she was so tired. "Do not deal with him too harshly." Her words faded.

Royce chuckled. "You know not what I speak of and you defend the lad. But I will keep in mind had he not known where you were taken, it is hard to say what might have happened."

Lifting heavy lids, she glimpsed his smile.

"You need to rest and get well." He brushed his lips over hers.

Her eyes popped open. "Royce, I need to tell you about Lyndle and Clarice."

"Not now. When you are well, there will be plenty of time for that. Lyndle is locked up, and Clarice is dead. You have been delirious for nigh on ten days now. If you are stronger on the morrow, I will tell you all that has transpired. But for now, rest, my love, you are safe."

†††

Brithwin was pleased that Royce finally allowed her to sit in the solar with him and his brother. She had not the strength to walk unassisted, even though three days had passed since she woke. Royce cheerfully carried her everywhere, claiming he didn't want to take a chance on her falling. She smiled. God had a sense of humor. All these years worrying about being strong, now here she was, weak as a babe. And this man became only more tender to her in her weakness.

Her smile faded as her hand went to her belly. "Why the sad face, love?" Royce's voice held concern.

Brithwin sighed and glanced at her belly. "I was thinking about the babe."

His eyes softened, giving her comfort. She was not alone.

"It was a sad day when we lost our child, but I thank God he spared you." He brushed the back of his finger tenderly over her cheek. "We must trust God that He knows what is best for us."

Bryce coughed. "So, Royce, why did you remain at Hawkwood after you married? I would have thought you would want to be here, where you grew up."

Royce turned his attention to his brother. "The memories were more than I cared to confront. 'Twas painful to be here and know I would never see any of you again." He winked. "And I had a wife I needed to tame."

Brithwin harrumphed.

Royce chuckled.

"Looks like you did a good job." Bryce grinned.

Brithwin shifted in her chair, uncomfortable with the attention on her. And furthermore, since she had lost so much weight, prolonged sitting became difficult. "Did you talk to Lucas and find out why he was in the woods?"

Royce stretched out and crossed his ankles. "Thomas had sent him to the village to bring back one of our horses. You could say he took the long way back to the castle once he found himself on a horse. 'Tis hard to get angry with the lad when I think from what he may have saved you."

Bryce leaned back. "Who would have thought our own uncle would betray us? I would like to know what he intended to do with Clarice, had his plan succeeded."

"I think your death addled Clarice's brain. She could not accept you were gone and that her hopes and dreams of becoming Lady of Rosen Craig and escaping her brother's cruelty had disappeared. I can understand that." Brithwin shivered.

"What of Edmond?" Bryce asked.

"He intended to betray Lyndle. Originally, he had planned to let Lyndle have Brithwin. But when Montfort escaped, he told Edmond what he had heard when we believed he was unconscious." Royce's gaze caught Brithwin's. "I am sorry. I was the reason they kidnapped your father. I spoke with Jarren and mentioned he had been a follower of Wycliffe. Edmond had wanted to get in the king's good graces and get Rosen Craig. He thought to do that by giving the king a Lollard. He abducted Pater and then planned on marrying Brithwin to insure Rosen Craig went to him." Royce shook his head. "There is no honor among thieves. They both planned to betray the other."

Bryce held the goblet in his hand and swirled the liquid in it. "They have changed our lives forever with their wickedness. I have trained my whole life to rule Rosen Craig, but I never believed I would have to do it so early."

Royce chuckled. "Can you imagine how I felt when I suddenly had two fortresses to run? You will do well. Trust in God. He will see you through."

Bryce shifted and broke his eye contact with Royce. "It will be a lonely place when you two are gone." Bryce tipped the goblet and took a swallow.

"Then come see us." Royce pushed himself up. "But now I need to put my wife to bed before she falls asleep and slides off her chair."

Royce walked over, scooped Brithwin into his arms, and strode to their chamber.

†††

Two weeks later, Royce sat on Shadowmere as they readied to leave Rosen Craig.

Bryce handed Brithwin up to sit in front of him. "You take care traveling to Hawkwood."

"I will see this trip is as easy as possible on her." He shifted Brithwin to make her more comfortable. "We will be lucky to reach there before darkness falls on the morrow."

Royce gazed at his brother—his friend. He had healed—at least physically. Clarice's betrayal had hit him hard. God alone knew how long it would take him to be able to trust again. How he wished Bryce would open up to God's love. He could only lead Bryce to God. His brother would have to choose for himself, as he had. Hopefully his brother would be less stubborn than he.

Royce reached out and clasped Bryce's outstretched hand. "Do not make yourself too scarce now. We are not far."

"Once I get settled in here and caught up on my duties, I will make a trip to see you and Lady Brithwin."

"If you wait until the work around here is done, it will be nigh on a year before you come." Royce grinned. "Hmm, that may work out. You can come see your new nephew."

Bryce arched a brow.

Royce nodded emphatically. "Oh, aye, I plan to have an heir before a year passes." He turned and winked at Brithwin.

A rosy hue crept up her face and she frowned.

Bryce chuckled. "I think you have gotten yourself in trouble, dear brother."

"That is the way it appears." Royce smiled back.

Brithwin sat straight and put her hands on her hips in mock disgust. "If you two are through."

"It looks like you need to turn on the charm, old boy." Bryce slapped him on the leg.

"And we all know I have plenty of that."

Brithwin laughed.

Royce grew serious. "If you need me for anything, do not forget I am but two days' ride."

They spurred their horses out the gate and headed for home.

††††

Nigh on three months had passed since their return to Hawkwood, and Brithwin's strength had restored. She felt quite well—a smile crept across her face—at least most of the time.

Brithwin touched the cloth that covered her eyes. "Why may I not see where we are going?"

Royce's breath tickled the back of her neck. "I told you, how many times now? It matters not how you ask the question, the answer remains the same. 'Tis a surprise."

"Are we almost there?" She squirmed in her seat.

Royce brushed her hair away from her neck and nibbled. "I can think of better things to do than talking."

Brithwin attempted a stern voice. "Royce, we are on a horse! Behave yourself."

He chuckled. "I am trying, love, but it is hard with you sitting in front of me."

Brithwin sniffed and lifted her chin. "If you had not insisted I be blindfolded, I could be riding my palfrey."

He nibbled some more. "Hmm, but then think of all the fun we would be missing."

Brithwin folded her arms and pouted. "But I want to know where we are headed. 'Tis driving me mad."

"Do you not like surprises?" He sounded shocked, and she envisioned him with his eyebrows raised.

"I love surprises, as you well know." She shifted again.

He tightened his arms around her. "Aye, I do know, and that is why I kept it secret."

"You should not have told me last night. I hardly slept at

all, and this trip seems as if it is taking forever."

Royce groaned. "We left half an hour ago, Wife."

Brithwin bit her bottom lip to keep from smiling. He was becoming exasperated with her. "If you could see nothing, you would feel the same way."

"'Tis five minutes longer, no more." He let out a gust of breath.

She leaned against him and sighed. "Then I can wait."

A few moments later, Shadowmere stopped on Royce's command. His arms loosened. "We are here."

Brithwin reached to take the cloth from her eyes. Royce grabbed her hand. "Not yet."

His feet hit the ground with a thud, and then he lifted her from the horse. He carried her a few steps and let her down. "Let me do the honors." He plucked the blindfold from her eyes.

Brithwin gasped. "You remembered!" Her gaze slowly took in her surroundings. He had brought her to the river and to her favorite spot. And before her, spread out on the ground, a blanket, and on it, a feast. She smiled, for sitting in the center was a bouquet of flowers that held a multitude of colors.

She heard a cough and spun around.

Lucas leaned against a tree. "I see as you made it, m'lord."

Royce looked around as if he were searching the area. "Did you hear something?"

Brithwin giggled and gazed at a frowning Lucas.

Lucas cleared his throat. "I meant to say, I am pleased you have arrived safely, my lord."

Royce smiled, and his eyes twinkled with merriment. "Much better. If you are going to be my squire, I expect you to speak correctly."

"Yes, my lord." Lucas stepped toward a small palfrey.

"Very good. Now you can take the horse and be on your way. I appreciate your watching things here."

Lucas climbed onto the mount next to him. "I hope as you have a time of it, m'lord," he blurted, then rode off.

Royce rolled his eyes. "I think he does it to annoy me." Brithwin giggled. Her husband was a different man. One filled with compassion, forgiveness, and love. Thomas and Father were both right. He was a good and honorable man. God had not simply seen her through everything, He had richly blessed her. "'Twas kind of you to take him on as your squire and give him a horse."

Royce's eyes softened. "He helped save your life." He coughed. "And he uses one of *my* horses."

Brithwin grinned. Lucas was full of mischief, but Royce was good to the lad.

Royce pulled his sword from its scabbard and placed it on the ground. He helped her onto the blanket and joined her. After they had eaten their fill, he lay back, resting his head on a log. He tugged her down beside him.

Brithwin watched his hand cover the hilt of his weapon, and she shivered. She could still feel the stabbing pain of the cold steel as Lyndle thrust his blade into her. Her gaze rose to Royce's, and she knew he had discerned her thoughts.

"'Tis a part of life we have to accept, my love." Royce stroked her hair.

She sighed. Aye, it was. But there was another part of life they could embrace. Brithwin couldn't keep the smile from her face. His surprise for her worked to her advantage. She had waited for the right time and place to share her own surprise with him. "While we are talking of life, I have something to tell you." She lifted her head so she could see his eyes.

Royce continued to stroke her hair. "And what would that be?"

Brithwin's smile grew. "In seven months, you shall be a papa!"

"I am to be a father." His brows drew together. "Is it too early for you? You almost died. How do you feel?"

Brithwin laughed. "I am fine, the babe is fine, and never forget, God is in control. We must only trust Him."

Royce cupped her chin with his hand as he gazed into her eyes. "I love you." He gently pulled her toward him and brushed his lips over hers.

"Oh, Royce, I love you. I could not be happier than I am right now, here in my two favorite places."

Royce raised one eyebrow. "I know this is your favorite place—that is why I brought you here. But where is this other favorite place?"

Brithwin drank in the man who filled her with so much joy. "Why, wherever you are."

Author's Historical Note

John Wycliffe, born in 1330, was a lay preacher, university teacher at Oxford, and reformer in England. Wycliffe, a dissident in the Roman Catholic Church and extremely influential amongst the people, gained followers known as Lollards. Wycliffe's belief was that if individuals understood the bible it would lead to moral living. He didn't believe the church should be rich and have luxuries, but should be more like the church of the apostles. John Wycliffe and the Lollard campaign was a precursor to the Protestant Reformation. Wycliffe was one of the first to challenge the papal authority over secular power. His and the Lollard's beliefs were considered a threat to the Catholic Church.

Debbie Lynne Costello has been writing since the young age of eight. She went to college for journalism. She enjoys medieval settings and settings set in nineteenth century Charleston, South Carolina. She loves the Lord and hopes to touch people's lives through her stories. Debbie Lynne lives in the beautiful state of South Carolina with her husband of 35 years, their 4 children, their Tennessee Walking horses, Arabians, miniature donkey, four dogs, and cat.

If you enjoyed reading *Sword of Forgiveness* you might enjoy two of the novellas in the Winds of Change Series, *Sword of the Matchmaker* and *The Perfect Bride*.

One of the best ways to let me know you enjoyed *Sword of Forgiveness* and say "thank you" is to write a favorable review on Amazon as well as other sites! Thank you so much!

I love hearing from my readers. If you have any comments or questions please feel free to contact me at debbielynnecostello@hotmail.com.

Catch me online at:
My website: DebbieLynneCostello.com
Facebook: https://www.facebook.com/debbielynnecostello
Twitter: https://twitter.com/DebiLynCostello

42237953R00199

Made in the USA
San Bernardino, CA
08 July 2019